FOREIGN AFFAIRS

Fiery flirtation...

Sophisticated seduction...

The world's most eligible men!

Dreaming of a foreign affair? Then, look no further!
We've brought together the best and sexiest men the
world has to offer, the most exciting, exotic locations
and the most powerful, passionate stories.

This month, in *French Kiss*, we bring back two best-
selling novels by Catherine George and Helen Brooks
in which irresistible Frenchmen are on a mission to
seduce. But it's only the beginning...each month in
Foreign Affairs you can be swept away to a new
location – and indulge in a little passion in the sun!

Look out for a tantalizing taste of Italy in
ITALIAN WEDDINGS
by
Jacqueline Baird & Rebecca Winters
coming next month!

CATHERINE GEORGE

Catherine George was born in Wales, and early on developed a passion for reading which eventually fuelled her compulsion to write. Marriage to an engineer led to nine years in Brazil, but on his later travels the education of her son and daughter kept her in the UK. And instead of constant reading to pass her lonely evenings she began to write the first of her romantic novels. When not writing and reading she loves to cook, listen to opera and browse in antiques shops.

Look out for *Legally His* by Catherine George
on sale next month in Modern Romance™!

HELEN BROOKS

Helen Brooks lives in Northamptonshire and is married with three children. As she is a committed Christian, busy housewife and mother, her spare time is at a premium but her hobbies include reading, swimming, gardening and walking her two energetic, inquisitive and very endearing young dogs. Her long-cherished aspiration to write became a reality when she put pen to paper on reaching the age of forty and sent the result off to Mills & Boon®.

Don't miss *Sleeping Partners* by Helen Brooks
on sale now in Modern Romance™!

french kiss

CATHERINE GEORGE & HELEN BROOKS

PROPOSALS PARISIAN-STYLE!

MILLS & BOON®

*MILLS & BOON and MILLS & BOON with the Rose Device
are registered trademarks of the publisher.*
Harlequin Mills & Boon Limited,
Eton House, 18-24 Paradise Road, Richmond, Surrey, TW9 1SR

French Kiss © Harlequin Enterprises II B.V., 2001

Luc's Revenge and *Reckless Flirtation*
were first published in Great Britain by
Harlequin Mills & Boon Limited in separate single volumes.

Luc's Revenge © Catherine George 1999
Reckless Flirtation © Helen Brooks 1996

ISBN 0 263 83181 7

126-1101

*Printed and bound in Spain
by Litografia Rosés S.A., Barcelona*

french kiss

LUC'S REVENGE

CATHERINE GEORGE

CHAPTER ONE

THE call came late on a Friday evening, when everyone else had left for the weekend. On the way out herself when the phone rang, Portia was tempted to leave the call to the answering service. But with an impatient sigh she turned back at last and picked up the receiver.

'Whitefriars Estates. Good evening.'

'Good evening. I am flying in from Paris tomorrow to see one of your properties. Your name, please?'

The voice was male, French and imperious.

'Miss Grant,' said Portia crisply. 'If you'll just give me the details.'

'First please understand that the appointment must be tomorrow evening. At five. I arranged this with your Mr Parrish.'

Portia stiffened. 'That's very short notice, Monsieur—'

'Brissac. But it is not short notice. Mr Parrish informed me last week that one of the partners at your agency was always on hand at weekends for viewings. He said it was merely a matter of confirmation. You *are* a partner?' he added, with a pejorative note of doubt.

'Yes, Monsieur Brissac, I am.' Portia's eyes narrowed ominously. Ben Parrish, one of the senior partners, had just left for a skiing weekend in Gstaad without a word about this peremptory Frenchman. 'Perhaps you would tell me which property you have in mind and I'll do my best to make the arrangements.'

'I wish to inspect Turret House,' he informed her, and Portia stood rooted to the spot.

The property was not in London, as expected, but a three-hour drive away on the coast. But, more ominous than that, it was a house she'd hoped never to set foot in again as long as she lived. During the lengthy time it had been on their books Ben Parrish had always taken prospective buyers over Turret House. Not that there had ever been many. And none at all lately. The property was sticking. But personal feelings couldn't be allowed to lose a sale.

'Are you still there, *mademoiselle*?'

'Yes, Monsieur Brissac. This is very short notice, but I'll arrange my diary to fit the visit in.'

'You will come yourself, of course.'

Portia's eyes glittered coldly. 'Of course. My assistant will accompany me.' She saw no reason to tell him that Biddy was at home, nursing a cold.

'As you wish. I shall not, you understand, expect you to drive back to London afterwards,' he informed her. 'The Ravenswood Hotel is nearby. There is a double room reserved for you in the name of Whitefriars Estates. Please make use of it.'

'That won't be necessary,' she said at once.

'*Au contraire.* I shall require a return visit to Turret House very early the following morning.'

'I'm afraid that's not possible.'

'But this was the arrangement made with Mr Parrish, *mademoiselle*. It was made clear that someone would be available to escort me round the property.'

Ben Parrish might be one of her senior partners, but she would have a bone to pick with him when he came back from the *piste*. 'As I said, I'll cancel my private arrangements and meet you at Turret House, Monsieur

Brissac,' Portia assured him. 'But a hotel room is unnecessary. I'm used to driving long distances.'

'In this case it would be unwise. You must be available very early on Sunday. I return to Paris later in the morning.'

Heaping vengeance on the absent Ben's head, Portia had no option but to agree. 'As you wish, Monsieur Brissac.'

'Thank you, *mademoiselle*. Your name again, please?'

'Grant.'

'*A demain*, Miss Grant.'

Until tomorrow. Which threatened to be very different from her original plans for Saturday. Her eyes stormy, Portia put the phone down, checked that Whitefriars Estates was secure for the night, and went home.

Home was a flat in a building in Chiswick, with a fantastic view of the Thames and an equally fantastic mortgage. The apartment was a recent acquisition, with big rooms only sparsely furnished as yet. But the view was panoramic and the building secure, and Portia loved it. All her life she'd lived with other people in one way or another. But the moment she'd moved into the empty flat Portia had experienced such an exhilarating sense of liberation she never begrudged a minute of the years of hard work, both past and future, which made her pricey retreat possible.

Despite her protests to the peremptory Monsieur Brissac, Portia had no private appointments to cancel. Her plan had been to rent some videos, send out for her favourite food, and do absolutely nothing the entire weekend. And do it alone. Something her male colleagues at the firm viewed as eccentric in the extreme.

'A woman like you,' Ben Parrish had informed her once, 'should be lighting up some lucky bloke's life.'

An opinion Portia viewed as typically male. She liked her life the way it was, and the social side of it was busy enough, normally. But, as Ben Parrish had known very well, it was her turn to keep the weekend free, in case some well-heeled client should suddenly demand a viewing of one of the expensive properties handled by Whitefriars Estates. Her only cause for complaint was the fact that Turret House was the property in question this weekend.

'You're unnatural,' her friend Marianne had complained once. She was on the editorial staff of a glossy magazine, rushed from one hectic love affair to another, and came flying to Portia for consolation between bouts. 'All you care about is that job, and this place. You might as well buy a cat and settle into total spinsterhood.'

Portia had been unmoved. 'I don't like cats. And the term ''spinster'', Ms Taylor, is no longer politically correct.'

'Nor does it apply to you, darling, yet. But it might if you don't watch out!'

Portia drove home, had a bath, put some supper together, then opened her briefcase and with reluctance settled down to study the brochure of Turret House. The recent owners had renovated it throughout, but she was surprised the Frenchman was interested in it. Turret House was in immaculate condition now, according to Ben Parrish, but it was big, expensive, in a remote location, and not even pleasing to the eye unless one had a taste for the Gothic. Built as a dower house for the owner of Ravenswood, the architecture was typical of the latter part of Victoria's reign. These days Ravenswood was an expensive country house hotel, and

Turret House a separate property far too big to attract the average family. Portia eyed the brochure with foreboding. Tomorrow would be a deeply personal ordeal, but otherwise a complete waste of time. The man would take one look at the house, give a Gallic shudder of distaste, and race back to Paris on the next plane. She brightened. In which case she could shake off the dust of Turret House for ever, drive back to London and take up her weekend where she'd left off.

The February afternoon was bright with cold sunshine as Portia drove west next day along the crowded motorway. She made good time, eventually turned off into the West Country, and arrived well on schedule at the crossroads between Ravenswood and Turret House. Her reluctance deepened as she took the familiar right-hand fork to head for the house she'd hoped never to set eyes on again. But as she slowed to turn into the drive Portia sternly controlled her misgivings. She took professional note of the refurbished splendour of the gates and the well-tended air of the tiered garden as she negotiated the hairpin bends of the steep drive. At last, no matter how slowly she drove, she reached the gravelled terrace and came face to face with Turret House again.

Portia switched off the ignition, but remained in the car for a while. With time to spare before her client arrived, she put her feelings aside and tried to view the house with a purchaser's eye as the last rays of sunset light glittered on arched windows and flamed on red brick walls. It was a typical, rambling villa of its era, with a turreted square tower stuck on the end like an afterthought—the taste of the self-made industrialist who'd bought elegant, Palladian Ravenswood for his aristocratic bride. And promptly built Turret House three miles away for his mother-in-law.

Unable to put off the moment any longer, Portia got
out of the car, shivering more with apprehension than
cold. She belted her long winter white coat tightly,
pulled her velvet Cossack hat low over her eyes, collected her briefcase and crossed the terrace to the arched
front door. She breathed in deeply, then unlocked the
door, switched on the lights, and stood still in surprise
on the threshold. She had noted the renovations in the
brochure, but it was still strange to find the old red
Turkey carpet gone and the austere beauty of the black
and white tiles left bare. And the heavy dark wood of
the staircase had been stripped and sealed, the artistry of
the carving revealed now by the light from the stained-
glass window on the landing. Portia let out the breath
she'd been holding. The hall was so much smaller than
her memory of it. But, most important of all, it was
empty. No ghosts at all.

Almost light-headed with relief, Portia went through
the rest of the rooms, switching on lights, noting the
quality of the pale carpets and the padded silk curtains.
No furniture, which was a drawback. It was much easier
to sell an inhabited, furnished house. Which was probably why the place was sticking. And upstairs everything
was so unfamiliar it could have been a different house.
Smaller rooms had been converted into bathrooms to
connect with the larger bedrooms, and the pastel paint
everywhere was a far cry from the dark gloom of the
past. Portia glanced at her watch, frowning, then went
back downstairs. The client was an hour late. And Turret
House was not a place she cared to linger in after dark.

Nor, Portia found, could she bring herself to look over
the tower rooms alone first. A cold shiver ran through
her at the mere thought. She turned on her heel and went
back to the bright, welcoming kitchen instead, hoping

Monsieur Brissac was bringing the woman in his life. Kitchens were a very important selling point. These days very few clients wanted a formal dining room as the only place to eat. Fortunately the vendors had joined the old larder to the kitchen to form one vast room, with space for an eating area. In contrast to the old-fashioned, comfortless place of the past, the result was a glossy magazine vision of a country kitchen, complete with fashionable dark blue Aga stove.

Portia stood very still, staring at it. There had been an Aga stove in the past, coal-fired and ancient, its beige enamel discoloured with age and constant use. It had been a devil to load and rake out...

A voice outside in the hall plucked Portia back into the present. She went through the leather-backed door to find a tall man craning his neck to look up the staircase, impatience radiating from him like nuclear fallout.

Portia coughed. 'Monsieur Brissac?'

He swung round sharply, the impatience falling from him like a cloak as she moved forward under the bare central light of the hall. He bowed slightly, his eyes narrowing as he saw her face. '*Pardon.* The door was open so I came in. My plane was delayed. If I kept you waiting I am sorry.'

Even at first glance Portia doubted that penitence was part of this man's make-up. 'How do you do?' she said politely.

He was silent for a moment, taking in every detail of her appearance. 'You are Miss Grant from Whitefriars Estates?'

'Yes. Unfortunately my assistant's ill and couldn't come,' she admitted reluctantly, and returned his scrutiny with interest. He wore a formal dark overcoat, worn open over a city suit, and he was younger than she'd expected, with thick, longish black hair and smooth olive skin, a straight noise. But his mouth curved in strikingly sensuous contrast to the firm, dark-shadowed jaw. And something about him revived the feeling of unease she'd experienced at the first sound of his voice on the phone.

'I had expected someone older, *mademoiselle*,' he said at last.

So had Portia. But you're stuck with me, she thought silently, then stiffened as a sudden gleam in his eyes told her he'd read her mind. Reminding herself that her mission was to sell the house, not alienate the client, she exerted herself to please as she took him on a tour of the ground-floor rooms, extolling virtues of space and the wonderful views by daylight over the bay.

'A pity you arrived so late,' she said pleasantly. 'The view is a major attraction of Turret House.'

'So I was told.' He raised a quizzical eyebrow. 'Is it good enough to compensate for the architecture? You must admit that the exterior lacks charm.'

'True. But the house was built to last.' Portia led the way upstairs, pointing out the various selling points as her elegant client explored the bedrooms. On the way downstairs again she stressed the advantages of the immaculate interior decoration, the new central heating system, the recent rewiring, the curtains and carpets included in the price. In the kitchen, she pointed out its practical and aesthetic virtues, but at last there was only the tower left to explore. Portia preceded her client into the hall, her pulse racing and her hands clammy as she pressed a button in the wall beneath the stairwell. A door slid aside in the panelling to reveal a lift. 'This is set in the turret itself,' she said colourlessly. 'It takes you to the bedroom floor, of course, then on to the top room in the tower, Monsieur Brissac.'

He smiled. 'Ah! You saved the *pièce de résistance* for last, Miss Grant. Is it in good working order?'

'Yes,' she said, devoutly hoping she was right. 'To demonstrate this we can inspect the three floors of the tower on foot, then call the lift up to the top floor to bring us down again.'

Wishing now she'd forced herself to inspect the tower alone first, Portia preceded her client into the ground-floor room, a light, airy apartment, with windows on the three outer walls. And empty, just like the hall. She relaxed slightly. 'I believe this was used as the morning room by the lady of the house when it was first built. This door opens into the lift, and the one beside it conceals a spiral stair to the next floor.' Straight-backed, Portia led the way up the winding stair to a room similar to the one below, then, at last, her heart beating like a war drum, she ran quickly up the last flight to the top of the tower. She switched on the light, waved her client ahead of her into the room, then stood just inside the door, her back against the wall, feeling giddy with relief.

'The view here is quite marvellous in the daytime,' she said breathlessly.

The Frenchman eyed her with concern. 'You are very pale. Are you unwell, *mademoiselle*?'

'No. I'm fine.' She managed a smile. 'Out of condition. I need more exercise.'

He looked unconvinced. 'But not at this moment, I think. Is this the button for the *ascenseur*? Let us test its efficiency.'

In the claustrophobic, strangely threatening confines of the small elevator Portia felt hemmed in by her companion's physical proximity, very conscious of dark, narrowed eyes fixed on her face as they glided silently to the ground floor.

'Most impressive,' he remarked as they went out into the hall.

'Installed in the early part of the century, when the house was fitted with electricity,' said Portia unevenly, the blood beginning to flow normally in her veins once they were out of the tower. 'Have you seen everything you want, Monsieur Brissac?'

'For the moment, yes. Tomorrow, in daylight, I shall make a more detailed inspection. I believe there is a path down to a private cove?'

Portia nodded. 'But there's been no maintenance work done on it for a long time. I'm not sure how safe it is.'

'If the weather permits we shall explore and find out.' He frowned slightly. 'You have not shown other prospective purchasers round Turret House?'

'Oh, yes. Quite a number,' she contradicted him quickly. 'The property's attracted a lot of interest.'

'I meant you, personally, Miss Grant.'

'Myself, no, I haven't,' she admitted. 'My colleague, Mr Parrish, owns a weekend cottage in the area, so he usually does the viewing.' She smiled politely. 'Have you any more questions?'

'Of course, many more. But I shall ask them tomorrow.' He glanced at his watch. 'Soon it will be time for our dinner. Let us drive to the hotel.'

Our dinner?

Again he read her mind with ease. He smiled. 'I am entertaining some clients to dinner at the Ravenswood. Will you join us?'

Portia shook her head. 'You're very kind, but I won't, thanks. It's an early start tomorrow, so I'll have supper in my room, then get some sleep.'

'A boring programme,' he observed as Portia switched off the last of the lights.

'But very attractive to me after a busy working week,' she assured him pleasantly.

'Then I trust you will enjoy it. *Alors*, you will go first so I can make sure you arrive at Ravenswood safely.'

With no intention of telling him she knew the area like the back of her hand, Portia said goodbye, got in her car, and drove swiftly down the winding drive, then accelerated into the narrow road, intent on getting to the hotel before him. But by the time she'd parked under the trees in the courtyard and taken her overnight bag from her boot her client was at her elbow, to take the bag and escort her into the foyer.

'This is Miss Grant of Whitefriars Estates,' he informed the pretty receptionist. The girl greeted him warmly, consulted a computer screen and handed Portia a key.

'Twenty-four?' he said, frowning. 'Is that the best you can do, Frances? What other rooms are free tonight?'

'None, I'm afraid, Monsieur Brissac.' She eyed him uncertainly. 'Some of the guests haven't arrived yet. Shall I juggle a bit?'

He shook his head. 'No, *I* shall take twenty-four. Give Miss Grant my room. She appreciates a view.'

The obliging Frances dimpled. 'All the rooms have views, Monsieur Brissac.'

'But some are more beautiful than others,' he countered, smiling. Frances flushed and handed over a new key to her guest, something in her eyes which rather puzzled Portia. It was only later, in the large, inviting room with a tester bed and a view over floodlit parkland, that she realised the receptionist had felt envious. And, much against her will, she could understand why. Monsieur Brissac was a formidably attractive man, with a charm she was by no means wholly immune to herself.

But the charm was oddly familiar. Yet she was quite certain she'd never met him before. Her client wasn't the type of man women forgot.

Portia unpacked her overnight bag deep in thought. The dimpled Frances obviously knew this Brissac man very well. Was he the hotel manager? That didn't fit, somehow, if he was inspecting a nearby property. Maybe he was just a customer, regular and valued enough to ask a favour. In which case, what, exactly, *was* the favour? Maybe his room was next door, and this was the reason for the envy. Portia made a swift inspection, but there was no connecting door to another room. She frowned, annoyed with herself. Going back to Turret House again had addled her brain. Monsieur Brissac's impatience had quickly changed to something different—and familiar—the moment he'd taken a good look at her, it was true. But otherwise he'd been faultlessly circumspect. He'd tuned in sharply enough to her uneasiness in Turret House, though. Which was unsurprising. Her reluctance had been hard to hide as they entered the tower, and her relief equally obvious when they left it. Tomorrow she would be more in control, now the initial ordeal was over.

Portia had packed very little. With no intention of eating in the dining room, a suitable dress had been unnecessary. A couple of novels and some room service completed her plan for an evening spent in remarkably pleasant surroundings. The room was quite wonderful, with luxuriously comfortable chairs and sofa, and gleaming bronze lamps. On a low table magazines flanked a silver tray laden with glasses, a decanter of sherry, dishes of nuts and tiny savoury biscuits. And a refrigerator masquerading as an antique chest held soft drinks and various spirits and wines, even champagne.

Portia took a quick look at the menus on the dressing table, then rang for tea to tide her over until the lobster salad she'd chosen for dinner later on. Once the tea tray arrived Portia tipped the polite young waiter and locked the door behind him. She pulled off her hat, unpinned her hair and ran her fingers through crackling bronze curls which sprang free as though glad to escape. Then she removed her tailored brown suit and silk shirt and hung them up, pulled off her long suede boots and removed her stockings, then wrapped herself in the white towelling dressing gown provided by the hotel. With a sigh of pleasure she sank down on the sofa with a cup of tea, nibbled on one of the accompanying petits fours, and gazed out over parkland lit so cleverly it looked bathed with moonlight.

When she was young it had always been her ambition to stay in the Ravenswood, which featured in smart magazines, offering weekend breaks of unbridled luxury. The room was exquisitely furnished, and the bathroom was vast, with a tub big enough to swim in and everything else a guest could need, right down to a separate telephone. A bit different from her usual company-funded overnight stops when inspections or viewings took her too far to return to base overnight.

So now, surprisingly, she could resume her plans for the weekend right here. She could read, watch a television programme, even request a video from the list provided.

Portia got up to draw the curtains, then picked up her book and prepared to enjoy the evening just as she'd planned to at home. Only tonight, after a long, leisurely bath, she would read herself to sleep in the picturesque tester bed, and someone would bring her breakfast on a tray in the morning. Wonderful. When a knock heralded

the arrival of her dinner, punctual to the minute, Portia
tightened the sash on the dressing gown and went on
bare feet to open the door to the waiter. And confronted
the elegant figure of Monsieur Brissac instead.

They stared at each other for a moment in mutual
surprise, then his eyes moved from her bare feet to the
tumbled hair. She thrust it back quickly, heat rising in
her face as her pulse astonished her by racing at the sight
of him. The Frenchman was obviously fresh from a
shower, the dark shadow along his jaw less evident, and
he was wearing a different, equally elegant suit. 'Is your
room to your taste, Miss Grant?' he enquired, moving
closer.

Portia backed away instinctively. 'Yes, indeed. Very
comfortable. But I'm expecting my dinner to arrive any
moment, so if you'll excuse me—'

'My guests tell me they are suffering from jet lag and
wish to retire early,' he interrupted smoothly. 'Since you
will not dine with us, perhaps you would join me in the
bar later this evening, Miss Grant. I wish to discuss certain aspects of the sale of Turret House before we return
to it in the morning.'

Refusing to let the intent dark eyes fluster her, Portia
thought swiftly. Her partners were about to suggest a
price reduction to the owners. If she could make the sale
at the present price it would be a feather in her cap. As
junior partner, and a female, she was secretly driven by
the need to compete on equal terms with the men at
Whitefriars.

'After dinner, in the bar?' he prompted, obviously
amused by her hesitation.

Portia nodded briskly. 'Of course, if you feel further
discussion will be useful before seeing the house again.
Perhaps you'll ring me when you're free.' No way was

she hanging about in the bar until he was ready to join her.

'Of course, Miss Grant.' He smiled. 'Enjoy your dinner.'

Portia returned the smile and closed the door, then stood against it for a moment, giving herself a stringent little lecture as she waited for her pulse-rate to return to normal. Charm personified he might be, but Monsieur Brissac was just a client. And she was here solely to sell him a house.

When her lobster salad arrived Portia eyed it in surprise. Not only was it a work of art on a plate, but it was accompanied by a half-bottle of Premier Cru burgundy, a small mound of gleaming black caviare as appetiser, and an iced parfait of some kind to round off the feast.

'No mistake, Miss Grant,' said the receptionist when Portia rang to enquire. 'Compliments of Monsieur Brissac.'

Portia thanked the girl, shrugged, then began to spread caviare on crisp squares of toast, wondering why she was being entertained so lavishly. It was she who wanted Monsieur Brissac's business, not the other way round. What was his motive? On the phone he'd been demanding almost to the point of rudeness, but in person, once he'd actually met her, deliberate charm had quickly replaced his initial impatience. Yet something about him made her uneasy. Unable to pinpoint the reason for it, Portia despatched the last of the caviare, then helped herself to some mayonnaise from a small porcelain pot and began on the lobster she could rarely afford. Tonight it had been a reward to herself for her disturbing day. She had assumed she would pay for it herself, but Monsieur Brissac had taken pains to show he was footing the bill. Yet if Ben Parrish had been in charge of the viewing he would have expected to pay for both his own dinner and the client's to oil the wheels of the transaction.

But she was an attractive woman, so the situation was different. Portia had no illusions about her looks. An accident of nature had given her a face, hair and a shape most of her women friends envied. Because she'd been wearing a hat, and a long coat which covered her from throat to ankle, Mr Brissac would have had to guess about shape and hair. But his impatience had evaporated the moment he'd taken a good look at her face at Turret House. And a few minutes ago his eyes had gleamed with something else entirely at the sight of her in a robe, with her hair all over the place.

Portia frowned thoughtfully. Monsieur Brissac, she was sure, was too sophisticated and subtle a man to try to mix business with pleasure. Tonight he had taken her by surprise. But from now on she would be in control, totally poised and professional. And in the meantime nothing was going to spoil her pleasure in her dinner.

CHAPTER TWO

WHEN the telephone rang just after ten Portia decided on a little dressage. Monsieur Brissac might whistle, but she wasn't coming running just yet.

'Would you give me another fifteen minutes or so?' she asked pleasantly.

'But of course. As long as you wish,' he assured her.

Portia had taken time over a bath and washing her hair. Sorry now she'd been so frugal with her packing, her sole concession to the occasion was a fresh silk T-shirt with the suit worn earlier—her usual office clothes. She brushed her newly washed hair up into as tight a knot as possible and pinned it securely, replaced the amber studs in her earlobes, then collected handbag and key and went off to charm Monsieur Brissac into buying Turret House.

The bar was crowded with well-dressed people in convivial mood after the pleasures of the impressive Ravenswood dinner menu. When Portia paused in the doorway the elegant figure of her client rose to his feet at a small table in a far corner.

'I'm sorry if I've kept you waiting,' she said politely, as he held a chair for her.

'You did not,' he assured her, smiling. 'You are punctual to the second. May I offer you a cognac with your coffee?'

No way, thought Portia. She needed to keep her faculties needle-sharp since her companion was making it clear that though they were here to discuss business he was taking unconcealed male pleasure in her company.

'I won't, thank you.' She smiled at him. 'Just coffee.'

Even before she'd finished speaking a waitress had materialised with a tray and put it on the low table in front of her.

Monsieur Brissac smiled his thanks at the girl, then filled their cups and handed one to Portia. She added a dash of cream, refused one of the handmade chocolates he offered, then sat back, waiting for questions.

Instead he looked at her in silence, examining her face feature by feature in a way Portia found unsettling. 'So, Monsieur Brissac,' she began briskly. 'What can I tell you about Turret House?'

He leaned forward and added sugar to his cup, and almost absently Portia noted his slim, strong hands, the small gold signet ring on his little finger, the fine dark hair visible on the wrist below a gleaming white shirt-cuff fastened with a gold cufflink of the same design as the ring.

'First of all, tell me why the owners wish to sell,' he said. 'Is there some drawback to the house not immediately apparent?'

'No,' she assured him. 'Make any survey you want, but I guarantee you'll find the house is sound, and the wiring and plumbing in perfect order. The roof has been renewed, and unless it's a matter of conflicting taste, neither exterior nor interior need repair or redecoration.'

'Then why should the owners want to sell a house they took so much care to renovate and modernise?'

Portia smiled ruefully. 'Unfortunately a very common reason. Divorce.'

'Ah. I see.' He nodded. 'A pity. Turret House is meant for a large family.'

'Is that why you're interested in it?'

'No. I am not married.' He gave a characteristically Gallic shrug. 'At least not yet. And, since you are *Miss* Grant, I assume you are not married either.'

'No, I'm not.' She changed the subject. 'So, what else would you like to know?'

'Your first name,' he said, surprising her.

'Portia,' she said, after a pause.

He glanced down into his cup quickly, giving Portia a view of enviable dark lashes. 'So. Your parents were fond of your William Shakespeare.' He looked up again, his eyes holding hers. 'And do you possess the quality of mercy, Mademoiselle Portia?'

Portia willed her pulse to behave itself. 'My name is nothing to do with Shakespeare, Monsieur Brissac. My father was a car enthusiast.'

He frowned. *'Comment?'*

'He loved fast cars, the Porsche most of all. So I'm named after it. But my mother held out for Shakespeare's spelling.'

He gave a husky, delighted laugh. 'Your father had vision,' he told her.

'In what way?'

'The Porsche is small, elegant and very efficient. The description fits you perfectly. I like your name very much,' he said. 'Will you allow me to use it?'

If he bought Turret House he could call her what he liked. 'Of course, if you wish.'

'Then you must respond.' He half rose with a little bow, then reseated himself. 'Allow me to introduce myself. Jean-Christophe Lucien Brissac.'

Her eyebrows rose. 'A lot of names.''

''I am known as Luc,' he informed her.

She shook her head. 'It's not my practice to be on first-name terms with clients.'

'But in this case, if I purchase Turret House, you will have a great deal to do with me in future, Portia,' he pointed out.

She pounced. 'And are you going to buy it, then?'

'I might. Tomorrow, if my second impression is as good as the first, and if we can negotiate the price a little, there is a strong possibility that you and I may do business, Portia.'

She kept iron control on every nerve to hide her excitement. 'That sounds very encouraging.'

'But there is another condition to the sale,' he informed her.

Portia stiffened. 'Condition?'

'You must tell me the truth. Does Turret House possess a *revenant*? Is there a ghost, Portia?' His eyes held hers so steadily she discovered they were of a shade of green so dark that to the casual eye it was hard to distinguish iris from pupil.

'Not to my knowledge,' she said without inflection. 'The house isn't nearly as old as this one, remember. Ghosts are more likely at Ravenswood than Turret House.'

'Yet for a moment, at the top of that extraordinary tower, I thought you were going to faint,' he went on relentlessly. 'And do not tell me you were breathless or unfit. Your tension was tangible.'

Portia looked away, fighting down the formless, unidentifiable fear she experienced at the mere mention of the tower. Poised and professional, she reminded herself, and turned to look at him very directly. 'Monsieur Brissac—'

'Luc.'

'Very well, Luc. If you buy the property I guarantee that neither you, nor anyone who lives there, will be troubled by ghosts. Turret House is not haunted.'

Straight dark brows drew together as Luc Brissac tapped a slim finger against the bottom lip which struck Portia anew as arrestingly sensuous above the firmly clenched jaw.

'*Alors,*' he said slowly, his eyes intent on hers. 'If I decide to buy, will you tell me what troubled *you* there today?'

'Is that a condition of sale?'

'No. But I am—interested. I could sense your distress. It disturbed me very much.'

Portia gazed at him, rather shaken. 'All right. If you decide to buy, I'll tell you.'

Luc Brissac reached out a hand to shake hers gravely. 'A deal, Miss Portia.'

'A deal,' she agreed, and looked down at their clasped hands, not liking to pull hers away, but very much aware that his fingers were on the pulse reacting so traitorously to his touch.

'Goodnight, Portia,' he said, very quietly, and raised her hand to his lips before releasing it.

She rose rather precipitately. 'If that's everything for the moment, it's time for that early night I promised myself.'

He walked with her through the now almost empty bar. 'Sleep well.'

'I'm sure I shall. It's a beautiful room.' She hesitated, then looked up at him very squarely. 'Thank you for turning it over to me. And for the dinner. It wasn't necessary for you to provide it, but I enjoyed it very much.'

Luc Brissac frowned. 'But I told you I had reserved

a room, Portia. Naturally I would provide dinner and breakfast also.''

'If I was anxious for you to clinch the deal shouldn't I have been buying *you* dinner?' She paused at the foot of the wide, shallow staircase.

He smiled. 'Perhaps when I return to London to finalise matters you might still do that?'

Portia's heart leapt beneath the silk shirt. 'Of course,' she said quickly. 'The firm will be happy to entertain you.'

'I meant *you*, Portia.' His smile faded. 'Or is the deal the price I must pay for more of your company?'

'In the circumstances I can't think of a reply which wouldn't offend you.' She smiled to soften the words. 'And I try to avoid offending clients, so I'll say goodnight.'

He returned the smile and bowed slightly. 'Be ready at eight in the morning, Portia. Your breakfast will arrive at seven-thirty.'

Portia woke early next day, with more than enough time to shower and dress and pack her belongings before breakfast. According to Ben Parrish, other clients had declined a scramble down to the cove. But something about Luc Brissac's voice had warned her that this particular client would be different, so she'd come prepared, with a heavy cream wool sweater, brown wool trousers and flat leather shoes in her luggage. And an amber fleece jacket instead of her pale winter coat. When she was ready she enjoyed the freshly squeezed orange juice and feathery, insubstantial croissants, and went downstairs at the appointed hour, her overnight bag in one hand, her coat slung over the other arm. And experienced the now familiar leap in her blood at the sight of Luc Brissac.

'Such British punctuality,' he said, coming to meet her. '*Bonjour*, Portia. You slept well?'

'Good morning. I slept very well indeed,' she returned, with absolute truth. Which was a surprise, one way and another.

Conscious of discreet interest from the reception desk, Portia surrendered her bag to Luc, who was informal this morning in a rollneck sweater and serviceable cords.

When they went out into a cold, bright morning, Portia was thankful to see the day was fine. Turret House would make a better second impression in sunlight.

Luc stowed the bag in her car, then informed her he would drive her in his hired Renault. 'Last night you drove too fast along such a narrow road, Portia. Perhaps,' he added, looking her in the eye, 'because you know it well?'

'Yes, I do,' she agreed, and got into the car.

When they reached Turret House Luc Brissac parked the car on the gravel terrace, reached into the back for a suede jacket and came round to let Portia out.

'It looks more welcoming today than last night,' he commented, eyeing the brick façade. 'Sunlight is kinder to it than—what is *crépuscule*?'

'Twilight,' said Portia, and unlocked the front door, ushering him ahead of her into the hall, where the sunlight cast coloured lozenges of light on the tiled floor, an effect which found favour with her client.

'Most picturesque,' he said, then smiled wryly. 'But I should not make favourable comments. I must frown and look disapproving so that you will drop the price.'

Portia smiled neutrally, and accompanied him through the ground-floor rooms again, glad to see that daylight failed to show up any flaws her tension might have blinded her to the previous evening. Luc paused in each room to make notes, keeping Portia on her toes with pertinent, informed questions right up to the moment they reached the tower and she could no longer ignore the faint, familiar dread as he opened the door to the ground-floor sitting room.

'If you do not wish to go as far as the top floor again you need not, Portia,' he said quickly. His eyes, a very definite green this morning in the light streaming through three sets of windows, held hers questioningly.

She shook her head, exerting iron control on her reactions. 'I'm fine. Really.' She ran swiftly up the spiral stairs to prove it, and went straight across the top room to the windows. 'As I told you, the view from up here is breathtaking.'

Luc Brissac studied her profile for a moment, then looked down at the tiered lawns and shrubberies of the garden, with its belt of woodland, and beyond that the cliff-edge and a glimpse of sandy cove below, and the sea glittering under the blue winter sky. He nodded slowly. 'You were right, Portia. For this, on such a day, one can almost forgive the excesses of the Turret House architect.'

Almost, noted Portia. 'You mentioned going down to the cove,' she reminded him. 'Do you have time for that?'

He nodded. 'Yes. Did I not say? I was able to postpone my departure until tomorrow. We can explore this cove at our leisure, then later we shall lunch together to discuss the transaction.'

Portia, not altogether pleased by his high-handed rearrangement of her day, opened the door into the lift and went in. Luc followed her, frowning as he pressed the button to go down.

'You feel I am monopolising too much of your time?' he asked.

'No.' He's the client, she reminded herself. 'If you want a discussion over lunch then of course I'll delay my return to London. But I shall pay for the meal.' She stepped out of the lift into the hall, and made for the door.

'Since lunch was my suggestion I shall pay,' he said loftily, following her.

She shook her head. 'I'll charge it to my expense account. And,' she added with emphasis, 'I suggest we lunch in a pub somewhere, not at the hotel.'

He stood outside on the terrace, arms folded, watching as she locked the door. 'You do not like the food at the hotel?'

'Of course. It's superb.' She led the way down a series of stone steps towards the bottom of the garden. 'But Ben Parrish says the meals are good at the Wheatsheaf, a couple of miles away, so I thought you might like some plain British fare for a change.'

Portia laughed at his undisguised look of dismay, and Luc smiled in swift response as they reached the path that led through the copse of trees to the cliff-edge. 'You should laugh more often, Portia.'

'Take care down here,' she said, turning away. 'It's pretty steep.' She went ahead of him down the overgrown path which cut down the cliffside in sharp bends to the cove below, with loose shale adding to the hazards in places.

Portia made the descent with the sure-footed speed of long practice. When Luc Brissac joined her a few minutes later he was breathing heavily, a look of accusation on his face.

'Such a pace was madness, Portia!'

She shook her head, and turned to look out to sea, shivering a little as she hugged her jacket closer. 'The path was quite safe.'

'For mountain goats at such speed, possibly. Or,' he added deliberately, 'for someone very familiar with it.' He waited a little, but when she said nothing he looked away, gazing about him in approval at the rocks edging the sand in the secluded, V-shaped inlet. 'But this is charming. Is there any other access?'

'No. The path is Turret House property.'

Luc turned up the collar of his suede jacket. 'In summer this must be delightful. A great asset to the house.'

'The path could do with some work,' admitted Portia. 'But if it's reinforced in places, with a few steps cut in the cliff here and there, and maybe a handrail on the steepest bit, it could be a very attractive feature. Not many houses boast a private cove.'

'True.' Luc cast an eye at clouds gathering on the horizon. 'Come, Portia, we must go back before it rains.'

Portia found the climb up the cliff far harder going than her reckless, headlong descent. By the time she reached the top she was out of breath. 'As I said yesterday,' she panted, as Luc joined her, 'I'm out of condition.'

His all-encompassing look rendered her even more breathless. 'Your condition looks flawless to me. Come. It is early yet for lunch, but perhaps your English pub will give us coffee.'

'If I'd known you weren't going back today I would have asked for a later start this morning,' said Portia as they went back up through the garden.

He shrugged. 'My change of plan took much effort to rearrange. I was not sure until this morning that it could be done.'

'Why did you change your mind?' she asked curiously, as they got in the car.

'There would not have been time before my flight to go down to the cove after inspecting the house again. And this was necessary before I made a decision.' He concentrated on the steep bends of the drive. 'Also,' he added casually, 'I desired to spend more time with you. Now, give me directions, please. Where is this inn of yours?'

The Wheatsheaf served excellent coffee, and later provided them with a simple, but well-cooked lunch very different from the cuisine at the Ravenswood, but in its own way of a very high standard.

'But this is very good!' pronounced Luc, as he ate roast lamb cooked with anchovies and garlic.

Portia laughed. 'The compliment would sound better without the astonishment.'

Luc grinned. 'We take our food more seriously than you British.'

'And suffer far less from heart problems, I read somewhere. Though you drink a bit more than we do,' she added, then regretted it at the look on Luc's face.

'True,' he said quietly.

'I didn't mean you personally, of course,' said Portia hurriedly.

'I know.' His smile stopped short of his eyes. 'You would like dessert?'

She shook her head.

'Then perhaps we can return to the bar to talk business. Please excuse me for a moment. I shall order coffee.' Luc seated her at a small table, then went off for a word with the barman.

Conscious of unintended transgression of some kind, Portia resolved to put a guard on her tongue for the rest of their time together. Luc had flatly refused to discuss Turret House before lunch, so her only opportunity for clinching a sale was during the short time left before her drive back to London. And outside, she noted glumly, the rain was coming down in torrents.

'You look pensive,' said Luc, as he rejoined her.

'I was eyeing the weather. I'm afraid I'll have to cut things short. It's a fair drive back to London.'

'I know.' He put a hand on hers. 'Stay the night at the Ravenswood again, Portia, and drive back in the morning.'

So, Jean-Christophe Lucien Brissac was no different from the rest after all. Portia removed her hand abruptly, utterly astounded by the discovery that she was deeply tempted to say yes.

'No, I can't do that,' she said quietly. 'I'm quite accustomed to long journeys in any weather. So, shall we discuss Turret House, or have you made your decision already?'

'I was not asking to share your room, Miss Grant,' he said icily. 'My concern was for your safety, only.'

'Of course.' Utterly mortified, Portia began packing her briefcase. 'I shan't rush you. I didn't expect a firm answer today, anyway. Perhaps you'll get in touch as soon as possible and let me know what you decide. In the meantime—'

'In the meantime, sit down and drink your coffee,' said Luc, with a note of command. 'You mistake me,' he added as she resumed her seat. 'Also you insult me.'

She frowned. 'Insult you?'

'Yes. It is not my habit to force my way into a woman's bed. Even a woman as alluring and challenging as you,' he informed her.

Portia calmed down a little. 'My apologies,' she said stiffly.

There was silence between them for a moment.

'You have been troubled by clients before?' Luc asked.

'No. My clients usually come in pairs.'

'By men in general, then?'

'One or two,' she said without inflection.

His eyes lit with wry sympathy. 'A woman with looks like yours—' He shrugged. 'It is easy to understand why.'

'If that's a compliment, thank you.'

He gave her a sidelong, considering look. 'It was meant to be. Though now, knowing that you suspect me of dark and devious motives, I shall strive to be careful.'

'Careful?' she said, frowning.

'That I do not offend.'

'I can't afford to be offended,' she said matter-of-factly. 'You're the client.'

His smile was tigerish. 'And you want me to buy a property that remains on your books rather a long time.'

So much for hoping to sell Turret House without a reduction. If she sold it at all. 'Of course I do,' she said, resigned.

Luc spent some time looking through the details of the house again, checking off various points against the notes he'd made. At last he turned to her with a businesslike air, raising his voice slightly above the crowded, post-prandial noise of the Wheatsheaf bar.

'I will consider my options most carefully, Portia, and then this evening, after your return to London, I shall ring you and let you know my decision,' he said with finality.

'If you're staying over tonight you can have longer

than that,' she said quickly, suppressing a leap of excitement. He was going to buy; she was sure of it. 'You can ring me at the office in the morning.'

He shook his head. 'Give me your phone number. I shall ring you tonight.'

Portia hesitated for a moment, then scribbled a number on a sheet from her diary and handed it to him.

'Thank you,' he said, and tucked it in his wallet. 'And now I will drive you back to Ravenswood.'

Outside, they raced through the rain to Luc's car. '*Mon Dieu*, what weather!' he gasped, as they fastened their seatbelts.

'It's not always like this,' she assured him breathlessly. 'The climate here is the best in the UK.'

'Not so *very* good a recommendation!'

Portia smiled, badly wanting a hint from him as to his decision about Turret House. But prudence curbed her tongue. If he sensed she was desperate to sell he would expect a substantial drop in the price. Assuming he did want the house. She eyed his profile searchingly, but it gave her no clue to his intentions.

When they reached the car park of the Ravenswood, Portia refused his invitation to go inside for a while before she started back to London.

'I'd rather go now and get it over with.'

'How long will the journey take?' he asked, frowning at the rain.

'I don't know. In this weather longer than usual, I'm afraid.'

'I shall ring you at ten. This will give you time?'

'I hope so.' Portia held out her hand. 'Thank you for the room, and my dinner—and for the lunch. When I tried to settle up just now they told me you'd already paid.'

He took the hand in his, shrugging. 'I never allow a woman to pay.'

'An attitude that gets you in trouble sometimes these days, I imagine?'

He looked surprised. 'Never—until now.' He raised her hand to his lips. '*Au 'voir*, Portia Grant. I shall talk to you later. Drive very carefully.'

'I always do. Goodbye.' She got in the car, fastened her seatbelt and drove off quickly, dismayed to find she already needed her headlights in the streaming February dusk. As she turned out into the road she looked in her mirror, rather disappointed that Luc Brissac hadn't waited to watch her out of sight. Not, she told herself severely, that there was any reason why he should. Only an impractical fool would have hung about in the drenching rain. And her acquaintance with Jean-Christophe Lucien Brissac might be slight, but one thing was very clear. He was no fool.

CHAPTER THREE

PORTIA'S return journey to London was nerve-racking. After a slow journey to the motorway, the rest of it was a nightmare of pouring rain and heavy spray from other vehicles, all three lanes clogged by traffic, all the way to London. When she reached Chiswick at last Portia felt exhausted. She parked her car in the basement garage, went up in the lift to her flat, locked her door behind her, then took her cellphone from her bag and blew out her cheeks in relief.

Now she was home and dry, she had an hour to spare before the call from the charming, disturbing Monsieur Brissac. If he confirmed he was going to buy Turret House it might be best to ask Ben Parrish to deal with him from now on.

A minute or so before ten the cellphone rang, right on cue, and she hit the button in sudden excitement.

'Portia Grant,' she said crisply.

'Ah, *bon*, you are returned safely,' said Luc Brissac with gratifying relief. 'I was worried, Portia.'

'How nice of you. But quite unnecessary. I've been home some time.'

'Then you did drive too fast!'

'I couldn't. Once I joined the motorway I was stuck in the middle lane all the way to London.'

'*Bien*, it is established that you arrived safely. So now, Portia, we get to business.'

'You've made a decision?' she asked, trying not to sound too eager.

36

'Yes. I confirm that I will buy Turret House. But,' he added emphatically, 'only on certain conditions.'

Portia's flare of triumph dimmed a little. 'What conditions do you have in mind?'

'First the price.' He named a figure lower than she'd hoped, but higher than the reduction Whitefriars had been about to recommend to the vendors.

'I must consult my partners, of course, but I'm sure we can come to an agreement on that,' said Portia, secretly elated.

'Also,' he went on, 'I wish you, personally, to conduct the entire transaction.'

She frowned. 'But it's actually Mr Parrish's—'

'I want you, Portia,' he said with emphasis.

Or he wouldn't buy it. The words remained unspoken, but Portia, visualising his usual shrug, was left in no doubt.

'As you wish.'

'Next weekend I fly back to London. In the meantime I shall arrange for information about my lawyers to be faxed to you, also contact numbers where I can be reached until we meet again.'

'Thank you,' she said briskly, secretly thrilled at her success in getting rid of the property Ben Parrish had failed to move.

'Please arrange to leave next weekend free,' went on Luc Brissac.

She stiffened. 'Oh, but—'

'I wish to inspect the property again. I cannot take possession of the keys until the house is legally mine, Portia. You must come with me. I shall drive you down to Turret House early on Saturday morning.'

For a split-second Portia was tempted to tell him exactly what he could do with his conditions, *and* his purchase of Turret House. But common sense prevailed. 'Monsieur Brissac, I shall do as you ask, but with a condition of my own. I'll drive down to the house separately and meet you there.'

There was silence for a moment, then he sighed impatiently. 'Very well, if you insist. But please be there by mid-morning.'

'Of course.'

'Until Saturday, then, Portia.'

The following morning her news of the sale of Turret House was greeted with teasing surprise by her partners at Whitefriars, and deep respect by Biddy, who was still heavy-eyed and red-nosed, but slowly recovering from her cold.

'I thought we'd never get rid of the place!' Biddy had been with the firm for years and looked on every property sale as a personal triumph. She handed Portia a cup of coffee and lingered expectantly, obviously wanting details before she went off to start on the letters and valuations Portia had gone through with her on the Friday afternoon before sending her home to bed.

Before she'd ever heard of Luc Brissac, thought Portia. 'The client wants me to go down to Turret House again this weekend.'

'Was his wife with him?' asked Biddy.

'No, he's not married.'

'Then I'd better come with you.'

'No need,' said Portia quickly. 'But thanks for the offer.'

'I thought Mr Parrish always took people round it anyway.'

'Monsieur Brissac insists on my personal attention for the transaction,' said Portia. And, for reasons she pre-

ferred to keep to herself, she wanted to deal with this
particular client on her own. She shot to her feet. 'Heavens, is that the time? I'm due in Belgravia in ten minutes
to sell a pricey mews cottage to your favourite soap
queen.'

When Ben Parrish got back from his skiing trip next
day he was amazed to find Portia had managed to sell
Turret House while he was away.

'Though I suppose I shouldn't be surprised. Luc
Brissac probably took one look at you and said yes to
anything you wanted.'

Ben Parrish was only a few years older than Portia,
stocky, sandy-haired, and possessed of a solid brand of
charm that stood him in good stead in the property business. Without ever resorting to the hard sell, he nevertheless managed to move properties at a rate envied by
his colleagues at Whitefriars. But success with Turret
House had eluded him.

'You know him, then?' asked Portia.

He nodded. 'I sold a place in Hampstead to him quite
recently. He knows one of the partners is always on call
on winter weekends.'

'So why didn't you tell me he was coming?'

'I thought he was due next weekend.' He consulted
his diary. 'I'm right. He was supposed to come next
Saturday, in which case I'd have taken him round the
place. As I always do,' he added significantly.

'Yes, I know,' said Portia, softening. 'Anyway, he
turned up last weekend, and also commands my presence
down there next weekend as well. You owe me, Mr
Parrish.''

Whitefriars Estates was a thriving business, which
dealt with desirable properties at the top end of the market, all of them in fashionable, expensive locations. The

clients were often celebrities of one kind or another, and
Portia's day was rarely boring. The week progressed in
its usual way, other than a hiccup with her car. When
she took it in for a service she was told it needed parts
which wouldn't be available for a day or two, which
meant the car wouldn't be ready until late on Monday.

Portia travelled by Underground the rest of the week,
except for the evening she went straight from the office
to dine with Joe Marcus. Joe was a property developer
she'd met on her MBA course, a high-flyer, clever, with
a wicked sense of humour, and determined to avoid marriage until he was at least forty. He took Portia out regularly, secure in the fact that she shared his point of
view. And with Marianne in the throes of a new love
affair, Portia kept the other evenings free, to get as much
sleep as possible to prepare for another visit to Turret
House. And a meeting with Luc Brissac again. A prospect she found herself looking forward to more than she
wanted to admit.

On the Friday Portia snatched a half-hour at lunchtime
for a sandwich in her office. She was immersed in the
designs Biddy had prepared for a brochure, when her
cellphone rang. She eyed it for a moment. Marianne's
new idol probably had clay feet. Again. With a sigh, she
pressed the button.

'Portia?' said a voice with an unmistakable French
cadence. 'Luc Brissac.'

To her annoyance her heart missed a beat, then she
tensed, suddenly afraid he was going to pull out of the
deal. 'Hello. How are you?'

'Very well. I wish to confirm our appointment tomorrow.'

Portia let out a silent breath of relief. 'Good. Actually,

I'm glad you rang. I can't make it to the house until noon. Does that suit you?'

'It would suit me better to drive you there myself, Mademoiselle Portia.'

A little thrill of excitement ran through Portia. It was only practical to accept, she told herself firmly, now her car was out of action. The alternative was a train at the crack of dawn, and a taxi to take her to Turret House. Which would be sheer stupidity when she could enjoy the journey in the company of Luc Brissac.

'You are still there?' he asked. 'If you have an appointment tomorrow night do not worry. I will drive you back in time. Or are you only content when driving yourself, Portia?'

'No, of course not. Thank you. What time do you want to leave?'

'I shall pick you up at nine. Where do you live?'

'No need for that. I'll meet you somewhere.'

'I insist on coming to *you*, Portia. Your address, please.'

She hesitated, then told him where to collect her. 'I'll be ready at nine, then.'

'I look forward to seeing you again. *A demain*, Portia.'

Assuming Luc Brissac would want another climb down to the cove, Portia was ready well before nine next morning in sensible shoes, black sweater, black needle-cord trousers and her amber fleece jacket, shivering a little with combined cold and anticipation as she waited on the pavement.

When a Renault came to a halt at the kerb Luc Brissac jumped out, smiling. 'Portia—you should not be standing outside in such weather.'

'Good morning.' She smiled. 'I thought I'd save some time.'

Luc was dressed casually again, in suede windbreaker, cashmere sweater and elegantly battered cords, none of it any different from some of the men she knew. The difference, she decided, lay in nationality, and his air of supreme self-confidence.

'You look delightful this morning, Portia,' he remarked as he drove off. 'Did your week go well?'

'Socially and professionally very well indeed.' Portia smiled wryly. 'The only blot on my week was my car. It needed a bigger repair than expected.'

'Ah.' Luc sent a gleaming look in her direction before negotiating a busy roundabout. 'So this is why you so meekly allow me to drive you to Turret House?'

'Yes,' she said demurely, and he laughed.

'You are so bad for my self-esteem, Portia Grant. Could you not pretend you joined me for the sake of my company on the journey?'

'I don't do pretence,' she informed him. 'But I'll admit I'm very grateful for a lift. I didn't enjoy the drive home last Sunday.'

'I was most concerned. It was a long evening before I could ring to assure myself that you were safe,' he informed her.

Portia gave him a surprised look. 'How very nice of you.'

'Nice? Such British understatement!' He shook his head in amusement. 'Now. Tell me. What expensive properties did you sell this week, Portia? Is business good?'

Portia told him business was surprisingly good for the time of year. The rest of the journey was spent in easy conversation more concerned with the property market and current affairs than any personal details on either side, which Portia found rather intriguing. Usually her male companions were only too ready to talk about themselves. The journey seemed much shorter than usual, and all too soon, it seemed to Portia, they came to the familiar crossroads and took the fork to Turret House.

The day was grey and cold, and without the sunshine of the week before the house looked even less inviting as Luc parked the car outside the Gothic arch of the front door.

'It needs trees in pots and tubs filled with flowers to soften the effect of the brick,' said Portia, getting out.

This time, with Luc for company, it was easier to unlock the door and go inside. Portia snapped on the lights quickly, but before following her Luc turned back to the car and took two folded director's chairs from the boot, then reached in again for a picnic basket. 'This time we drink our coffee here,' he announced.

Portia eyed the basket in surprise. 'That's very big for just coffee.'

He smiled. 'There is also a picnic for later, should you disapprove of lunch at Ravenswood. Since the kitchen is the only complete room, let us establish ourselves there.' He paused, chairs in one hand, the basket in the other. 'Unless you cannot bear to remain that long?'

'But I thought the whole idea of getting me down here today was to give you access to the place,' she said, frowning.

The green eyes met hers very directly. 'Part of the idea only, Portia.'

Portia turned away, surprised to find she no longer felt in the least uneasy with Luc Brissac. And in his

company she was not as opposed to time spent in Turret
House as he obviously assumed. 'Let's have that coffee,
then.'

Luc placed the chairs near the window looking out
over the back garden, then opened one flap of the basket
and filled china beakers with coffee from a vacuum flask.
He added milk from another flask to Portia's, and handed
it to her with a bow.

'*Voilà*. That is the way you like it?'

'Yes, it is,' she said impressed. 'Thank you.' She sat
down in one of the chairs, looking at him questioningly.
'Do you need any help with measurements, or anything
like that?'

Luc smiled at her indulgently and shook his head.
'No. But it is most kind of you to offer.'

'Then why, exactly, am I here?' she asked.

'If *you* were not with me, legally I could not enter
Turret House.'

Portia drank some of her coffee. 'Monsieur Brissac—'

'Luc,' he contradicted.

'Luc, then,' she said impatiently. 'I've given up a
Saturday to come down here, so surely I'm entitled to
know what you want me to do.'

'But I told you that last time we met.'

She looked at him narrowly. 'You've brought me all
this way just to find out why I dislike Turret House?'

He shrugged. 'Partly. But surely it is obvious to you
by this time that I also desire your company?'

She stiffened. 'You could have had that in London.'

'Could I, Portia?' he said swiftly. 'If I asked you out
to a purely social dinner would you accept? *Non*, I think
not. So this way you are obliged to suffer my company,
also to keep your promise.'

Portia stared down into her coffee for a moment, then

looked up to meet the intent green eyes. 'As I said, I don't do pretence, so it's not a case of *suffering* your company.'

His eyes gleamed with open triumph. 'I am honoured, Portia. That was not easy for you to say, I think.'

'No,' she agreed, and smiled a little. 'It won't be easy to tell you what you want to know either, so I require something in return.'

'Anything you desire,' he said swiftly.

'I'm curious to know why you're buying Turret House.'

'D'accord,' he said promptly, then grinned. 'Better still, you can make guesses.'

'Right,' she said, feeling suddenly light-hearted. 'Let's see, you're getting married and intend to have a large family?'

He shook his head. 'Wrong, *mademoiselle*. Try again.'

Startled by how much his answer pleased her, Portia thought for a moment, then said, 'I've got it. You were interested in the elevator. You want the house for a retirement home!'

Luc chuckled. 'Wrong again.'

Portia threw up a hand. 'I give in.'

'The house is needed as an annexe for Ravenswood. Business there is brisk, and often the hotel is obliged to turn customers away. Turret House is only a mile or two away, and there could be transport from one place to the other. Also,' he added, 'the private cove is a great advantage for families with children.'

Portia smiled at him in delight. 'But that's a wonderful idea, Luc. It's exactly what the place needs, lots of life, with people coming and going.'

'I'm glad you agree.' He stood up. 'Come, let us make another inspection. You shall look at everything with the eye of a guest, and tell me if you approve my ideas. But afterwards,' he added with emphasis, 'I shall keep you to your promise.'

As though bent on banishing any lingering ghosts for Portia, the sun broke through the clouds as she went through the house with Luc again. This time, looking at it with an eye to its possibilities as a hotel annexe, the house took on a new personality to Portia as they discussed possible use for each of the rooms, and which alterations would be necessary before it could function as a hotel. She grew enthusiastic and animated, stray curls escaping round her face, but tailed into silence at last as she realised Luc was looking at her without listening to a word she was saying.

'What is it?' she asked suspiciously. 'Am I talking nonsense?'

'Some of your suggestions are very practical. They will be of much use.' He hesitated, then gave his familiar shrug. 'It is just that you are so beautiful like this, Portia—like a statue come to life. I am dazzled.' He grimaced as the animation faded from her face. 'I am also a fool. Now I have spoiled it all. You will demand to be returned to London at once.'

'No, I won't do that,' said Portia, secretly disarmed by the compliment. 'In any case you haven't seen everything yet. There's something I forgot to show you last week.'

'There is?' He looked at her warily. 'So. After you show me this you will share the picnic with me?'

'Yes, I will. I'm hungry.' She smiled at him mischievously, her eyes dancing, and Luc made an involuntary move towards her, then halted.

'Maybe,' he said with constraint, 'we should eat at Ravenswood—'

'No,' she said firmly.

'Or at the inn we went to last week.' His eyes met hers. 'But it was very noisy there, not a place easy for conversation.'

'True. So we'll picnic here—pity to waste the contents of that smart basket.'

He smiled. 'I am not sure what they are. I did not pack it.'

Portia felt a definite pang at the thought of some woman making up a picnic lunch for Luc Brissac. Hey, she told herself. He's just a client.

Portia led Luc back to the kitchen and out into a room used by the precious owners as a laundry. A door from it led out into a large porch, with an outer door into the garden, and another which Portia opened on a flight of steps leading downward. As she turned on the light Luc caught her by the arm.

'Is that a cellar? You need not go down there, Portia. I can explore alone.'

'I don't mind in the slightest,' she assured him, and led the way down to a large basement room which housed the oil-fired central heating boiler and rows of empty wine racks.

Luc looked at her searchingly as he joined her. 'The cellar holds no terror for you, then?'

'No,' she said cheerfully. 'There's not much to see down here, other than the boiler.'

He inspected it, frowning. 'This must be replaced. It cannot have served the entire house.'

'I suppose the vendors rarely needed heat in every room at the same time.'

Luc nodded, then waved her ahead of him. 'Let us go back to the kitchen and eat this lunch. I asked for something nourishing to suit the weather, so let us investi-gate.'

The picnic basket yielded more insulated flasks, con-tainers filled with bread rolls and several types of cheese, plates, and silverware wrapped in starched white nap-kins.

'Because you might be cold I asked for lobster bisque,' said Luc, opening one of the flasks. 'It smells good. And I know you like lobster, Portia, because you ordered it for your dinner the other night. There is no wine, alas. So we must content ourselves with mineral water and coffee.'

'What exactly do you do, Luc?' she asked curiously as he filled fresh beakers with the soup. 'Are you a rep-resentative for a hotel chain?'

He nodded absently, intent on his task.

'That explains why you're so well known at the Ravenswood.'

He handed her a mug of soup. 'Try that, Portia.'

She sipped, and smiled at him. 'Delicious.'

Luc put the basket down between them on the kitchen floor. 'The easiest way, I think, without a table.'

They ate rolls and finished the flask of soup between them, talking over the improvements Luc felt were nec-essary for the success of Turret House.

'But I do not like the name,' he said, cutting a piece of Roquefort for her.

'Ravenswood Annexe? Or Cliff House?'

He shook his head. 'It does not ring the bell.'

'The house is near the edge of the cliff—Edgecliff?' She wrinkled her nose. 'Sounds like a Victorian novel. You need something romantic, inviting. My schoolgirl French isn't very wonderful, I regret to say. How do you say cliff-edge, Luc?'

'Au bord de la falaise,' he said, and Portia smiled triumphantly.

'Perfect! Plant creeper to soften the brick walls, and fill some urns with flowers, call the annexe La Falaise and Turret House will be a thing of the past.'

'As it was once part of your past, I think?' he said, his eyes questioning.

Portia nodded, suddenly sober. 'Yes. At one time it was my home.'

CHAPTER FOUR

'TIME to keep my promise.' Portia was silent for a moment, then she got up to rinse out their beakers. 'Could I have some coffee first?'

Luc frowned. 'Portia, I have changed my mind. Do not disturb yourself by telling me more. If they are painful, leave your memories in the past.'

She hesitated, almost tempted to agree. But in some strange way she felt she owed Luc Brissac something for laying her ghosts—unknowingly, it was true. But if he hadn't demanded her presence at Turret House she would never have set foot in it again, and it would have continued to haunt her. Now the ghosts were exorcised. The proof of this was the very fact that she was picnicking here in the Turret House kitchen. A situation she would have laughed to scorn if anyone had predicted it.

'I've psyched myself up to it now,' she said, as Luc poured coffee from a fresh flask. 'And we made a deal. My past isn't something I discuss much, but if you'd like to hear about it I'm willing to tell you.' She smiled faintly. 'It's supposed to be easier to confide in strangers.'

Luc gave her an unexpectedly cold look. 'Is that how you think of me, Portia? As a stranger?'

Her eyes fell. 'If I'm honest, I've done my best to think of you solely as a client.'

'You have done your best, you say?' repeated Luc thoughtfully. 'Does that mean you did not find it easy? To think of me as just a client?'

Portia looked at him warily, not sure how to answer, and he smiled.

'*Alors*, Portia. Begin at the beginning. Were you born here?'

She shook her head. 'I come from a small village about twenty miles away. I lived in a house attached to my father's garage—a small place that did car repairs.'

'Of course! Your father named you for the Porsche.'

She smiled ruefully. 'Not that he ever owned one.'

'And your mother?'

'She was a born home-maker, a fabulous cook and very pretty. My father adored her—wouldn't hear of her getting a job, even though money was always tight. Dad was brilliant at his craft, but hopeless about getting people to settle their bills. When I won a scholarship to the local girls' school they were so delighted and proud.' Portia paused to clear her throat, and Luc put out a hand to touch hers.

'Do you want to go on?'

'Yes. You may as well know the rest.' She took in a deep breath. 'When I was fourteen my father was out test-driving a car he'd repaired. A drunken idiot in a pick-up jumped a red light and rammed into him. Dad died later in hospital.'

'*Mon Dieu!*' Luc moved his chair closer and took her hand firmly in his.

Comforted by his touch, Portia did her best to keep to the unvarnished facts as she told him that the garage had been losing money, there'd been a second mortgage on the house, and Christine Grant had been left virtually penniless.

'It was so terrible for her.' Portia swallowed hard. 'She was in despair, until Mr Radford came up with a solution.'

Lewis Radford had been the solicitor in charge of Paul Grant's affairs. He'd lived alone at Turret House, his housekeeper had wanted to retire, and in the circumstances he'd suggested Christine Grant might care to take her place.

'So we came here to live,' said Portia colourlessly.

'This man was unkind to you?' demanded Luc.

'No. I hardly ever saw him. I was told to keep out of sight and never disturb him.' Portia shivered. 'So Mother and I had security, but we both missed Dad so horribly and the first year was grim. I was so miserable I put on weight and came out in spots.'

'This is hard to believe!'

'I turned to junk food for comfort.' Portia smiled wryly. 'Then a new girl arrived at the school. Marianne was blonde, pretty, and great fun. We were opposites in every way, but we hit it off right from the first. My life—and my appearance—improved enormously. Then at eighteen I went off to Reading to study Land Management. Mr Radford, much to our surprise, offered financial help.'

'And your friend?'

'Marianne went to Oxford to read English. We kept in touch, always, but after her family moved to Kent there was no one here for me in the vacations. So in warm weather I spent most of my free time down in the cove.'

Luc released her hand abruptly and stood up to pour more coffee. 'I assume,' he said after a while, 'that you slept in the room at the top of the tower.'

'Heavens, no. Mother and I had tiny adjoining rooms upstairs at the back, bathrooms now. The tower was Mr Radford's private property. He used the first two floors as a sitting room and a study, but the top floor was kept locked. Not even my mother was allowed up there. When I first came here I had nightmares about it, imagined all sorts of horrors.'

'Did you eventually discover the secret of the locked room?' asked Luc.

Portia managed a smile. 'That sounds like the title of a Sherlock Holmes mystery.'

'I confess I am intrigued.'

'My mother said Mr Radford kept confidential files for special clients there.' She was silent for a while, her eyes heavy with memories.

'So, Portia,' Luc prompted eventually, 'you achieved your degree?'

'Yes. But soon afterwards my mother died...' She trailed into silence, fighting a losing battle with tears. She took a tissue from her bag and scrubbed at her eyes. 'Shortly afterwards,' she continued hoarsely, getting up, 'Mr Radford died too. He'd left my mother some money, and it came to me. End of story.'

Luc took her hands in his. 'Ah, *chérie*, do not cry. Was this money enough to make life bearable for you?'

The endearment seemed so natural Portia hardly noticed it. 'It meant that with a lot of economising I could wait for a while before the right job came along and when I'd gained enough experience I still had just enough money left to take time off to study for my MBA—my Masters in Business Administration,' she added.

He nodded. 'I studied for this also. It is a demanding course.'

'Without it I wouldn't be a partner—though a very junior one—at Whitefriars.' She turned away. 'There. The story of my life.'

'Not all of it, Portia.'

'No, not quite. The rest is pretty ordinary. Boring, even.' She began repacking the picnic basket.

'You could never bore me, Portia,' Luc assured her.

'You haven't spent enough time with me to be sure of that,' she said, and turned to smile at him.

'A situation I intend to remedy.' He touched a fingertip to the tearstains under her eyes. 'Ah, *mignonne*,' he whispered, and took her into his arms. For a long, timeless interval he held her lightly, and Portia leaned against him pliantly, liking the comfort of the embrace as his hand stroked her hair. But at last, with supreme confidence of his welcome, Luc bent to kiss her, his lips meeting hers with tenderness which quickly transformed to heat as his arms tightened, and she responded instinctively for a moment or two before summoning the strength to free herself.

'Is this why you insisted I came here today?' she asked unevenly, backing away.

Luc stared at her in disbelief, then his face hardened. 'No, it is not! If you are implying that a sexual encounter was my aim, *mademoiselle*, I could have achieved that without leaving Paris. My sole intention,' he added caustically, 'was to make certain that this property would be suitable for the purpose I described to you.' He shrugged. 'But your story was touching. My urge was to comfort you. An impulse I now regret.'

After that there seemed little more to say. By the time Portia had visited a bathroom and tidied herself up Luc was waiting in the car with such hostile impatience she cursed herself for confiding in him.

For the first few miles of the journey the silence in the car was so impenetrable there was no possibility of breaking it even if Portia had wished to. The brief sunlight of noon had given way to a cold, grey afternoon, with the threat of fog. It matched her mood. Luc's too, she thought, depressed, wishing now she'd made less of the incident and passed off the kiss with more finesse.

They reached the motorway before Luc spoke.

'You need not worry,' he said brusquely, his accent more pronounced than usual. 'I shall keep my word.'

Portia glanced at his taut, imperious profile in surprise, then turned her gaze back on the myriad of red tail-lights stretching ahead of them. 'Good. Though I don't imagine my story would interest anyone else.'

'I meant my purchase of Turret House. But, since you mention it,' he added curtly, 'your confidences are also safe with me.'

'Oh.' Her cheeks burned. The possibility of losing the sale had never occurred to her. 'Thank you, Monsieur Brissac,' she said formally. 'On both counts.'

'You told me less about yourself than I wanted,' he said, sounding less hostile.

'My mission was to help with the house, not bore you to death.'

'You could never do that,' he assured her. 'Yours is a sad story, Portia.'

'Not any more,' she assured him.

He gave her a swift, sidelong glance. 'There is some man who makes you happy?'

'Yes,' she said with truth. Her weekly outings with Joe were great fun. He made her laugh, so it followed that he made her happy.

'Is it because of this man you were so reluctant to give up your weekend?' asked Luc, then broke off to curse volubly as a car cut in front of him without warning. 'Well?' he persisted later. 'Was your man angry that you spent the time with me?'

'Clients often take up my time at weekends,' Portia
assured him. 'Joe understands perfectly.'

'So admirable,' said Luc Brissac with sarcasm. 'In his
position I would not be so understanding.'

'Business is business,' said Portia, and slid further
down in her seat and closed her eyes.

As a hint it was effective. Luc Brissac made no more
attempt at conversation. Instead he switched on the radio
and found a Vivaldi recital.

'I apologise for disturbing you,' he said later, long
after Vivaldi had given way to Ravel. 'We are nearing
London. I shall need directions to your apartment when
we leave the *autoroute*.'

She sat up, yawning, doing her best to behave like
someone waking from a deep sleep. 'Sorry. I was a bit
tired.'

'You were out late last night?'

'No. I just didn't get to sleep very early.'

'This man lives with you?' he demanded.

Portia glared at him. 'No. He doesn't.' Then her eyes
widened as she saw the familiar green sign looming up.
'Watch out—we get off at this exit.'

Cursing under his breath, Luc slammed a hand on the
horn, and with negligent panache shot across the lanes
of traffic down the slipway, braking so suddenly at the
stop sign that the car behind shunted into them and
Portia let out a screech as her temple hit the side window.

Luc killed the engine and pounced to release her seatbelt, blood trickling down his chin, his English deserting
him as he bent over her in a frenzy of anxiety.

'Speak English, please,' she muttered.

'Are you much injured, Portia?' he demanded. '*Mon
Dieu*, you are so pale.'

'I feel pale,' she said bitterly, and sat up, putting a hand to her throbbing head. 'Who's that outside, talking to the police?'

'It must be the driver who crashed into me,' said Luc with indifference. He dabbed at his mouth with a handkerchief, and, once Portia had managed to convince him she was relatively unhurt, got out of the car.

By the time names and addresses had been exchanged, and Luc, to his outrage, had been breathalysed by the police for his alcohol level, Portia had the worst headache of her entire life. She assured the police that she was in no need of an ambulance, and promised to see a doctor if she felt worse when she got home.

Luc assured them with arrogance that his companion would receive every care, and only Portia's hasty intervention averted an international incident when the policeman suggested that better care of the lady should have been taken in the first place.

When both cars were pronounced fit to drive, and they were finally allowed on their way, Luc put out a hand to touch Portia's. 'I ask your forgiveness.'

'Put your hand back on the wheel,' she gasped.

He obeyed promptly, sending a smouldering look at her. 'You cannot endure my slightest touch?'

'It isn't that,' she snapped. 'I'd just rather we got home in one piece.'

'Normally I am a very safe driver,' he said furiously. 'If you had told me which exit we took I would have been prepared.'

'All right, all right, I'm to blame,' she said irritably. 'Turn right at the next junction, please.'

Luc drove with exaggerated care for the rest of the way, and when they arrived handed Portia out of the car as if she were made of glass. 'Are you feeling better?'

he demanded. 'You must see a doctor at once. You could
be suffering concussion—'

'I've got a headache, Luc, that's all,' she said flatly.
'I'll make myself some tea and go straight to bed, and
I'll be fine.'

'I shall ring you later—' he began.

'Please don't—there's no need,' she said swiftly.
'Goodnight.'

'I will see you safely to your apartment,' he insisted.

Desperate for privacy and bed, Portia reminded herself
that Luc Brissac was a valued client, and let him go up
with her in the lift. When it stopped she held out her
hand. 'There. Safe and sound.'

Luc lifted the hand to his lips. 'I am so desolated that
the day should end in such a way. *Au 'voir*, Portia.'

She frowned as she noticed he was still bleeding from
the corner of his mouth. 'Does it hurt?' she asked.

He shrugged, and gave her a sardonic smile. 'Less
than my pride.'

When it became obvious that Luc Brissac was determined to wait until she was safely through the door,
Portia unlocked it, gave him a weary little smile and
closed the door on him.

Then she turned to face two people who rose from the
sofa to eye her in blank astonishment.

'Darling, do knock next time,' said Marianne, laughing. 'We could have been doing all sorts of sinful things
instead of watching television. This is Hal Courtney, by
the way. Hal, meet Portia Grant.'

'How do you do?' said Portia, as a strong hand
clasped hers. She smiled up into a thin, interesting face,
then muttered an apology and made for the bathroom at
speed.

After she'd parted with her lunch, washed her face,
drunk some water, and explored the bump on her temple,

Portia examined her discolouring eye with resignation, then went back to the living room, where Marianne had a tea tray ready, and Hal was nowhere to be seen.

'He tactfully took himself to the off-licence to get some wine for our supper. Now then, Portia, what *have* you been up to? You look ghastly.' Marianne fixed her with a steely blue gaze. 'And, not that it isn't lovely to see you, but for a moment there Hal thought someone was breaking and entering. You could have rung first.'

'I didn't mean to get as far as actually coming in,' said Portia, accepting a cup of tea. 'Thanks. I need this.'

'You've hurt yourself!' exclaimed Marianne, and turned Portia's face to the light. 'I didn't notice when you made your dramatic entry. What on earth happened to you?'

Portia gave a brief account of the day, and the circumstances which had led up to the bump on the head and the ensuing encounter with the police.

'Good heavens, darling,' said Marianne, aghast, 'are you sure you're all right? Shouldn't you go to a hospital to get checked?'

'That's what Luc Brissac wanted, but I'm fine. I just wanted to get home.'

'Who's Luc Brissac?'

'The man who's buying Turret House.' Portia met her friend's astonished stare with a grimace. 'That's right. Turret House. We were driving back from it when it happened. I was showing him round. He's going to buy it.'

Marianne leaned forward urgently and took her hand. 'You've actually been back to Turret House? Why didn't you *tell* me?'

'I meant to, but I knew you were busy with the new man—who seems very nice, by the way, from my fleet-

ing glimpse.' Portia grinned. 'Time enough for girl-talk
when you're at a loose end again.'

'That may be longer this time,' muttered Marianne.

Portia watched in awe. 'You're blushing!'

'It's not against the law, Portia Grant.' Marianne released her hand and sat back. 'And you wouldn't have
interrupted anything.'

'Why not?'

'Because he's not like the others. We talk all the time,
and enjoy just being together, doing things other people
do. Walking, watching television, going to the cinema.
Ordinary things.' She smiled radiantly. 'It's lovely.'

Portia was impressed. Marianne's men were usually
the kind who wined and dined her expensively and expected return for their outlay. 'I'm glad,' she said simply. 'Sorry I barged in like that.'

'Don't be silly. But before I expire with curiosity,
please tell me why it was necessary!'

'I didn't want Luc Brissac to know where I lived.'

Marianne sighed impatiently. 'Why ever not?
Honestly, Portia, that flat of yours might just as well be
an anchorite's cell.'

'Don't exaggerate. I hand my address out sparingly,
that's all.' Portia shrugged. 'Luc Brissac is just a business connection. If he wants to contact me he can ring
the office.'

'Is he nice?'

Portia thought about it. 'I don't think "nice" fits him,
somehow.'

'Loaded, then. If he's buying Turret House he must
have the odd penny or two.'

'He represents a hotel chain. He wants the house for
an annexe to Ravenswood.'

Marianne frowned. 'What's his full name?'

'Jean-Christophe Lucien Brissac—' Portia winced.

'Have you got any painkillers, Marianne? I've got a splitting headache.'

The doorbell rang and Marianne jumped up to let Hal Courtney in. 'Why didn't you use your key?' she asked him as he came in with a clinking package of bottles.

'I was trying to be tactful,' he said, chuckling. 'I wasn't sure you'd want your friend to know I had a key.'

Portia smiled. 'As you saw, I've got one myself. Marianne keeps one of mine, too. Sorry I came crashing in on you earlier.'

'Talking of crashing,' said Marianne, 'give her the once-over, would you, Hal?'

'What's the problem? Trust me, Portia,' he added, eyes twinkling. 'I'm a doctor.'

After Portia explained about the incident in the car, Hal produced a medical bag and gave her a thorough examination, feeling her pulse and holding up a finger as he shone a slim torch beam in her eyes and asked if she felt sick.

'I threw up when I arrived, and I still feel a bit queasy,' she admitted apologetically, 'but the headache's the major problem.'

He pushed back unruly fair hair, eyeing her thoughtfully. 'I'm not surprised, Portia. You've got mild concussion.' He looked up into Marianne's anxious face. 'Could you rustle up some plain biscuits, darling? Once Portia's got them down, with some weak tea, I'll give her a couple of mild painkillers.'

Despite Portia's protests about ruining their evening, Marianne made her stay until her headache eased and she felt up to walking back to her flat. When Portia's phone rang just as they were ready to leave Marianne snatched it from her.

'Yes, she's here. I'm a friend. She's feeling very unwell.' She pulled a face and handed over the phone. 'It's a Monsieur Brissac,' she said very clearly.

'Hello,' said Portia, resigned.

'Your friend says you are ill,' said Luc heatedly. 'I should have taken you to a doctor—'

'I've seen a doctor. Apparently I've got slight concussion.'

'*Mon Dieu!* I am so sorry, Portia—'

'I'll be fine,' she assured him. 'By the way, how's your mouth?'

'It is why I did not ring earlier. My teeth caused damage to my lip. I needed a stitch,' he said with deep disgust. 'It would not stop bleeding.'

'Bad luck. I hope it's better soon. Goodnight.' She switched off the phone and put it in her bag, swaying a little.

'Steady the buffs,' said Hal, taking her arm. 'Are you sure you can walk? I've got the car.'

'I live in the next road,' said Portia. 'A walk would do me good.'

'We'll come with you,' said Marianne firmly.

'Oh, please don't—I'll be fine!'' said Portia in dismay, but nothing could dissuade either Hal or Marianne until she was back in the sanctuary of her own flat.

'This Brissac man's got a very sexy voice; I love his accent,' said Marianne, as they kissed goodnight. 'Why won't you give him your address?'

'I told you. He's strictly business.'

'Pity.'

'Get to bed right away, Portia,' said Hal. 'And see your own doctor tomorrow.'

Marianne sighed ecstatically. 'He's so masterful—I just love it!'

Hal shook his head, chuckling, put his arm round her and pushed her into the waiting lift. As the doors closed on them Portia was left with an indelible picture of Marianne gazing blissfully into the eyes laughing down into hers.

Annoyed because she felt vaguely sorry for herself, Portia closed her door and ran herself a bath. When she got into bed at last, her aching head propped up on several pillows, she wondered how Luc Brissac was feeling at this moment. Feigning sleep in the car had been a bad move. If she'd pointed out the exit in good time Luc's death-defying dash through the traffic would have been unnecessary. Now the man was mortified, and his ego badly dented. Not that it mattered. She was home in one piece, and, even more important, Turret House was now out of her life for good. Probably Luc Brissac's minions would work on the rest of the transaction. She need never see him again.

Portia frowned, rather startled to find she regretted this. Luc was attractive, sophisticated, and his insistence on seeing her again had been flattering. Nevertheless, there was a faint, indefinable something about him that made her uneasy. Which was illogical. Far from threatening her in any way he'd set out to charm from their first encounter in the hall at Turret House. And, if she were totally honest with herself, for a moment his kiss had been as welcome as he'd expected it to be. She sighed irritably. One way and another life would be more peaceful if Luc Brissac played no part in hers in future.

CHAPTER FIVE

PORTIA stayed in bed until the telephone woke her next morning. She picked up the receiver and yawned a response, her voice foggy with sleep.

'Wake up!' said Marianne urgently.

'I am awake. More or less. What's wrong?'

'I've just received a visit from a very irate Frenchman armed with roses. He's on his way round to you as we speak.'

'Mari*anne*,' shrieked Portia. 'How could you?'

'Very easily. He's gorgeous. I'll have words with you later, Portia Grant. Bye.'

Head protesting, Portia leapt out of bed, splashed water on her face, pulled on jeans and a jersey, and tied her hair back with a scarf. When her buzzer rang she cast a despairing look in the bathroom mirror and hurried to pick up the receiver.

'Luc Brissac,' he snapped. 'I wish to see you.'

'Come up, then.'

When Portia opened the door her heart sank as Luc, eyes blazing, thrust a vast bunch of tawny roses in her arms and stalked after her into the room, very obviously in a towering rage.

He stopped dead as the winter sunlight fell on her face. '*Mon Dieu*, you have a black eye!'

'How observant of you,' she said militantly. 'What lovely flowers. Thank you. I'll just put them in water.'

She took her time in the kitchen, looking for something large enough to hold several dozen long-stemmed blooms. In the end she put them in the sink, ran water into it, and returned to find Luc pacing up and down the room.

'Why did you play such silly games with me?' he demanded. 'Did it amuse you to make me feel like an idiot at your friend's apartment? The apartment,' he added, eyes kindling, 'that I escorted you to last night in the belief that it was yours!'

Portia looked away. 'I prefer to keep my address private.'

'And not only your address,' he said furiously. 'I just checked the number on your telephone. It is not the number you gave me. Does that also belong to your friend?'

'I gave you my cellphone number.' Portia tried a conciliatory smile. 'Won't you sit down?'

'No, I will not.' Luc flung over to the window and glowered at the view. 'I arrived at your friend's place this morning as one of the other tenants was leaving, so I was not obliged to ring a bell to gain entry. Otherwise, of course, I would have found your name missing from the list outside. So I rang the bell of the apartment I so stupidly believed was yours, and a man opened the door to me.' He swung round to glare at her. 'Can you imagine my reaction?'

Since Portia could imagine the scene only too clearly, she had trouble in keeping a straight face as she thought of Hal Courtney confronted with a strange man bearing roses. After his first night actually spent with Marianne, by the sound of it, too, she realised guiltily.

'You think this is amusing?' He muttered something French and unintelligible under his breath. 'I do not. Nor did your friend's lover. Naturally I believed he was the man you talk about. Now, of course, I know that the flat belongs to your friend Marianne, and it was a Dr Courtney who mistook me for a rival.'

Portia bit her lip. 'I'm sorry you were embarrassed, but I never dreamed you'd call round in person.'

'I was responsible for causing you injury,' he said through his teeth. 'Did you really believe I would just go back to Paris and never give you another thought?'

'If I'd thought of it at all I'd have expected you to *send* flowers, not bring them yourself.'

He glared at her. 'So. Once you sent me away yesterday you dismissed me from your mind!'

'*No,*' she retorted, suddenly angry herself. 'I meant I didn't expect anything at all. Other than a phone call, perhaps, to ask how I was.'

'You credit me with that much courtesy, then? *Merci!*' he said bitingly. 'But you do not allow me to know your address. Why? Do you dislike me so much?'

'No, of course not. It was nothing personal. Oh, do sit down,' she added impatiently.

When Luc, not without some reluctance, took the other end of the sofa she noticed a bruise along his jaw, near the neatly stitched cut at the corner of his mouth. 'Nothing personal,' he repeated, and shrugged. 'You are so bad for me, Portia Grant.'

She looked away. 'I haven't lived here long. As you can see by the lack of furniture. It costs a lot to live alone in London in a place like this. And I tend to keep it to myself. No—please don't take offence,' she added as his eyes narrowed ominously. 'All my life I've lived with other people in one way or another. It was uphill work to save enough money for a place of my own when I can be completely private.' Portia looked at him in appeal. 'I never thought I'd see you again after yesterday, anyway.'

'So you pretended your friend's apartment was yours.' Luc frowned. 'But you had a key. I saw you unlock the door, and open it.'

'She keeps one of my keys, too. It's a habit of ours.'

Luc raised an eyebrow. 'Your friend must have been surprised when you arrived so unexpectedly yesterday?'

'Yes. Especially as I had to rush to the bathroom right away to throw up.' She flushed, wishing she'd kept that particular detail to herself.

He frowned. 'This was the result of the blow?'

'Either that or pure fright. Luckily Hal Courtney's a doctor, so he saved Marianne the trouble of hauling me off to hospital. Which she would have done, otherwise.'

'As I wished to do,' he reminded her, then looked her in the eye. 'Tell me, Portia. Is this man of yours allowed to know where you live?'

'Yes.'

Luc gave the elegant little snort she was getting to know. 'Then I suppose I am fortunate that he did not answer your door to me and take exception to the roses also.'

Portia let out an irrepressible giggle. 'Sorry,' she said unsteadily, 'but I would have loved to be there when Hal Courtney found you on Marianne's doorstep.'

'*I* was not pleased to be there,' he retorted, but after a moment he smiled unwillingly. 'You are right. It is amusing to look back on. It was not at the time.'

Portia's eyes danced. 'It was the first time Hal's ever stayed the night with Marianne, too.'

'*Mon Dieu*—no wonder he looked ready to kill me!'

'I'm sorry I caused you such embarrassment, Luc,' she said penitently.

'If it was the only means to learn your address I shall

survive, Portia.' His eyes met hers. 'Are you nervous now I know where you live?'

'Should I be?' she countered. 'You don't live in England, after all.'

'Not all the time,' he agreed, suddenly very much in command of himself again. 'But I own an apartment in London.'

'Do you come over often, then?'

'I do much business here, so I come often enough to need a base. Perhaps very often in future,' he added.

'I see.'

'No, you do not see,' he assured her. 'Tell me, would this man of yours object to this?'

Portia's eyes narrowed. 'Object to what, exactly?'

'To your friendship with me.' Luc's eyes held hers, like a cat about to pounce. He leaned forward and lifted her left hand. 'You wear no ring, so he is not your fiancé, Portia.'

'Maybe not. But I don't suppose he'd take kindly to the idea.' Which was an out and out lie. Joe Marcus took Portia's socialising with other men for granted. Which suited her perfectly. She had no desire for a close relationship with any man. Certainly not Luc Brissac. But an inner voice told her she wasn't being entirely honest with herself on that point. Luc was a type of man new in her experience. Which probably accounted for the odd feeling of unease he aroused in her. Not that the feeling was dislike. Or physical repulsion. His kiss, fleeting though it had been, had demonstrated that only too clearly.

'You are very quiet,' he remarked. 'Do you wish me to leave?'

'Don't you have a plane to catch?'

He shook his head. 'Not until tomorrow.'

She waved a hand at his formal suit. 'But you must have an appointment somewhere, dressed like that?'

'My other clothes were stained with blood.' He smiled smugly. 'And to be dressed formally was a great advantage at your friend's apartment. Dr Courtney was wearing only a bathtowel.'

Portia shook her head, laughing, then winced as her bruise protested. 'Oh dear, oh dear. How I *wish* I'd been there.' She pulled a face. 'But I'll have some explaining to do to Marianne.'

'Why?'

She gave him a wry little smile. 'I said I was with a client when I got the bump on my head, but I didn't give any details, so she wasn't curious about you personally, only the fact that you were buying Turret House. Now she's met you, of course, it's another story.'

He frowned. 'In what way? She did not seem to object to me.'

Portia grinned mischievously. 'I bet she didn't. She finds your accent irresistible, she tells me. You obviously bowled Marianne over.'

'If so I am flattered,' he said, frowning. 'But, although she is a beautiful lady, and no doubt very charming, I do not—'

'I meant she probably thinks of you in relation to me,' said Portia, looking away. 'She's not terribly keen on Joe.'

Luc chuckled. 'Ah! You mean she likes making matches for you.'

'Something like that.'

'So she, at least, would be pleased if I asked to see you when I come to London?'

'That's not the point. It's *my* feelings you should be worrying about.'

'And I am,' he said swiftly. 'Otherwise why should I take so much trouble to find you? I was most reluctant to leave you last night. But I could not force you to let me stay. Also I was beginning to feel a little strange myself by that time.'

'So where did you get treatment?'

'I met one of my neighbours in the lift at my building. He was much concerned at the sight of me, and insisted on driving me to a hospital,' Luc shrugged. 'It was unnecessary, but without the stitch there would have been a scar, the doctor informed me.'

'Would that have worried you?'

His eyes gleamed sardonically. 'From a cosmetic point of view, not at all. But it occurred to me that if the cut was slow to get better I would not be able to kiss anyone.' The black-lashed eyes narrowed with a look that quickened her pulse. 'And even as you look now, *chérie*, with that regrettable black eye, the urge to kiss you is so strong it is a miracle I am so tamely keeping my distance.'

Portia felt colour flood into her face, and she jumped to her feet, which was a mistake, since Luc rose swiftly to bar her way. He stared down into her eyes, then took her in his arms.

'Do not be afraid,' he muttered into her hair, and tightened his hold as though expecting her to pull away. 'Yesterday you pushed me away.'

'I know,' she said into his shirt-front.

'Today is different?'

'It appears to be.'

Luc put a finger under her chin and lifted her bruised face to his, a wry smile twisting his injured mouth. 'Next weekend,' he said huskily, 'my stitch will be gone. If I fly over on Saturday, will you dine with me, Portia? Or will this man of yours object?'

'I'm my own woman, Luc,' she said with emphasis. 'If I want to dine with you I shall.'

His eyes glittered. 'And do you?'

She thought about it for a moment. 'Ring me later in the week.'

He scowled blackly. 'Why can you not say yes right now?'

Portia gave him a crooked little smile. 'Because I'm not dining out anywhere with a black eye, Luc Brissac. I do have my pride. So if you ring me on Friday I'll let you know if I'm fit to be seen.'

'I care nothing for your black eye.'

'Possibly not. But I do,' she said firmly, and smiled up at him.

'Mon Dieu,' he breathed, closing his eyes. 'I want to kiss you so much, Portia.'

'I could kiss you,' she offered, surprising herself.

Luc's eyes flew open, staring down into hers in disbelief.

'I'll be very careful,' she promised, and reached up to place her mouth at the corner of his, where she couldn't hurt him.

Luc stood like a man undergoing torture, his eyes tightly shut as her mouth moved over his cheek, and touched the bruise on his jaw with exquisite gentleness. With a stifled groan he put her away from him, breathing unevenly as he looked down at her flushed face.

'I was angry when I arrived,' he muttered.

'I know.'

'I thought you disliked me so much you would not even tell me where you lived.' He let out a deep, unsteady breath. 'Whereas I—'

'Whereas you?' prompted Portia.

''I do not dislike you,' he said in a constricted voice. 'But if I say more—as you well know I wish to do— you will refuse to see me again.'

Portia was surprised to find how unlikely that was. Now. It must be the knock on the head, she decided. It was by no means a habit of hers to kiss any man of her own accord. But his protective embrace had been strangely seductive.

'No,' she said quietly. 'I don't think I'll do that.'

'*Bon*. I am pleased.' Luc's eyes locked with hers. 'I must warn you, Portia, that it is only our respective wounds that force me to such restraint.'

Portia looked at him in silence for a moment. 'Are you saying,' she said slowly, 'that you will expect to sleep with me afterwards if I accept your invitation to dinner?'

He stood very still, his eyes suddenly like ice. 'I *expect* nothing, other than the pleasure of your company. I am no schoolboy ruled by the demands of my body, Portia.'

She shrugged, to mask the little chill that ran through her at the sudden coldness in his expressive voice. 'It's best to make things clear.'

Luc eyed her with hostility. 'Does this man of yours submit so tamely to such restrictions, Portia?'

'Not that it's any of your business, but as it happens he does.'

Luc shook his head in wonder. 'What kind of man is he?'

'A friend.'

'I was a fool to delude myself that *I* could be your friend.'

Portia was suddenly as angry as Luc. 'It's obvious

we'd better keep our acquaintance on a purely business level.'

'Which, of course, is what you value most.' The green eyes shot sparks of fire at her. 'As long as I buy Turret House it is all that matters to you, *n'est ce pas*?'

'It matters, yes.'

He looked at her in silence for a moment. 'As I said before, Portia, you are bad for my self-esteem.'

'Or possibly good for it,' she contradicted tartly. 'I suppose other women in your life fall over themselves to do whatever you want?'

Luc's eyebrows rose tauntingly. 'Are you curious about the women in my life?'

'Not in the least,' she lied.

'Then I shall not discuss them. I must go. I arranged an appointment for noon today.'

'Then I won't keep you,' said Portia tightly, and went ahead of him to the door. 'Goodbye, Luc. Thank you again for the roses.'

'I am glad you liked them,' he said, looking down at her broodingly. 'They reminded me of you.'

Her eyes narrowed. 'In what way?'

'Their tawny beauty—and their thorns.' He touched a finger to her unbruised cheek, and left without another word.

Not even an *au revoir*, she thought bitterly, and wondered who, exactly, he was on his way to meet.

Portia's eye had progressed to an angry plum colour ringed with green by next day, and, as expected, it provoked ribald, predictable comments from her male colleagues. Portia was in a bad mood by the time Biddy provided her with strong black coffee to kick-start her day.

'Are you telling the truth, Portia?' asked the middle-aged, streetwise Biddy. 'I mean, you didn't have a run-in with some bloke, by any chance?'

'No. I really did hit my head on a car window.' Portia thought for a moment. 'And if Monsieur Brissac—the man buying Turret House—rings, just take a message.'

'You mean whether you're here or not?' said Biddy sagely.

'Exactly.'

'Whatever you say. Mr Parrish wants a private word, by the way, when you've got a minute.'

When Portia went into Ben Parrish's office he rose and pulled out a chair. 'Take five and sit down.'

She did so, eyeing him questioningly. 'What's up?'

He looked away, shuffling papers in front of him on the desk. 'How much do you know about Luc Brissac?'

Startled by a secret leap of reaction, Portia shrugged casually. 'He's French, and represents a hotel chain. Other than that, not a lot.'

Ben eyed her uneasily. 'I feel a bit responsible because you had to get involved in the Turret House sale with him. It occurred to me you might like to know more about his background.'

Portia looked at him in alarm. 'Don't tell me he's not good for the money!'

Ben shook his head. 'Quite the reverse. Luc Brissac was only twenty-something when he turned the family château into a hotel, and just went on from there. His speciality is snapping up country houses and turning them into hotels—I quote—"famous for individuality and luxury". Both here and in France. The man's a millionaire.'

Portia stared at him. 'But he beat me down on the price of Turret House.'

'Of course he did. He's a businessman, Portia. He probably knew to the minute how long we'd had the place on our books.'

'So he meant to buy it right from the start,' she said, eyes kindling.

'I'd say, yes, he probably did.'

Portia sat burning with embarrassment as she remembered how Luc had not only conned her into a second visit to Turret House, but had demanded her life story before making a definite offer for the property. But *why*? What possible interest could a lowly estate agent have for someone wealthy enough to buy a hotel whenever he fancied one? She jumped to her feet, thanked Ben for the information, and assured him that the black eye wouldn't keep her from the day's appointments.

'Dark glasses and a hat, and no one will see,' she said brightly, and shut herself in her office, composing various flaying speeches to deliver when Luc rang.

But there was no call from Luc Brissac, that day or any other. Which infuriated Portia. She cringed as she thought of the kiss she'd volunteered. No wonder he'd expected her to fall into his arms. A man with his money could have any woman he wanted. Her eyes flashed. He'd soon find Portia Grant wasn't one of them.

Fortunately business was hotting up at Whitefriars. Spring was just around the corner, and with the appearance of the first daffodils enough demands for houses came in to keep all the partners busy full time. When Portia returned to the office mid-afternoon on the Friday Biddy was waiting, as usual, to take dictation for the letters and valuations she would send out the following Monday.

Biddy handed her a few messages she'd taken while Portia was out, but none of them was from Luc Brissac.

Which annoyed Portia so much she found it hard to concentrate on the job in hand. When the session was over
she surprised herself, Biddy, and the rest of her colleagues, by announcing she was leaving early for once.

'Hot date?' said one of the senior partners, on his way
in from a viewing.

'You bet. See you Monday.' Portia smiled at him and
went out into the cold sunshine to make for the car park.

When she got home there was a message on her machine from Marianne.

'Hal's on call tonight. Fancy a film and supper afterwards? Ring me.'

The other message was from Joe. 'Fond hope, I suppose, but are you free tomorrow night? I thought we
might try that new club I mentioned.'

Comforted to find herself in demand, Portia felt grateful to Joe for a Saturday night spent clubbing rather than
alone, fuming over Luc Brissac. After an entire working
week of expecting to hear from him every day, Portia
felt let down, and disproportionately angry.

She admitted as much back at her flat, as she shared
a pizza with Marianne after their return from the cinema.

'You like him, then?' asked her friend.

'Yes, I do.' Portia sighed glumly. 'But it's the usual
story.'

'You mean he wants bed,' said Marianne bluntly.
'And you, of course, don't, as usual. Pity. Luc's not up
to Hal's standard, of course, but he's eminently fancia-
ble.'

'We hardly know each other.'

'What difference does that make? You can fall in love
in the blink of an eye.'

Portia chuckled. 'You should know; you do it often
enough.'

'Ouch! Put your claws away.' Marianne detached another segment of pizza thoughtfully. 'Actually, having
met Hal, I realise I've never really been in love before.
The others were just rehearsals. This is the real thing.'

Portia eyed her anxiously. This was something new.
'Does he mind about the others?' she asked. 'Or haven't
you told him?'

'Oh, come on, love. I'm the same age as you. Of
course he knows there were others. Do I look like a
nun?' Marianne smiled philosophically. 'Besides, he's
had relationships in the past, too. He knows perfectly
well it's rare to get it right the first time.' She wagged
her finger. 'And you weren't *always* so touch-me-not
where men are concerned. When you were in college
you had a boyfriend or two.'

'All right, all right,' said Portia irritably.

Marianne eyed her for a moment, then shrugged. 'I
understand why you're wary of close relationships, love,
but it's time you put all that behind you. In my opinion
you should see something of the sexy Monsieur Brissac
for a while.'

'Always supposing he wants to see me!' Portia
shrugged. 'He hasn't rung me, so he's obviously lost
interest.'

'And you mind?'

'Yes, I do.' With Marianne there was never any need
to dissemble. 'But not in the way you think. I mind
because he made a fool of me. He softened me up into
selling Turret House for peanuts, when he's actually
worth millions. He owns the wretched hotel chain,
doesn't just represent it.'

'Golly!' said Marianne, impressed. 'All that Gallic
charm and lots of dosh as well?'

'That's right.' Portia smiled brightly. 'Not that it matters. I'm going out with Joe tomorrow night. At least with Joe what you see is what you get.'

'Hmm.'

'Joe's a great guy, Marianne, with exactly the same ideas about fun as me. Which makes for an uncomplicated social life. So take that look off your face.'

'Sorry. It's just that I worry about you.'

'You needn't. Joe won't hurt me. If anyone's likely to it's Luc Brissac—' Portia halted, biting her lip, and Marianne nodded sagely.

'I told you. The blink of an eye.'

'I'm not in *love* with him. Just—attracted. Besides, something about him makes me a bit uneasy.'

'What, exactly?'

'I wish I knew.' The phone rang, and Portia jumped up to answer it, a tiny flicker of hope snuffed out as Hal Courtney enquired about her head, then asked to speak to Marianne.

Portia went off to the kitchen with the detritus of their meal, and a moment later Marianne rushed in, starry-eyed.

'Hal's picking me up here in a few minutes. Someone else is taking over for him.'

Portia eyed her friend's translated face with wry amusement. 'You're right. I've never seen you like this before.'

Marianne gave her a mega-watt smile and hurried off to the bathroom to do her face, as excited as a teenager.

When the buzzer ran Marianne catapulted to the door to lift the receiver, and called, 'Come up,' then put it back and gave her friend a hug. 'When shall I see you again?'

'When Hal's on call again, I imagine,' said Portia dryly.

They laughed together, then a knock on the door sent Marianne racing to fling it wide, her eagerness transformed to astonishment as she came face to face with Luc Brissac.

CHAPTER SIX

LUC smiled politely at Marianne, but his eyes were drawn to Portia's blank, unwelcoming face. 'Forgive me. I should have rung first, I know. But—'

The buzzer interrupted him, and Marianne kissed Portia, wished them both goodnight, and with a meaningful look over her shoulder at her friend hurried off to meet Hal.

'May I close the door?' enquired Luc, when it seemed unlikely Portia was ever going to say anything.

'Yes, of course.' She pulled herself together. 'This is a surprise.' And, because she was wearing jeans and a not very new sweater, topped by a shiny face and riotously untidy hair, she was furious.

'The surprise is not pleasant, I think,' he said, standing just inside the door. 'I apologise that it is so late.'

'Not at all,' said Portia formally. 'Come in. Do sit down. Can I offer you a drink, or coffee?'

'Nothing. Thank you.'

Portia sat down in her only armchair, and waved him to the sofa. Luc sat on the edge of it, looking tired, and not quite as elegant as usual. He had dark rings under his eyes and needed a shave, and instead of a formal suit he wore the familiar suede jacket with jeans and a blue chambray shirt.

'Your eye is better,' he said at last, when it seemed the silence would last indefinitely.

'Yes, thanks. How's the cut?'

'The stitch was removed, so it is better also.' He gave

her a look which clenched her stomach muscles beneath the denim. 'I am sorry I did not ring you.'

'No need for apologies. We're both busy people.'

'I was angry when I left you last week.'

'So I noticed.'

'I did not intend to return to London this weekend.' He breathed in deeply. 'But at last I came.'

'A business appointment?' she asked politely.

'You know I do not mean that,' he said with sudden violence. 'I came to see *you*, Portia. I could not keep away.'

She masked a leap of pleasure with cool indifference. 'If your idea was to spend time with me I'm flattered, of course, but you're out of luck. I'm tied up this weekend.'

His eyes blazed. 'With this *friend* of yours?'

'That's right,' she said evenly. 'With Joe.'

Luc jumped to his feet. 'Then of course I shall not trouble you further. May I ring for a taxi?'

'Of course.' Portia marched to the telephone, thrusting back her hair as she looked down the list of numbers for the cab-hire firm she sometimes used, her eyes blurred by a mist of angry tears.

Before she could dial the number a hand reached to take hers. Luc turned her towards him and held her wrists, his eyes burning down into hers.

'Portia, do not send me away without talking to me. For just a little while.'

'Are you sure you mean talk?' she said huskily, throwing down the gauntlet.

His jaw tightened. 'You look so irresistible tonight it would be a lie to say I do not want more than that. But if you wish me only to talk, and not to touch, then I shall obey. Are you not proud of taming me so, Portia?

I am not accustomed to—what do you say?—toe the
line.'

'No. I can well believe that,' she snapped. 'So what
do you want to talk about?'

He eyed her warily. 'I thought that friendship would
be the perfect subject for discussion.'

'You mean you want that, after all?'

'No, I do not. If you demand the truth, then, yes. I
desire more than that. But if it is the only thing possible
between us—' He gave his expressive shrug.

'I do want the truth,' she said flatly.

'I just told you.'

'No, you haven't. I'm talking about money, Luc.'

He frowned. 'You mean you are dissatisfied with the
price I paid for Turret House?'

'I'm not talking about Turret House,' she said with
sudden heat, wrenching her hands away. 'At least, only
indirectly. It's your devious approach I object to.'

'Devious?'

'Yes. Demanding details of my private life before you
would clinch the deal. Did it amuse you to make a fool
of me?' She flung away, but Luc caught her hand again,
turning her to face him.

'Portia, you are angry with me, and I apologise. It was
wrong of me to ask about your private life—'

'Particularly when you were so sparing with details of
your own,' she said bitterly.

He dropped her hand, his face suddenly set in harsh,
suspicious lines. 'What exactly do you mean?'

'You don't just represent the hotel chain, Monsieur
Brissac, you own it. A pertinent little fact you withheld,
no doubt, to make sure you got a good price for Turret
House.'

Luc shrugged, obviously relieved. 'I gave no instructions at the Ravenswood to keep my background secret. And the price was the most I was prepared to pay for Turret House, whether you knew my financial standing or not.'

'Are you denying you implied that my confidences were part of the deal?' she demanded.

His lips tightened. 'No. I am not proud of that. But you are so poised and reserved, Portia. So British. I knew there was no other way of learning more about you in so short a time.'

'But *why* did you want to know?' she persisted.

He moved nearer, his eyes holding hers. 'You know why, *chérie.*'

'No, I don't,' said Portia, retreating.

'You lie. You know very well,' he said inexorably.

They stared at each other in tense, thickening silence, then the phone rang, breaking it, and Portia blinked owlishly, like someone waking from a heavy sleep.

She muttered an apology, and made for the phone, but before she reached it a hoarse voice began leaving a message.

'Hi, Portia, Joe here. I've come down with a filthy cold. I'm afraid tomorrow's off after all—' He broke off to cough. 'Sorry to mess you about. I'll call you as soon as I'm fit.'

'So. It seems you are free tomorrow after all,' said Luc, close behind her. 'Spend the day with me instead.'

She turned, meeting his eyes very squarely. 'I might have done if you'd rung me beforehand, as you promised. Probably you know dozens of women only too ready to drop everything and run when you crook your finger, Luc Brissac, but I'm different.'

'Ah, but I know that, Portia. It is this very difference which attracts me.' He smiled, spreading his hands. 'But if we do not spend time together how can we hope to be friends?'

Secretly conquered by the smile, Portia held out a moment or two longer, as though thinking it over, then inclined her head. 'All right, since I'm suddenly at a loose end, why not?'

This time Luc's smile was so victorious his triumph almost changed Portia's mind. But he was clever enough not to press home his advantage. 'It is almost possible for me to feel sorry for this man of yours, since he is ill.'

'I don't think you mean that.'

'I said "almost",' he reminded her.

Portia smiled. 'Have you eaten?'

'No, but do not disturb yourself.'

'It will not disturb me,' she mocked, 'to make you an omelette, Monsieur Brissac. If that will do?'

'It will be an honour! And so much more than I expected when I arrived,' he added soberly. 'At first I thought you would send me away without a word.'

'I probably would have done if Marianne hadn't been here.'

'Then I am grateful to your friend. I would send her flowers to express my gratitude, but I think the doctor would object.'

'I bet he would!' Portia led the way into her functional little kitchen. 'I don't have a dining table yet, so you'll have to eat here. Do sit down.'

'May I take off my jacket?' With a sigh of pleasure which disarmed Portia, he sat back in one of her kitchen chairs and asked about her day. Portia took out omelette pan and butter, and gathered a handful of herbs from the pots on her windowsill, describing the property sales she was involved in as she whisked eggs in a bowl. While the butter heated in the pan she cut slices from a rustic loaf, arranged slices of tomato on a bed of spinach leaves, and dressed them with oil and vinegar. Once the eggs hissed in the hot butter it was only a minute or so before a perfect omelette was set in front of her guest.

'So you can cook also,' he stated indistinctly through the first mouthful.

'Also?' she queried, taking the other chair.

Luc helped himself to the salad. 'You are clever, beautiful, successful.' He smiled at her. 'Career women are not always good cooks.'

'My mother taught me to cook when I was young.' She sobered, and Luc reached out a hand to touch hers.

'Now I have made you sad.'

She shook her head, smiling. 'Not really.'

'Good.' He ate the rest of his meal with flattering relish, and at last sat back with a sigh. 'That was perfect. Sometimes the most basic, simple things in life are the best.'

'But it's nice to splash out on a bit of luxury now and then. I enjoyed the caviare and lobster at the hotel.' She raised an eyebrow at him and she took his plate. 'Though I didn't know then that I had the owner himself to thank for it.'

Luc stretched out his long legs and sat with his hands clasped behind his head, watching her with open pleasure as she restored the kitchen to order. 'When did you learn the truth, Portia?'

'Last Monday. Ben Parrish took it on himself to enlighten me.'

'To reassure you I was good for the money for Turret House?'

'That too, knowing Ben.' Portia turned to face him.

'But he also thought I might be interested in your background.'

'And you were angry when he told you, of course?' said Luc, resigned.

'Yes. Not that I had any right to be. I don't usually demand personal details from my clients.' She filled the kettle. 'Coffee?'

'Thank you. Yes.' He frowned. 'Why were you angry?'

Portia looked at him squarely. 'If we do become friends from now on—'

'As we will!' he assured her.

'How can you be sure it wasn't your money which changed my mind?'

'I am sure,' he said, with utter certainty. 'I was not always wealthy. *Vraiment*, there was a time when I had very little ready money at all. But...' He hesitated, a wry smile twisting his mouth.

She nodded, resigned. 'Your success with my sex has never depended on money.'

'Exactly,' he said simply.

Portia gave him a crooked little smile. 'Not much wrong with your self-esteem tonight!' She handed him a cup of coffee. 'Let's sit in the other room.'

Portia curled up in her chair and Luc sat down on her sofa, looking utterly relaxed.

'This,' he said, 'is worth all the trouble.'

'Trouble?'

He nodded. 'There was a late crisis at my Paris office. I barely had time to change before driving to the airport, only to find my flight was delayed. When I arrived in London I told myself to be patient, to wait until tomorrow to see you, but—' He shrugged, his eyes on hers.

'Since meeting you I am regressed to boyhood. I was impatient. I could not wait until then.'

Portia's heart skipped a beat. 'If you'd arrived earlier I wouldn't have been here. I went to the cinema with Marianne.'

'Then I would have waited until you arrived,' he assured her.

She stared at him, startled, and realised he meant it. 'Then now you are here, and I've agreed to spend the day with you tomorrow, what would you like to do?'

Luc leaned forward, his hands clasped loosely between his knees. 'You choose, Portia. This is your city. Lunch, of course, then perhaps a trip up the Thames, or a theatre matinée? If you were alone, what would you do?'

'I tend to be very lazy on winter weekends,' she admitted. 'At this time of year I generally hire a video or two, read a lot, go shopping sometimes.'

'That sounds good. With you I would enjoy such things very much.' He eyed her searchingly. 'If I suggest lunch in my apartment will you suspect me of dark and devious motives again, Portia?'

She looked at him levelly. 'And will you lose your temper and get very brooding and French if I say I'd rather not?'

He sat very still. 'Are you saying,' he began with care, 'that you have changed your mind?'

'No. I'd simply prefer to keep to my home ground for a while.'

Luc relaxed slightly. 'Whatever you wish, Portia. So, what shall we do tomorrow? Sunday, also,' he added firmly.

'When do you go back to Paris?' she asked, making

no attempt to lie about some fictitious Sunday engagement.

'Early Monday morning. Until then I want to spend as much time with you as possible. And,' he added, leaning forward to emphasise the point, 'I talk of the days only. I am not demanding your company in my bed. You see? I, too, am learning caution.'

Portia smiled, 'Something new for you?'

He shook his head. 'In matters of business I am never precipitate. In affairs of the emotions, of course, it is different.'

'Have you been in love very often, then?' she asked curiously.

A smile played at a corner of the wide, sensuous mouth. 'Of course. When I was young I was never *out* of love.' He sobered. 'Then my father died suddenly and my carefree days were over.'

'Something like me.'

He shook his head. 'I was more fortunate than you, *chérie*. With my mother's aid I at least found a way to keep Beau Rivage.'

'Your home? Ben told me you turned it into a hotel.'

'He was right. My mother sold some paintings, which aided the original changes, and from the first the venture was a success.' He shrugged. 'But there was no time any more for falling in—and out—of love, Portia.'

'You were too busy saving your inheritance?'

'Not solely mine,' he informed her. 'The estate was left to the entire family. But the others were young, so the responsibility was mine.'

'That must have been hard for you,' said Portia, fascinated by this glimpse into the Brissac past. 'Had your house been in the family a long time?'

'No. I was born in Paris. But my mother is Bretonne

from St Malo, so my father bought Beau Rivage for her about twenty years ago, with the intention of restoring it to its former glories. It was built in the early eighteenth century, and is changed remarkably little. My father regarded it as his life work. Unfortunately his life was cut short.'

'Had he completed all the restoration?'

'Most of it, yes. But the only way to conserve it was to make it pay for itself. The location of Beau Rivage is ideal for a hotel. From the first it became popular with tourists, many of them your countrymen from across La Manche.'

'You mean the English Channel,' she said, laughing.

'Another difference! Tell me, Portia, are such differences obstacles to friendship between us?'

'Why should they be?' She paused. 'Or are there any more dark secrets I should know, Luc?'

He was silent for a moment, then looked up to meet her eyes. 'I am not married, nor do I possess a fiancée. I own an apartment in Paris, another in London, and I visit Beau Rivage to see my mother regularly. It is no longer a hotel. Once the chain was established and successful this was no longer necessary. My sisters are married, so my mother lives there alone.' His eyes darkened, and Portia felt a pang of sympathy for the father who had died, like her own, too young. 'But my sisters visit Beau Rivage with their children, so my mother is rarely alone for long there.'

There was silence in the room for a while, and Luc's eyes focused inwards, as though remembering times past.

Portia got up and collected the coffee cups. 'Would you like a drink, Luc, or are you driving back to your flat?'

'No, I came by taxi. Is it possible to get one at this time of night?'

'As long as you're not in a rush, yes.'

'I am in no rush at all,' he assured her, and smiled. 'But I do not wish to outstay my welcome.'

'I didn't give you much of a welcome when you arrived,' said Portia wryly.

'No,' he agreed, and looked at her challengingly. 'You feel warmer towards me now?'

'A bit,' she admitted, and smiled. 'I'll sort out a taxi for you, then the choice of beverage is tea, coffee, some of your French designer water, or a glass of wine I doubt very much will come up to your standards. Joe brought it last time he was here.'

'Then I will not drink it,' said Luc instantly, and rose to his feet. 'If you will ring for the taxi, Portia, all I want until it arrives is to talk to you.' The look in his eyes took her breath away. 'Do not waste time in making coffee. Just sit with me for a while. Please?'

'All right,' she said unevenly, and went over to the telephone to ring the company she normally used, to be told it would be forty minutes or so before a cab was free.

'So,' said Luc, standing in the middle of the room where she'd left him. 'I am granted forty minutes more of your company.'

'That's just tonight,' she pointed out.

He moved closer and put out a finger to touch her cheekbone. 'The bruise is almost gone, or are you using some clever *maquillage*?'

'I don't have any make-up on at all,' she retorted. 'Which was one of the reasons I wasn't very welcoming when you turned up tonight.'

'But why?' he said, mystified.

'You're always so elegant. I was furious at being caught with a shiny face and my hair all over the place, not to mention these clothes—'

'But you are so appealing like this. So much more approachable than the businesslike Miss Grant with the severe *coiffure* and tailored suits.' He caught her hand and drew her down on the sofa beside him. 'And tonight I am not elegant at all. My clothes are just like yours, and I am very conscious that I need a shave.'

She grinned at him. 'We're just a couple of scruffs, in fact!'

'Scruffs?'

She explained, laughing, and he chuckled with her, then stretched out his legs with a sigh, and turned his head on the sofa-back to look at her.

'It is so good to be with you like this tonight. My week was disaster from the time I left you until now.'

'Why?'

'Turret House is not my only concern at present. I am negotiating the purchase of a small château in Provence.'

'What's it like?' asked Portia, curling up beside him.

'Very Provençal, with gold sandstone towers and wood shutters, and great bronze urns full of flowers on the terrace.'

'Sounds wonderful,' she said, with a sigh.

'If I buy it I will take you there,' he said softly, his eyes moving over her face to catch every nuance of the reaction she was determined to hide.

'So why the disaster?' she asked matter-of-factly. 'Are the owners reluctant to sell?'

'Their price is unrealistic, because the property is not in good repair. And, at the moment, my offer is too low for the lady who owns it.' He shrugged philosophically.

'But in the end, as always, there will be a compromise, and then the château will be mine.'

'And what will the lady do then?'

'Do not feel pity for her, *chérie*. She is anxious to retire to her apartment in Nice—and live very well on the money I shall pay her.'

'You do a great deal of research, I suppose, before you begin negotiations?'

'But of course. My lawyers have an office in Nice. Also I employ staff who—very discreetly, of course—stay in the area for a while, and find out as much as possible about the property I am interested in.' He slid his arm along the back of the sofa, not quite touching her shoulders. 'Do you disapprove of my business tactics?'

'Of course not.' She turned her head to smile at him. 'I'm in the same line of business myself, remember.'

'For which I am most thankful. Otherwise, Mademoiselle Grant, I might never have met you.' His eyes grew suddenly intent and dropped to her mouth, and, suddenly flustered, Portia said the first thing that came into her head.

'Is your mouth better?' she asked, then blushed vividly, certain he would take it as a blatant invitation.

'Your kiss would complete the cure,' he said huskily, then let out a long, unsteady breath and drew her very slowly into his arms. When she made no objection he pulled her close with one arm, his free hand threading through the tumbled curls as he brought her face up to his. For a long, searching moment he looked deep into her eyes, then at last laid his mouth on hers.

With Marianne's words ringing in her ears, Portia offered no resistance. Nor wanted to. Her lips opened to the seeking, skilled mouth, and her arm went up to encircle his neck, a tremor running through her as his tongue found hers and caressed it with slow, savouring delight at her response. Luc's breathing grew faster, his kisses gradually fiercer, then hungry with demand, until at last he tore his lips from hers to gasp incoherent French endearments as he buried his face in her hair.

The buzzer on Portia's door brought them both to their feet, and she hurried to pick up the receiver while Luc collected his jacket from the kitchen.

'Your cab,' she said breathlessly, pushing her hair back behind her ears.

Luc touched a hand to her chin, his eyes rueful. 'Last time I left you with a black eye. This time I have made your skin red, *chérie.*'

'It didn't hurt—or if it did I didn't notice it,' she assured him, smiling, and with a smothered sound he pulled her back into his arms and kissed her fiercely. 'Now I must go,' he said unevenly, and put her from him. 'Perhaps it is just as well the taxi arrived when it did. I will return early in the morning.'

'Not too early. I need a bit of a shop at the supermarket.'

'I shall drive you there,' he said promptly. 'Very carefully this time.'

'That's a relief,' she said, grinning. 'But if you don't go soon the cab will give up and take off without you.'

'If it did, would you let me stay?' he demanded.

'Certainly not.' She smiled to soften the refusal. 'Goodnight, Luc.'

He touched a hand to her cheek. 'Until tomorrow, Portia.'

CHAPTER SEVEN

NORMALLY Portia allowed herself extra time in bed in the morning on free weekends, but this particular Saturday she was up at first light to wash her hair and shower and give herself time to search in her wardrobe for something which would look effortlessly perfect for the occasion.

When she was finally ready for whatever the day promised, in cinnamon velvet jeans and creamy cashmere sweater, Portia ran a brush through crackling waves and curls and left them loose on her shoulders. And, because Luc had professed himself enchanted with her unadorned face the night before, she spent a shamelessly long time in applying various subtle aids to look as though she'd used no cosmetics at all. She was drinking her first coffee of the day when her bell rang.

Sure it couldn't be Luc at just gone nine she picked up the receiver and flushed with pleasure when a familiar, husky voice said, '*Bonjour*, Portia. Am I too early?'

'No. Come up.' When he knocked a little later she threw open the door, smiling in welcome.

Luc promptly dropped a large paper bag on the floor and took her in his arms, kissing her on both cheeks.

'That is a much better welcome than last night,' he said in approval, and handed her the bag, which was warm and gave out mouthwatering scents of hot pastry. 'Croissants,' he said, and sniffed the air. 'Do I smell coffee?'

'Yes. Just made it.' Portia chuckled. 'When you said the entire day you really meant it, then?'

'But of course!'

Portia normally disliked breakfast of any kind other than a cup of tea or coffee. This particular, surprising morning she found she was hungry, as she shared the croissants with Luc and made a second pot of coffee. 'I wouldn't have put you down as domesticated,' she commented, as he filled their cups for the third time.

'I am very useful in the kitchen,' he assured her smugly. 'If you like I will make dinner for you. This morning we shall go shopping for food, and afterwards we will eat lunch somewhere, then tonight, before we watch these videos of yours, I shall impress you with my skill as chef.'

Portia regarded him in amusement over her coffee cup. Luc was informal, but no less elegant than usual, in dark needlecord trousers, his wool shirt creamy white against his smooth olive skin and thick black hair. His eyes narrowed in response to her smile.

'You are laughing at me?'

'It's hard to believe you've ever cooked anything in your life.'

He shook his head. 'I was not always wealthy, Portia. Also my mother is a formidable cook, and insisted that all her children should be capable of creating one or two simple dishes at the very least. You and I share that in common, *n'est ce pas*?' He gave her a long, green look. 'I believe that as our friendship progresses we shall discover many more things in common.'

'It's possible,' she admitted cautiously.

'It is certain,' he contradicted. 'Where is your dishwasher?'

Portia chuckled, and held up her hands. 'These wash my dishes.'

Luc leaned across the table and seized them, planting a kiss in each palm. 'Not today,' he said firmly.

It was strangely sweet to Portia to dry dishes as Luc washed them, a chore never undertaken in this particular kitchen by any man. In her flat-sharing days some of the unwilling male tenants had sometimes been bullied into a few chores, but though Joe sometimes came back to the flat for coffee, or a nightcap, he'd never suggested setting foot in Portia's kitchen, nor had she wanted him to. The present situation was doubly welcome, because before Luc arrived Portia had worried that he might expect to take up where he'd left off, after the passionate leave-taking of the night before. Instead his exuberant greeting had been more affectionate than passionate. And reassuring, just like his insistence on washing dishes. As, she thought with sudden intuition, he'd meant it all to be.

'Those beautiful dark eyes look thoughtful,' observed Luc as he dried his hands. 'Is the price in England still one penny for such thoughts?'

'Not in this case,' she assured him. 'Mine are not for sale.'

'Perhaps one day you will give me all your private thoughts freely,' said Luc, and touched a hand to her cheek. '*Alors*, let us get on with the shopping. Do we drive far?'

'No. Nor, thank goodness, do we go on a motorway,' she teased.

Shopping with Luc was fun, other than his tendency towards extravagance which Portia tried in vain to curb.

'No, I don't want smoked salmon, nor truffle oil. I need things like breakfast cereal, and coffee.'

Ignoring her protests, Luc began filling her trolley with all kinds of delicacies, including a bottle of champagne, leaving Portia to add more prosaic staples. When they arrived at the checkout he paid before she could prevent him.

'You shouldn't have done that,' she scolded, as he loaded the car. 'We'll settle up when we get to the flat.'

Luc merely laughed at her, patting her cheek. 'Such an independent lady. Last week I bought you roses; this week I buy you groceries. What difference does it make?'

'And before that you paid for my room, dinner, lunch, provided a picnic—'

'And last night you made me an omelette. Should I have refused because I did not pay for the eggs?'

'That's sophistry,' she said, laughing, as he drove off.

'You talk as though I offer you a mink coat—'

'Bad move all round. Real fur's frowned on these days.'

'Do not change the subject,' he said severely. 'So listen, Portia, because I am going to be very, very blunt now you are captive in the car.'

She eyed him uneasily. 'What do you mean?'

Luc kept his eyes on the road. 'To buy you roses, or pay for a meal, gives me pleasure. But these are not the dark and devious motives you suspect. I know that the only way to become your lover is for you to want that as much as I do. If this is never possible for you I will just be your friend, and perhaps kiss you now and then, because to be in your company for long and not kiss you at all is an impossibility for me, you understand. So, if you do not permit even this please say so now while I still—' He stopped.

'While you still what?' she prompted.

'While I still possess the strength to say goodbye.'

Neither of them said any more until they reached her flat.

'So?' said Luc at last. He leaned in the doorway, arms folded, watching her neat, methodical movements as Portia put the food away.

She frowned at him fleetingly, then resumed her task. 'Are you giving me an ultimatum, Luc?'

'No. I am striving to be honest.' He looked at her steadily. 'Are you willing for a loving friendship? Or for you must the friendship be purely platonic?'

From the first moment he'd kissed her in Turret House Portia had known very well that a platonic relationship with Luc Brissac was impossible. But one thing became clearer with each moment she spent in his company. She wanted *some* kind of relationship with him. If he said goodbye and walked out right now she'd regret it, she knew with certainty. She turned to face the green assessing scrutiny.

'I don't want you to say goodbye, Luc.' Which was as near as she would ever get to the answer he wanted.

'Good. I do not want it either,' he assured her. 'So let us find a place to eat.'

'Right,' she said, suddenly practical. 'I know a nice, unpretentious little wine bar where they serve a couple of French dishes every day. The wine's not bad either. Are you game?'

'Game?'

'Willing, then.'

He brushed a hand over her hair and smiled down into

her eyes. 'I am willing to do anything you wish, Portia. Always.'

Later, with plates of warm tuna flan in front of them, Luc nodded in surprised approval as he tasted his. 'It was clever of you to find a place with Breton cuisine.'

'I didn't know it was Breton,' she confessed. 'This is gorgeous, though. I wonder what's in this sauce?'

Luc tasted it, eyes concentrated. 'Lemon juice, herbs, and crème fraîche, I think. It goes well with this particular fish. The giant tuna has been the goal of Breton fishermen since the Middle Ages.'

They lingered over coffee afterwards, relaxed in each other's company, talking without pause. And afterwards they raced from the car into Portia's building through pouring, sleet-filled rain, gasping for breath as the lift took them up to her flat.

'And now,' said Luc, as they took off wet coats, 'I must ask you a favour. Even though,' he added sombrely, 'it may put a great strain on our friendship.'

'Oh, yes?' said Portia, eyes narrowed. 'What is it?'

'I would very much like to watch television. France is playing England at Twickenham this afternoon. Do you dislike rugby, Portia?'

'No. I'm an ardent rugby fan, I'd have you know.' She smiled at him. 'In college I had friends who played in the first fifteen.'

'Of course you did,' he said, resigned, then his eyes lit with an unholy gleam. 'Let us make a bet. If France wins you will pay me two kisses.'

'Done,' she said promptly. 'What happens if England wins? As they will, of course.'

'Fighting talk, *mademoiselle*. For which I shall pay you one kiss.'

'Why do I have to pay you more than you pay me, Luc Brissac?'

'Because,' he said patiently, as though explaining to a child, 'I want your kisses more than you want mine.'

Portia flushed, and took his coat. 'I'll put this to dry.'

He smiled at her indulgently, and switched on the television. 'Hurry, Portia, it is nearly time for the kick-off.'

She hung their wet coats in the airing cupboard, then went into the kitchen, needing a moment to herself. Luc was wrong. She wanted his kisses every bit as much as he wanted hers. And, if she were brutally honest, kissing was just a euphemism for what both of them really wanted. But though her body urged her to say yes to anything Luc desired, her reason advised caution. Three weeks ago neither of them had known of each other's existence.

A sudden roar from her sitting room sent Portia hurrying in to join Luc. 'What's happened?'

'We scored in the first five minutes!' he informed her jubilantly. 'Come, Portia, your team needs your encouragement,' he added gloatingly.

She laughed and sat down beside him, then wished she hadn't, since Luc jumped up every time France took the game forward, and when they scored a second time raised the roof with his shout of triumph.

Then England fought back, and it was Portia's turn for jubilation. By half-time the scores were level, and in the interval she hotly debated every aspect of the game with Luc. When the match resumed there was no let-up in the excitement, which mounted with every minute until the French backs surged away in a brilliant passing move across the field, culminating in a rocket-like burst of speed by the full-back as he eluded clutching English hands to ground the ball behind the posts for France.

'*Formidable!*' roared Luc, punching the air with his fist as the outside-half converted the try with a ball sent over the crossbar, plumb between the uprights.

'There's time yet,' said Portia loyally, her faith rewarded when England equalised with only a minute or two to go. Then, just as it seemed certain the game would end, unusually, in a draw, the French outside-half sent the ball sailing between the posts for a textbook drop-kick, and won the game for France.

Luc cheered wildly, then turned to seize Portia by the elbows. 'So,' he said, eyes glittering, 'you owe me two kisses, *mademoiselle*.'

'So I do.' She eyed him challengingly. 'Want them now?'

'He shook his head. 'I will save your kisses until we say goodnight. Otherwise—' He released her abruptly. 'If I start kissing you now, Portia, I might not want to stop.'

Portia got up, secretly rather disappointed. 'Right,' she said briskly. 'Time for tea.'

He raised an eyebrow. 'Tea?'

'You can drink coffee, if you like,' she said, laughing.

But Luc gallantly drank tea, and ate more than his share of the scones and clotted cream Portia had brought from the supermarket, all the time discussing the game and how good it had been. Portia entered into the discussion with passion, defending her team with a ferocity which Luc very obviously found enchanting.

'*Mon Dieu,*' he said at last. 'If this is how you are when you lose, you must be unbearable in victory, Portia.'

'Sorry,' she said, laughing. 'I tend to get over enthusiastic.'

'Ah, yes. The rugby-playing boyfriends!'

'Did you play rugby?'

'As a boy, only. Later I had no time. Now, Portia,' he added, 'what is next on the programme?'

Portia drew the curtains against the darkening afternoon. 'I suggest we watch one of the videos until it's time for dinner.'

Luc watched as she put the film in the VCR, then held out his hand. 'Come and sit beside me, Portia.'

The film was a fast-moving comedy, and they laughed together, enjoying the film almost as much as each other's company. And afterwards Portia teased Luc unmercifully about his skill at cooking when she found this consisted mainly of arranging a platter with ham, salami and pâté, and several kinds of cheese, his only real creation a colourful salad and the dressing to go with it.

'Tonight, because it is the first time we do this together, I consider time spent over an elaborate dish as time wasted, *chérie*.' He looked at her. 'If you were alone tonight, what would you eat?'

'Something very like this,' she admitted, 'on a smaller scale.'

'Then to make this meal special we shall drink champagne,' he insisted, and took the bottle from her fridge. He removed the cork with a deft thrust of his thumbs, and filled the glasses she gave him. 'A toast.'

She raised her glass, smiling. 'What shall we drink to?'

Luc touched her glass with his. 'To us, Portia.'

'To us,' she echoed, and tasted the wine with respect, and a certain amount of caution. Luc Brissac and vintage champagne were a heady combination. She would do well to tread warily.

'What is going on behind those beautiful dark eyes?' asked Luc, helping her to salad.

'I was thinking how very pleasant this is,' she said, with complete truth.

'If you were with this man—'

'His name is Joe. Joe Marcus.'

'*Bien*. What would you be doing?'

'He suggested a new club he'd heard about.'

'You would like this club?'

'I don't know, I've never been there.'

Luc shook his head reprovingly. 'You know exactly what I mean, Portia. For me, an evening here with you like this is a delight, but if your preference was a night-club I would have been most pleased to escort you.'

Portia went on with her meal in silence for a moment. Unknown to Luc, she infinitely preferred being alone with him in complete privacy rather than in some crowded club, however fashionable. 'I've had a busy week. I'm rather glad to stay home.'

He reached a hand across the table and touched hers fleetingly. 'So am I. It has been a good day. Not,' he added, 'that it is over yet. There is still the other film to watch. It is about murder, you said. Do you frighten easily?'

She smiled at him. 'If I do you can hold my hand.'

Luc's eyes darkened, and he seemed on the point of saying something, then shrugged and pressed her to more ham, leaving Portia curious about the words he'd left unsaid.

Later Luc insisted on switching out all but one lamp, to aid atmosphere, and sat close beside Portia on the sofa. When she gave a gasp at a particularly scary scene, instead of taking her hand Luc put his arm round her and kept it there until the end of the film. By the time the credits rolled both of them were tense and silent, and the moment Portia aimed the remote control at the screen

Luc drew her back into his arms and turned her face up
to his.

'I want the kisses now, *chérie*,' he said huskily, taking
possession of her mouth with a ragged sigh of pleasure
at the contact. His lips moved over hers, coaxing them
open, and she shivered a little as his tongue began to
follow the same path over her parted lips, then slid between them, his mouth gradually more persuasive as he
sought her response. Startled by the leap of fire in her
blood, Portia gasped, and Luc crushed her close, his
mouth fierce with demand she responded to so utterly
that he tore his lips from hers at last and thrust a hand
into her hair, holding her still as he looked down into
her eyes with such heat her mouth dried.

'This is not easy, Portia,' he said harshly.

She stared at him, dazed. 'Does your lip hurt?'

'It is not my lip that troubles me! You are irresistible,
ma belle. It is impossible just to kiss and want no more
than that.' He smiled down at her crookedly. 'I am not
made of stone, Portia.'

'Neither am I,' she said deliberately, and felt secret
muscles clench as his eyes blazed his response.

Very slowly, his eyes looking deep into hers, he drew
a hand down her cheek, then followed its progress with
his lips, kissing her throat as he stroked the outline of
her breasts through the soft cashmere. Portia stirred restlessly, unable to sit still under his touch, and Luc, in
tune with every nuance of her response, slid his hands
under the thin wool, caressing her satin-covered breasts
with a delicacy so erotic Portia began to breathe shal-
lowly, uttering a hoarse little sound he smothered with
his kiss as his hands slid behind her to release the catch
and her breasts surged, bare and taut, into his waiting
hands.

Luc buried his face in her hair as his thumbs moved in soft, abrasive caresses over her nipples, causing such tumult inside Portia that she sat up suddenly and held up her arms. Luc drew a rasping breath and slid the sweater over her head. He tossed the scrap of satin aside, then gazed at her with a molten look so tactile she felt it on her skin as it roved over her in slow, pulse-quickening relish. Her nipples hardened, and her breath suddenly laboured in her chest as she thrust herself against him and buried her face against his shoulder, unable to endure his gaze a moment longer.

'Mon Dieu,' he said hoarsely. 'You are so beautiful, so alluring. Can you understand how you make me feel?' He held her closer, his breath catching in his throat as her breasts flattened against his chest.

Portia shook her head. 'Not like this,' she said gruffly, and began to undo his shirt. But he tore it open, sending buttons flying in all directions in his impatience to feel her naked breasts against his chest. Luc buried his face in her tangled curls, uttering a torrent of husky, erotic French into her uncomprehending ear as his hands moved restlessly over her bare back.

At last she pushed him away a little, smiling shakily into his smouldering eyes. 'In school my French teacher never used words like that,' she whispered.

'Then I must teach you the language of love, ma belle.' Luc bent his head, his hair brushing her skin as he kissed the slopes of her breasts, his tongue tasting the satiny curves. Then he took one of the quivering, diamond-hard tips between his lips, his teeth grazing delicately on the sensitised flesh, and Portia gasped as darts of fire found their target deep inside her. Her head went back, threshing from side to side as Luc played clever havoc with lips and teeth and fingertips, until her entire body was blazing with need. For a long, timeless interval Luc made love to her with relentless skill, until his own artistry finally defeated him.

Abruptly he jumped up and put his shirt back on, his eyes averted. 'If I take even one look at you, I am lost,' he panted. 'Have mercy, Portia. Cover yourself before I lose my head completely.'

Dazed, surprised, and utterly frustrated, Portia pulled on her sweater with trembling, uncoordinated fingers.

'I'm respectable again,' she told him, and Luc thrust his shirt inside his belt and turned to look down at her, his jaw set.

'I did not realise I possessed such strength of mind,' he said bitterly. 'To let you go just then was not easy, Portia.'

She drew in a deep, shaky breath. 'Then why did you?'

Luc sat down beside her, leaving a space between them as he took her hand in his, his eyes holding hers as he smoothed her skin with a caressing finger. 'Because I was afraid that if I followed my desire to its natural conclusion you would think this was my sole reason for coming here this weekend.'

A faint smile played at the corners of her mouth. 'But, as you told me before, Monsieur Brissac, if a sexual encounter was all you had in mind you could have achieved that in Paris and saved yourself the price of an airfare.' She looked at him levelly. 'Unless, of course, you are combining business with pleasure this weekend.'

'Of course I am,' he said promptly. 'I am a client spending time with a partner of Whitefriars Estates to clinch the sale of Turret House.' He laid a caressing fingertip on her bottom lip. 'That not one word about business shall pass our lips this weekend will be our little secret, *chérie.*'

'One I'll keep to myself, too,' she said with feeling.

'Do not look at me like that, *ma belle*, or your client's good intentions will vanish,' he advised hoarsely, and moved farther away. 'Perhaps I should leave now, while I can.'

'It's early yet,' she said quickly.

Luc's eyes glittered. 'You know very well I am delighted that you wish me to stay, Portia. But I warn you that you must keep your distance. I have no defence against your touch.'

'Then I won't touch you,' she assured him, and curled up in the safety of the armchair.

Luc smiled ruefully, and asked about the programme for next day. 'For myself, I would like nothing better than another day spent like this one,' he said, from the far corner of the sofa.

'Fine by me,' she assured him. 'Heaven knows we bought enough food today.'

'I would like to make one change, Portia.' Luc gave her a long, steady look. 'Now you can trust my self-control, will you come to my apartment tomorrow?'

'Yes,' she said without hesitation.

He eyed her in surprise. 'You know, Portia, I did not expect you to agree so quickly.'

'I'm curious to see your flat,' she said candidly. 'Besides, I've enjoyed today. All of it.'

Luc breathed in deeply. 'I, too, *chérie*. So come early tomorrow.'

CHAPTER EIGHT

Luc Brissac's London base was a first-floor flat in a large, handsome house built at the turn of the century. When he conducted her through it the following morning, early, as he'd insisted, Portia was deeply impressed by the large rooms and floor-to-ceiling arched windows, and envied him the conservatory he used as an office. The entire flat gave an instant impression of light and space, even on a cold February morning.

'This is lovely,' said Portia, her cheeks glowing from the kisses Luc had planted on them when she arrived. 'Is it all your own taste?'

'It is to my taste, but only the furniture is mine. The decor is the work of the interior designer who sold the flat to me—through your agency, of course.' He smiled at her appreciatively. 'You look very beautiful this morning, Portia.'

Since she'd been up at first light expending much effort on her appearance she was glad he thought so. 'Thank you,' she said demurely. 'You look pretty good yourself.'

'If I do,' he said, with a bow, 'it is because I spent such a perfect day yesterday.'

'So did I,' she said candidly. 'Now, where's this breakfast you promised me?'

The day proved no less perfect than the one before as they ate brioche and coffee at Luc's dining table, then went for a walk on Hampstead Heath to sharpen an appetite for lunch in a restaurant where Luc was obviously well known.

'Do you come here often to Sunday lunch?' she asked.

He smiled indulgently. 'Very rarely, Portia. Normally I do not spend my weekends in London. My business visits to Britain are made during the week. I dine here occasionally, but this is the first time for Sunday lunch.'

'Then why did you stipulate a weekend for the viewing at Turret House?' she asked, frowning.

'It was the only time I had free at that point. 'Ah, good,' he added as a waiter approached. 'Here is our meal.'

The pie he had suggested they share was filled with monkfish and bacon, flavoured with thyme and vermouth and topped with a featherlight crust, and it tasted sublime, Portia assured him.

'I like to see a woman eat,' said Luc with satisfaction, then frowned. 'Do you eat well during the week, Portia?'

'Not like this! Lunch is usually a sandwich, and dinner something simple. 'I eat a lot of soup in winter.'

He eyed her disapprovingly. 'It is plain I must come to London every weekend in future, to make sure you eat enough to last through the week. This does not meet with your approval?' he demanded, at the look on her face.

'*Every* weekend?' she asked quietly.

Luc put down his knife and fork and leaned forward, looking at her steadily. 'Perhaps I should have said every weekend that you consent to spare me.' He smiled. 'Now, you must eat dessert, Portia, Or pudding, as you Brits say. I insist.'

When he refused to take no for an answer she eventually consented to share the cheese he chose, and it was well into the afternoon by the time the meal was over.

'We shall drink coffee at the apartment, and maybe a cognac,' he suggested, as he drove her back. 'I propose we dine at home tonight, Portia.'

She blew our her cheeks. 'Luc, I won't be able to—'

'You mean you must leave early?' he said, frowning.

'No. I *meant* that after the lunch we've just eaten I won't be able to eat again until breakfast tomorrow.'

He gave her a sidelong glance that brought colour rushing to her face. 'I would very much like you to stay with me until then, *chérie*—but do not flash your eyes at me. I know very well you will say no.' He smiled straight ahead through the windscreen. 'I suppose I must content myself with the memory of the two breakfasts shared with you already.'

When they got back to Luc's flat neither of them felt energetic enough to do anything more demanding than talk as they idled away the rest of the afternoon together, until at last Portia was feeling distinctly drowsy.

'I'm sorry,' she said with contrition, after a second stifled yawn. 'It must be the lunch, and the warmth in here.'

'Also I insisted you came so early this morning,' said Luc, and swung her feet up on the chesterfield sofa they were sharing. He put cushions behind her head, then drew his finger down her cheek. 'I must work for a while, so sleep, *chérie*.'

When Portia woke the room was in semi-darkness, the only light the glow from the conservatory. At some point Luc had covered her with a light rug, and she lay quietly, feeling warm and relaxed and utterly disinclined to move. She would stay like this for a little while, she decided. Until Luc had finished what he was doing...

She woke the second time to find Luc lying full-length beside her, his eyes only inches from hers in the half-light. He smiled, and she smiled back, and he tossed the rug away and took her in his arms.

'This seems a little dangerous,' she said huskily, as his proximity made it very obvious that he wanted her.

'Dangerous?' he queried in amusement, the faint trace of accent causing a familiar tightening of muscles in that part of Portia in close contact with the corresponding part of Luc. 'You are in no danger, Portia. My intention was to wake you with a kiss, but you were so beautiful lying there I could not resist joining you instead.'

Portia lay silent and still in his possessive embrace for a long interval, very much aware that she was Luc's captive. One part of her was outraged to find she liked it. But another part, the one that had begun to get out of hand ever since her first meeting with him, gave instructions her body was all too willing to obey. Her hips thrust closer against his and her lips parted, her eyes lambent with invitation. Answering heat flared in Luc's, and he began to breathe more rapidly. Portia's heart thudded against his chest, and he inhaled sharply, his jaw tightening until she could see the muscles taut in his neck. She moved the fraction nearer that brought her mouth in contact with his throat, and Luc gave an explosive sigh and tipped her face up to his.

To her surprise he didn't kiss her senseless, as she wanted, but slid his hand into her hair to hold her face far enough away for his eyes to look deep into hers.

'You were right, Portia,' he said harshly. 'This is very dangerous. It will take only one kiss to light a fire impossible to control.'

It was a prospect which took Portia's breath away, and she finally surrendered to the truth she'd been hiding from since her first meeting with Luc. Marianne was right. Falling in love did happen in the blink of an eye.

Because it was something new in her experience she hadn't realised what was happening to her. How could she have been so blind? It was plain, now, why she'd been miserable when Luc hadn't rung. Of course she was in love with him. Otherwise she wouldn't be here, like this, eager to spend every waking second of this weekend, and as many more weekends as possible in future, in his company. She was no teenager with a crush. Men had wanted to make love to her often enough. But to be desired in this subtle, cherishing way of Luc's was something she had never encountered before. And probably never would again.

'Then in that case...' she whispered, and felt his body tense, as though he were sure she would push him away. She knew that if she did he would let her go without argument. Wasting no more time on words, she touched Luc's lips with her own, in a caress which acted exactly as he'd predicted—like a match thrown on kindling. He received the kiss with disbelief, then kissed her wildly, hungrily, crushing her close, the building tension of the past two days exploding into a passion Portia had been given a mere foretaste of the night before.

Luc muttered incoherent words against her parted, gasping mouth, his hands stroking her feverishly through the silk of her shirt. Portia's schoolgirl French wasn't up to understanding most of it, but she no longer cared. She said yes to everything he was demanding as he took her by the hand and raced with her to the bedroom he'd omitted from his earlier tour of the flat.

Holding her fast in the crook of his arm, as though she might change her mind if he broke contact, Luc switched on a lamp and turned down the covers of his bed with his free hand, then turned her in his arms and looked down at her, his eyes oddly stern.

'You must know that I am in love with you, Portia,' he said in French, and a tremor ran through her as her brain translated.

'*Amoureux* is such a beautiful word,' she said breathlessly, knowing that he wanted her to reply in kind, but unable, yet, to put words to feelings she'd only just discovered for herself.

'It is you who are beautiful, Portia,' he said hoarsely, and threaded his fingers through her hair. 'I am on fire for you.'

Then take me, she said with her eyes, and Luc began to undress her with hands clumsy in their feverish hurry to dispense with the barrier of clothes which separated them. When she was lying naked in his arms at last, Luc gave a ragged sigh of pure delight and held her tightly with one hand, the other smoothing and stroking down her spine and her thighs until every part of her was in such close contact with Luc's taut body that Portia realised, for the first time, what it meant to be one flesh, even before their bodies were united. And, instead of the immediate, passionate union she craved, Luc was inexorable in his intention to withhold the final intimacy until he'd kissed and caressed every part of her into a state of longing so intense she was sure she'd lose her reason if he didn't take her soon. Even when he did, at last, he was tantalising as he made their union complete, his body taking possession of hers with a subtle, gradual progression designed to give both of them every nuance of pleasure it was possible for them to experience together. The sensations he induced were almost unbearably intense as the rhythm slowly grew faster, then progressively wilder, until the final cataclysm of pleasure overwhelmed her seconds before Luc finally relaxed the iron grip of his own control and collapsed on her in utter abandonment to the ecstasy of his own release.

Portia lay beneath Luc's weight like a butterfly pinned to a board, so shaken and dazed she would have found it hard to breathe normally even if Luc's body hadn't been crushing the life out of her. He raised his head at last, and with reluctance rolled over, taking her with him so that she was held close in his arms, her head on his shoulder. He pulled the covers over them, then lay with one hand stroking her hair, giving Portia time to recover some semblance of calm.

'That,' he said at last, sounding shaken, 'was the most sublime experience of my entire life, *chérie*.'

Portia digested that in flattered silence, then twisted up her face to look at him. 'How old are you, Luc?'

'Thirty-seven.' He smiled down at her. 'Am I allowed to ask your age, Portia?'

'Of course. I'm thirty.'

He frowned. 'I thought you were younger than that.'

'I wasn't fishing for compliments,' she assured him.

'Nor do you need to.' The look in his eyes brought heat rushing to her face. 'You must know that to me you are the most ravishing creature I have ever met. That first day in Turret House, you were so elegant in that long coat and Russian hat I was captivated from the first. Then at the hotel I surprised you in your robe, with that wonderful hair cascading over your shoulders—' He shrugged his broad shoulders. 'I was *bouleversé*. How do you say that?'

'Bowled over?'

'Exactly.' Luc kissed her lingeringly. 'There was no escape for you from the first, Portia. You belong in my arms like this.' He paused, stroking a possessive finger down her flushed cheek. 'Why did you ask my age?'

Portia's lashes dropped to hide her eyes. 'You must have had a fair amount of experience.'

'True. I am male, and normal. But I have never known such desperation to make love to a woman. Nor,' he added, his voice deepening, 'such rapture in achieving my desire.'

Portia's eyes turned up to his. 'You're very good at it,' she said bluntly.

He laughed delightedly. '*Merci beaucoup*. It would be strange if I were not experienced in love at my age.' He raised an eyebrow. 'Unlike you at your age, Portia.'

'Oh? Why do you say that?' she demanded, bristling.

'Because of this famous experience of mine.' Luc pulled her closer and kissed her again, refusing to let her break free. 'No. I will not let you go.'

'Then tell me what you mean,' she said crossly.

'Very well. You were a delight in my arms, Portia, so ravishingly responsive once you lost your natural caution. But other than your kiss of consent you instigated no caresses of your own.'

'Oh, I see,' said Portia ominously. 'You mean you're used to women who crawl all over you.'

To her indignation, Luc threw back his head and roared with laughter. 'No, no, Portia,' he said unsteadily at last. 'That is not what I meant.'

She glared at him. 'Stop laughing at me!'

Luc kissed the tip of nose and settled her more comfortably against him, one of his legs thrown over hers in an attitude of such overt possession Portia's anger was deflected. '*Chérie*,' he began, very seriously, 'when did you last make love with a man?'

Instead of blowing her top, and telling Luc Brissac to mind his own business, Portia sagged in his embrace like a deflated balloon. 'Why?' she said gruffly.

He cradled her close. 'The lady who introduced me to love was older than me. She taught me patience. But since then such patience has never been necessary, until tonight, with you. I wanted you so much it was difficult to take things slowly. I know it was not your first time, but it was plain that I must take care not to cause you pain.'

'When I was in college I had a boyfriend all the time I was there, but no one since,' she said tersely, and felt Luc tense with surprise against her.

He raised her face to his, his eyes narrowed. 'Did this boy injure you in some way?'

'No.'

'Portia, is that the truth?'

She nodded. 'We just went our separate ways after college, that's all. I haven't seen him for years. He went abroad to work.'

Luc stared at her in astonishment. 'No one else in all that time?'

'Is that so hard to believe?'

'Yes,' he said flatly. 'You are so beautiful, Portia. It is truly amazing that no man has tried to make love to you in all that time.'

She shrugged. 'Plenty tried. But up to now no one succeeded.'

'Then why was I granted such a gift, Portia?' he asked quietly.

She looked at him thoughtfully for a moment. 'Because you're the first man since then who's possessed even a flicker of sexual attraction for me,' she said with candour. It was only one reason among several. And the only one she was willing to admit to as yet. But from the look of exultation on Luc's face he was more than pleased with her admission.

'You do me great honour, Portia,' he said, very soberly, and slid out of bed to put on the towelling robe thrown across the back of a chair. He came round the bed and sat on the edge of it to take her hand, smiling indulgently.

'Do you wish to get up for dinner, Portia, or shall I spoil you and bring a tray for you in here?'

'Good heavens, no,' she said at once. 'Besides, I thought we agreed to cancel dinner tonight—' She stopped, flushing, as she realised that the thought of food was more attractive than she'd expected.

Luc chuckled, and bent to kiss her cheek. 'But making love makes one famished, *n'est ce pas*? Especially loving of the intensity we found together. We both expended much energy.'

'I'd rather not discuss it,' she said, colouring. 'Though I would like something to eat. But first I'd like a bath, please.'

Assuring her that she could have whatever she wished, Luc waved a hand at the bathroom door, announced that he would take a shower in the main bathroom, and left Portia to scoop up her scattered clothes and shut herself in a bathroom decorated in surprisingly minimalist style. Not that Portia had much attention to spare for it. She was too eager to sink into hot, pine-scented water.

When Portia emerged, Luc was waiting for her. He smiled and planted a kiss on each cheek, then on the tip of her nose.

'I was beginning to think you would never come out.' He eyed her challengingly. 'I did not think you would like it if I came in to assure myself nothing was wrong.'

'How do you know I didn't lock the door?' she countered.

His look almost made her back away. 'You need

never lock a door against me, Portia. I will never demand anything you have no desire to give.'

'If I didn't believe that,' she said very deliberately, 'I wouldn't have come here today.' She walked into arms which opened to receive her, and lifted her face to his. 'But I am here, and I'm very happy to give you a kiss, if you'd like one.'

After deciding on sandwiches as the quickest, easiest supper, the rest of the evening was spent sitting close together on the chesterfield in Luc's sitting room, with music as a background for their discovery of each other. They avoided the painful area of personal bereavement, but otherwise no topics were barred from their conversation as they explored the differences in their respective cultures, and discovered a surprising amount of common ground.

'What I can't understand,' said Portia much later, 'is why you're not married.'

Luc gave his usual expressive shrug. 'My mother desires this, and I came near to it once or twice. But never near enough to marry.' He ruffled her untidy hair. 'It is a mystery to me that you also are single.'

Her face closed. 'Marriage has never appealed to me.'

'Why not, Portia?'

'I like my life the way it is.'

'This life of yours must adapt now to include me,' he informed her.

She turned her face up to his. 'Is that what you want?'

He kissed her swiftly. 'Is it not obvious, *ma belle*, that I want it very much? It is not my usual practice to spend so much time in London. But in future you will keep your weekends free for me, *n'est ce pas*? And sometimes you could come to me in Paris.'

'Perhaps,' she said non-committally.

'I see I must use persuasion!' Luc scooped her up in his arms and strolled towards the bedroom. 'I know a very good place for that.'

She rubbed her cheek against his shoulder. 'You mean you're going to make love to me until I give in?'

'Yes,' he said matter-of-factly, but the altered rhythm of his breathing betrayed him, and when he came down beside her on the bed he threaded his hands through her hair and looked deep into her eyes. 'The truth is, *chérie*, that I need to make love to you again to convince myself I did not dream the first time.'

Portia was in full agreement, and made this clear in a way Luc found so ravishing that this time his self-control was less absolute. Portia was no longer passive, but grew progressively more adventurous with caresses of her own, causing such havoc that glory overwhelmed them again all too soon.

'Stay with me,' said Luc unevenly, when he could speak.

Portia was deeply tempted, but in the end she sighed and shook her head. 'I need to be at work early in the morning. In fact, I must leave soon. Will you drive me, Luc?'

He shook his head. 'I will ring for a taxi. Then I can hold you in my arms until we part.'

When they arrived in Chiswick Luc told the driver to wait and went up with Portia in the lift, taking her in his arms to kiss her all the way up to her floor. When they reached it he unlocked the door for her and kissed her again.

'I cannot bring myself to go,' he groaned, holding her cruelly tight. 'It will be a long, long week until I see you again.'

'Then stay,' said Portia recklessly.

He raised his head, his eyes glittering in astonishment. 'You mean that?' Without waiting for her confirmation he raced from the flat to pay off the taxi-driver, and minutes later they were undressing feverishly and making love again in Portia's bed. And this time they fell asleep in each other's arms, and only woke when Monday's dawn brought them back to reality.

CHAPTER NINE

WHEN Portia finally arrived at her desk that morning, much later than usual, Biddy took one look at her and made pointed comments about burning candles at both ends. 'I heard about this new eye-cream,' she added. 'Does wonders for circles under the eyes.'

Portia didn't care about marks under her eyes, or the fatigue that made her day's programme harder than usual to carry out. The February day was dark and bitterly cold, but in Portia's heart it was spring.

'Someone's happy in their work,' commented Ben Parrish, when he heard her humming cheerfully on her way out that night.

'It's spring,' she reminded him.

'It's something,' he agreed suspiciously. 'If I didn't know you better, Miss Grant, I'd say you were in love.'

'Me?' she said innocently. 'I'm married to my work, Ben. Goodnight.'

When Portia got home she ran to the telephone to find the message button winking on her machine, just as she'd hoped, and Luc's unmistakable accents telling her that it was late, that she should be home, and that he would ring again later. When he did Portia subsided into her armchair, her legs dangling over the arm, as Luc demanded details of her day, her health, and told her how much he wanted to be there with her, holding her close and—

'Don't,' implored Portia breathlessly.

'Are you missing me?' he demanded.

'Yes.'

'Good. Keep that thought in your mind, *chérie*. And tell this Joe Marcus you are not available any more.'

'He's just a friend, Luc!'

'He's a man. If you need a friend keep your time for the so charming Marianne,' he ordered.

'How about you?' she retorted. 'How do I know you're not seeing women every night in Paris?'

He laughed indulgently. 'If I were, would you be jealous?'

'No. I'd just make sure I wasn't here next weekend.'

'I want no other woman, Portia,' he said, suddenly serious. 'I thought I made that very clear yesterday.' He let out a deep, audible breath. 'Yesterday was so beautiful for me. To hold you in my arms all night was a privilege beyond my wildest dreams.' He paused, listening. 'Are you still there, *chérie*?'

'Yes,' she said huskily. 'I'm here.'

'And you will be there when I arrive on Friday night,' he stated.

'Yes.'

Luc groaned. 'It will be the longest week of my life.'

Portia's week was a succession of cripplingly busy days, followed by evenings highlighted by Luc's call. Some nights, due to pressure of work, his call came later than usual, and Portia watched the clock with tense, anxious eyes, unable to eat, or read, or even watch television until she talked to him. Sometimes, when she found it hard to get to sleep in the bed she'd so recently shared with Luc, she made resolutions about keeping her head. Then forgot them the moment she heard his voice again.

When Joe Marcus rang her in work one day, to see if

she fancied a film that night, Portia braced herself and told him she'd met someone.

'So? It's not the first time.'

'Actually it is. Like this.'

'Are you telling me some guy's finally breached the famous Grant defences?' he demanded.

'It's not the way I'd have phrased it myself, but, yes, I do mean that.'

'Look, Portia, you know I'm fond of you. So take care, eh? Make sure he's on the level.'

'Of course he is,' she said crossly.

'Then bless you, my child, have fun.' He paused. 'But if you need me any time, you know where I am.'

Marianne's reaction was far more satisfactory. She demanded that Portia spent Thursday evening with her, to keep her up to date on the French connection.

'Ring me on my cellphone number tomorrow, Luc—if you are ringing me,' said Portia that evening. 'I'm going out.'

'Who with?' said Luc instantly.

'Marianne. Though Joe did ask me.'

'And what did you say?'

'That I'm seeing someone.'

'That is a very lukewarm way of describing our relationship,' said Luc hotly. 'Tell him I am your lover, Portia.'

'I can't tell him that!'

'Why not? It is the truth.'

'It's not a word I feel comfortable with. But don't worry, Joe understands perfectly.'

'Good. Otherwise I would make it clear to him myself.'

Because Marianne was the only person in the world

she could confide in about Luc, Portia thoroughly enjoyed their evening together.

'I've got a half-bottle of champagne to drink with supper,' said Marianne with satisfaction, and fixed Portia with a searching blue eye. 'So. You've finally found someone you like.'

Portia smiled luminously. 'It's a lot more than that. I'm head over heels in love.'

Marianne's eyes widened. 'Head over heels!'

'You told me I was wasting time.'

'Yes. But if I hadn't met the tasty Monsieur Brissac in person I'd find it pretty hard to believe you'd taken my nagging to heart so quickly.' Marianne bent to plant a kiss on Portia's cheek. 'I'm glad. I was beginning to think you'd never take the plunge.'

'Well, I have, with a vengeance.' At the mere memory of it colour rose in Portia's cheeks, but for once Marianne tactfully made no comment, and even took herself out of the room when Portia's phone rang with the expected call from Luc.

'Now I know it's true,' said Marianne, returning to resume her dinner. 'I recognise the starry-eyed look. I see it in my own mirror since I met Hal.'

Portia changed the subject to ask for news about Dr Courtney, and gazed at her friend, wide-eyed, when Marianne confessed that the champagne had a dual purpose.

'We're getting married,' said Marianne, and held out her left hand. 'Those starry eyes of yours never even noticed my brand-new ring.'

Portia should have been on standby at the weekend, but Ben Parrish, keeping his promise to make up for her consecutive visits to Turret House, took over for her.

'Because,' he said, wagging a finger, 'something tells me you've got plans this weekend. Dare I suggest they involve a man?'

'You may, and they do,' said Portia, hurling her belongings into her bag. Then gave him the surprise of his life by reaching up to kiss his cheek before plunging out into the freezing fog to make for the car park.

It was a slow drive home, and Portia was worried by the time she finally reached the flat. But there was no message from Luc to say his flight had been cancelled. To pass the time she prepared their meal as far as possible without actually cooking it, then embarked on the lengthy process of making herself as beautiful as possible for him. But by the time she was ready Luc was overdue. She told herself that the plane was delayed, or he couldn't get a taxi. Then why didn't he ring? Portia fiddled with the table in the kitchen, putting the cutlery straight and rearranging tulips in a small pottery jar. She gave a stir to the creamy sauce she would pour over the cooked chicken breasts when he arrived. She pushed buttery breadcrumbs around in a frying pan, then took them off the heat and checked her watch for the hundredth time.

At last she went back into the sitting room and turned on the television, then hit the Ceefax button to search for news of flights into Heathrow from Paris. Her heart sank when she saw there was up to two hours' delay on some, and others had been cancelled. Next time, she decided fiercely, he could come by train through the Channel Tunnel. No fog problems there.

By the time Luc was two hours overdue Portia had dusted and polished every inch of the flat to keep herself occupied, and convinced herself he'd either crashed into the Channel, or changed his mind about coming.

Memories of the previous weekend came flooding back, and she began to curse herself for breaking the rule she'd kept so long where men were concerned. She was on the point of throwing the half-prepared meal away when the buzzer rang and Luc's husky, weary voice asked her to let him in.

Her heart thumped wildly as she waited for the small bell which announced the arrival of the lift. She opened her door and Luc, in formal overcoat and suit, threw down his overnight bag and took her in his arms without a word of greeting, kissing her with a hunger she responded to with the same need, relief and joy flooding her in equal force as he held her close.

'*Mon Dieu,*' he said hoarsely at last, raising his head. 'I thought I would never make it.'

'Why didn't you *ring*?' she demanded breathlessly.

'Your line was engaged. Who were you talking to?' he demanded, gripping her shoulders fiercely.

'No one—' she gasped, then surrendered again to his kiss, euphoric in her joy that he was here. Tired, pale, and in need of a shave. But here.

'While I waited in line for a taxi at Heathrow I rang you again, but all I could get was the engaged signal,' he went on, still holding her close.

'I was so *worried*,' she said, burying her face in his shoulder. 'In the end I thought you weren't coming at all,' she added indistinctly.

Luc turned her face up to his. 'You thought I would not come?'

Portia nodded, her colour rising at the look in his eyes, and Luc pulled her close and kissed her until neither of them could breathe.

'This, and this, was all I could think of all week,' he

said roughly. 'Are you mad? Nothing would have kept me away.'

She smiled radiantly and danced away from him into the kitchen. 'I must put the dinner in.'

Luc took off his coat, and loosened his tie as he followed her. He leaned in the doorway, watching as she poured the sauce over sliced chicken and fresh green broccoli. 'I did not wish you to tire yourself cooking a meal after a long working day, *mignonne.*'

Portia scattered the crisp buttered crumbs over the dish, then slid it into the oven. 'There.' She smiled at him. 'Would you like a drink?'

'Not if it is the wine your friend brought!'

'How you do go on about Joe,' she said severely. 'I spent a long time in consultation about the wine I chose. It's white, dry, French and very expensive, so I hope it will do.'

'If I drink it with you, Portia, it will taste like nectar whatever it is,' he assured her, and accepted the glass she filled for him. 'To us.'

'To us,' she echoed.

Luc drank some of the wine, then frowned suddenly and went over to the phone 'I have solved the mystery, Portia. The receiver is not in place.'

She stared at the phone, then at Luc, her eyes full of remorse. 'What a fool I am! I could have saved myself a very bad couple of hours if I'd thought to check.'

He frowned. 'I also tried your cellphone, Portia, but with no success. By this time I was insane with worry, certain something was wrong.'

Portia ran to her bedroom for the large handbag she used for work, and rummaged through it, then rejoined Luc, her colour high. 'I must have left it in the office. I was in such a hurry to get home tonight.'

'Why, *chérie*?' he said caressingly. He put down his glass and held out his arms. 'Were you as eager to see me as I am to see you, by any chance? Come. Kiss me to make up for all the anguish you caused me.'

Later, when they'd eaten the dinner Luc pronounced delicious, and drunk the wine she'd paid such a scandalous price for, he rose from the table and held out his hand to her.

'I am tired,' said Luc, his eyes locked with hers.

'Then perhaps you should go to bed,' she said unevenly.

'You must be tired also?'

'Yes. A little.' Which was a lie. Portia had never felt less tired in her life.

'First, I would like to shower,' he informed her.

'Right. You do that while I clear up.'

Portia made herself take her time over washing dishes and putting them away. She was certain Luc would want to take her to bed the moment he emerged from the bathroom, but no way could she bring herself to undress in readiness. Which, she discovered, was just as well, because when Luc rejoined her his hair was damp from the shower, and he'd shaved, but though his long, narrow feet were bare, he was wearing black needlecord trousers and a fresh shirt. She smiled at him, secretly deeply grateful. Much as she wanted him to make love to her the feeling was still new enough to need tenderness and care.

'Now,' he said, holding out his hand. 'Come and sit with me on your sofa and tell me about your week.'

Portia curled up against him as he drew her close. 'Part of me was just marking time, waiting for this. The other part was out selling houses as usual.'

Luc ran a caressing hand through her hair, winding

gleaming strands of it round his fingers. 'It was the same for me, Portia.' He laughed a little. 'I am like a schoolboy with a crush. I could not sleep. After the magical night together in your bed my own was cold and lonely.' He paused. 'Though do not jump to conclusions, *chérie*. It is not just our bed I want to share, but your life. One day—because I know I must proceed very carefully with you—I want us to be together all the time.'

Portia lay very still. All the time? She raised her head to look at him. 'I think we should get to know each other better before we think of anything—'

'Permanent?'

'If that's what you mean, yes.'

'What else would I mean? A love affair for a while, then *adieu*, and on to pastures new?' He frowned at her, his eyes suddenly cold. 'Or is that your preference, Portia?'

She detached herself and moved away, to curl up in the other corner of the sofa. 'My preference,' she repeated quietly, 'is to take things one step at a time.'

Luc thrust a hand through his damp hair, his eyes narrowed. 'You mean you dislike the idea of a permanent relationship?'

'I didn't say that. I just consider it sensible to know each other better before—'

'Sensible!' he said with scorn. 'What man in love wants to be sensible? I am crazily in love with you, Portia—but it is very obvious that you do not return my feelings.'

She looked down at her tightly clasped hands. 'Actually, I do,' she said inaudibly.

Luc moved along the sofa and caught her by the shoulders. 'Say that again,' he demanded.

Portia took in a deep, unsteady breath, and looked him

in the eye. 'If I didn't have feelings for you, Luc Brissac, last weekend would have been very different.'

'You mean you would not have made love with me?'

She nodded.

'So your emotions must be involved before you give yourself to a man?'

'Presumably.'

He scowled and shook her slightly. 'Presumably? What kind of word is that?'

'The kind,' she said tartly, 'that you use when the situation has never occurred before.'

Luc's hands relaxed a little. 'What are you saying, Portia? Perhaps my grasp of the English language is not as good as I imagine. Explain.'

She sighed impatiently. 'I'm trying to. I was actually thinking of marrying the boyfriend I had in college, but it didn't work out. And then my mother died, and my life changed a lot, and since Tim I've never had the slightest inclination for anything more than the odd kiss or two.' She gave him a wry little smile. 'Then I met you, and fell in love for the very first time.'

Luc pulled her onto his lap and kissed her fiercely. 'Why could you not say that before? A man needs to know that his feelings are reciprocated.'

'It comes easier for you,' she muttered.

'Is that what you think?'

'You told me you were in and out of love all the time when you were young,' she reminded him.

'But I am not so young now. And it is a long, long time since I have been in love. And never before like this. Do you believe that, Portia?' he added very quietly.

'I want to believe you,' she said honestly.

He stood up and set her on her feet. 'If you are not sure it is obvious I must find a way to convince you. I want you so much, Portia. I longed for you every minute we were apart.'

'It was the same for me too,' she assured him, and reached up to kiss him. 'Last time that was enough to start the fire,' she whispered.

'This time also,' he said hoarsely, and took her by the hand. 'I will not carry you to bed, because I wish to save my energies for better things.'

'Better things?' she queried, dancing away from him.

'The very best in life!'

CHAPTER TEN

ALL too soon the demands of their professional lives interrupted the weekend idylls. A fortnight later Luc rang to say he was urgently required in Provence to cinch the deal on the property the owner was now willing to sell at a more realistic price.

'This week my diary is full, so I must go at the weekend. Fly to Paris on Friday and drive down to Provence with me, *chérie*.'

'Oh, Luc, I'd just love to, but I can't this weekend,' said Portia, anguished. 'It's my stint on standby. Ben's taken over for me twice lately. I can't ask him again.'

'You mean it is two weeks before we can be together again?' he said, incensed. 'This is impossible, Portia. I cannot exist like this.'

She went cold. 'You mean you want to end it?'

'No, I do not!' There was a sudden silence. 'Is that what you want?' he said very carefully.

'*No!*'

'*Bien*, because I meant,' he said with passion, 'that I want more of you, not less, you maddening woman.'

Portia let out the breath she'd been holding. 'I want it too,' she said sedately.

'If,' said Luc, with dangerous calm, 'we were together at this moment, *ma belle*, I would make you admit so much more than that.'

'I'm sick with disappointment, if you want the truth.'

'Ah, *chérie*,' he said caressingly. 'You cannot know how good I feel to hear you admit this. I am disappointed also. If I could I would delegate the Provence deal to someone else. But the owner of the château is being difficult. She insists on my personal attention—'

'I understand, Luc,' she said quickly. 'Really I do. But I'll miss you. Badly.'

'Then it is time we did something about it.' He paused. 'Can you take a day or two off the following week, Portia?'

'I suppose I could,' she said, thinking it over. 'I've got some time owing to me.'

'Then fly to Paris, and I shall drive you to St Malo.' He paused. 'I wish you to see Beau Rivage.'

'Luc's taking you home to Mother?' said Marianne in awe. 'Doesn't hang about, does he? You haven't known him long.'

'About a month or so less than you've known Hal,' Portia reminded her.

Marianne grinned. 'True. But almost from the first Hal and I have been seeing each other at least five days a week. A bit different from these mad, passionate weekends of yours.'

Portia coloured. 'How do you know they're passionate?'

Her friend shook her smooth blonde head pityingly. 'It's blindingly obvious, love. To me, anyway. You've never been like this before. Ever.'

'He wants me to live with him, Marianne.'

'And are you going to?'

'I don't know.' Portia shrugged. 'Maybe my trip to France will make my mind up. His mother may hate the sight of me.'

'Will that put you off?'

'I'd rather she didn't. But maybe she's old-fashioned. She might think of co-habiting as living in sin.'

Marianne frowned. 'But if Luc's taking you home to Mother, surely he's got marriage in mind?'

Languages had never been Portia's favourite subjects in school. But as a little surprise for Luc she embarked on a crash course to improve her French, with conversation tapes she played in the car wherever she went. A couple of long, stop-over trips to Cornwall and the north of England did wonders for her French conversation. Because Luc's English invariably deserted him the moment he took her to bed, she was determined to understand every word he said when he made love to her.

To Luc's surprise she told him she'd rather not fly to Paris. And that because she much preferred to travel on the Channel by ferry, rather than under it in the train, she would take her car to St Malo and drive herself to Beau Rivage.

'Only make sure you're there before me,' she implored. 'I'm nervous about meeting your mother.'

Luc laughed indulgently and told her that of course he would be there before her. 'Waiting impatiently until you are in my arms again, *chérie*.'

On the drive to Portsmouth that evening, after putting in a hard day's work to leave her desk as clear as possible, Portia began to regret her chosen form of travel. After a restless, disturbed night, nothing to do with weather conditions, Portia drove off the ferry at St Malo next day to find Luc waiting for her, dressed in jeans and a heavy sweater, his hair ruffled in the brisk breeze. His eyes lit up as he spotted her, and he jumped in the car when she halted, causing a hold-up in the traffic leaving the ferry as he kissed her hard before letting her drive on.

'I didn't expect you to be here at this hour,' she said breathlessly, her heart thudding at the devouring look he turned on her. 'You faxed me the directions to Beau Rivage—'

'But I could not wait, so I asked one of the gardeners to drive me in.' He laid a hand on her thigh, his fingers caressing it through the fine wool of the suit she'd bought specially for the occasion. 'You look so *soignée*, so perfect. Too perfect—I want to tear the pins from your hair and bring it tumbling down on your shoulders. Why did you wear it up today?'

'To look as presentable as possible to meet your mother, of course. Will she approve of me?'

Luc's face shadowed. 'I must warn you that my mother is not at her best with strangers. Do not worry if she seems formal. You have *my* approval, which is all that matters.' His fingers burned on her thigh. 'Ah, *chérie*, it is an age since I touched you—'

'Luc, please,' she said huskily. 'How do you expect me to drive when you say things like that? Give me directions!'

Portia's first sight of Beau Rivage was a glimpse of tall chimneys over the high walls surrounding the property.

'Which is not large,' said Luc, as they drove through the main gates. 'No more than eight hectares or so.'

It seemed large enough to Portia. She drove carefully along a formal carriageway, through gardens which sloped down to the river, with a statue here and there as focal points. The house itself was large and imposing, with walls picked out in granite and tall windows positioned to overlook the traffic on the river.

'You are very silent,' remarked Luc, as he helped her out of the car.

Portia gave him an expressive look. 'It's not surprising. You home is dauntingly grand, Monsieur Brissac. I'm speechless.'

'You don't like it?'

'Of course I do. It's very, very beautiful.' She smiled wryly. 'But I feel I should pay to see round it.'

Luc nodded matter-of-factly. 'People do. During the summer it is open to the public. The money is welcome. Maintenance is constant on a house built almost three hundred years ago.'

He picked up her bags and led the way through the double glass-paned doors into a flagged hall, with a central pillar and a stone staircase with a banister of wrought-iron as delicate as lace. As he dumped the bags down a woman in an expensively simple blue wool dress emerged through a door at the back of the hall.

Her greying blonde hair framed a fair, cold face which bore no resemblance at all to the olive-skinned features of her son. She came towards her guest with a faint, regal smile, her eyes taking in the quality of Portia's trousers and jacket briefly before resting on her face.

'Welcome to Beau Rivage, Miss Grant. I am Regine Brissac. You must be tired after so demanding a journey. Was the crossing very rough?'

Portia took the hand held out to her, relieved there was no need for her newly acquired fluency in the language of her hosts. Madame Brissac spoke English as well as her son. 'How do you do? The crossing was rather choppy but I'm a good sailor.'

'This is why you chose to travel by ferry?'

'Yes—I dislike flying,' said Portia, aware that Luc

was watching his mother intently. 'Won't you call me by my first name, *madame*?'

'If you wish.' Regine Brissac turned to her son. 'Bring your guest to the kitchen for coffee.'

'We shall take these to Portia's room first,' said Luc, with slight emphasis on the name. He picked up the bags. 'Then we shall join you in the kitchen.'

'Of course, *mon cher*.' Madame Brissac smiled glacially at her guest. 'It is a pity your stay will be so short—Portia. Luc tells me your job is very demanding.'

'She is a partner in a very grand estate agency,' said Luc, looking his mother in the eye. 'With the various pressures of our careers it takes much organisation to spend time together.'

'Then you must make sure she enjoys her stay here at Beau Rivage.'

Chilled by his mother's cool welcome, Portia shivered a little as she followed Luc up the curving staircase and along a corridor which led towards the back of the house.

'I thought you would prefer one of the rooms kept private from the public,' said Luc rapidly. He opened a door, and dropped her bags on the floor of a room with tall windows looking out over the river. Portia was allowed only a quick glimpse of beautiful faded carpet and a boat-shaped bed before Luc swept her into his arms.

'I trust you were not desperate for coffee, because I am desperate for this,' he muttered against her mouth, then kissed her with a heat she delighted in after the icy reserve in his mother's manner. Luc raised his head a fraction to look into her eyes. 'Tell me, Portia,' he said unevenly, 'did you long for me as I longed for you?'

'Yes,' she said simply, and gave herself up to an em-

brace which got out of hand, so quickly Luc put her
away from him with unsteady hands, his breath ragged.

'I want nothing more than to go to bed with you right
now, but—'

'This is your mother's house, and we can't do that,'
she finished for him.

'It is *my* house,' he corrected her with hauteur, then
shrugged wryly. 'But you are right. It will not do to
linger here too long. My mother would not approve if I
make love to you at this hour.'

Or at any hour, thought Portia, as they went back
downstairs. It was too soon to decide that Madame
Brissac actively disliked her, but it was obvious that the
lady had reservations about the foreign guest her son had
invited to stay.

Luc took Portia's hand to lead her into the kitchen,
which was a vast room with one end fitted with modern
appliances and a scrubbed table. At the other end a fire
crackled in a large hearth, with a group of comfortable
chairs drawn up to it and a long table close by, surrounded by dining chairs.

'Perhaps you would care to sit close to the fire,' said
Madame Brissac politely. 'Our Breton springs can be
very chilly, *n'est ce pas*?' She waved a hand towards a
woman preparing vegetables at the far end. 'Clothilde,
this is Mademoiselle Grant from England.'

Clothilde was small and round and in her forties, with
a pleasant smile and a rosy face. *'Bonjour.'*

'How do you do?' said Portia, deciding not to air her
French quite yet.

Luc seated her chose to the fire and brought her a cup
of the coffee his mother poured, then collected his own
cup and hooked a chair nearer to Portia's with his foot,
giving his mother a warning look she chose to ignore.

'Clothilde baked the brioche this morning, *mademoiselle*,' she said. 'Would you care to try it?'

'I'd love to,' said Portia warmly, and cast a smile at the industrious servant. 'It looks delicious.'

'Did you eat breakfast?' demanded Luc.

'There wasn't much time. I just had coffee.'

'But why did you not say?' said his mother at once. 'Clothilde shall make you an omelette—'

'No, please,' protested Portia quickly. 'The brioche is perfect.'

'As you wish,' said Madame Brissac. 'I trust your room is to your liking?'

'It's lovely,' said Portia, avoiding Luc's eye. 'Such a wonderful view.'

'*Bien.* Later Luc shall give you a tour of the house.'

'I'd like that very much.'

They chatted politely together, but after half an hour Luc got up and held out his hand to Portia.

'Come. I shall take you on the grand tour. Only you, of course, being a privileged guest, shall see far more than the clients who pay.'

Portia thanked Madame Brissac formally for the coffee, complimented Clothilde on the brioche, then escaped with Luc.

He began the tour of his home in the formal grand salon. Portia looked round her in silence, trying not to feel daunted by the museum-like effect of crystal chandeliers and tapestry chairs, fragile gilded tables and boule cabinets filled with pieces of rare porcelain.

'Your mother doesn't like me at all,' she told Luc.

He shut the door and took her hands. 'It is just her way. Do not trouble yourself. The important thing for you to remember, *ma belle*, is that *I* adore you. So much

I think these few days will not be as relaxing as my mother believes.'

'Why?' said Portia, knowing why, but needing him to tell her.

'Because I shall be forced to employ much cunning to have you all to myself. And even now I must not kiss you as I want to, because then your lips will be swollen and your cheeks red, and your eyes will grow heavy with the wanton look I cannot resist.'

Portia breathed in sharply, and detached her hands. 'No more talk like that, please, Monsieur Brissac. For now let's just enjoy being together while you tell me about the room. I'm determined to make intelligent, informed comments on everything I see to impress your mother at lunch.'

Luc laughed indulgently, and took his time over displaying his home, pointing out certain pictures of interest, telling her which were his mother's favourites. 'The most valuable were sold, of course, but I have since bought others she likes very much. She is also very proud of the panelling in here,' he added, as they entered a formal dining room. 'It was made by Breton carpenters on leave from their usual occupation of shipbuilding.'

The panelling formed the perfect background for a table set formally with sparkling crystal, Limoges china and silver flatware on an embroidered cloth, with a porcelain bowl of fresh spring flowers as the finishing touch.

'Do you eat all your meals here?' asked Portia, thinking of the meals she'd given him at her tiny kitchen table.

Luc laughed, and kissed the tip of her nose. 'No. We eat most meals *en famille* in the kitchen. My mother insists that we dine in here tonight in honour of your company, but lunch will be eaten at our kitchen table.'

He looked down at her steadily. 'But I will not enjoy that as much as the meals I eat at yours, Portia.'

She smiled luminously, touched that he'd sensed her qualms. 'How very graceful, Monsieur Brissac.'

He shrugged. 'No, just truthful, *chérie*. Now let us proceed.'

By the time the tour of Beau Rivage was over Portia just had time to unpack and tidy herself before Luc fetched her for lunch.

'This time,' he said, when she opened the door, 'I shall avoid temptation and remain outside.'

'Very wise,' approved Portia, and closed the door behind her.

'It is hard to be wise when I am mad with longing to hold you in my arms!' His eyes lingered on her face as they made for the stone staircase. 'You look very beautiful, but also very pale. I think you worked many hours extra this week.'

She nodded. 'To make up for the days I'm taking off. I felt a bit guilty about taking a holiday just as business is really hotting up.'

'But now you will enjoy it,' he commanded.

'I will,' she assured him, and he paused, taking her hand before opening the kitchen door.

'Why will you enjoy it?' he asked softly.

'Because I'm with you,' Portia whispered, giving him the answer she knew he wanted.

Luc's eyes flamed in response as he brushed her cheek with a caressing fingertip, then he opened the door and Portia, feeling like Daniel braving the lions' den, prepared to face her first meal at Madame Brissac's table.

In their absence the fire had been replenished and the table laid for three, the silver and china only a little less than in the panelled dining room.

'Ah, *bon*,' said Madame Brissac, appearing from an adjoining larder. 'I was about to send Clothilde to find you. Tell me your opinion of Beau Rivage—Portia.'

Glad she could say, with complete truth, that it was a quite wonderful house, Portia assured her hostess she was grateful for the privilege of seeing over it. 'Is help readily available?' she asked. 'It all looks so immaculate.'

'Some local women come in during the visitors' season, but at this time of year I manage with Clothilde and her two married daughters.' Regine Brissac turned to her son. 'Since we will drink cider with our lunch, Luc, I think an aperitif would not be wise beforehand. Unless,' she said, turning to Portia, 'you would care for one, of course?'

Portia was deeply tempted to say yes, just to be awkward. 'No, thank you, *madame*,' she said politely, and smiled at Clothilde as the little woman put down a vast bowl of green salad and a platter of bread.

'It is a very light lunch,' announced Madame Brissac, indicating the slices of terrine on their plates. 'We Bretons are known for our cider, of course, so I thought you would enjoy our chicken in cider jelly. We serve it with pickled·onions and *cornichons*, or gherkins, as you say in English.'

Portia respectfully surveyed the perfectly aligned pattern of chicken and vegetable slices in their jellied casing. 'This looks too exquisite to eat,' she said, as Luc helped her to salad.

'But you must, *chérie*,' he said firmly. 'You are losing weight.'

Aware of hostile reaction to the endearment by her hostess, Portia was glad of the covering flurry of activity as she accepted oil and vinegar and bread before beginning on the terrine, which possessed a strong flavour all of its own, due to the dry, fermented cider which gave it its particular personality.

Both Luc and his mother drank cider with the meal, but Portia kept to mineral water, afraid cider might be the last straw for a digestion coping with a combination of tension, pickles and the thinly veiled hostility of her hostess.

Conversation grew slightly easier when Portia showed sincere admiration for those areas of the house Luc had said meant most to his mother. Portia paid compliments to the panelling in the dining rooms, and the tapestry chairs in the grand salon, deeply thankful for Luc's guidance when Madame Brissac confessed that the most recent covers had been created with her own needlework.

'You do not sew, *mademoiselle*?'

'I can mend things, but I've never tried my hand at tapestry or embroidery.'

'In the winter the evenings are long,' said Madame Brissac pointedly. 'My tapestry gives me occupation, since I see so little of my son.'

Luc shot an angry look at his mother. 'I come to see you as often as I can, as do Ghislaine and Amélie and their families.'

'Of course,' agreed his mother, unruffled. 'Let me give you more terrine, *mademoiselle*. It takes three days of preparation to achieve the perfect flavour.'

Which gave Portia no choice but to accept a second slice she found hard to finish, particularly when Madame Brissac confided that calves' feet poached in the stock with the vegetables ensured that the jelly set properly. And afterwards, when the very special cabinet pudding of brioche with crystallised fruits and jam was served,

Portia was unable to refuse that, either, when she was informed it was Clothilde's speciality.

'Though I made the custard—the *sauce Anglaise*—for our guest's benefit,' observed Madame Brissac.

By the time lunch was over, and coffee served by the replenished fire, Portia could hardly keep her eyes open.

'You must rest for a while,' said Madame Brissac with a hint of command.

Portia was only too happy to agree, though it was the lunch, rather than her journey, which had done the damage. A contrast to her usual hurried sandwich, she thought ruefully, as she went alone up to her room. Luc's help had been requested by his mother, over some business matters to do with reopening the house for the summer, and with his parent's watchful eye on them he merely smiled down at Portia as he saw her to the door.

'One hour only,' he warned. 'Then we shall go for a walk in the garden.'

'After which we shall have some English tea,' promised Madame Brissac graciously.

'Thank you, I'll enjoy that,' said Portia, finding it an effort even to smile.

She fell asleep almost at once, and slept soundly for almost an hour before she woke to look at her watch and leapt out of bed to dress and tidy herself before Luc came to find her.

She was halfway down the stairs when he came in from the garden, looking windblown, with more colour in his face than usual. His eyes lit with the familiar possessive glow as he watched Portia run down to join him.

'You are on time,' he said softly as he kissed her. 'Were you afraid I would come to your room if you were late?'

'Yes,' she said bluntly. 'You know your mother wouldn't approve.'

'She makes this very clear,' he said grimly, and took her hand. 'She invented a task to keep me with her when you went upstairs.'

Portia nodded. 'I thought so. Is she always like this when you invite people to stay?'

'No.' He opened one of the glass doors to let her out into the garden. 'Because my guests are always men, or married couples. You are the only woman I have asked here to meet her.'

Portia stared at him in deep dismay as they went along a walk lined with lime trees. 'I wish you'd told me that before.'

Luc frowned, bringing her to a halt. 'Before what?'

'Before I came. Otherwise—'

'Otherwise you would not have come,' he said impatiently, and resumed walking. 'I knew that. But I wanted so much for you to see Beau Rivage.' His eyes took on a possessive gleam as he waved a hand at their surroundings. 'When my father bought it, I was already sixteen years old, but the moment he drove me through the gates I was enslaved.'

'I can understand that,' she said with feeling.

They paused at the low wall bordering the lawns, where the occasional, skilfully placed statue stood out against a backdrop of trees and shrubs framing views of the River Rance. The breeze was stronger here, and colder, and Portia shivered slightly.

'You are cold,' said Luc, taking her arm. 'Come. We shall go round to the other side of the house to admire the kitchen gardens, then you shall drink your tea. I brought it specially from Paris. Just for you, *ma belle*.' Luc eyed the curls the breeze had plucked from her tightly coiled hair. 'Tonight, Portia, indulge me. Leave your hair down.'

'She shook her head. 'I'd rather not, Luc. I'll feel uncomfortable with my hair all over the place.'

'Do it for me,' said Luc, in a tone which quickened her pulse.

'Oh, all right,' she muttered unwillingly.

'You will do as I ask?'

'It was more an order than a request,' she said tartly, then smiled at him. 'But for you, anything.'

Luc's eyes lit with a molten look which took Portia's breath away. '*Mon Dieu*, I want so much to make love to you! I will come to your room tonight.'

'No,' she said quickly. 'Please. Not here in your mother's house—'

'It is *my* house,' he said harshly. 'And I want you.'

Portia made no attempt to hide the longing in her eyes. 'And I want you. But not here. Don't ask me to, Luc. Please.'

He seized her hands. 'Are you saying I must wait until next time we meet before I can make love to you again?'

'Yes,' she said flatly. 'I am. I shouldn't have come. I don't belong here—'   '*Ne dis pas des bêtises!*' he said explosively. 'I mean—'

'I know what you mean. And it's not nonsense, Luc. In London I feel we meet as equals. Here I'm very conscious of our different backgrounds.'

'Do you mean because your parents were honest artisans?' he said, and flung away to stare blindly at the view of the river through a short colonnade of pines. 'Do you think I care about that?'

'No,' said Portia disconsolately. 'But your mother does.'

Luc turned and took her face between his hands. 'My mother does not rule my life for me, Portia. Nor is she ''to the manner born'', as you say. She comes from respectable Breton farming stock. And my father was an architect who left Paris to practice in St Malo to please her. Beau Rivage was in such disrepair he bought it for less than the price gained for our house in Paris. So no more talk of not belonging, Portia. You belong to me.' His lips met hers in a hard, emphasising kiss, then he took her hand. 'Now. Before we go in we must admire *les chartreuses*. They are my mother's pride and joy.'

CHAPTER ELEVEN

THE *chartreuses* were a series of small gardens enclosed by stone walls angled to catch the sun for the vegetables and espaliered fruit grown there. Portia, feeling a great deal happier after Luc's lecture, was charmed with them, and told his mother so over tea served in the grand salon.

'They were in ruins when we came here,' said her hostess, looking gratified.

Discussion of Madame Brissac's labours in her vegetable gardens not only came as a surprise to Portia, but eased the strain of partaking of the finest Darjeeling from fragile porcelain in a formal, chilly room, where everything smacked of restrained grandeur, from the Aubusson carpet to the mouldings on the ceilings.

'But do you do the digging as well?' asked Portia.

'I make sure she does not,' said Luc. 'I pay local men to do the rough work in the gardens.'

'I concern myself with planting and nurturing—and instructions,' said his mother, and went on to describe the types of vegetable she had experimented with over the years to add to the staple crops of potatoes and artichokes common to the region. 'Edouard, Luc's father, was no gardener. In the spare time from his profession he was concerned only with restoring the building.' Her cold blue eyes met Portia's very deliberately. 'Since his death Beau Rivage is my life.'

Later, in her room, Portia took no pleasure in getting ready for dinner. No matter how strongly Luc felt about her, Regine Brissac's message had been very clear. If

Portia Grant had any fancy ideas about coming to live at Beau Rivage with Luc she could forget them as far as his mother was concerned.

After the revealing little session in the grand salon Portia had needed time to herself before dinner.

'Why?' Luc had demanded at the foot·of the stairs. 'It is two hours or more until dinnertime. Why waste it alone, without me?'

Portia had looked at him levelly. 'I always need some time to myself, Luc, wherever I am. Normally our time together on weekends is so brief I don't expect—or need—this. But I don't leave until Tuesday morning, so I need space to myself for a while. I'm going to take a long bath, read a bit, and spend a lot of time making myself presentable for tonight.'

Luc had looked down his nose, his black brows drawn together. 'Very well, Portia. I will allow you your space. But I shall expect you downstairs at seven-thirty, and not a moment later.'

It was a few minutes short of that when Portia finally decided she was as ready as she was ever going to be for dinner with Madame Brissac. Her dress was severe in cut, made from velvet of a rich bronze shade which echoed the hair she swept back in wings above her ears and secured at the crown of her head with a gilt clasp, leaving the rest to curl on her shoulders as a compromise to Luc's wishes.

As she reached the head of the stairs Luc paused on his way up to gaze at her. He was dressed in one of his superbly cut suits, a dark blue silk tie at the collar of his gleaming white shirt, and her heart missed a beat at the sight of him, her eyes questioning as they met the oddly sombre look in his.

'You are so beautiful,' he said softly.

She smiled radiantly and went down to join him. 'So are you.'

Madame Brissac, wearing diamond studs in her ears and a plain black dress, was waiting for them in a small room kept private from the public.

'Come in, Portia,' she said politely, her eyes taking in every last detail of her guest's appearance. 'We use my own little room tonight, to enjoy a fire. I trust you had a good rest?'

'Yes, thank you, though I didn't actually sleep. I read for a while before my bath.' Portia spied a frame with a half-finished tapestry stretched on it. 'May I look, *madame*?'

'Of course. Luc, give Portia an aperitif.'

Luc handed a glass of wine to Portia, who took it with absent thanks as she looked at his mother's impressive handiwork. 'You're very accomplished, *madame*,' she said with sincerity.

Regine Brissac shrugged. 'Only in matters domestic. I have never been obliged to earn my own living as you do.'

Something pejorative in her tone stiffened Portia's spine, and, sensing it, as usual, Luc took her hand and drew her down beside him on the chaise longue drawn up to one side of the hearth, retaining her hand in his when she tried to pull free. Madame Brissac, sitting straight-backed in a small velvet chair, directed a cold glance at their clasped hands and announced that dinner would not be long.

'So what do we eat tonight?' asked Luc.

He never addressed his mother as Maman, Portia noticed.

'In honour of your guest I chose a truly regional dish.'

Madame Brissac smiled blandly at Portia. 'You like fish?'

'Very much,' said Portia, with fond memories of tuna flan. Dinner promised to be less daunting than lunch. With no calves' feet involved.

Luc began asking questions about his nephews and nieces, and described them to Portia, and with a topic so dear to his mother's heart the time passed pleasantly enough until Madame Brissac left them to supervise in the kitchen.

When they were alone Luc put his arm round Portia and drew her close. 'This is obviously difficult for you, *chérie*. We should have spent the time at my Paris apartment, where we could be alone together.' He sighed. 'As must be very plain to you, my mother and I are not close.'

Portia looked up at his sombre face. 'Why not?'

'Various reasons.' He touched a hand to her cheek. 'I will not burden you with them.'

When they were seated in the panelled dining room, with Luc at the head of the table, Clothilde came in with a vast steaming platter she set down with care in front of Madame Brissac.

'*Merci beaucoup*, Clothilde,' said Luc warmly, as the smiling little woman left the room.

'Luc says your appetite is modest, Portia,' said his mother as she served the meal. 'So there are no *hors d'ouevres* tonight. This is a dish of salt cod, soaked for several days in advance, then fried and served with sautéed potatoes, red peppers and artichokes.'

Luc handed Portia her plate. 'You like artichokes?'

'I've never tried them,' she confessed, and when they were all served took care to eat very slowly, just in case she was pressed to more. The flavours of the meal were more to her taste than expected, but so strong she was grateful when Luc supplied her with mineral water to augment her dry white wine.

While they ate Madame Brissac, very much the *grand dame* entertaining her guests, informed Portia that in times past the Bishop of Rennes would bless the fleet which sailed from St Malo to the New World in search of cod. The fleets would be gone for months at a time, some of them never to return.

'But the original owners of this house,' said Luc dryly, 'made their fortunes in less respectable manner.'

'Really?' Portia smiled at him. 'How?'

'They were corsairs—the polite term for licensed pirates—who sailed from St Malo to engage both in normal trade and to attack enemy ships and sell their plunder.'

Madame Brissac gave him an admonishing look, then told Portia that in time the St Malo corsairs became more respectable, and were given exclusive trading rights with the French East India Company. 'They moved out of the fortified town itself to build *malouinieres*, beautiful country houses like Beau Rivage, outside the city walls.'

'How romantic,' said Portia, fascinated.

'To look back on now, maybe,' said Luc, smiling at her. 'But I doubt that the corsairs themselves were romantic in any way at all.'

This time when Madame Brissac offered a second helping Portia refused with polite regret, adding that the meal had been delicious, but very filling. When Luc also declined, his mother rang the bell, and Clothilde appeared to set a chocolate-coated confection garnished with whipped cream beside her employer.

'This chestnut loaf is very light, Portia, and much

loved in Brittany,' said Madame Brissac as Clothilde bore the dinner plates away.

'This is utterly delicious,' said Portia after tasting her portion, and learned, unsurprised, that the dish had been made in advance and garnished just before serving.

No fast food at Beau Rivage, thought Portia, resigned. Everything she'd eaten so far had needed days of preparation, according to Madame Brissac, who was making it very plain that Luc's guest had caused a lot of extra work for the Beau Rivage household.

After dinner they returned to sit by the fire in the intimate little room Portia much preferred to the formality of the grand salon.

'You do not speak French, Portia?' said Madame Brissac as she poured coffee.

Portia smiled noncommittally. 'I studied it in school, of course, but nothing to compare with your command of English, *madame*. Or Luc's.'

Regine Brissac smiled complacently. 'When the children were young I engaged an English nanny. A most superior woman, with teaching skills. She came here with us from Paris, and stayed until she retired. We had all studied English in school, of course, but Miss Brown taught us the art of conversation.' Her face shadowed. 'It was useful when the house was a hotel for a while. But Luc uses it most these days.'

It soon became apparent that Madam Brissac had no intention of leaving her son alone with his guest. At eleven Portia rose to her feet, thanked her hostess for the meal, and wished her goodnight. But this time Luc rose to accompany her, something in his face deterring the objection his mother obviously burned to make.

In silence Luc escorted Portia upstairs and along the corridor to her room, and when they reached it he closed the door behind them and took her in his arms, holding her close in an oddly passionless embrace.

'Forgive me,' he whispered into her hair. 'It was a mistake to bring you to Beau Rivage yet.'

Portia leaned back a little to look up into his face. 'Yet?'

'Until you and I are together officially, when our relationship is *fait accompli.*'

'Personally, I doubt your mother will ever approve of me.'

Luc's eyes narrowed. 'She will, in time. I shall make very sure of it. But as yet this is new to her. I have brought no others to meet her.'

'Others?'

He shrugged. 'I am not a boy, Portia. Of course there were other women in my life from time to time. But you are the only one I have ever wanted in this way.' He drew in a deep breath. 'It was not my plan to mention it so soon, but you must realise I want you for my wife, Portia.'

When she gazed up at him in shocked silence his eyes glittered in disbelief. 'You do not want me?' he demanded arrogantly.

'You know I want you!' she said passionately. 'But I won't marry you.'

Luc released her and stepped back, looking as though she'd struck him. 'Tell me why, Portia,' he commanded.

She hugged her arms across her chest. 'It's nothing personal.'

'Nothing personal!' he repeated, his face suddenly taut with anger. 'To me a rejection of such a nature is very personal. Are you telling me you are married already?'

'No.' Portia turned away in despair. 'I've been a fool.

I should never have let it get this far. I never dreamed you'd actually want to *marry* me.'

'I am so frivolous a character?' he asked bitterly.

'No. But I thought you'd just want a love affair! With no strings, and no recriminations when it cooled down.' She turned to face him. 'As it will, Luc. What we've found together is wonderful, but it couldn't last at such intensity.'

'The "intensity", as you describe it,' he said with passion, 'is because I never see enough of you. If we were married, or even living together, this fire I feel for you would not die as long as I breathe, but it would diminish in time. It is hard for me to believe at this moment, it is true, but it will not matter because our minds are as much in rapport as our bodies.'

Portia gazed at him with imploring pain-filled eyes. 'Luc, please leave me alone now. When—if—you come to see me again in London I'll give you the explanations you want. But not here.'

He looked at her in silence for a moment, then gestured at the bed. 'If I made love to you now—'

'It would make no difference,' she assured him.

Luc's face hardened. 'Then I shall not trouble you further,' he said coldly, and strode from the room, closing the door behind him with a finality which put an end to Portia's self-control.

She stripped off the new dress, tears pouring down her cheeks as she hung it away. She pulled on a nightgown and sat huddled on the edge of the bed, wishing she'd never laid eyes on Luc Brissac. She mopped her eyes, sniffing miserably. For the first time in her life she was hopelessly in love, and that, of course, was the point. It *was* hopeless. She'd been a fool to let things go so far, and an even bigger fool to come here to Beau Rivage.

Giving up any attempt to sleep at last, Portia rose very early next morning and packed her clothes. When she was dressed in the new trousers and jacket she coiled up her hair very tightly, then made up her face in a vain attempt to obliterate the effects of the night.

Ideally Portia would have liked to steal away from Beau Rivage without a word to anyone. Knowing this was out of the question, she went downstairs early, intent on a private word with Luc before she said goodbye to Madame Brissac. After that, no matter what Luc said, she would leave to wait for the ferry in St Malo.

Halfway down the stairs she overheard conversation coming from the small sitting room. For a moment Portia hesitated, reluctant to eavesdrop, but when she heard her name she put her luggage down very quietly, surprised to find she could understand most of what was obviously a telephone conversation.

'Luc has been very successful,' said Madame Brissac with gloating triumph. 'He has achieved exactly the result I desired. The girl is obviously besotted with him. Unfortunately,' she added angrily, 'she has bewitched him in turn. He is madly in love with her. A great mistake.'

There was a long pause, then Madame Brissac interrupted angrily, 'No, Ghislaine, I am not wrong. And of course it was her fault. As far as I am concerned she killed him.'

There was another pause, then Madame Brissac continued, 'Luc is on his way to you at this very moment. I told him you'd had an accident, so he will be furious. Nevertheless, keep him there with you as long as you can.'

Regine Brissac rang off, then came hurrying out of the room to find Portia standing like a statue, halfway down the stairs. 'Ah. Mademoiselle Grant,' she said, without turning a hair. 'You are early.'

'Yes,' agreed Portia dully. 'I'm afraid I overheard your conversation.' She looked down very directly into the cold blue eyes. 'You know, then.'

'Of course I know,' said Madame Brissac scornfully. 'Otherwise Luc could not have carried out my plan. It was I who...' She paused, searching for the word. 'Who instigated the search.'

Portia stared at her blankly. 'Search?'

'I paid an investigator to look for you,' said the other woman matter-of-factly.

'But why?' Portia stared at her in astonishment. 'What possible interest did I have for either of you? I'm afraid I don't see the connection.'

Madame Brissac's face took on a sceptical expression. 'Then perhaps it is time we were honest with each other, *n'est-ce-pas*? You were leaving?' she added, catching sight of the luggage. 'Without telling Luc?'

'If necessary. I got up early to drive to St Malo to catch the ferry. I was going to leave a note if no one was around.'

'You shall not leave yet,' said Madame Brissac imperiously. 'Luc has gone on an errand to his sister. Before he comes back you shall listen to me. It is time your association with my son was revealed in its true light.'

Portia walked slowly down the stairs. *'Madame,'* she said formally, as she confronted her hostess in the hall, 'there's no need for this. I'm not going to marry him.'

Regine Brissac stared at her blankly. 'What is this?'

'Luc asked me to marry him, but I refused.'

'He asked a woman like you to be his wife?'

Portia felt like an actor strayed into the wrong play. The entire conversation seemed unreal as Regine Brissac turned on her like an avenging fury. 'A woman like you has no right to a man like my son.'

'*Madame,*' said Portia, icily formal to hide her anger, 'since my presence is obviously causing you distress, I'll leave now. I'm grateful for your hospitality, but—'

'No,' interrupted Madame Brissac. 'First you and I will have a little talk.'

'I can quite see, *madame*,' began Portia, 'why you consider me an unsuitable wife for Luc.'

'I imagine you can,' sneered the other woman.

'When I told Luc about my early life at Turret House—' Portia broke off. 'You know of the house, *madame*?'

'Oh, yes,' was the bitter response. 'It was your home, I believe?'

'Not my home, exactly. I merely lived there for a time when my mother took the post of housekeeper to the owner.' Portia braced herself. 'When I told Luc about it I had to leave a month out.'

'What happened during this month?' demanded Regine Brissac.

Portia gazed at her in despair. 'I haven't the faintest idea.'

'What do you mean?'

'I remember returning to Turret House after my mother's funeral, then nothing until a month later, when an ambulance arrived to take the owner to hospital.' Portia met the other woman's eyes without flinching. 'Mr Radford died in hospital later that day. I left Turret House the same evening and went to stay with my friend's family.'

'You are telling me you have no recollection of that September at all?' asked Regine Brissac in disbelief.

Portia looked at her, startled. 'You know it was September, *madame*?'

'Who should know better than I?' said the other woman bitterly. 'So. What caused this convenient gap in your memory?'

'The doctor I consulted believes I can't remember because I'm afraid I caused Mr Radford's stroke and subsequent death.' Portia shivered. 'This, plus a whole month of my life I can't account for, is why I won't marry Luc.' She frowned, puzzled. 'But why did you have me investigated, *madame*? Did you know Mr Radford?'

'No,' said the other woman with supreme indifference. 'I care nothing for this man, nor the manner of his dying. Me, I do not believe this fairy tale about your lost memory. But,' she added with significance, 'if it really is missing, it is possible I can help you.'

Portia stared into the implacable eyes. 'What do you mean?'

'I mean,' said Regine Brissac, breathing rapidly, 'that right here, in Beau Rivage, I have something that may restore your memory.'

Portia's chin lifted. 'Then perhaps you'd be kind enough to show it to me.'

'Very well. Follow me up to the *grenier*.'

The familiar, formless dread began to rise inside Portia like a smothering mist as Madame Brissac led the way up to the Beau Rivage attic, where she unlocked a door and held it open, motioning Portia inside.

With deep reluctance Portia went into the room, then stopped, transfixed, at the sight of two huge photographs on the wall opposite the bed. She stared incredulously, her heart thudding at the sight of herself in a brief bikini, smiling and sunburnt, her hair blowing in the wind. The other photograph showed a handsome boy with long blond hair, posed against a sailing dinghy drawn up on a sandy beach. The likeness to Regine Brissac was unmistakable.

Portia stared wildly from one young face to the other. Then the inexorable mist rose up and finally swallowed her.

CHAPTER TWELVE

WHEN Portia regained consciousness Madame Brissac was kneeling beside her.

'*Bon*, you have come round. Can you get up?'

With Madame Brissac's help Portia got to her feet, then stood swaying, her eyes on the photographs. She swallowed convulsively, and turned away, accepting the woman's helping hand as they went slowly back down the stairs.

'I will help you to your room, *mademoiselle*,' said Madame Brissac, sounding subdued.

Portia nodded dumbly, glad to rest on the pretty bed, even more thankful when she was left alone. But after a moment or two Madame Brissac returned with a glass.

'Drink this cognac,' she said briskly. 'You are white like a ghost.'

Portia sipped obediently, coughing as the spirit hit her throat. 'Thank you,' she said, and subsided against the pillows.

Madame Brissac looked less militant as she pulled up a chair close to the bed. 'I regret making you faint, *mademoiselle*, but now you must own to knowing Olivier.'

Portia nodded. 'The boy in the photograph looks very much like you, *madame*, so I assume he's your son. He called himself Olly. I never knew his other name. He worked at Ravenswood that year with the other French students.'

'Luc insisted, as part of his training. Olivier was there

until the end of this September you say you cannot remember.'

Portia's mind felt like a jigsaw puzzle, with a mael-
strom of discarded pieces flying together all at once,
forming a picture she couldn't bear to look at. 'Where
is Ol—Olivier now?'

'My beloved son is dead,' said Regine Brissac
fiercely. 'And you killed him.'

Portia jerked upright, staring at the woman incredulously.

'He was driving home from a party and lost control.
He had been drinking,' added Madame Brissac defen-
sively, 'because you broke his heart.'

'Madame,' said Portia, very deliberately. 'I hardly
knew your son.' She thrust a hand through her hair, her
head spinning with the onslaught of returning memories.
'I used to go down to the cove for an hour some after-
noons, when it was fine. And Olly often sailed round in
his dinghy. But always with one of the other waiters
crewing for him. He was charming, and good company.'
She met the other woman's eyes without flinching. 'But
it was nothing more than that.'

'It was nothing to you, perhaps, but Olivier was so
much in love with you that when you disappeared so
suddenly he was inconsolable,' said Regine Brissac bitterly. 'My child would spend hours up in that room,
staring at your photograph.'

Portia was coming to terms with so many things at
once she felt sick. The brandy tasted acid at the back of
her throat as pieces of the jigsaw jostled to fall in place.
'Poor boy,' she said unsteadily. 'I'm very sorry he died,
but it was nothing to do with me. He was years younger
than me. I honestly never thought of him in that way.'

'Then why did you not tell him that?' cried Madame

Brissac. 'He came home ranting of this girl, that you had been lovers and he wanted to marry you. He pleaded with me to try and find you.'

'Madame,' said Portia very gently, 'to me your son was a charming schoolboy. We were *not* lovers. We never exchanged so much as a kiss.'

Regine Brissac gave her a scornful glare. 'I do not believe that. For years I burned with the desire to find you, to tell you what you did to my son—'

'But I did nothing, *madame,*' said Portia gently. 'I'm deeply sorry Olivier died, but I had no idea he felt anything for me. He was just a boy.'

Madame Brissac's eyes glittered as she stared at the girl on the bed. 'Life is strange, *n'est ce pas*? Fate led Luc straight to you when he bought his London flat from the agency where you work.'

Portia's eyes narrowed suddenly. 'You mean Luc knew who I was before we met?'

'But of course,' Madame Brissac said gloatingly. 'When he decided to buy Turret House I instructed Luc to combine the business with the pleasure and make you fall in love with him.'

'Then you must be very happy,' said Portia, feeling sick. 'He did exactly as you wanted. Tell me,' she added bitterly, 'what was the precise plan, Madame Brissac? After I was caught in the trap you set me, what was to happen then?'

For the first time the other woman looked less sure of herself. She eyed Portia defiantly. 'I told Luc to—to seduce you, then abandon you. To inflict the pain Olivier suffered. Then my revenge would have been complete.'

Portia nodded slowly. 'I see. That's why Luc persuaded me to talk about myself, of course. To learn about Olivier. But I couldn't oblige.' She shrugged. 'Not that it matters. Even if I had remembered Olivier I doubt I'd have talked about him. I hardly knew him.'

Madame Brissac gave a choked sob, and put her head in her hands.

Portia eyed the downbent head with detached compassion. 'I wish I had remembered Olivier, *madame*. It would have saved a great deal of trouble, one way and another.' She sighed wearily. 'I hope you won't think me rude, but I'd deeply appreciate a little time alone now.'

'Yes, of course.' Madame Brissac got to her feet, looking haggard. She turned at the door. 'When Luc returns I will send him up to you. If I was mistaken about you,' she added with obvious effort, 'I apologise.'

When Portia was alone at last she got up and went to the bathroom to splash cold water on her face. Afterwards she made a few repairs, then looked at her watch blankly. So much had happened since she'd first got up, yet it was still only a little after nine. She controlled a sudden urge to throw herself on the bed and cry her eyes out, and went down to the hall instead, relieved to find her bags waiting there. After looking in Madame Brissac's small sitting room Portia went to the kitchen, then took a peep into a few other rooms, but with no result. She hesitated, then returned to the hall, wrote a brief note, and placed it on one of the hall tables.

In minutes she'd stowed her bags away in the car and was on her way into St Malo, praying tidal conditions would allow the ferry to leave on schedule. Her prayer granted, Portia was halfway across the English Channel before she finally relaxed. Right up to the last moment she'd been afraid Luc would appear to block her escape. But for the moment she couldn't cope with thoughts of Luc. Or of his mother. She needed time to come to terms with memories which had begun to rush back the moment she'd seen her photograph alongside Olivier Brissac's in the *grenier* at Beau Rivage.

During the crossing Portia went over and over the events of that lost, terrible September. She had chosen to spend the summer with her mother, instead of going to Italy with Marianne and her brother. Then, when Christine Grant had died suddenly of a heart attack, Portia had been desperately grateful to the instinct which had told her to stay home. The day of the funeral, still numb with grief, Portia had agreed listlessly when Lewis Radford had asked her to take care of Turret House for a week or two until he found a new housekeeper. And until today, in the attic at Beau Rivage, the period from her mother's funeral to the day she left Turret House for good had remained a complete blank.

In some ways, thought Portia, as the ferry sailed homeward, she wished it still was. Now, she thought with a shudder, she could recall only too clearly how Lewis Radford's manner had changed. While her mother had been alive he'd hardly deigned to acknowledge Portia's existence. But after the funeral he'd seemed to be watching her all the time, his eyes on her every move. Reminding herself constantly of the debt she owed him, Portia had told herself she was imagining things. But she'd felt Lewis Radford's eyes on her just the same, crawling like spiders on her skin, and though the weather was hot she'd taken to wearing long-sleeved shirts buttoned to the neck, and pushed a heavy chest against her door at night. And prayed that the morning would bring a reply to one of her job applications, or news of Marianne's return.

Portia had lived for the hour or two she took off each afternoon to swim and sunbathe in the cove. Sometimes

Olly, the charming young French waiter from the hotel, would sail round in his dinghy with one of the other young waiters, and Portia had enjoyed the brief, pleasant interludes in youthful male company which contrasted so pleasantly with Lewis Radford's.

She had always returned early from the beach every afternoon, long before Lewis Radford was due home from his legal practice, but that last day Portia had found him waiting in the hall, brandishing binoculars, his face suffused with anger. He'd spat terrible names at her, accused her of consorting with men on the beach, and told her it was now his turn. He'd seized her arms in a bruising grip and pushed her into the lift, ranting and raving like a maniac, terrifying Portia when he sent the lift up to the turret room he'd always kept locked. He'd flung her inside it, and Portia had stared in horror at the pornographic studies of young girls plastered all over the walls of the empty room. And in pride in place huge shots of herself and young Olly and his friends on the beach.

One look was all Lewis Radford had allowed her before he'd pounced on her, tearing at her clothes, bellowing it was time she paid her debt in full at last. She'd fought him off like a wildcat and run for the stairs, careering madly down the spirals with Lewis Radford in hot pursuit. Portia had burst out into the hall, screaming as he grasped her shoulder. The grip had slackened, he'd given an ugly choking sound, and collapsed, unconscious, on the worn red carpet.

Portia shuddered as she remembered feeling for his pulse to make sure he was alive. She had rung for an ambulance immediately, and afterwards, half out of her mind with horror and shock, had gone back up in the lift and torn down all the pictures, taken the remaining film from the camera standing on a tripod at the window. When she'd been satisfied nothing was left she'd taken the bundle down to the kitchen. She'd added her shirt, stuffed everything into the Aga bit by bit, and sent all evidence of Lewis Radford's hobby up in smoke.

During the voyage, as she looked back on that terrible afternoon, Portia still had no idea how long the ambulance had taken to arrive. When the paramedics asked what had happened she'd been unable to tell them a thing. Four weeks of her life had remained stubbornly blotted from her mind until she'd seen her photograph with Olivier Brissac's at Beau Rivage, and found the key to unlock the door she'd slammed shut in her memory.

When Portia finally arrived home in Chiswick after the drive from Portsmouth, she felt drained, desperately tired, and in no mood to answer the phone she could hear ringing as she unlocked the door. She let the machine take over and, just as expected, Luc's urgent voice demanded that she pick up the phone. She listened for a moment, then gave in and picked up the receiver.

'Hello, Luc,' she said wearily. 'I've just got in.'

'*Mon Dieu*, Portia, why did you run away?' he demanded, incensed. 'Can you imagine my feelings when I returned to find you gone?'

Portia could. Easily. 'I left you a note. Didn't you find it?'

'Of course I found it! Was it supposed to make me feel better?'

'Oddly enough,' she informed him bitterly, 'at that moment your feelings were not my main concern.'

There was a pause.

'Of course. Forgive me,' said Luc tightly. 'I am so angry with my mother I am not thinking clearly. I had forbidden her to mention Olivier and her obsession during your visit, you understand. Yet she deliberately lied about an accident to my sister to get me out of the way. Just so that she could take you up to the *grenier*. I apologise for her, and the distress she caused you—'

'No need. I'm grateful to her.'

'Grateful?'

'Yes. Thanks to your mother I'm now clear about a lot of things. Very interesting things,' Portia added significantly.

Luc breathed in audibly. 'You mean you are angry with me because you discovered that I deliberately set out to—to—'

'Seduce me?' she suggested coldly.

'If you mean I found great joy in your arms, then you are right, Portia. You expect me to feel sorry for that?'

'No,' she retorted, stung by the arrogance in his tone. 'I don't *expect* anything from you, Luc.'

'You know very well that I love you—'

'No,' she said inexorably. 'You want me. There's a difference.'

'Have you forgotten I talked of marriage?' he demanded hotly. 'Yet even before you knew about Olivier you refused me. Why, Portia? Is marriage to me so unthinkable?'

'You won't understand this,' she assured him, 'but when you first mentioned it there were certain reasons why I couldn't accept your proposal. Those, oddly enough, no longer apply, because my memory's decided to come back. Now I've got a different set of reasons for turning you down.'

'Tell me what they are!'

'For one thing you set out to seduce me out of revenge—'

'I did *not* set out to seduce you, Portia. Can you not accept that? Revenge was my mother's goal, not mine.' He took in a deep breath. 'Listen to me, please. I was growing more and more concerned for my mother's mental health. So when, by chance, I discovered you worked at the Whitefriars Agency, I decided to get to know you. But not out of revenge. I was convinced that if I heard your side of the story it would rid my mother of her obsession about Olivier's death.' He sighed heavily. 'It was never my intention to fall in love with you—'

'Nor I with you,' she retorted, stung. 'Goodbye, Luc.'

'Good*bye*?' he said incredulously. 'I cannot believe this. Are you saying you never wish to see me again?'

Portia pushed a tired hand through her hair. 'I had a lot of time to think on the crossing and the drive home. It became clearer with every mile that the gap between us is a lot wider than just the English Channel. Until I arrived at Beau Rivage I hoped it didn't matter. Now I know it does. You're a smooth operator, Luc. I really believed you were in love with me—'

'It is the truth,' he interrupted harshly. 'I keep telling you. Revenge was my mother's desire, not mine. I could never hurt you in such a way.'

'But you have, just the same. And I'm not only hurt, but furious with myself for being so gullible. I played right into your hands, didn't I? You made a fool of me. I can't turn off a switch and stop loving you right away. But at this moment, Luc Brissac, I dislike you intensely.' She cut the connection, took the phone off the hook, then switched off her cellphone, firmly putting herself beyond the reach of electronic communication.

*   *   *

Portia immersed herself in work when she got back to Whitefriars, parrying enquiries about her early return with the excuse of a cancelled holiday. It was no surprise to find there was a message on her machine from Luc when she got home that night. He sounded tired, the husky, accented voice affecting her so strongly she almost relented and rang him back. But instead she rang Marianne, and asked to see her as soon as possible.

'Right now, if you like,' said Marianne promptly. 'Hal's on call tonight. Why aren't you in France?'

Later Marianne listened in dumbfounded silence while Portia gave her a detailed account of the entire visit, ending with the photographs in the Beau Rivage *grenier*, which had triggered recall of her lost September. But long afterwards, when Marianne had stopped cursing Lewis Radford and had finally run out of questions, she eyed Portia searchingly and asked once more.

'But apart from all that, are you sure you never want to see Luc again?'

'No.'

'You mean no, you don't, or no, you're not sure?'

Portia let out a long, unsteady sigh. 'Part of me wants to see him more than anything else in the world. But the other part hates the way he deliberately set out to make me love him.'

'And succeeded. Because you do.'

Portia couldn't deny it. 'Illogical, I know, but I'd find it easier if he *had* been thirsting for revenge. The fact that he was humouring his mother makes it all so much worse, somehow—harder to forgive.'

'I don't suppose she told him to take you to bed!'

'As long as *madame* achieved her ends I don't think she was too fussy about the means.'

'Glory be! Just as well she's not going to be your

mother-in-law, then,' Marianne smiled thankfully. 'I get on rather well with Hal's mother.'

'You get on well with everyone,' said Portia with affection. 'So when's the wedding?'

'This very summer, and you're chief bridesmaid.'

Portia was very grateful for Marianne's wedding. The preparations helped fill the terrible aching emptiness left by Luc. At first he was merciless in his efforts to contact her, leaving messages on her phone and at the office, even sending faxes asking her to return his calls. Afraid to risk the seductive effect of Luc's voice, Portia arranged for a new unlisted telephone number, instead of leaving her phone off the hook every night, and bought a new cellphone. And she contacted Joe Marcus again, and arranged to have dinner with him. Only to learn that the occasion was an opportunity for Joe to tell her he was getting married.

'Joe Marcus, the serial bachelor?' said Portia, laughing, then insisted on treating him to champagne to celebrate.

She was genuinely glad for Joe, who was a good friend and would make his lucky lady a great husband. She would miss her outings with him. But for the moment going out with any other man who wasn't Luc was pointless, anyway. From now on she'd stick to evenings spent with friends of her own sex.

Inevitably Portia's security system broke down. She answered her telephone during Biddy's lunch hour one day and found she was listening to Luc's unmistakable accents.

'At last, Portia,' he said in triumph. 'Listen to me—'

But Portia, heart hammering, put down the phone,

then rang through to Reception and gave instructions regarding her non-availability to a Monsieur Luc Brissac. Just as she'd feared, one word from Luc was enough to breach all the defences she was trying so hard to build against him.

For days after that Portia expected Biddy to tell her Monsieur Brissac had asked for her again. But eventually she realised that this wasn't going to happen.

'He's given up,' she told Marianne despondently.

'I don't blame him. Do you mind?'

'Of course I don't.'

'Oh, come on, Portia, this is me you're talking to.' Marianne looked her in the eye. 'Ring him. Tell him you've thawed.'

'Not a chance.'

'You prefer your life the way it is?'

Portia smiled ruefully, unable to lie to Marianne. 'No. I prefer it the way it was, before I went to Beau Rivage.'

In her heart of hearts, something barely admitted to herself, let alone to Marianne, Portia had fully expected Luc to fly to London when his phone calls failed to reach her. When he didn't her life felt horribly empty without him. She filled it with visits to the cinema and theatre, and one weekend went to the party Joe Marcus threw to celebrate his engagement to his Sarah. But when she got home the flat seemed more lonely than before. At which point Portia looked the unwelcome truth in the face. She missed Luc so badly she no longer resented the reason for their first meeting. Because no man, not even Jean-Christophe Lucien Brissac, could have made her fall in love against her will.

The moment Portia arrived in the office next morning, she put through a call to Luc's Paris office, and in careful French gave her name and asked if Monsieur Brissac would speak with her. After a wait Portia was informed that Monsieur Brissac was away for a few days, and would *mademoiselle* care to leave a message? *Mademoiselle* was so disappointed she could hardly muster enough French to decline.

Portia had prepared herself for the fact that Luc might refuse to talk to her. After her recent behaviour she could hardly complain if he did. But the discovery that he was away came as such an anti-climax Portia sat staring blindly at the work on her desk, until Biddy came in to remind her she was due at the first viewing of the day.

Portia was brooding over an uneaten sandwich in her office during the lunch hour when Ben Parrish came in, yawning, and perched on her desk.

'I don't suppose, Miss Grant, ma'am, that you could possibly do me a favour?'

Portia eyed him warily. 'It depends, Mr Parrish, sir, on the nature of the favour.'

He gave her a wheedling smile. 'The thing is, Portia, it's my anniversary, and my five-thirty client can't get here until an hour or so later. Sue booked dinner in our favourite eating place weeks ago. She'll blow her top if I'm late getting home.'

'As long as you don't expect me to go chasing off to some remote part of the British Isles.'

'Now would I do that?' he said injured.

'Ben, if the alternative was losing a sale, of course you would.' Portia relented and grinned at him. 'So where do you want me to go?'

'Darkest Kensington, to sell "a beautifully presented maisonette with south-facing terrace and patio garden" et cetera, et cetera. The owners are on holiday, so it's all yours. Are you sure this won't interfere with your plans?'

'Very sure,' she sighed. 'My dance card's empty to-night.'

After a final session with Biddy Portia had half an hour to fill before driving to Kensington, and spent it on her face and hair to make a good impression on the people interested in the expensive property.

Portia let herself into the smart maisonette with the key Ben had given her, and went on a quick tour of inspection before her clients arrived, making notes of the features most likely to recommend the property to a pro-spective buyer. She was eyeing a rather gaudy specimen of modern art over the drawing room fireplace when the buzzer rang. She pressed a button to hear a voice with a pronounced East End accent announcing the arrival of a Mr and Mrs John. Portia pressed the release button and opened the door. Then stood staring at the tall, elegant figure of the man she'd been trying to contact that very morning.

'Luc?' she said incredulously, and looked out into the street. 'What are you doing here? I'm expecting cli-ents—'

'I am your client,' he informed her.

'So who spoke on the intercom?' she demanded, fight-ing to hide her ecstatic pleasure at the sight of him.

'The taxi driver.' He smiled crookedly. 'If I had an-nounced myself you would not have let me in.'

Not ready yet to tell him how mistaken he was on that point, Portia led the way into the drawing room. 'Have you given up your place in Hampstead?' she asked po-litely.

'No.'

She frowned. 'You need two places in London now?'

'No,' he said absently, his eyes moving over her with such unconcealed hunger Portia flushed, finding it hard

to believe that Luc Brissac was actually here in the irresistible flesh.

'Then what's your interest in this place?'

Luc tore his gaze from her with obvious effort, and
looked around him indifferently. 'I have no interest in it
at all.'

Portia blinked. 'Am I missing something? If you don't
want a flat why are you here?'

Luc turned his green, hungry gaze on her again. 'It
was the only way I could think of to see you. Are you
not proud of your power over me? That I should go to
such lengths to see you again?'

'How did you arrange it?' she asked, not really caring
how, only why.

'Your Mr Parrish was most helpful.' Luc moved
nearer. 'He told me you changed your telephone numbers.'

'Did he now?' said Portia militantly.

Luc's eyes glittered. 'You have been very cruel,
Portia. Did you enjoy your revenge?'

She stared at him, shocked. 'I wasn't out for revenge.
I was just angry.' Her eyes fell. 'And hurt.'

'I know. I wanted so much to make amends. But you
would not talk to me. And I was sure that if I came to
your apartment you would tell me to go away.'

Portia, not nearly so sure, raised her eyes to his. 'Probably.'

His mouth twisted. 'So I employed a different strat-
egy, and lured you here tonight. Are you angry?'

'No.' Portia smiled a little. 'Not angry.'

'Are you saying you are glad to see me?'

'I rang you this morning,' she said elliptically.

Luc's eyes blazed incredulously. 'You rang Paris?
Why, Portia?'

'Last night I made a discovery.' She looked at him steadily. 'I've taken all this time to discover something that was staring me in the face.'

'And what is that?'

'That no man, not even you, Luc, can *force* a woman to fall in love with him.'

He nodded gravely. 'That is true. Love is very dangerous. There is no defence against it. I went to meet you at Turret House out of concern for my mother. But from the moment I first saw you I was determined to put an end to my mother's dramatic nonsense about revenge. Can you believe that, Portia?'

'I want to,' she admitted.

'I just wanted you for myself.' Luc moved nearer still. 'I still do. So very much, *chérie*.'

Portia's heart skipped a beat. 'Shall we discuss it somewhere else?' she said breathlessly. 'It doesn't seem polite to stay in someone else's house under the circumstances.'

Luc looked at her for a long moment. 'Do you know a restaurant nearby where we can dine?'

'Is that what you want?'

'Not exactly, Portia.' He smiled crookedly. 'But at this moment it is *your* wishes that concern me most.'

'I've got my car,' she said, collecting her briefcase. 'I suggest we buy some food on the way back to my flat. There are things I need to say to you I can't discuss in a restaurant.'

On the drive to Chiswick, Portia talked determinedly about Marianne's wedding, the upsurge in the property market, and asked Luc about the work in progress on the château he'd recently acquired. But Luc was abstracted with his replies, apparently content just to look at her, undermining her concentration with the gaze he kept fixed on her face throughout the journey.

Portia called in at a delicatessen on the way, and bought French bread, ham and pastrami. When they got to the flat she gave Luc a bottle of wine to open, and, determinedly brisk, told him to sit down while she tossed a salad, sliced bread and arranged the meat on a plate.

'Not much like your Breton cuisine, I'm afraid,' she said lightly.

Luc held her chair for her, then poured the wine. 'As you remember, Portia, *charcuterie* like this is very much to my taste' He looked her in the eye as he seated himself opposite her. 'Not that it matters what I eat, now I am with you again. But I must not assume too much, I know, just because you agreed to talk to me.'

She smiled a little. 'Not your usual way, Luc.'

'No,' he agreed sombrely. 'Normally I am not so patient. But I learned a lesson at Beau Rivage, Portia. When I returned to find you gone I—' His jaw tightened. 'I do not possess the English to describe my feelings.'

'You understand why I couldn't stay?'

'Of course I do. When my mother confessed that she had disobeyed me I was insane with worry until I knew you were safe.' His eyes held hers. 'And then you would not talk to me.'

Portia reached out a hand to touch his. 'Let's eat, then afterwards we'll talk, Luc. The things I want to say are not exactly an aid to digestion.'

Luc tensed, his eyes narrowed in suspicion. 'I will obviously not like these things. Do they concern our relationship, Portia?'

'No. Not directly, anyway.'

He relaxed slightly, eyeing the food on the platter.

Then he looked up at her. 'It is useless, *chérie*. I cannot eat until you tell me these mysterious things.'

'Neither can I,' said Portia in relief, and jumped up. 'Let's go into the other room, then.' She curled up in a corner of the sofa, and patted the cushion beside her in invitation. Heat leapt in Luc's eyes for a moment, but he sat down gingerly, very careful not to touch her. 'How is your mother?' she asked.

'Since your visit she is much changed,' he said soberly. 'Now she has faced the truth about Olivier at last she no longer wishes to live at Beau Rivage. Her plan is to make a new home for herself, somewhere near Ghislaine or Amélie, and expend her care and energies on her remaining family, instead of the son who died.'

'I'm glad. Now I've had time to recover I can feel sympathy for her. And for poor young Olly.'

'Portia, it is you I am concerned with at this moment, not my mother, nor Olivier.' Luc turned towards her and took her hand. 'Am I right in assuming you remember what happened that September?'

She nodded. 'The moment I saw those photographs in your attic it all came rushing back. Although in some ways it began before then. From the day I met you, I suppose. I couldn't understand why your voice, your accent, was so familiar. I knew I'd never seen you before, yet in the beginning I felt so wary, as though you spelt danger for me in some way.'

'Do you still feel like that?'

'No. Because I know now that your voice reminded me of your brother. I found it tantalisingly familiar, but I couldn't remember where I'd heard it before.' She leaned against him, and Luc tensed, then put his arm round her, waiting, Portia knew, to see if she would push him away. When she merely settled herself comfortably in the crook of his arm he let out a deep breath, then drew her close as she began, hesitantly at first, to tell the unpleasant story of her lost September.

When she'd finished Luc sat very still for a moment, his face set in grim lines. Then he lifted her onto his lap and cradled her against his shoulder. 'And I am to blame for bringing that back to you,' he said bitterly.

Portia raised her face to his, her eyes shining. 'But I'm glad, Luc. All those years I was sure I was responsible for Mr Radford's death. I felt like a murderer. I knew he was alive when he went to the hospital, but I couldn't remember what happened before I was found in the hall with him.'

'*Mon Dieu*, it is no wonder you feared a return to Turret House!'

'I tried to make myself go back several times, convinced I had only to cross the threshold and it would all come rushing back. But I couldn't bring myself to do it, terrified of what I'd find out. And in the end it didn't work, anyway. I dreaded setting foot inside the tower most of all, but when I did, even the turret room was just an empty space. I felt something,' she added, 'when I saw the new Aga. But not enough to remind me of what I'd done with the old one.'

Luc's eyes locked with hers. 'Tell me, Portia. Was this gap in your memory the reason why you refused to marry me?'

'Of course it was. But I couldn't stop myself falling in love with you. Or staying in love,' she added huskily, her eyes falling.

Luc let out a long, unsteady breath, then kissed her with such tenderness tears leaked from the corners of Portia's eyes. 'Do not cry, *mon amour*,' he said against her lips.

'I'm crying because I'm happy,' she whispered, and said nothing else for a long time as Luc kissed her with a mounting passion she responded to with a rush of desire fuelled by the relief of telling Luc her secret. When she felt Luc draw away she opened her eyes in protest, to find his eyes glittering with determination in his set face.

'First there are confessions to make, Portia—'

'No, please, you don't have to,' she interrupted.

'Yes, *mignonne*, I do,' he said heavily. 'In future there must be no shadows between us.'

She reached a hand to his cheek, then put her head on his shoulder. 'All right, Luc. Though nothing will make any difference to the way I feel about you—'

Luc's mouth came down on hers to cut off her words as he kissed her with passionate thanksgiving. Then he smoothed her head down against his shoulder again, silent for a moment as he searched for words to explain. 'First, Portia,' he began, 'you must understand how it was with my mother and Olivier. She idolised him. All his life she gave him everything he wanted the moment he asked, first toys, then later boats and cars. So when he wanted you, *chérie*, he made my mother pay someone to search for you. When this failed, he grew wild, began drinking heavily.'

Portia took his hand and held it tightly.

'Olivier,' continued Luc harshly, 'drove too fast always, believing himself immortal, as boys of his age always do. One night his luck deserted him when he took a corner too fast on his way home from a party. No one else was hurt, *Dieu merci*. But my mother was mad with grief, and perhaps guilt also, because it was she who bought him the powerful car he was driving. She needed someone to blame—'

'So she chose me,' said Portia quietly.

Luc nodded. 'She persuaded herself that Olivier killed himself because of you. It became an obsession with her. I became truly afraid for her reason. My sisters, also. When I bought the Hampstead flat from Whitefriars and found you worked for the agency it seemed like fate. So I decided to end this nonsense of my mother's. Your Mr Parrish had given me details of Turret House, giving me the perfect way to meet you, but I had not expected to fall so desperately in love, *mignonne*,' he added huskily, and Portia drew his head down to hers, kissing him passionately to show she felt the same.

'At first,' he said unevenly, when he could bring himself to continue, 'I merely intended to ask if you'd been in love with Olivier. But once I met you I was more concerned with making you love *me*. When my mother heard I'd found you,' he went on heavily, 'she insisted I take you to Beau Rivage. I planned to tell you everything that weekend, certain that when my mother met you she would know at once that you had nothing to do with Olivier's death.'

Portia shivered. 'Instead your mother said I virtually killed him. She told me her plan was for you to seduce me, then abandon me, to inflict the pain Olivier suffered.'

Luc's mouth twisted in distaste as he pulled her closer. 'Portia, I did not agree to this, I swear. Can you believe that?' He brought her face up to his, his face relaxing slightly as she smiled up into his eyes.

'Of course I do. Now. But that horrible day I was trying to cope with far too many things at once. My missing memory would have been enough on its own, but when your mother implied you were a willing accomplice to her revenge I was so shattered I just got in the car and took off for St Malo.'

'My mother sent me off on a fool's errand, with some story of an accident to Ghislaine,' said Luc bitterly. 'When my sister confessed Maman had told her to keep me there I broke the speed limit back to Beau Rivage. Then I arrived to find you gone and learned my mother had disobeyed me. I was so enraged with her that she was frightened into facing reality at last.'

'Luc, don't blame her too much,' said Portia quickly. 'If she hadn't taken me up to the attic I might still be in the dark about the gap in my memory. In which case,' she added, 'there would have been no hope of—of anything permanent between us.'

Luc smiled, looking suddenly younger, as though a great weight had rolled from his shoulders. 'Why can you not say marriage?'

She flushed, her eyes falling from the look in his. 'It seemed to be taking too much for granted,' she muttered, and he laughed outright, and bent his head to kiss her. But after a moment he put her away, breathing hard. 'I cannot kiss you like this without wanting so much more. And I am determined to show you that it is not just your beautiful body I desire. I want all of you, Portia.'

'I want all of you, too.' She smiled at him with such undisguised love in her eyes Luc crushed her to him.

'These past weeks have been a torment,' he muttered into her hair.

'For me too,' she assured him, and pushed at his restraining hands.

He dropped them at once and Portia got to her feet, her hands going to the pins securing her hair. Luc watched as she took them out, one by one, then she shook her hair free and smiled at him, and he leapt to his feet and swept her up into his arms.

'Until you did that I thought I could exist without making love to you, but it is impossible—'

'I thought it might be,' she admitted, then blushed vividly as Luc threw back his head and laughed joyously, and she laughed with him.

They were still laughing when they fell on her bed together, undressing each other with caressing, unsteady hands. But when she was naked in his arms Luc's laughter died, and he laid his face between her breasts, his breath hot against her skin.

'I persuaded myself I would not expect this,' he said indistinctly.

Portia balanced on an elbow and ran her free hand through his thick dark hair. 'This morning, when I rang your office and found you were away, I was sure this would never happen again.'

Luc smiled up at her in triumph. 'I was on my way here to find you. We were meant to be together, Portia. Fate led me to find you that day. And I am keeping you.'

He began to caress her, his hands cool and his mouth hot as they enticed her into a response made all the fiercer by their separation. As she began caresses of her own Luc stiffened and muttered something French and indistinct in her ear.

'Yes, please,' she said breathlessly. 'I'd like that.'

Luc raised his head to stare down into her glittering eyes. 'You understood?'

She smiled exultantly. 'I've been studying in secret.'

He held her arms wide, keeping her pinned beneath him. 'Is there anything else you should confess?' he demanded.

She nodded, and he waited, poised tense above her.

'Tell me, Portia!'

'It's just something I've been practising in secret.' She took in a deep breath, her eyes holding his. '*Je t'aime beaucoup*, Luc.'

He let out an unsteady breath and released her hands to bury his face in her hair for a moment, then he kissed her with an urgency he could no longer control, her response so explicit he lifted her hips and took possession of her, their need for each other so overwhelming they were swiftly consumed by the fierce heat of their reunion.

They stayed locked in each other's arms for a long time afterwards, luxuriating in the bliss of reconciliation. But at last Portia struggled free.

'What is it, *mignonne*?' demanded Luc.

'I'm hungry!'

On a beautiful early summer day a few weeks later Portia walked down the church aisle, smiling up at the man beside her. The smile stayed through all the kissing and hugging, and the photographic session outside the church, but once the photographer pronounced himself satisfied Portia found herself firmly detached from the wedding group.

'Who is that man you were clinging to?' demanded Luc.

'Hal's friend. And I wasn't clinging. The chief brides-maid always walks arm in arm with the best man,' said Portia happily. 'Besides, you know perfectly well you're the best man where I'm concerned.' She gave him an approving head-to-toe look. 'You look wonderful.'

'I like your dress, also,' said Luc, eyeing her narrow sheath of midnight-blue silk. 'Very elegant, *ma belle*. However,' he added conversationally, 'I would like very much to tear it off you right now. It is two endless weeks since we were together.'

'What on earth are you saying, Luc Brissac?' called Marianne. 'It's the bride who's supposed to blush, not the bridesmaid.'

The reception at the Taylors' home was a happy, informal affair, where most of the guests mingled at will. But Luc flatly refused to move from Portia's side the entire time, to the amusement of all concerned.

'Can't say I blame you,' said the bride's father, patting Portia's cheek. 'You're a lucky man, Luc,' he added, and beckoned a waiter to refill their glasses.

'I know this,' Luc assured him.

Mr Taylor winked, then went off to see to the rest of his guests. Soon it was time for speeches, and toasts to the bridesmaids, then the cake was cut, and at last Marianne went off with her mother to change.

'Soon,' said Luc, 'we shall be able to go, *n'est ce pas?*'

'Yes,' said Portia, and smiled up at him. 'What do you think of a traditional British wedding?'

'Most charming. But very long. I have made so much conversation my English is beginning to desert me.'

'Like it does in bed,' she whispered, and his eyes darkened.

'It no longer matters, since you now understand everything I say.'

She smiled demurely. 'Not quite everything.'

'Tonight I shall translate every word,' he promised, sliding an arm round her.

'Luc, can you let Portia go for a minute?' called Hal. 'Marianne wants her.'

'Not as much as I do,' muttered Luc, but he released

his hold on Portia's waist and watched her go upstairs before joining Hal and his best man.

Marianne was waiting in her room, ready for her honeymoon in the suit they'd chosen together. 'Well, then, Portia. It's done. The knot's tied.'

'Are you happy?' said Portia.

'Very. Luc looks happy too. I take it things are settled?'

Portia nodded. 'Beau Rivage is reverting to a hotel again. Madame Brissac has found a house near Ghislaine and her family, and Luc and I are going to alternate between his apartment in Paris and the one he's bought in London.'

'So it's happy-ever-after time for us both,' said Marianne with satisfaction.

'I never really thought it would be for me,' said Portia soberly, and they hugged each other convulsively, until a knock on the door broke them apart.

'Come *on*, Mrs Courtney, or we'll miss our flight,' yelled Hal. 'There's another impatient guy out here too. Luc wants his wife back.'

The two friends looked at each other, blinked a little, then smiled and went to join the men waiting for them outside on the landing.

'I hope you haven't been putting my bridegroom off the joys of wedded bliss,' said Marianne, laughing up at Luc.

'*Au contraire*, Madame Courtney.' Luc grinned wickedly. 'I am as eager to resume my marriage as Hal is to begin his.'

'I'm surprised you let Portia work out her notice alone in London,' said Marianne, as the four of them went downstairs together.

'It was the only way I could get her to marry me so

quickly,' he said with regret. 'It is no way to conduct a marriage, with the bridegroom in Provence and the bride in London.'

'We had a honeymoon at that gorgeous château first,' pointed out his wife.

'True. But it was not long enough.'

Later, after Luc and Portia had waved off the bridal pair and taken protracted leave of their hosts, Luc got into the car with a sigh of relief. 'A mile or two only, *chérie*, and we can be alone at last.'

Portia gave him a startled look. 'I thought we were going back to London tonight.'

'No, we are not.' Luc smiled smugly as they drove away from the Taylor home. 'I booked a room at a very pleasing little country hotel not far from here, *mignonne*.'

Portia began to laugh. 'You are a very high-handed man, Luc Brissac.'

'Do you mind that I am so eager to be alone with you?'

'No. Not a bit. It's a brilliant idea. I can't think why I didn't think of it myself.'

'Because you are a woman, *chérie*.'

'What's that got to do with it?'

'A man who exists without his very new wife for two long weeks is naturally obsessed with thoughts of taking her to bed the moment he sees her again. With a woman it is sadly different.'

'Not this woman,' said Portia, and gave him a wicked little smile. 'Your wife is in complete accord, Monsieur Brissac. Can't you drive a bit faster?'

RECKLESS FLIRTATION

HELEN BROOKS

CHAPTER ONE

'MRS CHALLIER? How do you do?' The cool, deep voice was as distant as the dark, handsome face staring down at her. 'You are Mrs Ann Challier?' The attractive French accent, so like Emile's, was chilling.

'I—' Sandi hesitated for a split second, her mind racing.

'I was informed this was the residence of Mrs Ann Challier.' The aristocratic face was as cold as ice, and the fine aquiline nose almost wrinkled with distaste as he spoke the word 'residence'. 'This is not so?'

'Who are you?' Sandi ignored the niceties of social intercourse as the fine hairs on the back of her neck stiffened warningly. This was one of them, she just knew it. But which one?

'I think you know who I am.' The hard face didn't give an inch. 'Emile must have mentioned me, surely?'

Sandi stared at the tall, broad-shouldered stranger as she searched her mind quickly. It had to be either André or Jacques. The likeness to Emile was too strong for there not to be a blood tie, but which brother was it? Whichever one, that lean, muscled body and hard, ruthless face spelt trouble with a capital T—and no way was this man coming within three feet of her sister. 'I'm not in the mood to play games, Mr—?'

'Games?' For a moment she almost closed the door in his face as the dark eyes glittered menacingly. 'I do not play games, Mrs Challier. I am Emile's brother Jacques. I regret the imposition at such a delicate time, but I trust you understand we need to talk—'

'You have got to be joking!' So this was the great

and venerable Jacques Challier, was it? She might have
known. The flood of pure undiluted rage that swept
through her slight form brought her chin jerking upwards
and her eyes flashing blue sparks as she surveyed the
immaculately dressed man in the doorway. 'I wouldn't
talk to one of your despicable clan if you were the last
family left alive on earth, Mr Challier,' she said tightly.
'And for the record I'm not Ann, I'm her sister, Sandi.
But you can take it as read that I'm voicing my sister's
thoughts as well as my own.'

'I beg your pardon—' The frosty, icy voice was cut
off in mid-stream.

'No, you don't!' She was almost crouched in the doorway now as she spat her rage and anger and bitter hurt
at him. 'The illustrious Challier family have never
begged in their life. Force is more in your line, isn't it?
That and nasty not so subtle manoeuvring of people's
lives and happiness. Well, you should all be happy now,
back in your wonderful, precious château, shouldn't
you? Emile is dead and you've broken Ann's heart—
what more do you want?'

'You dare to talk to me like this?' The French accent
was very pronounced and his face was as white as a
sheet, but nothing could have stopped her from speaking
her mind to this unfeeling block of stone.

'Oh, yes, I dare, Mr Challier. I most certainly dare,'
she hissed hotly, straightening sharply as he made to
push past her into the tiny flat and barring the way with
her small body like an enraged tigress defending her
young. 'No further!' Her voice, quiet as it now was,
stopped him in his tracks as he recognised the throbbing
hate in its depths.

'You're not coming into this flat. I'd rather die than
let you soil Ann's home with your filthy presence,' she
said softly. 'You can leave her alone now; the only thing
that linked her with your family has gone. We're not
intimidated by your wealth or influence, Mr Challier, not

any more. My sister wasn't good enough for your precious family, was she? She didn't have the right connections and she wasn't French.' Her lips had drawn back from her teeth as though she was looking at something repugnant, and the tall man standing in front of her was as still as a statue.

'Well, let me tell you something—something you can take back home with you for the rest of them. She's worth more than all the Challiers put together. In fact, you aren't worthy to lick her boots, any of you. Emile knew that. At least they had a few months of happiness together, and none of you can take that away. If you're worried we'll make any claims on the Challier fortune, you can forget it. We despise and detest you all. There is nothing—*nothing*—we want from you. Have I made myself clear?'

'Transparently so.' The black eyes were narrowed slits, but otherwise the hard face was expressionless. 'I could even say dramatically so.'

'You can say whatever you like,' Sandi answered softly. 'You can't hurt Emile any more and I won't let you hurt Ann.'

She saw the import of her words register in his eyes at the same moment as a faint female voice reached out through the door separating them. 'Sandi? Sandi, who's there?'

'It's all right, Ann. I'll be with you in a minute.' She turned back to him and her hand moved to close the door. 'Goodbye, Mr Challier.'

'And this is your final word?' He stiffened as her intention to send him on his way unheard hit home.

'You'd better believe it,' she said tightly, a small part of her mind acknowledging that this was probably the first time in his life that he had been actively thwarted— and by a female at that. Ann had told her that Emile had often joked that Jacques, as the older brother and partner in their father's huge and successful wine business, had

more women than he knew what to do with. Having seen
him, she could believe it.

'The conversation would have been to your sister's
financial benefit—'

'What is it with you people?' she asked with horrified
contempt, not bothering to control her scorn. 'Is money
your god? Is that it? Well, rest assured it isn't ours. Ann
has her memories and—' She stopped abruptly and bit
her lip as she realised what she had been about to say.
'And that's enough,' she finished carefully. 'So you've
fulfilled your obligation to your brother's widow, Mr
Challier. You've made the gesture of a blood-offering to
appease your guilt, and now I would like you to leave.
My sister hasn't been able to sleep for days. This is the
first time she's rested during the day and now you've
woken her up—'

'Oh, come, Miss—?' Sandi ignored the request for her
name with a raising of her chin and a narrowing of her
eyes as she stared back into the dark face looking down
at her so contemptuously, and after waiting a few seconds he shrugged coldly. 'This is the age of sleeping
pills and other such medication for difficult circumstances. I'm sure her doctor has prescribed—'

'She can't have sleeping pills—' Again she stopped
suddenly and took a deep breath, furious with herself for
being provoked into responding to his scornful cynicism
without thinking about what she was going to say first.
'Look, just go away, will you?' she hissed tightly as her
voice returned along with her wits. 'We don't want you
here.'

As she made to slam the door a large male foot moved
quickly into the opening. At the same moment his body
took the force of her action, his shoulder effectively
checking the door's momentum. 'Not so fast, Ann's sister,' he said softly, his voice like liquid steel. 'There is
something here I do not understand—'

'There's nothing *to* understand,' she spat back quietly,

her voice shaking. 'I don't want you upsetting Ann, that's all. Just leave us alone—'

As the door to one side of the small hall opened her voice stopped abruptly, and both their faces turned to the young girl standing swaying in the doorway. And even though her thin, slender body emphasised her swollen stomach, heavy with child, a young and vulnerable girl was still exactly what Ann Challier looked like. A beautiful, pale, lost child, with long, tangled strawberry-blonde hair and haunted dazed eyes the colour of a summer sky that widened on fastening on the tall, silent man in the doorway.

'No...' The bewildered, frightened gaze moved fleetingly to Sandi. 'Sandi? No...'

And as she slipped helplessly into a dead faint they both moved as one—Jacques reaching Ann just a second before Sandi and catching her body before it hit the floor. He sank to his knees with her in his arms.

'Look what you've done.' Sandi, too, had crouched down over her sister's inert body, and now they faced each other across Ann's unconscious form. 'Oh, why did you have to come here today? You didn't even bother to acknowledge the funeral—why come here now and upset her like this?'

'She's having a child.' The heavily accented voice was as stunned as the dark face. 'Is it Emile's?'

'Of course it's Emile's.' Sandi glared at him so savagely that he blinked. 'Who on earth did you think—? Oh, you Challiers!'

'I didn't mean it like that.' He shook his head slightly. 'But I didn't know. We were not informed—'

'Why should you have been informed?' she asked tightly. 'You and your family made it perfectly clear that if Emile married my sister he was, to all intents and purposes, dead in your eyes. Well, now he is, isn't he?' Her face was as white as his, but her eyes were scorching with the force of her emotion.

'The poor boy was working all hours—doing his degree by day and a job at night, catching a few hours' sleep whenever he could. But you don't care, not really. You've never cared. What do your type, with all your millions, know about hard work anyway?' she asked scathingly. 'He was killed while driving back to his depot, if you're interested. The police think he fell asleep at the wheel of the van, because there was no reason for it to plough into the brick wall he hit.'

'I have read the police report,' he said stiffly.

'But you couldn't make the funeral?' she asked slowly. 'But why should you, after all? He was only your brother, the black sheep who had stepped outside of the Challier regime and was therefore less than nothing.'

'I came as soon as I found out,' he said sharply, his eyes glittering as they met hers. 'We were away. My mother has not been well and needed a complete rest away from all outside contact.'

'And this "complete rest" was without telephones?' she asked disbelievingly. 'The police must have tried to contact you—'

'They did, and eventually they succeeded,' he said coldly. 'As you see.'

'What I see—' The harsh retort she had been about to make was cut off as Ann moaned softly and her eyelids flickered and moved.

'Could you carry her to the bedroom?' Sandi asked quickly, hating the necessity but knowing that she couldn't leave Ann lying on the threadbare carpet in the small hall. 'She's been ill ever since it happened. Since Emile's accident,' she added quietly but with a wealth of bitterness in her voice.

'Of course. If you will permit me?' He moved a hand under Ann's limp body and lifted her into his arms as though she weighed less than nothing, and as he rose Sandi led the way into the flat's minute box of a bedroom, drawing back the quilt and covering her sister's limp body as soon as Jacques had laid her on the bed.

As she did so, Ann's lovely eyes opened slowly, her fist going immediately to her mouth as her gaze centred on Jacques's dark face, which was an older version of Emile's.

'It's all right, Ann, it's all right.' Sandi crouched over her sister, blocking her from her brother-in-law's gaze. 'You've fainted, that's all.'

'Who—?'

'It's Jacques,' Sandi said quietly. 'But it's all right, I promise. He just wanted…' She hesitated and forced herself to go on in a neutral, steady voice. 'He just wanted to see if there was anything he could do to help.'

'Help?' There was a touch of hysteria in her sister's voice that the tall man standing so silently just behind them heard and recognised.

'Mrs Challier?' To Sandi's fury he moved round to the other side of the bed, drawing Ann's gaze to him as he looked down at her, his face amazingly gentle and quiet. 'I wish you no harm, please believe me.' Sandi saw her sister flinch as her exhausted gaze took in the remarkable likeness to her dead husband, but Jacques had continued speaking before she had time to react. 'We had no idea of Emile's accident until just a few hours ago,' he said quietly. 'It is important that you understand this. My mother is unfortunately not well herself, and the news—naturally so—proved a great blow to her—'

'Look, what exactly do you want?' As Sandi spoke again the dark eyes turned to her, and she was immediately conscious of her faded T-shirt, old, worn blue jeans and the fact that her face was devoid of make-up. The deep brown eyes that had been so quiet and intent as they'd looked at Ann now hardened into glinting onyx as they fastened on her face.

He, on the other hand, was dressed with the unmistakable elegance of limitless wealth. His clothes—casual, but screaming an exclusive designer label that put them in the unattainable bracket—sat on the big male frame in a way guaranteed to make most red-blooded females take a second look.

'My sister is very tired, and the funeral yesterday was the worst sort of ordeal in her condition.'

'Of course—'

'She needs rest and quiet, and I have to say that your presence is not conducive to either,' Sandi continued quickly, before she lost her nerve. There was something very intimidating about Jacques Challier—a fact she felt that he was well aware of and used to good advantage—but she was blowed if she was going to be terrorised by him or any other member of the family who had treated her sister so cruelly.

She saw dark red colour flare briefly under the high classical cheekbones, but other than that there was no trace that her words had hit home; his whole stance was one of cold contempt and autocratic imperiousness as he faced her over the bed. 'This attitude is not helping any of us,' he said coolly. 'Your sister least of all.'

'I think you can safely leave my sister's welfare to me,' she answered just as coldly, and her heart thudded so hard that she felt he would hear it.

'I'm sure she is in most capable hands.' His eyes had narrowed to black slits, his gaze sweeping again over her slight figure and the mass of corn-coloured hair tied high on the top of her head in a voluptuous ponytail of silky gold curls.

'Yes, she is.' Sandi's gaze didn't waver, even though she knew he was speaking tongue-in-cheek. 'So, if you don't mind…?' She waved her hand towards the door in a gesture of dismissal.

'Not at all.' He turned quietly to Ann, nodding his head in a formal little bow that was pure French. 'There are one or two formalities, you understand, but as it seems your sister is dealing with such things I will talk to her, yes?'

It wasn't quite what Sandi had had in mind, but as long as he left Ann alone she didn't much care, she thought shakily as she noticed her sister's strained white face and tense eyes. At this rate she would lose the baby, and if that happened—

'Yes…' Ann's voice was a mere whisper, but it seemed to satisfy him because he turned in the next instant, leaving the room after another nod at them both and shutting the door carefully behind him.

'I'll go and see what he wants.' Sandi forced a smile as she spoke, patting her sister's hand reassuringly. 'It won't take long.'

'I'm sorry, Sandi.' Ann had half raised herself in the bed when the door closed, and now her eyes were bright with unshed tears. 'But he looked so much like Emile that for a minute I thought… Oh, I shouldn't involve you like this.'

'Don't be silly.' Sandi plumped down on the bed, taking her sister's too thin body in her arms and giving her a quick hug before standing again. She was too slender, she thought worriedly. Even before Emile's accident the pregnancy had been a difficult one, and although the doctors were satisfied that the baby was getting all it needed it was clear that Ann was suffering in consequence. 'If you can't involve me, who can you, for goodness' sake? I told you yesterday—I'm staying as long as you need me here and I mean it.'

'But your job—?'

'No job is as important as you,' Sandi said firmly. 'If they won't keep it open for me until I get back that's their loss, not mine.' Brave words, but her stomach lurched at the thought of what she might be throwing away.

She had had to leave university eight years ago, halfway through her degree, to look after Ann when their parents had died. She had known that a career would be that much more difficult without the necessary qualifications, but she had done it gladly, knowing that her sensitive, delicate sister would have wilted and pined with strangers.

After getting a foothold on the ladder of advertising she had proved herself both gifted and tenacious, and when her chance had come eight months ago she had reached out and grasped it. And the job, based in America, was a dream. Her own flat, car, and a monthly salary that had made her gasp when it was first offered. But…Ann still came first.

She smiled at her again as she left the room. Dreamy, impractical Ann, who persisted in seeing the world through rose-coloured glasses, whereas hers were as clear as crystal—sometimes painfully so.

And Emile, in spite of his youth, had been like her, she thought quietly as she walked through to the tiny lounge. Determined and obdurate and wholly devoted to her sister. When Ann and her Frenchman had decided to get married eight months ago, at the same time as the American offer had materialised, she had had no qualms about entrusting her quiet, gentle, sensitive sister to Emile's care and leaving for the States.

Jacques Challier was waiting in the middle of the room as she entered, his tall, immaculate figure somewhat incongruous against the threadbare carpet, the diminutive two-seater sofa and the old rocking-chair that made up the sum total of the furniture besides the small portable TV on a rickety chest of drawers. A good third of her salary each month had gone straight over the Atlantic into Ann and Emile's joint account, but even so, being two students on a limited budget, they had struggled to get by. But they had been rich in love. Her throat tightened at the thought.

'I'm going to make Ann a cup of tea; would you like

one, Mr Challier?' she asked coldly, indicating for him
to be seated. She would get through the next few minutes
with a modicum of dignity, she thought tersely, in spite
of the fact that she would have given the world to scream
all the abuse that had been mounting for the last few
days into his handsome, superior face.

'Thank you.' He didn't smile. 'That would be most
welcome, Miss—?'

'Gosdon—Sandi Gosdon.' She waved her hand at the
sofa behind him again. 'Do sit down, Mr Challier. I'm
sorry that the furnishings are not quite what you're used
to, but—'

'Miss Gosdon, I'm fully aware that at this moment in
time you would like nothing more than to wipe all trace
of the Challier name from the face of the earth,' he said
flatly, his eyes glittering at her sarcasm, 'but don't you
think that in the circumstances we could try to communicate?'

'Why?' She faced him directly now, her eyes sparking. 'Exactly why?'

'Because of your sister.'

'She doesn't need you—any of you,' Sandi said
tightly. 'The only Challier that mattered to her is dead,
so what can you do for her now? And don't mention
money,' she warned furiously as he opened his mouth
to reply. 'Don't you dare.'

'You think she can live on fresh air?'

How could someone who looked so much like Emile,
although admittedly an older version, be so hateful? she
asked herself silently as she stared at him with all the
dislike and bitterness in her heart evident in her eyes. 'I
can look after her.'

'You?' There was a wealth of contempt in his voice,
and as he waved a disparaging hand she noticed a heavy
gold watch that would have paid the rent on the flat for
a year or more gleaming on one tanned wrist. 'I hardly
think so, although I am sure you are well intentioned.

Ann is twenty years of age, I understand, and you are—
what? Twenty-one? Twenty-two? And with the child—'

'Ann's child!' Sandi's voice was shaking with rage.

'And Emile's.' In comparison, his was icy cold.

'But Emile is dead and Ann is alive,' she said tightly.
'And as it happens, Mr Challier, I am twenty-eight years
of age and have an extremely highly paid job in
America. I can more than adequately support my sister
and her child for the next few years.'

'Really?' He didn't move an inch, although she saw
the flash of surprise in his eyes before he had time to
conceal it.

'Yes, really.' She had seen something else there too—
a hot, dark anger, like black lightning, that had turned
the handsome face stony hard before a mask had settled
over the autocratic features, concealing his thoughts.

So you don't like to be foiled in your plans, Mr
Jacques Challier, she thought silently as she stared her
dislike. And you don't like me much either. Well, that's
good, that's very good—because the only thing that
could give me any satisfaction at this moment in time
would be to frustrate that cold, logical mind and send
you back to your socially élite family with your tail very
firmly between your legs!

'And you think it fair—wise—to deny your sister's
child the comfort of its father's family?' he asked
smoothly after a long, still moment when they faced each
other like two gladiators about to enter the ring. 'I understood from Emile that your parents are dead and there
are no close relatives. That being the case, do you think
one aunt can compensate for the loss of a host of grand-
parents, aunts, uncles, cousins?'

'If they are Challiers then the answer has to be yes,'
she said bitterly.

'But your niece or nephew will bear this hated name,
surely?' he asked with deceptive mildness. 'As did its
father.'

'I've got no intention of bandying words with you.' She drew herself up to her full five feet five and wished with all her heart that she were a statuesque, model-type six feet, so that she could have glared at him eye to eye. 'I think I've made the position clear.'

'And it would seem I have failed in this respect.' He smiled, but it was a smile utterly without warmth. 'I came here today on behalf of my family to offer our respects to Emile's widow, but now—' He stopped abruptly as he glanced towards the bedroom. 'Now everything has changed.'

'Like hell it has.' She couldn't match his cold, austere bearing or air of ruthless command and she didn't even try. Instead she faced him like a small, enraged lioness, with her teeth all but bared. She knew exactly what he meant. The baby. Ann and Emile's unborn baby. It was that and that alone that had captured his interest.

She had heard about these old and noble families— and the Challiers were certainly that—had heard stories of their obsessional desire for male heirs that sacrificed everything in its path. André, the other brother, had five daughters, and Emile had been of the opinion that Jacques would never marry, was the eternal bachelor— so that left… 'When Emile died all ties with the Challier family were cut—'

'Don't be naïve, Miss Gosdon.'

Now the deep, rich voice was definitely nasty, and as he moved closer, staring down at her from cold, narrowed eyes, a whiff of frighteningly expensive after shave caused her stomach to contract in fear. It spoke of wealth and power and influence, all formidable weapons, but there was something else… A sudden realisation of the overwhelming maleness of this man, the sensual force and vigour that were apparent even when he was absolutely still, like now.

'Because I know you aren't. I think it is time for both of us to acknowledge exactly where we stand, yes?' She didn't say a word; she couldn't. She just remained frozen before him like a mouse before a snake. 'My parents are entitled to know that they will have another grandchild in the not too distant future—I think even you would agree with that?'

'Then you think wrong,' she snapped hotly, stung to speech by his infuriating command. 'And if you're going to suggest that it would be all sweetness and light on the Challier side just because Ann's expecting Emile's child, I don't believe you. As you just pointed out, I'm not naïve, and there is no way I'm going to stand by and see her treated as some sort of second-class citizen—'

'I know, I know.' He interrupted her with a raised hand and sardonic face. 'My family are not worthy to—what was it? Ah, yes—lick the boots. I have, as you say, received the message.'

'Good.' She eyed him warily. 'So you accept there is no point in your family visiting Ann?'

'But there is no question of that.' His voice was cool—too cool, and the determined set of the hard jaw was not exactly reassuring either. 'It would be far more...appropriate for your sister to accompany me to my parents' home in France and take up residence with my mother until the child is born.'

'You've got to be joking...' She gazed at him open-mouthed until his mocking gaze informed her of the fact, whereupon she shut her mouth with a tight little snap.

'I never joke, Miss Gosdon; I consider it a singular waste of time,' he said softly, his French accent making the words attractive even as their content chilled her blood. 'My family are wealthy and secure and can provide Ann with all she needs. You would really rather see her have the child in these conditions?'

'*These conditions?*' She glared at him angrily. 'I can assure you there are a lot worse, Mr Challier. This flat might be small, but it's—'

'No fit place for a Challier to be born,' he said tightly, his face contemptuous.

'But you didn't care whether Emile and Ann were alive or dead this time last week,' she protested furiously. 'And now, just because Ann's pregnant, everything has got to be done as you wish it? You can't force her into something she doesn't want—take her to a strange country with people she doesn't know—'

'Miss Gosdon—' He took a deep breath and suddenly relaxed his big body, sinking down onto the sofa behind him and leaning back with one leg crossed over his knee. He stared up at her with glittering black eyes. 'Shall we have that tea?' he asked smoothly. 'I'm sure Ann is waiting for hers. And perhaps when we have both calmed down we can discuss this matter rationally. I can understand that you are apprehensive, and your concern for your sister does you credit, but there are things you do not understand—things I must explain to you.'

'I...' She stared at him helplessly. He obviously had no intention of leaving, and he was too big to manhandle out of the flat, but every instinct in her body was screaming at her to do just that. He was dangerous. Her violet-blue eyes widened at the thought, but it was true. Her sixth sense had told her just that the second she had opened the door to him, and part of her antagonism had been a form of self-protection against the overpowering magnetism that was inherent in the man...

But this was no time for fanciful wanderings. She pulled herself together sharply. She had to handle this in the best way she could. He could have his darn tea and then she would listen, very meekly, to everything he said, and agree where necessary, and then she would usher him out of the flat and never let him or any other of the Challier brood set foot in the place again.

If it hadn't been for their meanness in cutting Emile off without a penny towards his education he wouldn't have had to take that punishingly tiring job which had ultimately killed him. And his crime? He had married the woman he loved. A woman they had despised and loathed whilst refusing even to meet her.

'I'll get the tea,' she said flatly.

He was sitting exactly as she had left him when she returned with the tea, and, although her stomach muscles clenched at the sight of his big, relaxed body and dark, sardonic, handsome face, she betrayed none of her inner agitation as she carefully set the tray down on the floor— the flat being devoid of niceties such as coffee-tables and the like. 'How do you like your tea?' she asked quietly, without raising her eyes to his face.

'Black.'

She might have guessed. Like his soul. She poured the tea into a mug and handed it across, taking care not to come into contact with his flesh. 'There aren't any cups and saucers,' she said briefly.

'No matter. This is most acceptable.' He leant back in the seat after reaching for the mug, and after she had poured her own tea she was forced to lift her gaze to his, her face expressionless. 'May I call you Sandi?' he asked softly.

'What?' The hard-won composure fled.

'Your name—may I call you by your name?' he asked again. 'It is a little ridiculous, this Miss Gosdon and Mr Challier, do you not think? And we have much to discuss.'

'I don't think we have anything to—'

'Please.' He raised an authoritative hand and she was furious at her instant obedience to the command. 'Let us deal with the immediate problems one by one, Sandi.' His accent gave her name a life all of its own. 'Ann has her tea?' She nodded silently. 'Then let us talk.

'The first thing I have to say is that my mother is devastated by the turn of events.' She noticed that he didn't mention his father, and wondered why for a fleeting second before he went on. 'I understand Emile's sup-

port from my parents was terminated on his marriage?'
She nodded again, her eyes tight on his dark face. 'This,
I knew nothing about.'

'You didn't?' She shook her head slowly. 'I'm sorry,
but I find that very hard to believe. Why wouldn't your
parents tell you what they had done?'

'Because they knew I would have paid the cost of
Emile's education myself,' he said quietly. 'Sandi...' He
shifted in his chair, as though he was finding the conversation difficult. 'There are matters—personal matters—which I find it painful to discuss. Suffice it to say,
my parents bitterly regret their action in view of the
present circumstances. The knowledge that they will
have to live with the consequence of what they have
done is punishment enough, surely?'

She shrugged without speaking. There was nothing
she could say, after all.

'My brother André and I were told of Emile's relationship with your sister when it first began fifteen
months ago, and at that time I warned him to go carefully.'

'I'm sure you did.' Her voice was bitter and tight, and
he shook his dark head at the pain and contempt in her
face.

'Not for the reason you imagine,' he said quietly.

'No?' She eyed him hotly. 'What was the reason,
then?'

'I am not at liberty to say.'

'Oh, really!' She turned away with a gesture of contempt. 'This is ridiculous. I don't believe—'

'The reason was a good one—or it seemed so at the
time,' he said levelly. 'When matters advanced and
Emile told the family that he intended to marry your
sister it was not well received, as you know. My brother
André and I were of the opinion that once it was *fait
accompli* the natural order of things would take their
course. Time is a great healer—'

'Of what?' she asked tightly. 'The fact that Emile had married so far beneath him in your parents' eyes? Or was it that Ann is not French? I understand André's wife is the daughter of a count. I suppose she was welcomed with open arms!'

'We are not discussing Odile—'

'We're not *discussing* anything at all,' she said angrily. 'You're talking *at* me without telling me anything substantial. Look, I really think it would be better if you left—'

'I have no intention of leaving, Sandi.' The dark eyes were chips of black glass as they stared into hers. 'And you will listen to everything I have to say. There are certain confidences that are not mine to divulge, but once Ann meets my family—'

'*If* Ann meets your family,' she corrected tightly. 'The decision is hers, after all.'

'Quite.' The black eyes bored into hers. 'Hers and hers alone. I am glad you mentioned that.' His meaning was unmistakable, and she flushed hotly before meeting the challenge.

'You're quite right,' she said as coolly as she could, considering that the urge to rise and empty her tea over his immaculate head was fierce. 'If it was left to me Ann would never meet any of you, but she is a grown woman in her own right and, although I shall make my opinion clear, the final decision will be hers. She loved Emile very much and your parents hurt him badly. Whether that will colour her judgement I don't know.'

'He also loved them very much, you know,' Jacques said softly. 'As they did him. I am thirty-six years of age and André is thirty-four. Emile was the baby of the family, the late arrival, and my mother doted on him.'

'She had a funny way of showing it.' She couldn't have stopped herself speaking if her life had depended on it, but strangely he didn't react as she had expected—with anger and blazing indignation. Instead the black eyes narrowed still further on her flushed face and he rose slowly, moving across the room to stand in front of her. She, too, rose—she was at a distinct disadvantage seated as she was in the old rocking-chair—and raised her chin as she stared back into the handsome, cold face watching her so closely.

'All this righteous scorn and resentment...' he muttered softly as his eyes stroked over her hot face, their darkness unfathomable. 'You give the appearance of being hard and worldly—one would even think that you have worked at this image.' She said nothing, fear at his intuitiveness rendering her dumb. 'But your eyes tell another story,' he continued quietly. 'A quite different one. Why this hard shell, Sandi Gosdon? What has happened in your twenty-eight years to make you so hostile, so ready to see the dark side?'

'I am seeing what's under my nose,' she retorted stiffly, 'and I don't like being soft-soaped. If, in your opinion, that makes me hard and worldly, then so be it.'

'I didn't say I thought you were hard and worldly,' he corrected softly. 'I said that I believe this is the image you like to project. I am wrong in this supposition?'

'Quite wrong.' She glared at him angrily and forced her eyes not to flicker at the lie. And it wasn't a lie, not really. After what she'd been through, after Ian, she preferred to keep the world in general and men in particular at arm's length. There was nothing wrong in that, was there?

He smiled slowly, as though she had confirmed his opinion rather than denied it. 'I will return this evening, and then I would like to speak to Ann directly—if I may?' he said quietly.

'Ann will see things as I do.' Sandi's heart gave a little jump as she spoke. Since she had been able to toddle her sister had been the easiest person in the world to manipulate—her sensitive gentle nature shying away from any kind of confrontation or disagreement. She

would be putty in this man's hands, even without him
having a head start in looking so startlingly like Emile.

'We will see.' The deep brown, almost black eyes
were suddenly ruthless. 'But I *will* put my case to your
sister, Sandi, with or without your blessing. In this I shall
be most determined; you understand me?'

'Perfectly,' she ground out through clenched teeth.

'Good.' He smiled again as he held out his hand in
farewell, but for the life of her she couldn't voluntarily
respond to the goodwill gesture.

She didn't want to touch him. Her mind raced at the
thought. And yet he was handsome—probably overwhelmingly so to some females—but not to her. Oh, no,
not to her. She had had her fingers burnt too badly by
men who thought they only had to smile and the world
rocked on its axis.

'I don't bite, Miss Sandi Gosdon.' The dark voice was
mocking and amused, and it was the thread of laughter
in the deep tones that brought her hand out to meet his.

'I'm sure you don't, Mr Challier,' she said coldly.

'Till this evening, then.' His flesh was warm and firm
as it enfolded hers, and as he raised her small hand to
his lips for a fleeting moment an electric shock shot up
her arm, causing her to snatch her hand away as though
he had burnt her. For a split second she saw surprise in
the dark face, and then it closed against her, his eyes
hooded and remote.

'I shall return at seven,' he said coolly. 'Please do not
think of advising your sister not to be here. It would be
most unwise.'

'Really?' So he was a mind-reader as well?

'Really.' He walked towards the door, turning in the
doorway to survey her through narrowed eyes. 'It is only
fair to warn you that I am a stubborn man—stubborn
and determined. And I always get exactly what I want.'

'But do you always get what you deserve, Mr

Challier?' she asked with honeyed sweetness, looking straight into the autocratic face.

For a moment she thought she had gone too far as he stared back at her, a small flame glowing in the depths of the black eyes, but then the cold, beautifully shaped mouth twisted in an amused smile and he shrugged slowly. 'Now, of that I am not sure,' he murmured softly as his gaze wandered over her hair and face. 'Perhaps I will be able to give you an answer to that one day—who knows?' He smiled again, his dark maleness intimidating and virile in the small room, and as her breath caught in her throat she realised that the palms of her hands were damp. With what? Fright? Sexual attraction? Panic?

But she wouldn't let herself feel any of those emotions for a man like him, she thought angrily. What use was the past, in all its painfulness, if she hadn't learnt well from it? 'I doubt it,' she said, and stared back at him, unaware of how young she looked in the middle of the small room, a ray of sunlight from the narrow window behind her turning her hair to glowing gold and her eyes to a deep, stormy blue. 'I would think our paths won't cross again after today.'

'Perhaps.' He shrugged again and turned to leave. 'And perhaps not. Life has a way of surprising us when we least expect it. Till seven...'

As she heard the front door of the flat close she stood perfectly still, her hands clenched tight against her sides and her heart pounding furiously. Oh, she knew all about surprises, she thought bitterly. He'd be amazed at how much she knew. She shut her eyes to banish the images of the past that were suddenly stark and savage on the screen of her mind, and when Ann called, her voice nervous and faint from the bedroom, it was a relief to come back to the present and hurry to her sister's side.

CHAPTER TWO

WHEN Jacques Challier returned at seven all Sandi's worst fears were realised. He was charm itself as he talked to Ann, his voice persuasive and soft as he explained how distraught and stunned his parents—his mother in particular—were at their youngest son's untimely death.

Their remorse at the way things had turned out, their sorrow for his young widow and their bitter-sweet joy on hearing of their future grandchild from Jacques that afternoon—all was relayed with great sensitivity and appeal, and, in Sandi's eyes at least, utter ruthlessness to further his own ends. He worked on Ann like a master musician with his instrument until he had her eating out of his hand, her large blue eyes dark with sympathy and distress and her mouth soft with compassion.

'Emile would have wanted you to be with his family at this time,' Jacques said quietly, 'even though you perhaps feel you can't forgive us for the way we have behaved. I can understand that you blame us for his death—'

'No, not really.' Ann twisted uncomfortably. 'Maybe at first, but not now. It was an accident, I know that—but he had got so tired, you see, working for his finals all day and with the job at night. But we needed the money. Even with what Sandi sent us—'

'You sent them money?' Jacques asked sharply, turning to Sandi, who was standing to one side of the sofa, looking down at him with bitter eyes as she watched the little scene in front of her.

'Of course.' She glared at him without explain-ing further.

'Even with what Sandi sent us we couldn't manage,' Ann continued quietly. 'Not once I'd left the university and my grant had stopped.'

'Ann's pregnancy was difficult from the outset,' Sandi said flatly. 'There was no way she could continue to work for her degree, although she and Emile had planned that she would return to her studies later—once the baby was born and he had finished university and had a job.'

'I see.' Jacques turned to Ann again, taking one of her hands in his. 'The rest of the family did not know that Emile's support had stopped, Ann; please believe that. And when I spoke to my mother this afternoon she asked me to tell you the reason why they took this step— this foolish step that they now regret so much. It is a matter of great delicacy, and I would be grateful if you would not speak of it to anyone.'

'I'll get some coffee—'

'No, please, Sandi.' He quickly stopped her move to leave the room. 'It is necessary that you understand this, for the future—yes?'

No, she thought tightly, but nevertheless she found herself sitting gingerly on the rocking-chair, facing them both as he talked.

'When Emile informed my parents that you were go-ing to get married they were upset—my mother partic-ularly so,' Jacques said slowly. 'She thought if his grant was threatened he would see what she considered to be reason and put off the wedding until he had finished university. In that way she was hoping this relationship between you would perhaps fail the test of time and come to nothing.

'She was concerned about the result a marriage might have on his studies, also that the two of you were so young, but there was another, more important reason that overshadowed all that.' He paused, rising from the sofa where he had been sitting next to Ann and moving to stand with his back towards them as he looked out of the window into the grimy London street below.

'Two years ago my father was foolish enough to have an *amour* with a young English girl who had recently come to work for us,' he said expressionlessly. 'And even more foolishly he was indiscreet enough for my mother to suspect what was happening. She confronted my father, who admitted the affair and immediately agreed to end the liaison.

'But the damage, as far as my mother was concerned, was done. She suffered a nervous breakdown from which even now she is not fully recovered.

'As my father's business partner, I was told the full facts, but no one else in the family—including André and Emile—had any idea what had caused my mother's illness. This, both my mother and father wanted. When Emile fell in love with you so soon after all this had happened she just couldn't—how do you say?—handle it.' Jacques turned to face both women now, but his face could have been carved in stone, so devoid was it of any visible emotion.

'Her behaviour at this time was not rational or wise, but she was still suffering greatly and my father was consumed by guilt—he still is, I think. This girl had flattered and cajoled him, persuaded him into the alli-ance, but it was a thing of the flesh, not the heart. She was sent packing with a cheque which amply soothed her ruffled feathers.' Now a flash of searing bitterness lit the black eyes for a brief moment. 'And my mother has tried to pick up the pieces of a life which has been smashed apart. She wants you to know this not so that you will excuse her actions, but perhaps understand them.' He was standing very straight and stiff, his face set and proud.

'I—' Sandi saw Ann take a gulp and swallow before

she tried to speak again. 'I'm so sorry, Jacques; she must have been very hurt.'

He nodded grimly. 'She was.' The black eyes narrowed on Ann's pale face. 'But nothing could compare to the loss of her child. My father and I have not told her the full facts of the accident. She thinks merely that Emile was killed whilst riding in a car. If she knew the accident was a direct result of the job he had taken to make ends meet—'

'I won't tell her,' Ann responded quickly. 'There is no point, after all, and Emile wouldn't have wanted it.'

'Thank you.' Jacques nodded quietly, his eyes flashing to Sandi's face as she watched them.

She had been as shocked as Ann at the revelation, but her mistrust of the Challier family as a whole, and Jacques Challier in particular, was unaffected by his explanation—although she couldn't have explained why. She couldn't help feeling that, genuine though his account of the circumstances obviously was, he was using it to persuade Ann to do exactly what he wanted. And his next words confirmed her fears.

'And now I must ask you an even greater service. My mother would very much like to meet you, to speak to you herself. Would you accompany me to France for this purpose?'

'I—' Ann's eyes shot to Sandi. 'I don't think so. I haven't been feeling too well, and there's the baby—'

'All the more reason to be in the comfort and safety of my parents' home,' Jacques returned smoothly. 'Their doctor is excellent and the nearest hospital is just a few miles away—you would receive exemplary care, should it prove necessary. Here the facilities are a little…basic?' His face was expressionless but his meaning clear. 'And I understand Sandi has a demanding job in the States. I'm sure she would rest better at nights knowing you were well taken care of.'

'I told you, I'm going to look after Ann,' Sandi said

tightly, deciding she had had more than enough of this subtle manoeuvring. 'There is no question that she would be alone.'

'But your work?' Jacques enquired with suspect concern, his eyes gleaming as they took in her angry face. 'Surely this could prove difficult? If you stay in England with Ann this must put your job in jeopardy, and if she returns with you to America she will have long periods of being left alone.'

'A certain amount of my work is done from home—'

'But not all of it.' He stared at her, his face impassive as he tied her up in knots. 'You would not be able to relax when you were not with her, whereas in France there would be my mother and the servants—'

'Don't tell me what I would or wouldn't be able to do,' Sandi shot back immediately. 'If it's necessary I can resign.'

'Oh, no, Sandi!' Even as her sister spoke Sandi realised she had played right into Jacques's very capable hands. The worst thing she could have done was suggest that there might be a possibility of her leaving her job. Ann knew how she had worked for her success, how thrilled she had been with her new appointment, and her sister's soft heart wouldn't be able to bear the thought of it all being lost—especially as she was aware of the therapy it had provided after Ian... 'Please, I don't want you to worry about me any more—and besides, I'd like to meet Emile's parents. Really.'

'Ann—'

'I mean it, Sandi.' Ann cut into her protest with unusual firmness. 'It's got to happen sooner or later, and perhaps it's best to meet them now. You know I'm not very good at facing things, but with the baby...' She shook her head slowly. 'It's only natural they would want to see it when it's born, and I'd prefer to meet them first. I'll just come for a few days, Jacques.' She turned to the tall, dark man who had remained silent through the little exchange. 'If that's all right?'

'Of course.' He bowed his head in a little gesture that was very French. 'You must stay as long as you wish.'

Once Ann was out there she would be kept there—at least until the baby was born, Sandi thought darkly. Couldn't her sister see what was happening? She looked into Ann's pale, lovely face thoughtfully. Or maybe it was easier for her not to. Ann had always been so very good at hiding her head in the sand.

'That is settled, then.' Jacques's eyes mocked her as he looked down at her sitting so stiff with rage in the rocking-chair. 'If it fits in with your plans, perhaps you would like to accompany Ann to France? I'm sure she would find that most…reassuring.'

'Sandi? Could you?' Ann's voice was eager.

'Of course.' She smiled at her sister but her eyes changed to splintered blue when they met Jacques's. 'I've taken some leave to sort things out here.'

'Excellent.' The cold voice held a thread of amusement that made her want to kick him—hard. 'Then perhaps if I could suggest I pick you up tomorrow afternoon, say, two o'clock? That should give you time to make all the necessary domestic arrangements and organise passports and so on. I do not think it wise that Ann flies at this time, you agree?'

She nodded silently, having been about to make that point herself.

'My parents' château is only a few hours' drive from the Channel, so this will not prove a problem. I will arrange to have one of the cars waiting for us.'

Sandi continued to stare at him, her thoughts whirling. She was experiencing the most awful sense of *déjà vu*. This could have been Ian talking. Ian, with his forceful, cool air of authority that she had thought so attractive at the time and which had hidden such treachery. Ian…his big body lean and virile, confident of his power to subject and subdue, to command without question. And she had fallen for it. Utterly. And how she had paid for her naïvety…

'Sandi?' She came back to the present with a violent sense of having been on a nightmarish journey as Ann touched her arm tentatively. 'Are you all right?'

'I'm fine.' She forced a quick smile and turned away from the intent pair of dark eyes across the room. 'I'll get that coffee now.'

When, a few moments later, she heard the door to the tiny lounge open and close she looked up from the coffee-cups expecting to see Ann in the doorway, her mouth already open to order her back to her chair. 'Can I help at all?' Jacques's undeniably attractive smile did not reach the glittering blackness of his eyes.

'No.' She qualified the blunt refusal with a quick shake of her head. 'No, thank you. I can manage, Mr Challier.'

'Of this I have no doubt.' She glanced across at him once, her eyes distant, before resuming the preparation of the tray. 'You do not think it appropriate that we drop this formality in view of developments?' he asked quietly after a long moment of silence.

'Developments?' she asked coldly, raising her head to meet his dark gaze. 'If you mean by that the fact that my sister and I shall be guests in your home, I hardly see—'

'Not my home, Sandi.' The deep voice was infuriatingly smooth. 'My parents' home. I have my own establishment some distance away. But, of course, if you would prefer to stay with me…?' Her face spoke volumes and he chuckled huskily, shaking his head as he leant lazily against the doorpost. 'What a bad-tempered little pussy-cat you are…' he drawled thoughtfully. 'All claws and teeth.'

'Not at all.' She drew herself up to her full height and

spoke through clenched teeth. 'Just because I don't happen to approve of your blackmailing technique—'

'Blackmail? This is not a nice word,' he reproved softly.

'It's not a nice act,' she returned tersely.

'And this is how you see my family's wish to help your sister?' he asked slowly. 'As something intimidating? Suspect?' There was a grimness about the handsome face now that made her hesitate for a moment, but then she shook off its menacing effect and spoke her mind.

'Considering that up to a few hours ago the Challier name was synonymous with rejection and pain, how do you expect me to feel?' she asked tensely. 'Ann is six months pregnant, and in all that time not one of your family has even sent a postcard!'

'But Ann is prepared to be reasonable—'

'Ann is too trusting,' she said flatly.

'And you—you are not,' he stated quietly, moving to stand in front of her and holding her eyes with his own in a vice-like grip she was powerless to break. His bronzed skin, the smooth blackness of his hair, the big, lean body that was intimidatingly male—it all served to hold her mesmerised under the dark, glittering gaze as he leant towards her. 'What was his name, Sandi—this man who has put the fear and mistrust in those beautiful blue eyes? Do you still love him?'

'I don't know what you're talking about.' She had wanted her voice to be acidic, but it was merely shaky.

'No?' He lifted her chin with the tip of one finger and she felt the contact right down to her toes. 'From the first moment we met you have been fighting me—and do not tell me it is because of Ann, because then I would have to call you a liar.' His face was close now, too close, the firm, sensual mouth an inch or two from hers. 'Is it because you sense I want to do this?'

She was totally unprepared for the feel of his lips on

hers, standing stunned for one breathtaking moment as his mouth took hers and then jerking away so violently that she felt her neck muscles snap.

'How dare you?' She backed another step before bringing her hand to her mouth in a harsh scrubbing action. 'How *dare* you?'

'I dared because I wanted to, very much,' he said softly.

'And that makes it all right?' she asked scathingly as pure rage flowed through her veins. 'You see, you like, you take—is that it? The original macho man? Well, I'm immune to all such rubbish—so you can just forget that old line and you can keep your hands off me too. You ever try a number like that again—'

'Zut!' The oath was soft but intense. 'It was merely a kiss.'

'I know what it was,' she answered tightly, 'and I'm not interested, OK? Is that plain enough?'

He growled something under his breath and she was heartily glad that she knew no French. 'I was not asking you to come into my bed,' he said darkly, 'or even into my life. The kiss was an acknowledgement of your beauty, of the age-old attraction between male and female—'

'Oh, spare me…' She glared at him furiously. 'How many other poor sops have you tried this one on? I really can't believe—'

'Miss Gosdon, if you say one more word I really think I will not be responsible for my actions.' She could see that he was fighting for control under that icy exterior and it gave her enormous satisfaction. Just to have rocked that amazingly arrogant stance a little, to have punctured that thick male skin and imperious self-esteem, was wonderfully gratifying. For a moment it was Ian's face there in front of her, his hard, lean body that was held so stiffly to attention. And then the image faded, and with it her rage as she heard Ann call from the lounge.

'Sandi?'

'I don't want anything else to upset Ann,' she said quickly as she heard the lounge door open. 'She's been through more than enough—'

'What on earth are you doing out here?' Ann's voice held more than a touch of apprehension although her face was smiling as she appeared in the open doorway, her eyes darting from Jacques's face to Sandi's.

'I—' Sandi found that her mind was a complete blank.

'Your sister was telling me about her work,' Jacques said easily at her side, his voice cool and lazy and his manner relaxed. 'You must be very proud of her.'

'Oh, I am.' Ann smiled back at him, completely reassured. 'Sandi left university to get a job when Mum and Dad died so we could stay together. She's worked her way up from the bottom rung of the ladder, and she deserves everything she gets.'

'Really...?' Jacques's voice was very dry.

'Did she tell you how...?'

Sandi let Ann lead him back into the lounge, and once she was alone leant back against the painted wood cupboards in the very basic kitchen. The nerve of the man, kissing her like that! Who on earth did he think he was— God's gift to womankind?

The glug of the coffee-maker reminded her of the task in hand, and she quickly finished setting the tray and poured three cups of coffee once the machine was ready. Well, here was one woman who wasn't going to melt into a little pool at his feet—although that was obviously what the little charade had been all about. Were there still women about in the world who fell for old lines like that?

It was much later, as she lay wide awake at Ann's side watching the bedside clock tick the minutes and hours away, that she gave in to the searing memories from the past that had been at the forefront of her mind since she had first set eyes on Jacques Challier. Of course there were still women who were taken in by a handsome face and a soft, tender voice—she of all people should know that.

Once the floodgate in her mind was open there was no stopping the tide...

She had been almost twenty-five years of age when she had met Ian Mortimer, and as innocent as a babe. They had met through a friend of a friend at one of the numerous advertising parties that were commonplace in London, and from the first moment his smoky grey eyes had smiled into hers she had been lost. His charm had been considerable, his technique polished to perfection, and she had never doubted one thing he had told her about himself—even though, with hindsight, there had been plenty of question marks.

Ann hadn't liked him. Sandi shut her eyes for a moment in the darkness. Funny, that, when you considered that Ann usually liked everyone. But she hadn't liked Ian Mortimer, and how right she had been.

They had been together for four months when he'd asked her to marry him, and that had been accomplished, via the registry office, within weeks. Their joint bank account had been a declaration of their love and trust, Ian had assured her, despite the fact that all the money in it had come from the account she'd had from her half-share of her parents' estate, Ann's portion being held in trust until her sister reached the age of twenty-one.

Sandi twisted restlessly and then froze as the movement disturbed Ann's steady, regular breathing at her side. Although her sister had cried herself to sleep in the same way she had done each night since Sandi had arrived back in England, she had slipped into a deep slumber within minutes—which was a definite improvement on all the previous nights and one that Sandi wanted to continue.

That awful morning… Her thoughts drifted back to the sunny May morning, almost exactly three years ago, when she had run to answer the ring of the bell at the front door of the small flat she and Ian had been renting. Ann had already left for college and she had been late for work, but the thought that it might be Ian, due back that day from the business trip that had taken him away for two weeks, had put wings on her feet. He'd forgotten his key again, she'd thought happily as she'd swung open the door. He had a head like a sieve…

But it hadn't been Ian. The tall, attractive woman who had faced her had had short dark hair and gentle brown eyes, and the eyes had continued to be gentle as she had begun to talk. It was strange that her world had been devastated by someone with such gentle eyes…

'Mrs Mortimer?' The woman held out her hand. 'How do you do? My name is Carol Prescott. I don't suppose Ian's told you about me?'

'Ian…?' Sandi shook her head slowly. 'No, I'm sorry. You know my husband?'

'Unfortunately.' Sandi was nonplussed by the grimness in the soft voice. 'Yes, unfortunately I do. Look, we really need to talk. Can I come in a minute?'

'Well, I'm already late for work—'

'This won't wait, Mrs Mortimer.' The woman smiled regretfully. 'And please believe me, I am really very, very sorry.'

And so the nightmare began. It appeared that her husband, wonderful, dashing Ian, with his liquid grey eyes and dark, romantic good looks, was a confidence trickster of the first order. Carol Prescott had brought a sheaf of papers with her—a history of his activities over the past few years that she had made it her business to investigate.

It made sickening reading. Ian preyed on young, and

in some cases not so young women who had a certain
amount of money—the amounts ranging from a few
thousand to much higher figures in one or two cases—
making them believe he loved them and then departing
with his ill-gotten gains once he had milked each one
dry. His explanations were various—business problems,
an ill mother, a temporary hold-up in funds—but the end
result was always the same. A broken-hearted woman
with no Ian and no money.

'But I don't understand…' Sandi's heart was thudding
like a drum as she faced Carol Prescott in the sun-filled
lounge. 'Why haven't the police got involved if all you
say is true?'

'It's true,' Carol replied quietly, 'and the police *are*
involved—at least in two cases where Ian forged sig-
natures. As for the others…' She shrugged bitterly. 'If
silly women want to make gifts of money or jewellery
to their current boyfriend that's between the two of them,
according to officialdom. The police are busy—they haven't got time to chase all over England searching for
one man, besides which he uses a wide variety of names
which makes everything more difficult.'

'But why—?' Sandi stopped abruptly as the full realisation of what was happening to her began to make
itself felt and the room swam and dipped. 'I mean—'

'Why am I on this crusade?' Carol asked flatly. 'Because someone had to do it—someone had to try and
stop him. I met him five years ago, just after my mother
had died and left me the house and a tidy amount in the
bank. Ian wormed all the money out of me, and when I
began to suspect that something wasn't right he disappeared one night with all my mother's jewellery—even
her wedding ring. That's what I really can't forgive him
for.'

Her eyes were deep wells of pain as she stared at
Sandi. 'A solicitor friend with a million and one contacts
helped me begin to search for him, and then we discov-

ered a veritable can of worms. He's in his thirties now, and he's been at this game since he was fresh out of school.'

'But—' Sandi took a deep breath and then forced herself to speak although her throat was dry and her chest tight. 'But we're married. Or is that a lie too? Is he already married to someone else?'

'No, you're legally married,' Carol said quietly. 'Although frankly, if I were you, I'd prefer that to be false too. As far as I know he's never actually married anyone before—I don't think he's had to, to be honest. Most women fall for him so badly they can't wait to shower him with gifts. Have you given him much?' she asked gently.

'No.' Sandi shook her head slowly. 'I haven't given him anything.' But he *had* wanted her to live with him, wanted her to be his lover. It had been she who had held out for marriage, she thought blindly, wanting to give herself to him for the first time on her wedding night, wanting him to be the first and only. Oh... She shut her eyes tight. Let this be a mistake, she prayed. A terrible, ghastly mistake. He couldn't have done all this; he couldn't.

'Joint account?'

Sandi opened her eyes wide at the quiet voice. 'What?'

'Have you a joint account?' Carol asked patiently, shaking her head at Sandi's nod. 'And where's Ian now?'

'On a business trip...' Sandi's voice trailed away.

'There is no business,' Carol said softly, 'and I think he knew I was closing in on him—which meant the police would be informed as to his whereabouts. I think you'd better get on to the bank...'

The bank manager was very kind when she saw him later that morning. He said that he had wondered why she and her husband had decided to close the account so abruptly, but Mr Mortimer had explained that they were moving abroad. He hoped everything had gone through satisfactorily.

Twenty thousand pounds. Was it worth ruining someone's life for twenty thousand pounds? she thought now helplessly. Obviously Ian had thought so. He had vanished without trace.

She couldn't bear to brood on the months that had followed. Without Ann she wouldn't have got through. But by the time she had started to pick up the pieces, six months later, life was beginning to return to something like normality. Which had made that other knock on the door so much harder, somehow.

'Mrs Mortimer? Mrs Ian Mortimer?' The policeman and policewoman had been very kind too, she remembered with painful irony. 'It's about your husband. I'm very sorry to have to tell you...'

Ian had died in a drowning accident off the coast of France while staying on his current girlfriend's yacht. Apparently Sandi's name had been found among his papers. He had had exactly five hundred pounds to his name when he had died. Most of her twenty thousand had gone on riotous living and expensive presents to his new fiancée, who was worth a mint, so it had appeared. How exactly he had planned to marry her too wasn't clear.

Perhaps he wouldn't have gone through with it—who knew? And who cared? She shook her head in the warm darkness. But that final blow had welded the lock and key onto the door of her heart for ever.

Never again would she trust a man, any man, be he rich or poor. Ian had killed the happy, trusting girl she had once been as completely as if he had driven a knife through her heart. And the new Sandi Gosdon? She was her own woman, utterly and totally, and that was the way she intended to remain. No romances, no liaisons, no involvement.

She shook her head as hot tears coursed down her face. Never again. That one savage encounter with love had taught her one thing—she couldn't trust her own heart and still less any man. Her career would be her life, and with that she would be content. Content? The word mocked her, but she thrust the weakness back into the recesses of her mind. She *would* be content. She'd have to be. It was the only course open to her now.

CHAPTER THREE

'WE WILL stop shortly for some refreshments.' Jacques glanced at Sandi briefly before his gaze moved to the mirror, in which he could see Ann stretched out on the back seat of the big car. 'You are comfortable, Ann?' he asked politely.

'I'm fine,' Ann answered drowsily.

They had been travelling for two hours through the lush French countryside on their way to the Challier château in the Loire Valley, and Ann was beginning to show the strain of the journey—although she was bearing up far better than Sandi had anticipated. The May evening was warm and still showing to full advantage the green pastures, the colourful orchards and vineyards, the old towns with their slate roofs and the spectacularly beautiful châteaux. The powerful Mercedes that had been waiting for them on the other side of the Channel ate up the miles with little effort.

It had been sensible for Ann to stretch out on the back seat with her legs raised—her ankles were swollen most days now—but Sandi had been less than comfortable when she'd realised that that meant she would be sitting in close proximity to Jacques in the front of the car. And although she hadn't said a word he had known.

She glanced at him now as he sat, big and dark, at her side. Yes, he had known. The deep brown eyes had glittered with silent amusement and there had been a ruthless twist to his mouth that had told her he was enjoying every moment of her discomfiture.

Why did he affect her so badly? She forced herself to concentrate on the natural beauty of the French countryside. She had thought no man would ever affect her again after Ian, and until Jacques no man had. Everything about him grated on her. Everything.

She bit her lower lip hard. Even when he was being solicitous over Ann the dark power of the man was evident, like a great wild beast that had temporarily sheathed its razor-sharp claws. He was arrogant and imperious and utterly sure of himself and the authority he commanded, and since that incident in Ann's kitchen Sandi had been unable to wipe the feel of his mouth on hers from her consciousness. It was driving her *crazy*. She wanted to be aloof and detached, to pretend he didn't exist, but Jacques Challier was not a man one could ignore.

Thank goodness he had his own home, separate from his parents'. She clung onto the thought like a lifebelt. Hopefully, after this one torturous journey, she wouldn't have to be in his company again.

'I was going to stop at the little tavern down there, but it looks as though Ann has fallen asleep.' His voice was soft and deep at her side, rich and attractive with its broken accent. 'You are happy to carry on with the journey, Sandi?'

'Yes, of course.' She forced a stiff smile from somewhere as she glanced his way, and then wished she hadn't as the hard profile did strange things to her nerves that both alarmed and surprised her.

The way Ian had treated her, the fact that he had taken her youth and her innocence and then used her as carelessly as an old glove, to be tossed away once he had got what he really wanted, had caused a humiliation and debasement so deep that it had taken her months to be able to look in the mirror again with any sense of self-worth. She didn't want to feel anything for any man ever again, and even this…awareness of Emile's brother was frightening.

'It is still some way to the château; couldn't you try

to relax a little?' His voice was cool and quiet. 'Even a Frenchman would not try to take a woman against her will in a car travelling at seventy miles an hour when he is the driver.' He glanced at her briefly, and although she didn't turn her head to look at him the black eyes burnt her flesh.

'Don't be ridiculous—'

He cut off her soft but furious voice with a raised hand. 'We do not seem to have—how you say?—hit it off—yes?' he said quietly. 'This is unfortunate, but I am sure we can both live with it. However, the present situation between my mother and Ann is a delicate one and I do not want further complications. My mother has suffered enough—'

'And what about Ann?' She was too enraged now to feel any emotion other than anger. 'She's lost her husband—'

'And my mother has lost her son,' he said grimly.

'And whose fault was that?' The second the words had left her lips she was horrified at their content, but it was too late. The dark face hardened into pure granite and his tone was icy when he spoke.

'Her suffering equals her crime; of that I can assure you. If you want your pound of flesh you will have it when you see my mother's face.'

'I don't want any pound of flesh,' she said bleakly, unaware of the throb of pain in her voice. She had experienced enough suffering in the last three years to last a lifetime; she wouldn't wish such an emotion on any living soul.

He glanced at her swiftly, his eyes narrowing on the taut line of her mouth before his gaze returned to the road. 'No?' He waited a moment but she didn't speak. 'Then perhaps a compromise? We will both do our best to be civil to each other and let the grown-ups sort out their own difficulties?'

He was trying to lighten the situation and she was

grateful for it, but just for a moment she couldn't respond, fighting as she was to hold back the flood of tears that was threatening to erupt. 'Yes...' When she did speak her voice was a mere whisper.

'Then this is a deal.' His teeth flashed white in his face as he glanced her way once more, his smile dying at the look on her face as she stared ahead. 'Sandi?' He reached out a hand to touch hers for a fleeting second before returning it to the steering wheel. 'You are OK?'

'I'm fine.' Control, control... What was the matter with her anyway? She'd got her life back the way she wanted it—things had been wonderful before Emile's death. It was that—her sorrow for Ann and her deep sadness for her young husband who had had his life cut short so abruptly. It was enough to make anyone desolate.

In spite of their tentative agreement they continued for the next hour or so in a silence that was anything but comfortable, and Sandi breathed a sigh of relief once Ann woke. 'Have I been asleep?' Ann asked apologetically. 'I'm sorry; I didn't mean to.'

'No problem,' Jacques said easily. 'You are perhaps ready for some refreshment now?'

'I'd love a long, cool drink,' Ann answered gratefully.

They stopped at a small country hotel with a pretty beamed restaurant, and a flower-filled courtyard with a fountain that led directly from the dining area, sitting for a while in the dusky perfumed air with their drinks before returning to the restaurant for their meal, which was simple but delicious.

Sandi was aware of one or two interested glances in their direction. The tall, dark, handsome Frenchman and the two small, blonde and obviously English women had obviously caused a little stir among the locals. They probably thought Ann was Jacques's pregnant wife, Sandi thought with a wry twist to her mouth. And what did that make her? The gooseberry? But she was more than happy to be the gooseberry in this case, she told herself drily. More than happy.

Jacques entertained the two women with an easy courtesy and lazy humour that was dangerously attractive—or would have been if she hadn't known better, Sandi thought cynically. After the meal he escorted them back to the car with a hand on each of their waists, and, light though the contact was, Sandi was inexpressibly thankful when it ceased.

'And now we drive to the Château des Rêves, yes?' Jacques turned to smile at Ann after settling her on the back seat of the car again, and then the dark, glittering gaze moved to Sandi's face at the side of him.

'Château des Rêves?' Ann asked, a note of interest in her voice.

'The castle of dreams,' Jacques replied quietly. 'My parents' house is very beautiful, as you will see—something of a fairy tale, in fact—and dates back to the fourteenth century. I was most fortunate to be brought up in such a place.'

'Emile loved his home,' Ann said quietly from behind them. 'But after…everything that happened he found it difficult to talk about France.'

'This is understandable.' Jacques turned to give her a swift smile before starting the car and drawing carefully out of the small car park. 'I hope you will love it as much as he did.'

I just bet you do, Sandi thought silently at his side. It would make the job of persuading Ann to stay in France until the baby was born so much easier…

The night sky was like black velvet by the time they reached the Loire Valley, but the air was still warm and moist from the heat of the day, without the chill that would have been evident in England. Jacques drove the big car off the main road on which they had been travelling and onto a long drive lined on either side by massive oak trees. After a full minute Sandi saw the spires and turrets of a great house in the distance, but the darkness shrouded the image, the moon merely a thin hollow of light over the sleeping landscape.

They approached a high stone wall in which vast iron gates stood open and ready to attention as they passed through, and immediately a host of lights were triggered on each side of the drive, lighting the night as brightly as if it were day.

'The château,' Jacques said briefly, indicating the enormous sculptured building of honeyed stone in the distance that was the epitome of all the magic castles that one heard and read about in childhood rolled into one. Spires and turrets, arches and fine lace balconies all joined with breathtaking affect in the old château, its curves and arcs majestic and proud against the black sky beyond.

'It's beautiful,' Ann breathed from behind them.

'It's greedy.' Jacques smiled at her wide-eyed face in the mirror. 'It costs a fortune to maintain, but it's been in the family for generations—my father was born in one of the bedrooms on the second floor.'

He brought the car to a standstill on the vast drive and turned directly to Sandi as he cut the engine. 'What do you think?' he asked quietly as he waved towards the château. 'Do you approve?'

'One could hardly disapprove of such a lovely building,' she said carefully. 'I'm amazed you decided to leave. How long have you had your own house?'

'Eight years.' Anything else he might have been about to say was lost as the enormous carved oak doors opened and a small, slim, exquisitely dressed woman appeared in the lighted doorway, with several other people just behind her.

'My mother,' Jacques said quietly. 'André and his family live in one of the wings of the house, so I'm afraid it will be the family *en masse* tonight.' He opened his door, moving round to the other side of the car and opening both Ann's door and her own and helping them to alight.

'Maman—Ann and Sandi.' He took Ann's arm and ushered her forward slightly in front of Sandi, his hand moving protectively to her waist as he sensed her hesitation. 'Ann, this is your mother-in-law.'

'Ann…' Madame Challier's dark brown eyes fastened on Ann's face, and no one could have failed to read the muted appeal in their depths. 'Thank you for coming, my dear. I'm really so sorry—' Her voice broke and she shook her head helplessly. 'You look exhausted— I think…'

As the soft voice floundered again Sandi saw Jacques stiffen, but Ann was there in front of him, reaching out to the woman who had caused her such misery and holding her close for a long moment. 'I'm so sorry…' There was a sob in Jacques's mother's voice now. 'Can you ever forgive us for the way we have behaved?'

'Come on into the house, Maman.' As Jacques motioned to the tall, grey-haired man just behind Ann and his mother he stepped forward, his own eyes moist. 'I'm Emile's father, Ann,' he said softly. 'And I'm very pleased to meet you—but you must be quite drained from the journey. Please, Arianne, let us take our guests into the house.' He turned to Sandi. 'And this must be Sandi? It was good of you to accompany your sister at this time; you must be a great comfort to her.'

Once in the house, the splendour of which rendered both women dumb, André and his wife were introduced—the former a smaller and plumper version of his handsome brother and his wife dark and pretty. Coffee was served by a small maid in uniform in the magnificent drawing room, the walls of which were hung with beautifully restored tapestries, but André and his wife declined to stay, returning to their own apartments once the introductions were over.

'You had a pleasant journey?' It was clear that

Madame Challier was trying to act the perfect hostess, but her eyes were luminous with unshed tears as she looked at Ann and the atmosphere crackled with tension and embarrassment.

'Yes, thank you.' Ann put down her coffee-cup, clearly not knowing what to say. 'It was kind of you to ask us to stay…'

'I think it would be opportune to leave Maman and Ann alone for a few moments, Papa?' Jacques took charge of the situation again, his dark face autocratic. 'I will show Sandi a little of the house if you could organise Pierre into getting the cases from the car?'

'Of course, of course.' His father was patently glad of the opportunity to escape.

'But—' Before Sandi could object further she found herself whisked out of the room by a very firm arm at her elbow, and as Claude Challier disappeared to raise the said Pierre she turned to Jacques indignantly, her violet-blue eyes sparking.

'Ann's exhausted—she should be in bed. She needs—'

'She needs to talk with my mother.' The cool voice was inflexible. 'The first few minutes of a relationship are vitally important. You do not know this?'

'What I *know* is that you're the most overbearing man I've ever met,' she said tightly.

'This I do not consider a fault.' He leant against the wall, his eyes cool on her hot face. 'It is good for a man to know what he wants.'

'Is it, indeed?' She thought of the devastation Ian had caused in so many lives and her voice was bitter. 'You'll excuse me if I don't applaud that sentiment.'

'You know, Sandi Gosdon, for such a sophisticated woman of the world you have the most filthy temper,' he drawled lazily. 'You prefer your men to be little lap-dogs, is that it?'

'I don't "prefer" anything,' she answered hotly. 'In fact—'

'In fact, it is not only Ann that is tired.' He uncoiled himself from the wall so swiftly that she was being ushered down the wide panelled hallway before she had time to think. 'You have been very brave for your sister, very protective of her rights, but now it is time for her to make up her own mind about this unfortunate state of affairs and you must let her.'

They had reached another set of ornate winding stairs, a replica of the ones which had faced her as she'd entered the house, but as he took her arm to lead her upwards she jerked away, her head turning backwards.

'I'll wait for Ann.'

'I think not.' The determined jawline hardened. 'My mother will not keep her long and then she will join you in the suite that has been prepared for your arrival and to which I am taking you now. She is your sister, Sandi, not your child, and very shortly she will have a child of her own to care for. It is time to cut the cord. You have your own life to lead.'

As she opened her mouth to fire back a hot reply he took all the breath from her body by whisking her into his arms and beginning to carry her up the stairs. 'I know, I know,' he said. 'I am this overbearing Frenchman that you cannot abide. This is sad, very sad, when I am sure we could have had fun together.'

'*Put me down!*' She didn't dare struggle in case they both toppled backwards. 'Now!'

'In a moment.' His voice was quite expressionless.

The sensation of being in his arms was fast taking all lucid thought from her head, his hard, lean body firm against her curves and the delicious smell that emanated from the dark, bronzed skin causing her head to whirl. She couldn't believe her body was reacting like this to a man she both despised and disliked. Even with Ian, at the height of her infatuation, she hadn't been in danger of losing control like this, and the knowledge was frightening.

'I said now,' she hissed angrily, risking one small struggle and then stiffening immediately as she glanced over his shoulder at the drop beneath them.

'And I said in a moment.' She turned her head to argue but it was a mistake. He had been waiting for the moment and capitalised on it immediately, his mouth hard and electric as it captured hers and his arms like bands of steel as they held her close. And then, almost immediately, his mouth was coaxing and warm against her lips, parting them as he penetrated the inner sweetness of her mouth and produced an exquisite torture that turned her fluid against him.

Her months with Ian told her that this was a man of vast experience, a connoisseur in the art of lovemaking, but even that knowledge was no defence against the wild response of her body. She wasn't aware that she had shut her eyes; she wasn't aware of anything except the feel of his body against hers and the drowning pleasure his lips were inducing. As he set her down at the top of the stairs against the wall some sanity returned, but then he leaned over her, both hands on the wall either side of her, as though he sensed her intention to escape, and his head came down again, his mouth searching.

'No…' She pushed against him but his answer was to move his long, hard body against hers, stopping all movement and creating sensations in her frame that made her legs tremble and her thighs hot. She knew she was returning the kiss, she also knew it was madness—but the force of her sudden desire, the demands of her body were too fierce to ignore.

His hands moved down her body in a light but passionate caress that made her flesh tingle under its layer of clothes and long for more direct contact, and her breasts swelled and ripened against his hard frame as her breath caught in tiny pants against his face.

'*Ma chérie…*' His groan of desire was soft and warm against her mouth, but somehow the fact that he hadn't said her name, that she had been regulated to the anonymity of '*ma chérie*', turned her to ice.

What was she doing? *What was she doing?*

The sudden twist she made to escape his arms took him totally by surprise, and in a second she was free. She knew what sort of a man he was. Emile had said that women couldn't keep their hands off him, so what was she doing playing with fire like this? Hadn't she learnt the hard way that men could go from woman to woman without it meaning a thing? And he had said himself that he thought they could have had 'fun' together—a brief affair, no doubt, where he would use her body until he tired of it and then move on to the next woman with no second thoughts, no regrets.

Like Ian. Just like Ian. Oh, she was such a fool, such a fool…

'Sandi?' As he went to reach for her she jerked back so violently that she hit the opposite wall.

'Don't touch me. Don't you dare touch me,' she ground out furiously. 'And keep your hands to yourself in future. I'm sure you think you're totally irresistible, but this is one female who is unimpressed by your undoubted talents.' Let him believe it, she prayed desperately as she spoke. Please don't let him guess how he's made me feel. Please…

'What the hell is this—?'

She waved her hand frantically as he made to move towards her again. 'I know your type, Jacques Challier— a woman for every occasion, is that right? I'm sure you can't even recall their names. Well, here's one that doesn't want to play.'

'Ah, I see.' He stared down at her, his eyes glittering with rage. '*Dans la nuit, tous les chats sont gris?* This is the way you suppose I think? The sort of man you assume I am?'

'What?' She had no idea what the French words, spoken with such biting contempt, meant.

'At night, all cats are grey,' he translated softly. 'You think I am a womaniser, a philanderer—the sort of man who is without morals, sensitivity?'

'Well, aren't you?' She was glad of the wall behind her; it was the only thing that was keeping her upright.

'Do not worry, Sandi.' He straightened suddenly and it was as though a veil had been drawn down over his face, masking all emotion. 'I have no intention of repeating what proved to be an interesting but all too easy experiment. I am male enough to appreciate something of a challenge in my love-life—you understand?'

The cruelty momentarily robbed her of speech, and then he was striding down the corridor in front of her, his words thrown over his shoulder through grim lips. 'This is the door to the suite which you and Ann will be sharing while you stay with my parents,' he said icily as he opened a door set in the long wall which was hung with ornate, expensive paintings and fine prints. 'It is quite self-contained and I trust you will find it comfortable.'

It took her a few seconds to find enough strength to follow him, but then she walked stiffly, her head up and her back straight. 'Thank you.' She walked past him into the luxuriously furnished room beyond. 'I'm sure it will be adequate.'

Adequate? The beautiful surroundings mocked such a meagre word with their magnificence, but she only had time to take in an enormous sitting room in blue and gold before she turned to face him again as he spoke.

'One of the maids, Charlette or Claire, will bring a cold supper once Ann has finished speaking with my mother. Breakfast is normally at eight here, but if you prefer to have it in bed just tell the maid when she brings the supper.'

'Thank you.' Go, go. For heaven's sake just go, will

you? she screamed at him silently as she stared into the handsome face that was as cold as ice, his eyes glacial. She had made a terrible fool of herself; she hadn't needed him to spell it out in words. The way she had responded to him... She almost shook her head as the humiliation flowed through her, hot and fierce, but controlled the gesture just in time, although she knew her cheeks were burning. 'Goodnight.'

Once alone she put her hands to her hot cheeks and shut her eyes tightly, forcing back the stinging tears by sheer will-power. How could she have behaved like that? She didn't even like the man. He was arrogant, domineering and far too handsome for his own good, and if his ego was jumbo-size she had certainly done nothing to deflate it, had she, falling into his arms like an overripe peach?

She groaned out loud and forced her trembling legs to move as she got a tissue and blew her nose defiantly. Well, she wasn't going to crumble over this or any other stunt that Jacques Challier might pull. She'd come through far worse in the last three years and there was no way she was going to let him get under her skin— besides which she probably wouldn't have to see him again until she left France, if then.

She glanced round the elegant room slowly. She had a distinctly uneasy feeling that she would be leaving France alone, and if that was the case she would hire a taxi to the airport and fly back to England.

When Ann arrived at the suite a few minutes later it was clear that she had been crying but also clear that she was happier than Sandi had seen her since Emile's death.

'Your talk went well?' Sandi asked quietly as she left the unpacking in the big twin bedroom and walked through to the sitting room, where Ann had collapsed in one of the big easy chairs that were dotted about the room.

'Oh, Sandi…' Ann shook her head slowly. 'What that poor woman has gone through—and she's so full of remorse now about Emile's accident. She feels totally responsible, even not knowing the full circumstances.'

'So you're going to stay here until the baby's born,' Sandi stated flatly.

'I don't know… She wants me to.' Ann rose as easily as her bulk would allow and walked across to Sandi. 'Would you mind if I did? I think it's what Emile would have wanted.'

'Ann—' Sandi took her sister's hands in her own and looked full into the lovely face she knew so well. 'This is *your* life, *your* baby—you've got to do what you think best. It doesn't matter about me or anyone else; how do *you* feel?'

'I want to stay,' Ann said softly.

'Then stay.' Sandi smiled as she let go of her sister's hands.

'With your blessing?' Ann asked hesitantly.

'Of course with my blessing, you idiot!' Sandi hugged her close for a moment before she indicated the bedroom with a wave of her hand. 'Now, go and have a shower and get into your nightie; I understand our supper's arriving in a minute. And, in case I don't get the chance to mention it again, I shall expect to be informed once junior is on the way.'

'Of course.' Ann looked shocked.

'And you'll have to do some serious thinking over the next few days,' Sandi said quietly, 'about whether you want to keep the flat in England on or not. You can't just let things drift.'

'You'll stay here for a few days more?' Ann asked quickly. 'Like we'd arranged? Emile's mother wants to get to know you—she felt awful at the way Jacques bundled you off tonight.'

'He thought it was important that you two got to know each other.' Now, why had she said that? Sandi thought crossly. As though he needed defending! If there was anyone in the world who could look after himself it was Jacques Challier!

'Thanks for being so understanding, Sandi. I don't know what I'd have done without you the last few weeks,' Ann said huskily, her eyes misty. 'You've been such a support.'

'What else are big sisters for?' Sandi purposely kept her voice bright and her manner easy. One way or another there had been far too much emotion flying about tonight, and what Ann needed now was a meal and sleep. As did she!

She grimaced to herself when Ann had left the room and she was alone. She had never felt so emotional and exhausted in her life, not since— She shut her mind to all thoughts of Ian and marched into the bedroom to continue the unpacking, finishing both Ann's and her own just as Ann emerged from the large and very luxurious bathroom and the pretty little maid, Charlette, appeared with enough food to feed a small army.

Later that night, as she lay wide awake despite an exhaustion that was making her bones ache, her mind replayed the last scene with Jacques over and over again until she felt like screaming. This was ridiculous, absolutely ridiculous.

When the clock ticked to two o'clock she climbed quietly out of her bed and, after checking to make sure that Ann was fast asleep, padded onto the small balcony that led off the full-length windows in the sitting room. The night air was cool on her hot, troubled face and she breathed in its sweetness gratefully before curling up in one of the large cushioned cane chairs and letting the peace of the night steal over her taut nerves.

She would have given the world to go downstairs to the kitchens and make herself a drink of hot milk, but, apart from the fact that she didn't have a clue where they were situated, the thought of wandering about the huge château in the dead of night when she was a temporary guest, and a definite afterthought at that, squashed the idea flat. She'd help herself to a drink of mineral water from the small fridge in the sitting room in a minute, she thought tiredly as she pulled the quilted bedcover she had brought with her more closely round her shape. Or maybe a long glass of orange… It was her last coherent thought before sleep washed over her in a thick blanket of warm oblivion.

'Sandi?' The soft feminine voice at her elbow brought her out of a deep sleep, and as she opened dazed eyes it was to stare straight into the concerned countenance of Arianne Challier. 'You are unwell?'

'I—' She glanced round helplessly, realising as she struggled to make sense of her surroundings that she must have slept the night away curled up in the chair on the balcony. 'I couldn't sleep. I came out here to sit a while…'

'Is that all?' Relief made the dark brown eyes velvet-soft at the same time as the early morning sunlight emphasised the lines running from the older woman's eyes and mouth. It was a nice face, Sandi thought light-headedly as she battled to come fully awake. Still unusually attractive, but natural, warm…

'I'm sorry.' Sandi moved to sit up straight, wincing as cramped muscles twinged in protest. 'I didn't mean to fall asleep.'

'No, it is I who should apologise,' Jacques's mother said quickly as she sat down facing her on one of the other chairs. 'Normally the maid would bring the breakfasts, but I wanted to do it today. I was worried when your bed was empty and then I saw the curtains waving in the breeze from the open windows.'

They continued to talk for some minutes, and as they did so Sandi felt the most peculiar feeling stealing over her. She found herself warming to Arianne in a way she would never have dreamed possible this time yesterday, but at the same time she was conscious that she was fighting the emotion—frightened of it, even.

She didn't want to be drawn to this family, to this gentle mother-figure or her handsome, arrogant son. She wanted to be as the last three years had taught her it was wise to be—distant, aloof, remote, keeping herself separate from all sentiment, warmth and susceptibility, drawing her self-reliance round her like impenetrable armour to repel invaders. But these people were finding chinks in that armour.

She stood up suddenly, softening the action with a smile. 'You said something about breakfast?' she asked lightly.

'Oh, my goodness, yes.' Arianne jumped up quickly, her face stricken. 'I've left the trolley just inside the door. I do hope the food won't be cold now. There are warming dishes, but—'

'I'm sure it'll be fine.' Sandi found herself reassuring the older woman as if their roles were reversed, and caught herself up abruptly. There was something very endearing about Jacques's mother; she could see why he was so protective of her. 'Shall we go and see if Ann is awake?'

In the end the three women had breakfast together on the light-filled balcony that the sun was already warming with its mellow rays, and although there was the odd uncomfortable moment and awkward silence the meal went well. They were just finishing coffee when a knock sounded at the outer door. 'That will be Claire for the dishes,' Arianne said quietly, before she raised her voice to bid the maid enter.

However it wasn't the plump, pretty maid who stepped through the curtains a moment later but Jacques, devastating in black jeans and a grey silk shirt that revealed just enough of the broad, hair-roughened chest to make Sandi choke on her last mouthful of coffee.

'Good morning, ladies.' The black eyes roved mockingly over Sandi's pink face. 'I said I'd save Claire a job,' he said easily to his mother, 'and at the same time inform you that your presence is required in the kitchen regarding the menus.'

'*Oui, oui.*' Arianne touched her son's face in a little gesture of welcome as she rose. 'You slept well?' she asked softly.

Jacques nodded before glancing across at the breakfast table. 'Is there any coffee left?' he asked smoothly.

'No.' Sandi had answered a trifle too quickly, but the thought of sitting any longer in her dishevelled state, with only the doubtful comfort of the bedcover between her and those wicked black eyes, her nightie being wafer-thin, was too painful to contemplate. He, on the other hand, was as cool as a cucumber, his hair damp and slicked back from an early morning shower, freshly shaven and looking quite...quite... Her thought process faltered and died. What was he doing here anyway? she asked herself weakly. He had his own home. He'd *said* so.

'No problem.' His sardonic smile told her that he knew exactly what she was thinking, and the urge to hit him hard, kick him—*anything* to ruffle that overwhelmingly arrogant assurance—was so fierce she could taste it.

'I think you ought to leave Ann and Sandi to get dressed.' Arianne sounded a trifle shocked and Sandi blessed her for it. 'Jacques stayed here last night,' she added unnecessarily. 'I felt he had done quite enough driving for one day and that, knowing the road between here and his own home as well as he does, there was the possibility he might be...careless.'

'Not I.' Jacques hugged his mother close for a moment and Sandi knew he had seen—as she had—the shadow that had turned the brown eyes into pools of pain. The ghost of his brother straightened the hard mouth and wiped the mocking smile from his lips in an instant.

'And now you can come and make me some coffee,' he said firmly. 'The brew Claire served last night reminded me why it was necessary to find my own place. Why you have a housekeeper who arrives after breakfast and leaves at eight every night is beyond me.'

'You know Madame Jenet has worked for me for years,' his mother said placatingly as they left, after a nod at the two younger women. 'Did I tell you her daughter...?' As their voices dwindled away and the door closed behind them Ann turned to Sandi with a wry smile.

'He handles her very well,' Ann said thoughtfully.

'He loves her very much.' The way Jacques had distracted his mother from her pain had touched Sandi and she didn't like it; she didn't like it at all. He had so many facets to his personality, so many guises that she was beginning to feel quite bewildered. And she didn't like that either.

How soon could she leave? She pondered the thought as she showered and dressed, hardly aware of the wide-eyed, ethereal reflection in the mirror as she brushed her shoulder-length hair until it shone like liquid gold, fastening it high on her head in a cloud of curls. Ann would be fine here—she could see that now—so perhaps after one or two days, when she was completely settled?

Yes. She nodded to herself firmly. Two days at the most. She needed to get back to America, to her job, to the normality and routine it represented. She wanted to be safe.

She didn't dare question that thought when it materialised, a sixth sense deep in her subconscious warning her that it was best left alone.

CHAPTER FOUR

'I CAN picture Emile here, you know, Sandi—much more so than in England.' Ann was lying on one of the thickly upholstered sun loungers scattered round the wonderful pool under the shade of an enormous spreading copper beech. 'Don't you think that's strange?'

'Not really.' Sandi raised herself on one elbow as she stared back at her sister through dark sunglasses. 'He was very French, wasn't he?'

'Yes.' Ann turned her head away and silence reigned for a few moments before the sound of children's laughter broke into their solitude. Both sisters turned to look towards the far end of the massive pool, which was surrounded by trees and bushes, with just one entrance through which they had walked an hour or so earlier, and as they did so three small children ran hopping and skipping through the inlet, causing Sandi to leap to her feet, only to relax a moment or so later as they were followed by Jacques's tall, lazy figure.

'I thought they were going to fall into the water.' Sandi found that her hand was clutching at her throat and brought it sharply to her side. What was Jacques doing, letting those tiny children dash about near such potential danger anyway? She wasn't aware of the scowl on her face as the little group approached, but when Jacques was a few feet away she saw that a mocking, sardonic smile was twisting his mouth.

'You are going to frighten them to death with such ferocity.' He indicated the little trio at his side who had pressed into his legs, their small faces solemn now and their black eyes saucer-wide.

She glared at him for one more moment before forcing a smile to her face as she crouched down in front of the three little girls, aware that Ann had twisted onto her side and was viewing the proceedings with more interest than she had shown in anything that morning. 'Hello there, what are your names?'

'Bonjour. Comment allez-vous?' The eldest of the little mites, who couldn't have been more than four years old, spoke what was obviously a rehearsed welcome, but, not understanding a word of French, Sandi looked up helplessly at Jacques.

'She asked how you are.' He too crouched down at the children's side, his muscled brown thighs in their brief swimming trunks and broad, hair-roughened chest far too close for comfort now. 'They speak a little English—but only a little. They will learn more when they go to school.'

He spoke rapidly to the girls in their native tongue, which caused them all to grin at Sandi and then turn to Ann, their eyes wide again, and the eldest one repeated her little speech.

'Je vais très bien, merci. Et vous?' As Ann replied in their own language the three little tots took a step nearer, clearly intrigued. 'Emile taught me some basics.' Ann smiled at Jacques and Sandi before swinging her legs over the sun lounger and patting the empty space beside her, an invitation which the children were quick to take up, leaving Sandi and Jacques briefly crouched side by side in close proximity.

'You slept well?' As Sandi straightened he rose too, towering over her and causing a fluttering in her chest that she despised herself for.

Why did he have to walk round practically naked anyway? she thought testily. He was hardly decent! Those swimming trunks revealed more than they hid. And then she was astonished at herself for having noticed—well, more than *noticed*, she admitted grudgingly—exactly how his big frame was put together. And it was put together well. Very well.

A heat that had nothing to do with the beautiful weather brought the colour surging into her cheeks and she lowered her head quickly, letting her hair cloud about her face in a concealing veil.

'Fine, thank you.' She forced her voice into a cool tone that she was quite pleased with—until she glanced up again and saw the wicked sparkle in those deadly black eyes. 'The children? They are André's, I presume?' she asked coldly as she held the mocking gaze that seemed able to read her mind with no effort at all.

'You presume correctly.' He turned slightly and gestured to the three small girls who were giggling with Ann on the sun lounger. 'The smaller two, Anna-Marie and Suzanne, are twins, although not identical, and they are three years old. The elder one is Antoinette, who is a very precocious four-year-old, soon to be five. The other two girls, Ghislaine and Chantal, are at school, but you will meet them this evening, no doubt. I understand there was some resistance this morning to leaving the house before meeting their new aunts.'

Aunts? Now she did turn away, gazing out over the blue expanse of sparkling water. She made no reply. Aunt, *singular*, she thought. She had no intention of getting involved with this family, none at all.

'You have swum this morning?' The quiet tone fooled her and she turned to make a light rejoinder to find the dark brown eyes with their thick dark lashes tight and intent on her face.

'I—I—' She stuttered a little and heard herself with a wealth of contempt. 'No.' She took a deep, long, silent breath and tried again. 'No, I haven't. Ann and I forgot to bring costumes.'

'That is not a problem.' The deep voice was even, but as his gaze moved consideringly over her slight figure, which was clad in a brief suntop and long white skirt, her breathing was anything but. 'I do not think Odile's swimwear would fit you—five children in eight years of marriage has made her figure a little...rotund. But my mother has a host of costumes that would fit you. She, too, is slim and petite. I will arrange for some to be brought to your suite later.'

'No, no, it's all right, really. I shan't be here long—'

'You do not like the water?' he asked softly. Again that quiet tone deceived her, until she looked into the glittering black eyes that saw too much.

'Not particularly.' It was a lie, and as she shrugged gracefully she felt that he knew it. Exactly why she had lied about such an unimportant thing she wasn't sure, except that the need to ensure that this man learnt nothing about her, however insignificant it might be, was paramount. She had to protect herself from him. Her recognition of the fact wasn't reasoned knowledge but pure instinct, and all the more powerful because of it.

'That is sad. I feel a good swim is most satisfying—although there are other pleasures, of course, that more than equal it.' The tone was wickedly innocent and the look on his dark face more so, but before she could reply—if she could have replied with her composure shot to ribbons—he had gone on. 'Of course, with the pool in the grounds Odile and André have taught their children to swim from birth, and the girls are more at home in the water than out of it.'

He called the children by name then, and they immediately slid off the lounger and bounded to his side, divesting themselves of the short towelling robes they had on over their tiny black swimsuits and following him down the rounded sloping steps into the shallow water as they chattered like little magpies in rapid French. Within seconds the three tiny figures were shooting through the water in a way that left both Sandi and Ann open-mouthed.

'Well, would you look at that?' Ann smiled quietly.

'You needn't have worried about them falling in after all, Sandi. They're like little fish.'

'Mmm…' There was only one figure in the pool as far as she was concerned at that precise moment in time, and he was fascinating. The big, powerful, almost naked body was cutting through the water with such aggressive masculinity that it was literally making her toes curl, and although it made her furious with herself she was quite unable to tear her eyes away from his dark shape. A great wave of alarm swamped her as she realised she was positively ogling him. What *was* the matter with her?

She turned so suddenly that she almost lost her balance. 'I'm going back to the house for a moment; there's a book I meant to bring down.'

'Oh, right.' Ann was still sitting on the lounger with her eyes following the children, and the look on her face made Sandi hesitate before she left and give her sister a quick hug.

'All right?'

'Oh, Sandi, seeing those three has made me realise I've still got part of Emile with me.' There were tears in her sister's eyes, but Sandi heard a note of anticipation too. 'I'm so glad we came here.'

'It doesn't upset you? The fact that Jacques and André are so like him?' Sandi asked quietly.

'No. Perhaps it should do, but it doesn't,' Ann answered thoughtfully. 'In fact, I find it comforting.'

'Good.' Sandi hugged her once more before straightening. So she had been proved wrong and Jacques right about what was best for her sister, but she didn't mind— not after seeing Ann's face. Anything that gave her sister a modicum of peace at this time was fine by her. And Ann, with her placid, amenable nature, would fit perfectly into the Challier household—that much was becoming patently clear. As clear as the other indisputable fact that she, most certainly, would not. Not when Jacques Challier was around, anyway.

She took her time in returning to the pool and met Odile on the way back. She had gone down to fetch her children and was now returning with the three little girls, their dark curls damp and shining in the warm air. They talked for a few moments, Odile proving to be as warm and pleasant as her mother-in-law, and then Sandi continued down to the pool, where she found Ann fast asleep under the shade of the vast tree and Jacques, much to her annoyance, just pulling himself out of the water.

He'd done that on purpose, she thought waspily. Waited until she got back so that he could display that magnificent body to its best advantage, with the water gleaming on his dark skin like diamonds and the brief wet trunks leaving nothing to the imagination. It was just the sort of trick Ian had used, although she hadn't been aware of the calculated intent at the time. But she was now. Oh, yes, she was now.

'Stop frowning.'

'What?' Her mouth opened in a little O of surprise as he approached, before she had the sense to close it with a little snap.

'This ferocious expression that you adopt whenever I am in the vicinity,' he said mildly as he passed her and stretched himself out on a lounger in the full blaze of the sun just a stone's throw from hers. 'It is most unsociable.'

'Unsociable?' She was still standing to one side of her own lounger, which was only partly in the sun, and now moved it closer to Ann's as she glared at the inert figure a few feet away, her lips pursed tight.

'Unsociable.' He raised himself on one elbow to glance her way briefly, his eyebrows raised quizzically. 'There was no need to move. I wasn't going to bite.'

'I don't want to get sunburnt,' she said stiffly.

'How wise.' It was a mocking drawl as he lay back down again, his hands beneath the back of his head—which brought the broad male chest into muscled relief. 'But I would have thought a little attempt to bring some colour to that pale English skin would have been…practical?'

'Would you?' she asked with tight sarcasm. So he didn't like the colour of her skin, did he? Well, she really couldn't care less. She was burning with rage as she flopped down on the lounger, and once settled she lay stiffly for long minutes as she tried to force herself to relax. But it was no good. The motionless male figure to one side of her had her nerves twanging like guitar strings, and there was no way she could just pretend he wasn't there. He, on the other hand, seemed to have fallen asleep.

She glared at him angrily. Why was he here anyway? He'd told her he had his own home to go to. She could understand him staying the night after the long travelling hours of the day before, back across the Channel, but it was nearly midday now. She grimaced to herself at the unfairness of her thoughts. She really was getting this thing out of all proportion. He seemed to have the ability to turn her into something even she objected to.

'I have never known a woman who could twist her face into so many unpleasant expressions,' the dark voice drawled again, causing her to almost jump out of her skin. 'And such a beautiful face, too. You really have no appreciation of what God has given you.'

She met the black eyes without flinching even as her cheeks flooded with the colour he had lamented the lack of minutes earlier. 'But you, of course, fully appreciate everything God has given you,' she stated with bitter meaning. 'And no doubt use it to its fullest advantage.'

'Now, what exactly does that mean?' he asked lazily. 'I am sorry to be obtuse, but I'm not quite sure what

I'm being accused of here. You English have a way of making the most simple statement into an indictment.'

'I—' She stared at him helplessly, suddenly aware of the hole she had dug for herself. If she told him she thought he was flaunting his body for her benefit he would know that she was aware of him in a way she very definitely did *not* want him to know she was—but how else could she explain her cryptic statement?

'Yes?' He was clearly thoroughly enjoying her discomfiture, and she was just preparing to throw caution to the wind when the sound of his name being called brought his dark head jerking upright. She thought she heard him groan softly, but in the next instant he had risen to his feet and was walking swiftly to the entrance of the pool, where a tall, slim redhead had just appeared, closely followed by Arianne and another older woman.

There was a babble of French just as Ann stirred at the other side of her, opening dazed blue eyes slowly. 'Who is it…?'

'Looks like Jacques has visitors,' Sandi murmured in a dry undertone as she glanced from Ann back to the effusive redhead, who had now draped herself round Jacques, her slim brown arms wound round his neck in such a way that the front of her body was pressed suggestively into his, her face uptilted for his kiss— which, Sandi noticed, was full on the lips.

As the party made their way towards them both girls rose from the sun beds, and Sandi had a brief impression of large brown eyes set in a heart-shaped face surrounded by a mass of wonderful red hair before she concentrated on Arianne as she made the necessary introductions.

'Ann, Sandi, I would like you to meet my dear friend, Simone Lemaire, and her daughter, Monique. Simone, Monique—my new daughter-in-law and her sister, Sandi.'

'How do you do?' As both girls murmured a greeting

Simone stepped forward to embrace them in the traditional French fashion, kissing both cheeks as she held them to her.

'It is good that you have come.' It might have been her imagination, but Sandi felt that the remark had been addressed solely to Ann and that Simone's dark eyes had hardened briefly as she'd turned her head in her direction. The next moment Monique had followed her mother's example, and this time she knew for sure that her presence in the Challier household wasn't appreciated as deep brown eyes held hers for one split second, their depths as hard as jet-black coal.

'Simone and Monique are staying to lunch. Do you think it might be nice if Pierre arranged a barbecue by the pool?' Arianne asked Jacques as the six of them walked across to a table and chairs under the shade of a huge striped umbrella. 'It will be more relaxing for Ann. I'll get Charlette and Claire to serve drinks shortly.'

'You aren't working, Monique?' Jacques's voice was cool as he glanced at the redhead, who had positioned herself very firmly in the chair next to his.

'I've just returned from Bermuda.' Monique's voice fitted in with the whole package—sensual, rich and silky smooth, with the sort of sexy French accent most women would kill for. 'I'm quite exhausted, darling. I need lots of tender loving care.' Her eyes were hungry on his dark face.

'Monique is a model.' Arianne supplied the information helpfully. 'And really doing very well.'

'How interesting.' Sandi smiled, but there was no answering warmth in the beautiful face as Monique glanced her way. 'You get to travel often?'

'Too often.' Monique shrugged almost sulkily before her gaze slid from Sandi and fastened on Jacques's face, where it brightened considerably. 'I need to be home more.' There was no question about what she was insinuating, and Sandi found that she was keeping the smile in place through sheer will-power.

Talk about obvious! She met Ann's eyes for a moment and read both amusement and distaste in her sister's face at Monique's blatant statement of possession. So Jacques and Monique were an item, she thought silently as the conversation ebbed and flowed around her. It shouldn't surprise her. The other woman was exactly the sort of sensual, bold, beautiful female he would admire.

The fact that the knowledge bothered her hit her a second later, and almost instantly she dismissed it. Of course it didn't. Who he was involved with was none of her business—*none*. He could be sleeping with half of the country for all she cared, and probably had if what Emile had hinted about his brother was true.

'Sandi?' She suddenly became aware that the others had gone quiet and that everyone was looking at her.

'I'm sorry?' She smiled quickly, aware that the frown that Jacques had pointed out twice already was again in evidence. 'I was daydreaming, I'm afraid.'

'Monique asked you what your job entails,' Arianne said quietly. 'She has spent some time in the States and feels you must be very good at it to survive out there.'

'I don't know about that, but I enjoy my work anyway.' Sandi spoke directly to the young Frenchwoman just as Claire and Charlette arrived with a trolley of drinks and crushed ice and took the others' attention. 'It's very hectic, though.'

'Yes, I can imagine this.' Monique slanted her dark eyes thoughtfully. 'You have a boyfriend? In America?'

'I have friends who happen to be male, but nothing of a personal nature.' She knew it wasn't what the red-head wanted to hear—those lovely eyes had flickered to Jacques even as she had voiced the question—but it was the truth. 'My work is all-consuming at the moment.'

'It is?' The finely shaped eyebrows rose just the merest fraction. 'So you are…how do they say?…fancy-free?'

She was persistent, Sandi thought grimly as she kept the smile in place. She had to give the Frenchwoman that at least. With a hide like a rhinoceros too—albeit an extremely beautiful rhinoceros. 'Yes.'

'Hmm…' Monique had been leaning forward slightly in her chair, Jacques having stood to help the maids with the drinks, and now she leant back, crossing her long, slim legs as her eyes narrowed still more. 'How long do you intend to stay here with your sister's in-laws?'

From anyone else it would have sounded, and probably have been, a perfectly legitimate enquiry, but coming from Monique's pursed red mouth it was a clear statement that she was in danger of outstaying her welcome, and Sandi recognised it as such. For a moment the carefully veiled rudeness had her lost for words, but the training she had received in the school of life over the last few years stood her in good stead, and she smiled coldly as she shrugged gracefully. 'I've no idea, Monique.'

She turned away as she spoke, signalling that the subtle questioning by the other woman was at an end, and as she did so she became aware that Jacques was looking down at them both, a dark frown on his face—although quite whom he was displeased with she wasn't sure.

'Monique.' He handed the redhead a glass of what looked like brandy and sparkling wine, and Sandi noted, with a little kick in her heart region, that he hadn't had to ask what drink she would prefer. He obviously knew her well, very well—but then she'd already worked that out with a little help from the lady in question, hadn't she? 'Sandi? What would you like?' As he turned to her, Claire hovering at his elbow, she looked directly at the maid as a sudden violent, and in the circumstances quite unreasonable, anger rendered her blazing mad.

'I'll have a glass of dry white wine, please, Claire.'

The smile she gave the young girl was the best piece of acting she had ever done. It was as she'd thought—*just* as she'd thought. He was the type of man who enjoyed playing around, who liked women, most women, and that was fine. It was. It was just fine, she assured herself tightly. It didn't mean a thing to her. *He* didn't mean a thing to her, and—

'Here.' His fingers touched hers as he handed her the glass of wine Claire had poured, and she all but dropped it as the slight physical contact shot through her arm like a bolt of lightning.

'Thank you.' In direct contrast to her innermost self her voice was cool and contained as she turned away to speak to Ann at her side. She hated this man, this virile, blatantly aggressive male, who thought he only had to crook his little finger and women went down like ninepins. He was too handsome, too rich, too powerful and he knew it. Oh, yes, he knew it all right.

The barbecue continued well into the afternoon, Odile and the three younger children joining them just as they began to eat, which Sandi, at least, found a blessing. The three girls were little bundles of live wires, and Sandi found that by entertaining them she could keep herself slightly apart from the other adults without appearing rude.

The small children were delighted at her attempts to learn a few basic words of French, and there was much hilarity from the little corner by the pool they had moved to. By the middle of the afternoon, when Odile announced that they were to return to the house for their nap, the three tiny girls were totally won over, putting up quite a protest at the thought of having to leave their new friend.

'You are very good with children.' There was a note in Jacques's voice she couldn't quite place as he pulled out a chair for her when she returned to the table where the others were seated.

'They're fun,' she said lightly as his words brought the old twist to her heart that she had thought she'd had victory over. When she had married Ian she had dreamed of having his babies—several of them, if finances permitted—and when he had gone, and the dream had been so brutally smashed, the loss of those unborn children had been almost as hard to come to terms with as his betrayal and death.

'Fun?' Monique's voice was a mixture of laughing contempt and mockery. 'All those grubby little fingers and the oh, so shrill screams? You think this is fun?' She looked directly at Sandi as she spoke, and the extent of the other woman's antagonism, hidden from the others behind her smile but clear in the dark hardness of her eyes, paralysed Sandi's tongue for a moment.

'Oh, I love children.' Ann entered the conversation, her calm voice gentle and sweet as she placed her hand on Sandi's arm. 'Which is just as well, really.' She laughed quietly as she patted her swollen stomach meaningfully, at which point the conversation shifted to babies' names and everyone's preferences. But Monique was tenacious and the diversion only lasted a few minutes.

In a slight lull in the conversation the Frenchwoman surprised Sandi for the third time that day by turning to her, her voice clear and almost expressionless as she spoke. 'You did not consider a career with children, then? Caring for them like you do?'

Why her playing with Odile's children should have bothered Monique so much Sandi wasn't sure, but it was quite apparent that it had: the dark eyes were alive with dislike.

'Or perhaps the advertising world was more… lucrative?' Monique continued sweetly. 'Even though you have to be so tough to survive. I know how impossible it is to succeed as you have apparently done.'

On a scale of one to ten she would have to give her

ten for sheer nerve, Sandi thought, with something akin
to wonder tingeing her mind. With just a few well-
chosen words Monique had implied, with perfect innocence, that she was both money-grabbing and ruthless—
the sort of callous businesswoman who would make it
to the top whoever she stepped over to do it.

'Yes, Monique would know this.' Even as Sandi
opened her mouth to formulate some sort of a reply
Jacques spoke. 'The modelling world is second to none
for sheer heartless insensitivity. Is that not so, Monique?'
He was smiling but there was something in his expression which Sandi couldn't quite place. 'Simone is very
proud of the way her daughter has risen in such a com-
petitive, dog-eat-dog environment.'

'Oh, I am. I am very proud of my little girl.' As
Simone gushed on happily Jacques was still smiling, but
whatever message he had endeavoured to convey to the
young Frenchwoman had been understood; that was apparent in the set stiffness to her face, and her smile was
tight and sharp.

The lunch party broke up just after that, when Simone
mentioned an afternoon appointment and Ann decided
that she was returning to the house for a lie-down. By
unspoken mutual consent they all began to walk towards
the entrance to the pool, beyond which stretched large
bowling-green-smooth grounds with fountains and several small rose-entwined bowers of latticed wood—
shady retreats from the heat of the sun—together with
magnificent well-attended flowerbeds, perfumed and
ablaze with colour under the blue sky.

Simone and Arianne were either side of Ann as they
walked out of the pool area and as soon as they had
risen Monique had taken Jacques's arm in a proprietorial
gesture that reeked of ownership, her smile very much
in evidence again when she flashed her eyes up at him
as they walked. Sandi fell just a step or two behind as
she followed the others out into the grounds.

'Sandi?' She wasn't quite sure if Monique let go of Jacques's arm or if he shrugged himself free of the Frenchwoman's grip, but in the next instant she found herself between them, Jacques's hand very firmly under her elbow. She blinked up into his face. 'You would like me to show you the grounds in a moment?'

'I—' She was vitally aware of Monique on her other side as something indefinable but definitely hostile communicated itself without words from the other woman. 'I— No—no, thank you. I think I'll go up with Ann and—'

'Nonsense.' The dark gaze swept over her face as it probed her mind. 'You have been resting all day and you are not with child; you have no excuse to be lazy. We will have a short walk before dinner, yes?' He gave her no chance to reply as his gaze moved from her slightly bemused face to Monique on the other side of her, the tall Frenchwoman almost on a level with his own considerable height. 'You drove your mother, Monique?'

'Yes.' The one word was curt and short, and then Monique underwent the lightning chameleon-type change that seemed an integral part of her make-up. 'Darling?' She had swung to Jacques's other side and taken his arm in one graceful movement, speaking softly in rapid French of which Sandi couldn't understand a word.

'English, please, Monique.' Jacques's deep voice was cool.

'A party. We are having a party this evening.' Monique glanced briefly at Sandi before her eyes returned to the man next to her. 'Nothing formal, just a celebration for my mother's birthday next week. You would like to come?'

It was quite clear that the invitation was meant exclusively for Jacques, and just as they reached the vast drive, on which was parked a small and very expensive red sports car, Simone turned round, overhearing what her daughter was saying.

'*Oui, oui*. Of course you must come, Jacques.' She smiled graciously. 'There are few people of Monique's age; it would be good if you came.'

'But of course we will come,' Jacques responded innocently as he turned to look down at Sandi by his side. 'It will be a chance to show you a little of the French countryside while you are here, yes?'

She knew that he knew she hadn't been included in the invitation, and she also knew, for whatever reason and in spite of his casual air and relaxed smile, that he was angry about it. Perhaps such unnecessary rudeness had grated on the excellent good manners which the Challier family had extended to their guests so far? Or maybe he just felt sorry for her? Whatever, she had no intention of going anywhere alone with Jacques Challier, and especially not to Monique's family home, where it would be very much a case of stepping into the lion's— or, to be more accurate, *lioness's*—den.

'I don't think—'

'Oh, do go, Sandi. It will do you good.' There were few times when Sandi wished her sister in another place, but this was one of them. 'You've been so wonderful to me over the last week or so and you need a break—you know you do—before you go back to America.'

'I'm having a break.' Sandi forced a smile that almost cracked her face. 'I'm thoroughly enjoying my time here—'

'And you will enjoy it all the more tonight.' There was a sardonic note in Jacques's voice that she didn't miss, and as her eyes rose to meet his she saw a definite challenge in the cool, shuttered gaze. He was *daring* her to go with him? The shock of it put fire in her eyes. He was. He was daring her to spend the evening with him.

'If Sandi doesn't want to come…' Monique allowed her voice to trail off with a faint trace of regret as she dropped her eyes, and that hypocrisy more than anything else brought quick words to Sandi's lips which she had never intended to say a minute before.

'I'd love to come, Monique,' she said brightly, tilting her blonde head in a little gesture of defiance that she was quite unaware of. 'If it's not inconvenient, of course.'

'No, no. As I said, the evening is informal.' The words were forced through lips that had suddenly set in a tight, hard line, and as Sandi glanced from Monique to Jacques she saw a small smile of satisfaction curve the well-shaped mouth for a moment.

What game was he playing? She glanced at him suspiciously as Monique and her mother slid into the snazzy little car. Did he imagine he had two females fighting over the chance to be with him? Or was there some deeper meaning to all this? Perhaps a lovers' tiff with Monique? Something along those lines? And this was intended to bring the redhead to heel?

She found herself wishing with all her heart that she hadn't agreed to go, but when, in the next instant, Monique's brilliant red head popped out of the driver's window and she called out the time the party would start she didn't say that she had changed her mind. And as the little car roared off down the drive any opportunity to escape from an evening that was bound to be a disaster of unprecedented proportions went with it.

CHAPTER FIVE

'YOU look gorgeous, Sandi—absolutely gorgeous.' Ann breathed a sigh of satisfaction as she lay on her bed watching Sandi put the last touches to her discreet eye make-up. 'And please, just go and have a good time without worrying about me. I'm fine here.'

'You weren't fine earlier, when I came back before dinner,' Sandi accused her sister softly as she turned to look straight into her pale face. 'I always know when you've been crying.'

'I'm going to cry, aren't I?' Ann's voice didn't hold a trace of self-pity, rather a mature knowledge of her way of working through her grief that she hadn't expressed before. 'I loved Emile, Sandi, and I'll always love him. But that doesn't mean life has to stop for everyone else. I want you to go out tonight and have a wonderful time with Jacques—I mean it.'

A wonderful time? Sandi just stopped herself repeating the words in a tone that she knew would have been full of amazed contempt. She didn't expect to have a wonderful time; she expected— She expected something quite different, she told herself flatly as she shut off her mind from the route it was following. But thinking about it wouldn't help. She had to take the proverbial bull by the horns and get on with it. And the bull in question was at this moment in time waiting for her downstairs.

'You think this dress is OK, then?' she asked as she turned back to the mirror and had one last glance at her appearance. She had chosen a simple sleeveless dark wine-coloured dress in pure silk that she had bought a few weeks previously in America, the cut of which was

78

exquisite. Quite why she had thrown it into her case at the last moment before leaving for England she wasn't sure—she hadn't been thinking straight at the time, after the distraught telephone call from Ann, who had been hysterical with shock and horror—but now she blessed the impulse.

She had fixed her hair into a high loose knot on the top of her head, allowing a few wispy golden curls to fall about her neck to soften the severe style, and had added a touch of violet-blue eyeshadow to her eyelids that emphasised the unusual hue of her eyes and the clear honey-coloured skin that surrounded them. Tiny stud earrings and high-heeled shoes in the exact shade of the dress completed her ensemble, and now, as she checked the wide-eyed reflection in the mirror, she was satisfied with the cool, worldly and remote image it presented.

And that was how she intended to be tonight, she told herself flatly. Cool, cosmopolitan and definitely—*definitely*—remote.

'Go on, go and wow them, Sandi.' Ann's smile was warm. It had been a long time since she'd seen her sister get ready for a date—over three years, in fact—and her soft mouth hardened as she thought of Ian Mortimer.

'I don't know about wowing them.' Sandi gave her sister a quick hug before straightening her shoulders as though she was preparing to do battle. And that was exactly how she felt, she told herself nervously. The tight tensing of her muscles, the rapid heartbeat and ridiculous flow of adrenalin were all down to the fact that she had been forced into a situation she both disliked and resented. That was all. There was no excitement mixed up in this feeling. *There was not.* And she was not attracted to Jacques Challier—in fact, he was everything she despised in a man.

He watched her every step as she came down the stairs, and Sandi had never found it so difficult to put one foot in front of the other. She purposely kept her eyes straight in front until she reached the foot of the winding staircase, when she turned and faced him for the first time, her eyes widening slightly as they met his, but otherwise her face concealing her thoughts from him.

He looked magnificent! She wanted to lick her suddenly dry lips as he moved towards her but forced herself to stand absolutely still and remain the ice-cool blonde. But he *did*, her brain told her with traitorous disregard for her thudding heart. She had never seen a man whose body carried an evening jacket the way this one did. His curly hair, as black as jet, had been persuaded into a more conservative style than normal and his skin could have been sculpted in bronze against the snowy white of his shirt, but the black eyes, as they held hers, were the same. Wicked, amused and mockingly aware of every thought in her head—or so it seemed to her feverish mind.

'You look very beautiful, Sandi.' His voice, with its sensual accent, was like liquid fire on her overwrought nerves, and she found herself blinking like a startled rabbit before she forced a light smile to her lips as her mind replayed the sight of him as he had been earlier, dripping wet and almost naked. She had to stop this—oh, she did, she told herself desperately. The only way to get through this evening was to match him in every way.

'Thank you.' She glanced at the small gold watch on her wrist as she spoke without raising her eyes. 'You look rather nice yourself.'

'"Rather nice"?' The tone of his voice brought her head up with a little snap, and as she had expected the dark eyes were alive with wicked amusement. 'That is very English, is it not? "Rather nice"?'

'I *am* English,' she said stiffly, and was further affronted when he laughed softly, his eyes lingering on the swell of her breasts through the thin material of the dress.

'But not as aloof and cucumber-cool as you would

have me believe, I think,' he said softly. 'I have seen you with your sister, and a little tigress could not defend her young so admirably, and with the children this afternoon... You were not the cold English woman of the world with them.'

'Children are children.' She had wanted her voice to be mocking and light but it was merely breathless, and the slight tremble in its depths had her wanting to close her eyes with mortification.

'And what makes them different from the adult population in your eyes?' he asked quietly, all trace of derision gone now and his eyes deadly serious as they fastened on her flushed face. 'The fact that they are small, helpless? That you have no need to keep the formidable armour in place with them? Is that it?'

'Don't be ridiculous.'

His face hardened, a dark flare of anger in the midnight-black eyes as they held hers. 'I am never ridiculous.' It was said with such arrogance, such utter male authority that on any other occasion it would have brought a smile to her lips. But not now, and not with this man. 'You are hiding from life. I know it and you know it,' he stated coldly. 'Everything about you holds a subtle message that you are unattainable—'

'And that's why you wanted to take me out tonight?' she flashed back, with both pain and rage in her voice. 'Because you thought I was a challenge—'

'Partly.' He cut through the angry tirade with a cool smile as he spoke, her apparent lack of control restoring his perfectly. 'But only partly. I have to confess I find you intriguing, Miss Gosdon. I would like to know how someone so exquisite could have escaped the male jungle this long—how it is that some brave soul more courageous than the average man hasn't taken it upon himself to put a gold band on the third finger of your left hand.'

'Someone did.' Her voice was utterly flat now, but

there was a wealth of pain in the violet-blue of her eyes
that stunned the man in front of her into total silence.
'And the brave soul is dead now. Shall we go?' So saying, she walked past him and to the front door.

It was a good ten seconds before Jacques Challier
could bring himself to move, and even then it was quite
automatic, his mind on a different plane altogether.

'Sandi?' He caught her arm as they walked across to
the silver-coloured Ferrari crouching on the drive.
'Please, look at me.'

She turned because there was really nothing else she
could do, but her face was closed against the appeal in
his, her mouth tight and buttoned as she looked up into
his dark, handsome face.

'I had no idea. You believe this?'

'It doesn't matter.' She moved slightly, the gesture
indicating to him to remove his hand from her arm. 'It
all happened three years ago. It's history now.'

History? Jacques Challier was suddenly filled with an
emotion he had never experienced in his life before, and
he had no way to describe it other than as a compilation
of burning curiosity, regret, dark anger and a hundred
other emotions besides raging through his frame. She
had been married? *Married?* And she still loved him
even though he was dead, if the look on her face was
anything to go by. Why that should bother him in the
way it did he didn't know, but he did know that he didn't
like it, and the knowledge tightened his jaw and brought
a thread of harshness to his deep voice.

'Nevertheless, I had no wish to cause you pain,' he
said with a formal little nod of his head that was very
French. 'You accept my apology, Sandi?' His voice was
quiet now, quiet and low and very controlled, all emotion absent.

'Yes.' She answered automatically, and then her eyes
rose to meet his.

The stillness of his body and the strange unfathomable

expression on the hard male face momentarily pierced the shock and pain that his words had induced. If she hadn't known better she would almost have imagined there was something defensive about the posture of his body and tilt to his chin, but she was imagining it—she had to be—and when she blinked in the next instant the impression was gone.

'Yes, of course I do,' she said softly now as she forced her heartbeat to return to normal. 'Let's forget it, shall we?'

He nodded almost coldly before gesturing towards the car, and opened the door of the Ferrari without looking at her.

As she slid into the luxurious depths of the beautiful car she was aware that she was seeing a side to him she hadn't seen before. Earlier that evening, as they had strolled round the immaculately tended grounds before dinner, he had been the perfect host—courteous, attentive and very correct. She had expected— She didn't know what she had expected, she admitted to herself as he joined her in the car and the powerful engine purred into life, but it hadn't been the formal politeness he had shown at the time.

Ian would have capitalised on such an opportunity by making a subtle or maybe not so subtle attempt to make love to a woman, but Jacques Challier had returned her to the château with nothing more threatening than a cool, light hand at her elbow. And now? Now he was yet another person in addition to the dark, mocking philanderer he had appeared to be at the poolside—cold, reserved, with an almost visible aura of aloofness that sat on the big male body like a dark mantle.

They drove to the party in a silence that vibrated with electricity, and it wasn't until they were almost at the Lemaire residence that Sandi relaxed enough to take in any of the beautiful scenery through which they had been travelling. Charming villages, gently dozing in the late evening air, and warm, rolling hillsides dotted with sweet-smelling orchards and vineyards were virtually at every bend in the winding road, and after they had passed one particularly impressive vineyard that seemed to stretch for miles she forced herself to break the silence that had reached screaming-pitch.

'I understand from Ann that the Challier family have been in the wine-making business for centuries,' she said quietly as she turned towards the dark profile at the side of her.

'This is correct.' The beautiful car, the lovely evening and the handsome dark man at her side were too intoxicating, she told herself tightly, leading her to all manner of foolish imaginings. She had to keep the conversation on a more mundane, ordinary level, like now. There was nothing at all mysterious about Jacques Challier. In fact, she could read him like an open book—like all his type. He liked women, plural—that much Emile had made clear—and he was involved with Monique—*that* much the tall, beautiful redhead had made clear. End of story.

'Your vineyards are close by?' she asked carefully.

'Yes.' He glanced at her for one brief moment and her heart thudded at the eye contact. 'I can arrange a visit before you leave if you wish?'

'That would be fun,' she said lightly. 'I'm sure Ann would be interested to see how things are done.'

'I'm sure she would,' he agreed drily, the lazy drawl in his deep voice telling her that he was aware of her intent not to be alone with him again and found it amusing. Well, that was fine, just fine, she told herself tightly. She didn't mind how the message got through as long as it was received.

Dusk had given way before the onset of a black velvet night as they drew into the enormous drive of the Lemaire château, but the moon washed the imposing house with a bright silver glow as they drew to a halt in a drive already jam-packed with similar cars. The wealth of these people!

Sandi glanced round her as she stepped from the car after Jacques had opened the door, and found Ian in her mind again—much to her annoyance. These were the sort of people he had craved in his search for wealth and fun and high living. She shook her head slightly at the thought, unaware of glittering black eyes watching her every move.

'Something is the matter?' His voice was calm and controlled, but there was a thread of something hard and silky that brought her eyes snapping immediately to his.

'No, no—of course not.'

'No?' He stepped back a pace, crossing his arms across his hard-muscled chest as he surveyed her from cold, dark eyes. 'I saw disapproval on your face—distaste even. I was wrong in this?'

'I—' She didn't know what to say. Good grief, what *could* she say? And then the temper this man seemed to ignite with such little effort came to her rescue. 'I am entitled to the privacy of my thoughts, surely?' she asked with a coldness that matched his. 'And I hardly think they would be of any interest to you.'

She had a warm, sensual mouth, whatever that ice-cool-blonde image said to the contrary, he thought. He stared at the full lower lip for one second more before he crossed the yard or so separating them and took her in his arms, his mouth taking hers in a hard, vital, burning kiss before she even had time to realise what was happening.

One hand was round her waist, the other at the nape of her neck to give his searching mouth greater power of invasion as he held her head at an angle that suited him. There wasn't a trace of hesitancy in the kiss, no suggestion of permission being sought, merely a bold taking of something he desired that took her completely

by surprise and numbed all thought of resistance for a
few incredible moments.

'No—' As her speech returned along with her senses
she began to struggle, jerking her mouth from his, but
even as he made a small gruff sound in his throat his
lips claimed hers again, and he moulded her into his hard
body in a way that made further resistance useless.

And then the kiss became one of sweet exploration,
his tongue working with his hungry lips to send her
senses reeling. This kiss was how she had always imagined a kiss could be—should be, she realised as her body
made an instinctive arch into his. And her body was responding as it had done the night before when she had
been in his arms—wantonly and without thought. But
she *needed* to think.

This time when she struggled he let her go at once,
moving her to arm's length with his hands dropping to
her waist as he stared down into her flushed face.

'You said—' Her voice was shaky and she raised a
trembling hand to her hair as she tried again. 'You said
you wouldn't do that again.'

'I lied.' He smiled slowly, his dark eyes stroking
across her golden hair before returning to her face. 'I am
very bad.'

'I don't want—' She shook her head slightly as she
searched for the rage that should have been there at his
autocratic assumption that he could kiss her. 'I don't
want this, Jacques—I mean it.'

'You do not want what?' he asked softly, his hands
still refusing to release her. 'A kiss? You do not want a
kiss? But what is so bad about that, little one?'

How could he change like this? she asked herself
helplessly. During the drive here she had almost felt the
dark waves emanating from the big male body at her
side, and when they had first stepped out of the car he
had been angry with her, she knew it. But now—now
his mouth was curved in an attractive half-smile that

caused the breath to constrict in her throat as she stared up at him, his broad, muscled shoulders and height dwarfing her slender, diminutive frame. Monique's tallness would suit him so much better.

The thought, coming from nowhere as it did, put iron in her backbone and gave her the strength to move away with a firmness that made his arms drop to his sides. 'There is nothing bad about it,' she said with a coolness she was far from feeling. Bad? it was glorious, wonderful and terribly, terribly dangerous. 'But I'm not into brief affairs or one-night stands, so if you don't mind—'

'*One-night stands?*' Well, she'd certainly got rid of the warm, ardent lover, she thought wryly as he metamorphosed in front of her eyes, his brows drawing together over glittering black eyes in an unholy frown as his mouth thinned and straightened. '*One-night stands?*'

'Or whatever the equivalent is in France,' she said coolly as her stomach jerked and dipped like a roller coaster. 'Apart from the social sense it makes these days, I've always thought there should be more between a man and a woman than lust. Now, shall we go in to the party...?' Her voice trailed away when she saw the blackness in his face.

He stared at her for a full thirty seconds without speaking, and then took her hand in a tight grip that almost broke her fingers and practically ran her up the rest of the drive towards the huge steps fronting the massive studded oak door.

'What are you doing?' she asked breathlessly as she trotted along at his side, almost unable to keep her balance in the three-inch heels she was wearing.

'You want to go to the damn party?' he asked tightly. 'So we are going, yes?'

She arrived at the front door in a panting gallop, and was immeasurably glad that it was a few moments before their ring was answered as she endeavoured to bring her breathing under control. The pig. The arrogant pig!

To manhandle her like that, just because she had objected to his lovemaking.

'And smile.'

'What?'

'Smile!' She had never heard anyone shout without raising their voice before, she thought weakly. 'There is no way I am walking through that door with you looking as though you are with the Marquis de Sade on a bad night,' he growled through gritted teeth.

As the door opened and a small maid ushered them into the baronial hall she found a smile from somewhere. It faltered for a moment as Monique appeared almost immediately from the edge of the throng of people in what looked like a vast drawing room. Her smile was radiant as she caught sight of Jacques, and her tall, slim body was encased in a black cocktail dress that made her slender legs endless and her red hair a mass of vibrant colour that was quite breathtaking.

'Darling…' She reached out slim arms in a gesture that should have looked theatrical—and would have done from anyone else—but which merely added to the Frenchwoman's charm. 'You're here. And Sandi…' When, in the next moment, Sandi found herself in a brief, highly perfumed embrace she forced herself not to show her surprise. 'It is so nice to see you again,' Monique said sweetly, her brown eyes wide and soft. 'You must come and meet everyone.'

And meet everyone she did. Simone was at her elbow the minute they entered the drawing room, slipping her arm through Sandi's and drawing her away from Jacques and Monique in a warm gush of words, then personally introducing her to every person in the place—which necessitated a great deal of smiling and nodding and desperate concentration to keep pace with the broken French accents.

After almost half an hour, with Simone's arm still tightly holding hers, Sandi was just thinking that she really couldn't smile again without her face setting in concrete when a dark voice at her elbow brought her head swinging round and up to meet Jacques's lazy smile.

'Introductions completed?' he asked Simone silkily.

'I think so.' Simone's eyes searched for Monique as she spoke.

'Then let me relieve you of your duties as hostess for this particular guest,' Jacques drawled smoothly, and drew Sandi into his side, taking the empty glass she had been holding as he spoke. 'Was that wine?'

'I— Yes.' She turned from him to smile her thanks at Simone, but the older woman was exchanging a glance with her daughter across the room, and as Sandi saw the almost imperceptible flick of Simone's head she followed her eyes to Monique's face.

They had engineered that, she realised with stunned surprise. Simone had deliberately kept at her side under the guise of hostess making a stranger welcome to give her daughter time with Jacques, and now she was calling her over. Simone surely didn't regard her as a threat to her daughter's relationship with Jacques, did she?

As she saw Monique begin to make her way over to them, Jacques's arm at her waist turned her round, drawing her out of the room and into the huge hall, where the sound of the music she had been hearing for the last ten minutes became louder.

'First a drink and then we dance, yes?' He guided her along the hall and into another vast room, one wall of which was lined with tables groaning with food and an army of waiters dancing attendance on yet more folk.

'I thought this was supposed to be a small, informal party?' she asked a trifle breathlessly as the touch of his hand burnt through the thin silk of her dress.

'It is. Believe me, by Lemaire standards it is,' he said softly. 'Monique and her mother are social animals of the first degree, and Philippe Lemaire indulges them both—it makes life simple,' he added cynically. 'You've met our host?'

'In the drawing room.' He had steered her over to a corner of the room where a large bar was being attended by four uniformed waiters as they'd spoken, and now requested a glass of dry white wine which was immediately placed in her hand.

'What did you think of him?'

'Think of him?' She stared up into the dark face as she took a sip of the chilled wine. 'He seemed nice. Friendly and warm,' she added quickly on seeing the flash of mocking amusement in his eyes at her choice of words.

'He is nice. He is also friendly and warm.' She began to simmer gently at the laughter in his face, but kept her face open and blank and her body still. She would not let him get to her. *She would not.* 'It is Philippe who is a friend of my parents rather than his wife. My father and Monique's father were boys together many years ago, and now the two families are closely linked with business ties.'

'Really.' How very convenient, she thought waspily. For Monique, that was. Not only did she have parental backing for her claim on Jacques but the two families' financial fortunes were entwined too. The tall redhead had had it handed to her on a plate, all things considered. She was surprised at how much the thought hurt.

'Come. We are going to dance.' He took the glass from her hand and placed it on a small table before pulling her with him out through the massive French doors at the end of the room and into the grounds of the château, which were lit as brightly as day. A small band was playing with both finesse and flair under a large striped marquee in one portion of the smooth green grounds that seemingly stretched for miles, and already the lawn was full of slowly moving couples dancing to a romantic ballad.

'I don't want—'

He put his finger on her lips as she protested. 'Come, come, little one, there must be some things you enjoy,' he said silkily. 'You do not swim, you do not dance—'

'I didn't say I didn't dance,' she shot back quickly, incensed at the mockery.

'But you don't want to dance with me.' Now all laughter and amusement were wiped clean from the dark male face and his eyes held hers in a penetrating grip she couldn't break. 'As you did not want to swim with me.'

'Jacques—'

'No, no, Sandi.' As he drew her against him she knew that he was perfectly controlled and absolutely determined to have his own way. 'You will dance with me. I want to hold you in my arms, and as you have made it perfectly clear this is the only opportunity I shall have for such pleasure I intend to make the most of it.'

'You're a pig,' she said weakly.

'Not the most inspiring of phrases for such an occasion, but for the lack of anything else it will have to do.'

This was a game to him, just an amusing game, she thought helplessly as he drew her against him, holding her so close against his broad chest that of their own volition her hands crept up to entwine round his neck as they danced. She was aware of the waves of pleasure moving from her head to her toes as she drank in the smell and feel of him but she fought them—desperately.

She had been here before, only once before in her life, and look where that particular road had led—straight into hell. She had never thought she would surface from the despair and black pain that Ian had plunged her into but she had—admittedly by the skin of her teeth, but nevertheless she had clawed back a life for herself and had learnt to live again, on her terms. And they didn't include flirting with a tall, dark, handsome man of the world who was already involved with at least one woman that she knew of and possibly several more. It was emotional suicide. And she didn't have a death-wish. Not any more.

'Stop fighting me, Sandi.' The shock of hearing him read her mind brought her head back, and as she looked into his face he kissed her full on the lips, but lightly this time, his mouth stroking hers with a warm, thrilling caress before he raised his head.

'I'm not.' The protest was weak and she knew it.

'No?' The sardonic voice and dark brows raised in mocking disbelief made her want to kick him—hard. 'However much you try to disguise your femininity from me you can't hide it from yourself, you know. You are attracted to me. I know it and you know it, although you don't want to admit it yet.'

'How dare you?'

'Oh, I dare much more than this, little one,' he drawled silkily as his eyes gleamed darkly. 'Your husband has been dead three years, is this so?' The shock of his words brought her jerking way from his body but the strong, steel-clad arms didn't relax their hold for a moment. 'Is it?'

'This is nothing to do with you—'

'And if I read all the signs correctly you have in effect been on top of the funeral pyre all that time.' It was cruel, he knew it was cruel, but it was the only way to get through that iron reserve that was holding him at bay. And he wanted to get through it—badly. The feel of her body next to his was affecting him in a way he couldn't believe. When had he been hit by such raw desire before? Not in a long time—a long, long time. 'Burying yourself in your work, holding everyone at bay as you carve a career for yourself—'

'There is nothing wrong in having a career.'

'There is if the personal cost means that you become isolated, a robot—'

'You know nothing about me,' she said hotly, her cheeks scarlet. 'Nothing.'

'Something I would like to remedy,' he said softly.

'You're talking about sex.' She spat the words at him, her face and body taut. 'That's all. Just a bodily satisfaction.'

'Am I?' He considered her through half-closed eyes for a moment before pulling her close against him again, his muscled strength too hard to withstand. 'You think this is all? Of course the physical aspect of a relationship is important—'

'How many women have you had, Jacques?' He had been blunt—well, so could she be, she thought angrily. 'How many?'

'*What?*' She wasn't to know that she had done what most people would have considered impossible—surprised Jacques Challier twice in one evening—but nevertheless she did get a measure of satisfaction from the amazed glitter in his eyes.

'You heard what I said. I asked you how many women you have had in your life—liaisons, affairs, call them what you will,' she said with brittle control. 'I want to know.'

'*Zut!*' The oath was short and sharp as the smooth control faltered for a moment, but then, as he caught the disapproving glance of a portly matron at one side of them, he breathed harshly before tilting his head to look deep into her eyes again. 'More than I would like at this moment in time.' The honesty surprised her and she remained silent as he stared down at her. 'But I am a grown man of thirty-six, Sandi, and I am no saint. I have never pretended to be. I would say in my defence that I have lived my life by my own rules and never knowingly taken what was not mine to take.'

'And that makes it all right?' she asked flatly.

'As far as I am concerned, yes.' He eyed her darkly. 'And now I will ask you something. From the moment we met you have made it clear that you dislike me. You are attracted to me—' he raised his hand to her lips when she would have interrupted '—but you dislike me. This is a fact. Now I think I deserve to know why.

'It cannot be Ann any longer; you have seen yourself that she is welcome, more than welcome, and loved by my family. I expected this…antagonism to diminish when Ann made her decision to stay but it has increased—with me, that is. I could suppose that you are sulking at being proved wrong, but you are too strong a character for such petulance.'

She should have been pleased at the veiled compliment, but strangely she wasn't. In fact, at that moment her whole self was taken up with the fight not to burst into tears. She hadn't wanted this—she hadn't wanted any of it, she thought wildly. She had flown to England just over two weeks ago with one thought in her head and that had been to comfort Ann. The Challier family, Jacques, they had forced all this on her, and she wasn't ready to handle it—not any of it—and especially not Jacques.

Her life was settled now, orderly, in control, and although she wasn't exactly happy she had regained her peace of mind—which meant the world to her after losing it for so long after Ian. If she had thought about the future at all it had been with regard to her work, not her love-life. In fact she didn't want a love-life—not ever. The old adage of once bitten, twice shy still held good in this day and age, and especially with a man like Jacques, who was already deeply involved with another woman and had made no effort to pretend otherwise.

Some women could handle casual affairs, relationships that asked for nothing more than a little fun and excitement, but she wasn't one of them. She never had been, even before Ian.

'All right, all right, we will talk later.' The expression on her face caused him to move her close to him without another word as they continued to dance to the music, and, although she was glad of the respite from those piercing dark eyes that saw far too much, his closeness was having a dire effect on her metabolism.

What was it with her? she asked herself angrily as the warm heat in her lower stomach transferred itself to different parts of her body. It was as though she had a self-destruct button that fired with a certain type of man— the Ian Mortimer, Jacques Challier type. She had heard of women who were attracted time and time again to real swines, but until now hadn't put herself into that category.

'You are enjoying the party, Sandi?' As the deep-throated, sexy, feminine voice sounded just over her left shoulder she shut her eyes tightly for a second, before lifting her head and turning to face Monique and her partner.

'Very much, thank you,' she said politely as Jacques's arm slid to her waist and they surveyed the other couple. Monique's partner was a tall, good-looking young man with dark brown hair and deep blue eyes and the sort of physique that suggested a great deal of weight-training.

'Let me introduce Jean-Pierre,' Monique continued sweetly as she placed a red-taloned hand lightly on the other man's arm. 'He works with me.'

'You're a model too?' Sandi asked when the brief introductions were over.

'No, no.' Jean-Pierre laughed as he grimaced disarmingly. 'Me, I could not stand all the pirouettes and panics if I got a spot on my nose, you know?' Sandi couldn't see the suave, impeccably dressed individual in front of her ever having something so mundane as a spot on his nose, but she nodded anyway. 'I photograph—you know—click-click?' He made a little gesture as though he had a camera in his hands. 'This suits me.'

'And he's excellent at it, aren't you, Jean-Pierre?'

Monique was at her most gushing. 'In spite of some of the...how shall I say?...bimbos you have to work with.'

'That is naughty.' Jean-Pierre shook his head at her before turning back to Sandi. 'She is a bad girl, this one.' Oh, she believed it, Sandi thought wryly. She really didn't need to be convinced.

'You would like to dance with me, Jacques?' Even as she spoke Monique took Jacques's arm and dimpled up into his face. 'Jean-Pierre will look after Sandi—won't you, darling?'

'Of course; it would be a pleasure.' The young Frenchman looked as though he meant what he said, and Jacques surveyed him through cool, shuttered eyes for a long moment before he allowed himself to turn and take Monique in his arms as the music began again. 'You would like to dance, Sandi? Or maybe something to eat and a drink?'

Jean-Pierre was a little smaller than Jacques, she noted as he smiled down at her, but there was something open and engaging about the young man's face that she liked. And as they danced she found that her first impression had been right, for Jean-Pierre proved both an amusing and very natural companion, his rather caustic wit and quite wicked sense of the ridiculous making her laugh more than once as they circled the lawn.

She didn't glance to left or right, keeping her eyes very firmly on the handsome face in front of her. Somehow the prospect of seeing Monique in Jacques's arms was to be avoided at all costs. But it was Jean-Pierre who forced the issue some minutes later.

'They make a handsome couple, do they not?' When he inclined his head to the side she followed the gesture without thinking, and then found that her stomach seemed to have risen up into her throat as she caught sight of Monique draped all over Jacques as they danced. 'Whenever I see them together like this I am always surprised Monique does not quit the rat race of modelling and concentrate on the Challier fortune instead.' His tone was slightly astringent.

'You see them together often?' Her voice was as light as she could make it, and it seemed to satisfy Jean-Pierre because he didn't even glance her way as he kept his eyes on the beautiful redhead.

'Now and again, at social functions like this one,' he said absently. 'You will find the beautiful people's set is quite a small one. The cost of the entrance fee is too high for mere mortals.'

'You're here.' She hadn't meant it quite as it had sounded, but now the vivid blue eyes did snap back to her face for a startled moment before he burst out laughing, throwing back his head as he let out a delighted bellow that brought more than one head turning in their direction—and in particular a pair of dark, glittering black eyes.

'This is true. This is very true.' He laughed again as he looked down into her lovely face. 'But I am something of a cheat, you know? It just so happens my father has an inordinate amount of money—which is very bad taste to mention, incidentally, but true nevertheless.'

'So you're one of the beautiful people too?' she asked with a wry smile.

'So it would seem.' His eyes moved back to Monique. 'But not beautiful enough.' He spoke the words almost to himself before his gaze snapped back to her watchful face. 'But enough of this. I am sure you would like a drink now, yes? And perhaps something to eat?'

'Yes, please.' The brief revelation that Jean-Pierre was head over heels in love with Monique further dampened her spirits as she walked hand in hand with him to the edge of the lawn. There he found two seats before disappearing, only to return a couple of minutes later with a small tray containing two plates of food and two glasses of chilled white wine.

The knowledge of how Jean-Pierre felt about Monique

somehow strengthened Monique and Jacques's relationship, although she couldn't quite explain how. Did they
see other people as well as each other? she thought flatly
as she sipped at the expensive and delicious wine.
Perhaps it was one of those modern affairs where they
both indulged in any sexual flirtations they felt like when
they were apart, knowing that what they had would stand
such behaviour? She gave a mental shake of her head.
She knew there were people who could cope with such
relationships but she didn't understand them.

'You look sad.' As Jean-Pierre spoke at her side she
smiled up at him quickly and shook her head.

'No, no—of course I'm not. How could I be when
I'm in such good company?' He bowed at the compliment and his eyes laughed at her.

'Not too bad for one of you reserved English, I think,'
he teased smilingly, spearing a large juicy prawn from
his plate and offering it to her as she smiled back at him.

She really did like him, she decided suddenly, and the
knowledge that he was in love with Monique and was
asking nothing more of her, Sandi, than a little light
amity and conviviality made her relax with him in a way
she could never have done with Jacques, her face open
and warm as she laughed with him when the prawn
slipped off the fork, narrowly missing her cleavage to
land with a plop on her plate.

'It must be a good joke to make you laugh like that.'
The dark voice was like a heavy douche of ice-cold water, and the plate almost jerked off her lap as she jumped
and then raised her eyes to see Jacques and Monique at
their side.

'Not really.' Jean-Pierre rose swiftly, offering his seat
to Monique. 'Can I get you some food?' he asked the
lovely redhead after one lightning glance at Jacques's
tight face.

'Thank you, darling.' Monique sounded sulky, and the
next few minutes until Jean-Pierre returned with

Monique's plate were spent in an uncomfortable silence which Sandi couldn't break for the life of her. She nibbled at the food on her plate with her eyes downcast and her thoughts in turmoil. How dared he object to her laughing with Jean-Pierre when he had been doing goodness knows what with his mistress? How dared he?

Almost in the same instant that Jean-Pierre returned with the food she found herself lifted to her feet with a firm hand under her elbow. 'A most enjoyable evening, Monique...' Jacques's voice was cool and contained and controlled.

'You are leaving? But it is so early—'

Jacques cut into Jean-Pierre's remonstrance with a smile that would have chilled ice. 'Nevertheless, it is time that we said our goodbyes,' he said grimly. 'You will thank your mother for us, Monique?'

It was noticeable that the lovely Frenchwoman barely raised her head as they left, and also that Jean-Pierre's expression held something of surprise and awareness in its depths as he bent over her hand in a continental gesture of farewell. In the next moment, Jacques whisked her along towards the house and through the noisy throng filling the downstairs rooms with laughter and chatter, and she barely had time to catch her breath before they were out of the front door and into the relative quiet of the enormous drive.

'Is anything wrong?' She shook his hand off her elbow as he prepared to lead her down the steps, refusing to be intimidated for a second longer.

'Wrong?' He paused for a moment two steps below her to look into her face, his voice cold and civilised. 'What could be wrong, *ma chérie*?'

'I don't know, but you seem...annoyed at something,' she said a trifle breathlessly. Standing as he was on the lower steps, his head was just above hers but almost on a level, and she found the nearness of his hard, firm mouth disturbing, her eyes leaving the thin, well-shaped lips with difficulty to fasten on the glittering black eyes that were looking directly into hers.

'I do?' His smile held no warmth. 'Then this is a puzzlement to us both. Now, shall we?' As he gestured to the Ferrari some way down the drive the motion of his hand was sharp and fierce, and she knew, she just knew that he was holding onto that iron self-control with an effort.

But why? What had bothered him? Had he had some sort of a row with Monique? Perhaps she had voiced her objections to her lover bringing another woman to the party—even though he had merely been fulfilling the obligation that had been virtually foisted on him by the fact that Monique had mentioned the party in front of her in the first place. The Challier family were excellent hosts, she would give them that, and, looking back, she could see that it would have been the height of rudeness on Jacques's part not to include her in his reply. He probably hadn't really expected her to come at all.

When she still didn't move he gave her one last long glance of grim exasperation before turning and walking down the drive towards the car, and as she followed, her footsteps quiet and slow, she suddenly felt that she had never been so miserable and alone in all her life.

CHAPTER SIX

'JACQUES?' The grim profile was not exactly encouraging, but Sandi felt she had to voice the suspicion that had been growing in her mind for the last twenty minutes or so. 'I didn't think the journey here was this long.'

'It wasn't.'

'But I don't understand—' She stopped abruptly as he swung off the main road on which they had been travelling for almost three quarters of an hour and onto a dark, wide lane that was bordered on both sides by the outlines of huge leafy trees. 'Where are we? Where are we going?'

'We are exactly two miles from my home—which is also our destination,' he said coolly, with a low silkiness that told her he knew exactly how his words were going to be received.

'Your home?' He didn't need to wince to tell her how shrill her voice was, and she didn't care. She couldn't believe this. She just couldn't believe it. 'You're taking me to your home?' she asked furiously. 'Without even telling me—asking me?'

'Which would you have preferred?' he asked frostily. 'To be told or to be asked?'

'You can turn this car round right now.' She glared at the implacable profile when he made no reply. 'Did you hear me, Jacques? I want to go back.'

'Of course you do, and so you will…later.' He turned to smile at her for one brief moment, his face a dark bronze in the night and his teeth flashing white. 'I only want to show you my home, Sandi—this is no crime, surely? I was finding the party a little…boring, but the

night is still young. We will worry my parents if we
return so soon. They will think we have had a disagreement.' The last words were said with a mocking note of
irony that was not lost on her.

'I don't care what they think,' she grated furiously. 'I
want to go back.'

'Don't be tedious.' His voice was lazy now, with a
shred of amusement that told her he was thoroughly enjoying her reaction. 'I will show you my home, we will
have a quiet cup of coffee like two civilised people and
perhaps even talk to each other without fighting.' He
glanced again at her angry face and sighed loudly. 'Or
maybe the last part is too ambitious?'

'You had no right to bring me here without asking
first,' she said tightly. 'No right at all.'

'I know.' The admission brought her head swinging
round, and she saw to her immense irritation that he was
smiling. 'But if I had asked you to accompany me to my
home this evening we both know exactly how you would
have replied.' He quirked his eyebrows sardonically. 'Do
we not?'

'You're impossible.' It was a *fait accompli*, and there
was nothing she could do but try and get out of this with
a little dignity.

'I know that too.' And there was a satisfaction in the
sensual French voice that made her want to hit him with
concentrated force in the place where it would hurt most.
As it was, and mainly due to the fact that the Ferrari
was travelling at a speed well over seventy miles per
hour on an unlit road in the middle of the night, she
contented herself with a loud 'huh', an icy lifting of her
head and a tight stiffening of her body.

Within a few minutes the road narrowed to little more
than a dirt track, and then they were passing through
wide-open wrought-iron gates into a large courtyard,
complete with duckpond and resident ducks, which was

lit up as brightly as day as soon as the car approached the building in front of them.

'My home.' Jacques brought the car to a halt in front of a large, sprawling thatched-roof farmhouse of mellow, honey-coloured stone that was partly covered with sweet-smelling roses and trailing ivy. Diamond-leaded windows and dark wood doors completed the air of timelessness about the place, and on the top storey the windows peeped from the overhanging thatch, with tiny balconies filled with a profusion of scarlet and mauve bougainvillea.

'Oh, it's lovely. It's really lovely.' She turned to him impulsively as the sound of the engine died away. 'What a wonderful place to live.'

'Yes, it is.' The dark eyes were watching her intently even as his mouth curved in a warm smile at her sincere praise of his home. 'Not exactly on the lines of the château but I like it.'

'Oh, it's much nicer than the château.' She spoke without thinking, only to blush a deep red as she realised what she had just said. 'Not that your parents' home isn't beautiful, of course—it is—but this is more homely. I mean—'

'I know what you mean.' He interrupted her rush of embarrassed words with a nod and a reproving finger on her lips. 'And I agree, utterly. Now, come and see inside.'

A few geese waddled across to their side, cackling a protest at having their slumber interrupted, but they were all bark and no bite, and although Sandi gave a little squeal at their approach they merely surveyed her through bright black eyes before gathering together again like noisy, gossiping old women. 'Ducks and geese?' she asked Jacques as they walked across to the old studded wooden door.

'They came with the place originally and then I found I liked having them around,' he said quietly. 'My lifestyle is not conducive to pets of any kind—sometimes I don't return home for days at a time—but they survive quite happily with the pond and the food I leave for them. I have a lady from the village a couple of miles away who comes in twice a week to clean and so on, but otherwise I fend for myself.'

'I see.' She didn't ask if it was business or pleasure that took him away from home so often; she didn't want to think what his answer might be.

She had somehow sensed what the interior of the farmhouse would look like, and she wasn't disappointed as her eyes took in the plain whitewashed walls filled with fine paintings, the beamed ceilings, the thick dull-rose-coloured carpet that stretched through all the downstairs rooms and the dark wood antique furniture. The kitchen was huge and beautifully restored in a way that kept its olde-worlde feel at the same time as providing all mod cons—even down to a large dishwasher hidden behind carved wooden doors.

Everything seemed to blend together into a perfect whole, accentuating the initial impression of quiet repose and serenity that the exterior of the house had given. She found that it disturbed her that Jacques had chosen such a place for his home. She would have preferred to find him living in a brash, modern bachelor pad or a luxurious apartment close to the city's nightlife, not in this peaceful old farmhouse with its air of tranquillity. And the fact that she was thinking such thoughts disturbed her even more. It was nothing to her where he lived—of course it wasn't. *He* was nothing to her.

'You are frowning again.'

'What?' She came out of her reverie to find him standing in the middle of the wide square hall, from which a twisting flight of stairs led upstairs, with his eyes tight on her face.

'You are frowning again,' he repeated grimly. 'I was going to ask you if you would like to see the bedrooms, but with such a fierce expression on your face perhaps that would not be a good idea?'

'I'm not frowning.' The protest was weak and they both knew it. 'Your home is lovely—enchanting—and I *would* like to see upstairs, if it isn't too much trouble.'

'What has displeased you?' He didn't move as she walked slowly to the foot of the stairs.

'Nothing—I told you.' She turned and faced him, keeping her voice bright and her face smiling.

'This home of mine does not fit in with what you expected of me?' he asked, with the devastating intuitiveness he had displayed more than once. 'You expected something less…harmonious?'

'Not at all.' She had never found it easy to lie deliberately, and it was all the more difficult with those piercing black eyes holding hers.

'I do not think you are telling the truth but, as you reminded me on another occasion, your thoughts are your own.' His voice was deep and quiet, and as he moved over to where she stood his hands went round her waist and he looked down at her. 'For such a tiny little thing you have a heart and mind of iron, do you not?'

'No—'

'But yes.' As she tried to slide out of his grasp his hands tightened. 'Iron.' His eyes were half-closed as he surveyed her, dark and gleaming in his tanned skin. 'When I first saw you at the door of Ann's flat I thought you were a fragile little slip of a girl—young and curiously innocent in spite of being, as I thought, my brother's wife. And then…then I learn you are the sister, the older sister, who is a force to be reckoned with in the advertising world, fierce and ambitious—'

'Jacques—' He ignored her interruption as though she had not spoken, his voice still low and deep but with an inflexion that made her weak.

'A career woman, hard and uncaring. But almost immediately that illusion is dispelled as the tigress defends her young—or in this case her sibling—and I learn that you sacrificed much for your sister when your parents died, at a time when no one would have blamed you for carrying on with your education, for putting yourself first.'

'Look, this is all history—shall we go upstairs? I mean… You—you were going to show me the rest of your home,' Sandi stammered weakly as the nearness of him began to do crazy things to her shaky composure.

'And then I see the ice maiden as you come with me to my parents' home—the cool English blonde who is disdainful and haughty and proud—'

'Jacques, *please*—'

'And just when I think I have made a mistake, that you are really as cold and remote as you wish me to think, I learn you have been married—married and widowed—that you have loved a man and agreed to commit your life to him—'

'*Jacques!*' Now she did jerk out of his hold, her face fiery.

'And at that moment I see another side of this slender, tiny will-o'-the-wisp who has exploded like a meteor into my life. A passionate, fiery, fierce side—but a side that is full of pain—'

'I don't want to continue this conversation, Jacques.' And now her voice did stop him and she stared, trembling and white, into his face. 'I will not discuss this with you.'

'And Jean-Pierre? Is he the type of man you would discuss such things with?' he asked tautly.

'Jean-Pierre?' For a second she didn't recognise the name, so completely had she forgotten the other man.

'That was still another Sandi, there in front of me tonight,' he said tightly. 'You laughed with him, looked at him in a way—' He stopped abruptly, taking a deep, hard breath before he spoke again. 'In a way I had not seen before.'

It hadn't been what he had intended to say, she felt sure, but she didn't pursue it.

'He was amusing, that's all.' She couldn't quite believe she was having this conversation. In the last three years she had made it her business to keep the male population very firmly at arm's length, and now somehow she was in the home of a man she had only met a few days ago, it was the middle of the night, and, worse, he expected her to bare her soul to him!

Panic hit her like a hard punch in the chest. It was obvious that she represented something of a challenge to him—that much he had made plain himself—but it was also crystal-clear that any lowering of her guard would result in a brief, no doubt torrid affair that he would be able to dismiss as easily as he would dismiss her when the time came for her to leave. He would return to Monique's eager arms and she—she would be crushed, devastated.

But that wouldn't happen; of course it wouldn't, she told herself as she surfaced from the mindless darkness that had briefly taken hold of her. Because she wouldn't let it happen. It was up to her. Most men would take what was on offer, so she wouldn't offer. It was as simple as that.

'Sandi—'

'You brought me here to show me your home.' Now she didn't have to engineer the coldness in her voice. 'So show me.'

He straightened as she spoke, reached across the space separating them and took her in his arms, kissing her fiercely and angrily and without restraint. And, like before, despite her fears and panic, her alarm at the thought of where it might lead, she couldn't help kissing him back. She wasn't sure what happened to her when he touched her—this mindless yearning that sprang up from the very depths of her hadn't been there even with Ian—but it was strong and potent and so sweet that she had no defence against it.

'You are beautiful—so, so beautiful…' His voice was husky and soft as he put her from him, and the trembling that had taken over her body almost seemed to have affected his too, before she blinked and the illusion faded away. 'And I want you very much. So if we go up-stairs…' He let his voice trickle away as she flushed hotly. 'You understand? So, this is not a good idea. But it is not good if we talk either, because then we fight—you know?'

Sandi gave him a level look, noticing the faint sparkle of amusement in the black eyes with a tight frown.

'Oh, that look again. *Ma chérie*, we will have to work on that. But for now? For now, we swim. I have to admit to a little subterfuge. I asked Ann if you liked the water and she assured me that you do, that you swim like a little golden fish. My pool is large and warm and very…nice.'

His eyebrows quirked at the last word but she still didn't speak. Their conversation had all but reduced her to a weeping mess and his lovemaking had her body quivering like an unset jelly, and now—now he was the cool, debonair, cynical man of the world again, and it hurt far more than it should. But it just proved what she had suspected—that she was nothing more than a mo-mentary pastime, a game, a distraction in his busy life.

They stared at each other for long electric moments without speaking, and then she forced her lips to respond to her mind. 'I don't have a costume.'

'This is no problem. I do not bother with such incon-venient things when I am at home,' he said softly.

'You don't—?' She remembered the dark bronze tex-ture of his magnificent body as he had got out of the pool earlier that day and her face flamed. 'Well, I do,' she said hotly.

'Oh, you English…' He shook his head, his voice wry. 'So conservative, so ashamed of what God has given you. But, as you stated before, I am not ashamed of what He has given me, am I, my reproving little siren? So, you will not be as nature intended, free and silky-smooth in the water? It is wonderful to swim without the constriction of clothes. You have never tried this?'

'No, I have not.' Her tone was vehement and brought a dark sardonic chuckle from the curved mouth.

'Then I am sure we can find you a large concealing T-shirt that will reach down to your knees. Will that do?'

'I'd really rather not,' she said stiffly.

'But you will.' He was absolutely still as he looked down at her, tiny and defiant, in front of him. 'I want you to. Please, Sandi?'

It was the tone in which he spoke rather than his words that crumpled her resistance. He had said she had shown many aspects of her personality, but now she was seeing another side to his—an appealing, almost little-boy-lost side—if a six-foot-plus giant of a man with muscles to match could ever be considered in that light. It was powerful persuasion and she had no defence against such subtleness.

'I—' She hesitated and then shrugged as casually as she could. 'Well, just a quick swim, then. I don't want Ann worrying. And I do want the T-shirt,' she added warningly as he took her hand with a mocking smile and walked her through the back of the house towards the garden.

'Stop worrying. You will have your T-shirt.' They passed through the large French doors of the breakfast room, which directly overlooked a stone patio with hanging baskets and a profusion of flowers in terracotta pots, and then she saw the still waters of the pool glittering under the night sky as Jacques flicked some switches that lit up the whole area with warm golden and pink lights.

The pool was a large one, kidney-shaped, with several tables and chairs and bright parasols at the far end. Behind it stretched a long, low stone building which had obviously once been a barn but was now divided into two rooms. The larger one served as a bar and dining area and the other one, reached through a door from the first, contained several small changing cubicles and showers, complete with a host of swimming costumes to fit every shape and size, numerous thick towelling robes and a large shelf that ran the whole length of the room and was filled to overflowing with different types of shampoo, shower gel, talcum powder and everything else a would-be swimmer could possibly desire.

'Oh...' She glanced up at Jacques as she stepped into the room.

'You see?' He waved his hand expansively at the costumes. 'Happy now? You can cover up that delectable body as much or as little as you wish. I will wait for you in the pool,' he added with mocking amusement. 'In case you think I may be tempted to peek.' She felt she ought to glare at him, but instead she found herself giving a weak smile that she immediately despised herself for. 'And if you feel the need for still further protection there are plenty of T-shirts in the cupboard at the end of the room,' he drawled lazily.

'I'm sure a swimming costume will be more than adequate,' she said primly, her face flushing still more as he gave a chuckle of deep, sardonic amusement before leaving her alone.

How on earth had she come to be here? She stood for a moment, gazing at her reflection in one of the long, narrow mirrors that were dotted about the room. The expensive cocktail dress gave her a poise that she had badly needed tonight, and now she was going to strip off both the dress and her inhibitions and make herself vulnerable. She must be mad. She *was* mad. She blinked at the slender, golden-haired girl in the mirror. She was playing with fire here, she really was—and yet she didn't seem able to drop the matches…

'Oh, hell.' She grimaced into the violet-blue eyes as panic clutched at her throat. 'What are you doing, Sandi Gosdon?'

Jacques was already in the water when she emerged, with slow, tentative steps, from the barn, his dark figure cutting through the water with a power that made the panic rise again. He was so masculine, so virile, so… So in control. As Ian had been in control. Cool, suave, cynical—but with that edge that made them both different from the normal run-of-the-mill man.

She met lots of men in her working life, some handsome, some interestingly attractive and some just plain creeps. But Jacques was different. He had a certain something that she couldn't put a name to but which held a potency that would affect any female from sixteen to sixty. Ian had had it too.

However much she despised the thought of the man she had married, loathed the fact that she had given him a right to her mind and her body, she had to acknowledge that he had been devastatingly attractive. But it had been skin-deep, only skin-deep. Underneath there had been the putrid stench of betrayal, dishonesty, trickery and a treachery that was unimaginable to the normal mind.

She didn't imagine that Jacques was capable of the sort of cruelty Ian had exacted, but… She stood in the shadows watching the powerful, steady strokes of his arms through the rippling water. But his values weren't hers. He had had women, lots of women; he lived a bachelor life that he revelled in, apparently with Monique's blessing.

Monique. She thought again of Jean-Pierre's words spoken so innocently a few hours before as they had watched the two entwined in each other's arms. 'They make a handsome couple, do they not? Whenever I see them together like this I am always surprised Monique does not quit the rat race of modelling and concentrate on the Challier fortune instead.' Well, one day she would. Sandi's mouth hardened. Of course she would. They were suited, after all.

The water was as silky-soft as Jacques had promised, and icy-cold on her overheated skin. She gave a little gasp as she slid carefully into the water and then a startled scream as Jacques's head popped up beside her in the next instant, pulling her against him and kissing her hard with wet lips. 'You were at the other end of the pool,' she accused him when his mouth left hers, and then all further thought left her as the feel of his body next to hers broadcast the fact that he, unlike her, wore nothing but his skin.

'You look wonderful.' His eyes were glittering black orbs in the dim pink and golden lights, his face dark and strangely alien. 'Why did you hesitate before you came in?'

'You were watching me?' She had thought he was absorbed in his swimming and hadn't noticed her in the shadow of the building as she had contemplated his dark body in the water.

'All the time,' he said huskily. 'I like to watch you.' His body was providing ample evidence to corroborate his words, and she was glad of the cooling effects of the water as her skin burnt hotly at the feel of his arousal against the smooth silk of her swimsuit.

And then he let her go, turning from her to swim with measured, powerful strokes down the pool, his dark head just visible above the water. 'Come on.' He stopped halfway and raised his arm as he called her. 'Show me how golden-haired temptresses swim.'

She had always been a strong, vigorous swimmer and now she put everything she had into the exercise, driving her body through the water as hard as she could and passing him with a fluid grace that made her honey-coloured limbs appear weightless. She was aware of him at her side as she continued to the far end of the pool, but didn't stop until she reached the smooth marble wall, where she flicked back her hair, which had worked loose from its high knot at the violent movement.

'I'm impressed.' He touched a wayward curl that had fallen across her forehead as he spoke. 'You swim like a man.'

'Is that supposed to be a compliment?' she asked with mock seriousness.

'Not a feminist too?' He shut his eyes for a second, and when he opened them they were bright with suppressed laughter. 'I really don't think I can take much more—my ego is in tatters as it is.'

'That'll be the day.' Now she was laughing openly, and for the next half an hour, as they swam and dived and enjoyed the freedom the water gave their bodies, she almost forgot that she had to be on her guard with this man—almost, but not quite.

'Coffee?' She was just beginning to shiver and he immediately noticed, pulling himself out of the pool with a supreme disregard for his nakedness and offering her his hand as he bent down to the water's edge.

She tried to concentrate her gaze on his upper torso but it was difficult. Her eyes seemed to have a will of their own and she suddenly felt like a naughty little schoolgirl who was spying on her elders. Ridiculous! She blinked at the thought. Absolutely ridiculous. But the sight of that big male body was doing something to her hormones that was creating a soft, moist warmth at the core of her being and sending her heartbeat haywire.

He pulled her out of the pool with effortless ease and then she was standing by him, her limbs shaking and quivering—and not just with the cold. 'The more I see of you, the more I want you,' he said softly. 'You have bewitched me, my cold little English blonde who turns to fire in my arms.'

She wanted to speak, to make some clever, cynical remark that would defuse the sudden electricity and make him turn from her, but her mouth was dry and her heart was pounding like a sledgehammer as she stared up into his face. She was vitally aware of every part of his big masculine body even though her eyes were fixed on his, and the knowledge of his male power over her soft femininity was both intimidating and thrilling, making her helplessly afraid and fascinated at the same time.

'I don't like the thought that other men have touched you, kissed you,' he continued huskily. 'You know that? I have never felt this way before and I don't like it, but I can do nothing about it.'

He meant Ian, she knew he meant Ian, and suddenly the name was a talisman to hold off this feeling that was utterly new to her, this fierce, deep, primitive desire that had a vibrant sexual awareness at its base, and something else—something she didn't recognise.

'You mean my husband?' she asked flatly, forcing the words out of her mouth.

'Your dead husband,' he corrected softly, his face hardening at her tone. 'He's dead, Sandi. Dead. Whatever you shared, however good it was, it is over.'

'I know that.' She swung away from him, the pain in her eyes at the terrible irony visible.

'No, no, I do not think you do.' He caught her arm, forcing her to turn and face him, his eyes black pools in the shadowed light. 'You cannot live on memories; do you not understand this yet? I am not suggesting that you forget this man—I know that would be impossible— but you have to accept that it is over—'

'*Leave me alone!*' She had thought she could use Ian as protection against Jacques's advances, but she realised now that she was not as strong as she had thought. The bitter humiliation, the doubt, the uncertainty of herself as a woman, the sense of abject failure—they all crowded in on her as though it were yesterday.

Ian had made her feel as though she was less than dust on the ground when he had taken her innocence and used her before leaving without a word. She had trusted him, loved him, and suddenly it had all been proved a monstrous illusion.

For weeks and months she had walked the streets at night, too tense and emotionally raw to sleep, looking at other women—ugly women, plain women—and wondering what they had that made them so different from her, how men could love them and feel such disgust for her. Because that was what Ian had done for her, she realised now, with a stab of pain that blinded her to Jacques's face. He had made her feel as though she was only fit to be despised, rejected, at best pitied. She was nothing. He had proved it. She was some sort of freak, unlovable and unloved.

'Sandi?'

'No!' Suddenly, Jacques faded and Ian stood there, and she reacted with all the hurt, pain and bitterness in her heart. She flew at him, pounding his chest with her fists as she wailed her agony to the moon, and he was still for one stunned moment, then moved swiftly, gathering her up against him as he trapped her wrists in one broad hand and lifted her off her feet with the other, carrying her quickly towards the house.

When she had felt her feet leave the ground the urge to bite and kick and destroy had left her in one blinding surge of tears, and now, as she was carried, she continued to cry, not in acceptable ladylike sobs, but in great convulsive bellows of grief and pain and rage that she had never allowed herself before. She raged against the unfairness of it all, against the agony that should never have been hers to endure. She hadn't done anything— she *hadn't*. She was innocent of it all and yet it was she who had paid the price. It wasn't *fair*...

'Drink this.' She wasn't aware that they had entered the house, but a moment or two after she had felt herself being laid on something soft she found that her hand was being raised and made to grasp a glass. Jacques's hold was still tight on her fingers as he raised it to her lips. 'Drink it, Sandi, all of it.'

The neat brandy hit the back of her throat like fire and she spluttered most of the first mouthful all over him, but after trying again, more slowly this time, she managed to swallow several mouthfuls of the raw alcohol before falling back against the soft upholstery of the sofa Jacques had placed her on, her eyes still streaming.

'Now stop crying—that's enough. Do you hear me, Sandi? This is enough.'

She didn't hear the actual words, but the tone of his voice and the feel of his warm flesh against hers as he put the glass down and took her hands in his caused the weeping to subside into hiccuping sobs and then soft, shaking shivers. 'That is it. It is finished—over. Now, you sit here, you do not move, and I will get a cup of coffee, yes?'

As he spoke she forced her swollen eyelids open, knowing that she must look as bad as she felt. She had never been able to cry prettily, not even tears of happiness. Her nose always went red and ran, her eyes swelled and her face turned blotchy. 'I— I'm sorry.' A late and lone sob caught at the words. 'I didn't mean to do this. I don't—'

'It is I who should apologise. I was stupid and clumsy and I spoke of things I had no right to speak of.'

'No.' She peered at him, a thread of surprise at the quiet, almost tender note in his voice piercing her misery. 'It was me. I don't know why I reacted like that. You must think I'm mad, crazy.'

'No, I do not think this.' He was kneeling in front of

her, his hands still holding hers. 'What I do think is that all that pain has been held in too long—far, far too long.'

'I—' The sympathy was too much, and as her eyes swam with tears again he stood up briskly, his voice firmer now.

'Coffee. This will make you feel better.'

With Jacques standing as he was, it was impossible for her to concentrate on anything other than his body, and now she surprised them both as she gave a weak smile, her face still wet with tears. 'Are you going to put anything on first?' she asked shakily. 'If you're handling hot liquid?'

'I see your point.' He smiled, a dark, rueful smile directed against himself, and it was in that moment that something in her leapt and sprang into life, but she didn't question what. 'The big seduction scene did not go quite according to plan, did it?' he said mockingly. 'I do not usually have the effect of reducing women to tears when I undress.'

'I'm sure you don't.' The dry humour was restoring her equilibrium, but with it the knowledge that she had just made the most terrible fool of herself began to gather steam. She shut her eyes tight against the sight of him and leant back against the sofa, giving a little shiver that came from the turmoil within her rather than the cool air.

'You are cold.' She heard him move away as he spoke, his bare feet light on the thick carpet, and when in the next instant she found herself enveloped in something soft and warm she still didn't open her eyes.

'Thank you.'

'And now I will get the coffee.'

He was still standing in front of her—she could feel it—and when the silence continued she opened her eyes warily to see him looking down at her with a strange expression on his dark face as she lay curled up in the folds of a blanket.

'It is not a crime to show your feelings, Sandi—you understand this?'

'I know.' She wished to goodness that he would put some *clothes* on, she thought frantically as he remained in front of her. She knew the French had few inhibitions, that *au naturel* was commonplace on the beaches of France, but right now his total disregard for his nakedness was causing her severe breathing problems—and he wanted a conversation about feelings?

'No, you do not know this. You are like the oyster that is tightly closed against the sea of life, holding onto its pearl at all costs.'

'And what happens when the oyster is forced to let go of its pearl?' she asked as coolly as her racing emotions would allow. 'It loses everything.'

'And this is what you feel?' he asked slowly. 'That if you open up, start to live again, you will lose everything for the second time?'

He didn't understand—she knew he didn't understand—but in spite of that he was so near the mark that she stared at him with huge violet-blue eyes opened wide in her tear-stained face. 'Jacques—' She shook her head slowly as her eyes wavered and then fell from his. 'I really can't talk about this right now—I just can't.'

Was he really concerned about the way she was feeling for her sake, or was it the ultimate goal of getting her into his bed that was prompting all this solicitude? she asked herself faintly. He had made no secret of what he was, how he ran his life and more especially his love-life.

Just an hour or so ago, when they had arrived at the farmhouse, he had mentioned the fact that he was often away for days at a time, and irrespective of whether it was because of business or something of a more personal nature he couldn't have made it more clear that a permanent relationship was out of the question. Some women could enjoy such a man, take the time they had together and savour it to the full and then move on when the time came for a parting of the ways with a kiss and a hug.

But she wasn't like that. She never had been. She couldn't envisage ever opening up her mind and her body to anyone again, but if she did ever come to such a point it would have to be with a man who would commit himself to her totally.

She felt him move silently out of the room and when she raised her head she felt almost bereft for a moment. But that will pass, she told herself fiercely. It will.

When he brought in the tray of coffee a few minutes later he was clothed in tight black jeans, his upper torso and feet bare, and although her senses still gave a hard kick at the sight of his muscled, hair-roughened chest and broad, masculine shoulders it wasn't so bad as having all of that magnificent body on display. He didn't speak until he handed her the coffee, but she had felt his eyes intent on her wan face as soon as he'd entered the room.

'Sugar?' His flesh was warm as it touched hers, and she felt the contact with a jolt.

'Two, please.'

He seated himself next to her when he had poured his own cup and as she went to move her legs to the floor he caught at them, his hand resting on top of the blanket. 'No, don't move; it is all right.'

His hand remained on her upper leg, and although the soft cloth was between his flesh and her body she felt the contact begin to burn like fire. She had expected further questioning, or maybe a follow-up on the seduction scene he himself had mentioned earlier, but as they sat in the quiet, beautiful room in the soft, dim light he said nothing, seemingly lost in his own thoughts as he drank the coffee.

She glanced at him once or twice from under her lashes. His hard profile was just a foot or so away, and

she found it gave her pleasure to watch him. After the
swim his hair was ruffled across his forehead in unruly
curls that were as black as jet, and his dark lashes and
hard jaw, where the stubble was already showing black
under the skin, were curiously sensuous. She wished
things could have been different. She wished she had
met him years ago, before Ian, when she had still had
the ability to believe in love and happy ever after—

The dangerousness of her thoughts suddenly brought
her up sharp, the breath catching in her throat. What was
she thinking? What *was* she thinking? It didn't matter
when she might have met him—he would still have been
the same. He wasn't a slippers-by-the-fire man any more
than Ian had been. How many times did she have to
learn the same lesson before it sank in?

Her thoughts made her swing her feet to the floor
abruptly, dislodging his hand, and then she stood up, still
keeping the blanket swathed about her.

'I'll go and change now, if that's all right?'

'Of course.' He rose too, his voice cool, but then, as
he looked down at her, his eyes crinkled in a smile. 'You
look remarkably like a small, worried child, standing
there wrapped in that thing,' he said mildly.

'Do I?' She didn't like the simile; she didn't like it at
all. She couldn't imagine any man ever saying that to
Monique. The tall redhead would look every inch a
woman no matter how much or how little of her slim,
perfect body was hidden.

'Sandi…' And then his voice changed, thickened, and
he drew her against him, his eyes soft. 'Are you warm
now?'

'Yes…' Warm? She was on fire, she thought helplessly as she felt his hands move under the folds of the
blanket and slide down her body in a slow caress that
brought an immediate languorous warmth snaking
through her limbs. She had been waiting for this. The

thought hit her like a small electric shock. Waiting for it, wanting it—

'I don't know what it is about you that makes me want you so much,' he muttered thickly. 'Oh, Sandi…'

His mouth drove down on hers and at that point all coherent thought stopped. She felt the blanket slide to the floor but hardly registered the fact, although it meant that she was pressed against him in nothing more than a brief black cut-away swimming costume which, in spite of its lack of material, had been the only garment she'd been able to find that went even a little way towards covering her body.

But now that didn't matter—nothing mattered but the mindless pleasure she was experiencing as his powerful body subdued all resistance. The kiss was deep and slow as he invaded the tender, secret places of her half-open mouth, his tongue devastatingly sensuous, and as his hands continued to wander over her skin she felt her breasts fill and harden, their peaks becoming rock-hard when his fingers paused in their exploration of her quivering softness.

'I cannot believe what you do to me…' The sultry French accent added to the magic of what was happening to her. 'You are incredible, incredible…'

His kisses were burning her now as he moved from her mouth to her throat, her ears and then lower, to where the swell of her breasts was straining against the thin fabric of the costume. She knew the thin straps had been pulled down over her shoulders, but still the shock as his lips branded the heavy fullness of her breasts was fierce.

She hadn't known she could feel like this—that the combination of hard male strength and tender lovemaking could reduce her to a quivering, helpless mass of sheer sensation. She had heard of such things happening to other women, read about the experience second-hand in romantic novels and books, but it was real, *real*…

Her hands were laced in his hair now, and as he raised his head again she knew she was murmuring little, soft, incoherent pleas against his lips. But she could no more control her mind than her body. She was on fire, on fire, and she had no idea how it had all come about.

'Sandi?' For a moment she couldn't believe that he had moved her gently from him to arm's length, but as she opened dazed blue eyes and saw him looking down at her she was quite unable to speak. 'One more moment and I shan't be able to stop. You understand what I am saying? Whether you want me to or not I shall have you, but it will be *me*, Jacques Challier, not some shadow that you have conjured out of your mind. Listen to me, Sandi…'

Listen to him? She stood swaying, her skin flushed a deep, warm pink, as she tried to make sense of what he was saying.

'I will not be used as a substitute. This I will not allow.' A substitute? she thought faintly. What on earth was he talking about? 'When I have you—and I *will* have you—it will be because you want me as badly as I want you. Whatever you shared with your husband, however much you loved him, he will not be a spectre at our union. I will not have it.'

'I—' She tried to speak, to communicate in some way, but both her mind and body seemed transfixed and her eyes fell from his as she tried to focus her thoughts.

'*Look at me.*' His voice was harsh now, in direct contrast to the softness of before. 'Look at *me*. I am alive. I am flesh and blood—feel.' He took one of her limp hands and banged it against his chest. 'You see?'

'Don't.' She shrank from him, from the anger in his face.

'I want you, Sandi.' His voice was tight and strained. 'I want you so badly I can taste it, but not at the cost of my self-respect.'

He took her arm now, leading her from the room and

through to the grounds at the back of the house without speaking. He opened the door of the changing room, almost thrust her inside and turned to leave.

'Jacques?' She was stunned, bewildered at the sudden turn events had taken.

'Get dressed, Sandi.' His voice was harsh and cold now, his self-control visible in the steely tightness of his jaw and the way he held his big, hard body rigid and taut. 'I'll wait in the car.'

And then he left her, slamming the door behind him with a viciousness which indicated that the self-control was only just holding out.

CHAPTER SEVEN

'YOU'RE leaving today? But why?'

Sandi reached across the small table on their suite's balcony and took Ann's hands in her own as her sister stared at her, her face and voice heavy with disappointment. 'I need to get back to work, Ann,' she said quietly. 'They have been very good about all this, but it's been nearly three weeks now, and there are a hundred people who would be only too pleased to step into my shoes— you know how things are in the advertising world. You are happy here, settled, and that's all I wanted to be sure about before I left. There's no need for me to stay here now.'

'I'll miss you.' Ann looked at her, her voice flat. 'It won't be the same with you gone.'

'But you knew I couldn't stay.' Sandi squeezed her sister's hands. 'That was never on the cards, was it? You get on so well with Arianne and Odile, besides which it won't be two minutes before I'm back to see my nephew or niece.'

'Yes, I know.' Ann sighed and looked down at the table on which the remains of their breakfast were sitting. 'And I do appreciate you coming over here with me instead of going straight back to America—it helped enormously.'

Not me, Sandi thought wryly with silent pain. It hasn't helped me at all.

When Jacques had brought her back to the château the night before she had expected him to come in, but he had merely left the car to open her door and see her across the threshold before turning to leave. 'Where are you going?' Her voice had been high with surprise as she had spoken to his departing back.

'Home.' He had turned halfway to the car as she had stood in the doorway watching him. 'My home.'

'But—' He wasn't going to leave like this, was he? she thought miserably. Without a word being exchanged? Without things being sorted? 'I thought—' She stopped again. The glittering black eyes weren't conducive to conversation.

'You thought what?' he asked as he moved to stand in front of her, his great height dwarfing her petiteness. 'You thought I would beg, is that it?'

'Beg?' She reared up in surprise and distaste. 'I don't know what you mean.'

'Do you not?' He was looking at her intently, his eyes narrowed and dark in the shadows of his tanned face as he stood with his back to the moonlight. 'Well, perhaps you do and perhaps you do not, my English rose, but it really doesn't matter one way or the other. You have made it perfectly clear how you feel and, unlike many others of my sex, I have never indulged in the strange fancy of banging my head against a brick wall.'

'Banging your head...?' She was still staring at him in bewilderment as he gave a harsh sigh of deep exasperation then leant forward and kissed her—a hard, bruising kiss that spoke of anger and fury—seconds before he turned from her and strode to his car. The engine started immediately, and in almost same instant the Ferrari swung in a violent semi-circle to roar off down the drive in a flurry of screaming tyres and silver metal, leaving her small and forlorn on the doorstep.

Those feelings were soon replaced by a multitude of others as she got ready for bed in the luxurious sitting room to avoid waking Ann, who was fast asleep in the bedroom. Bewilderment, rage, bitterness, fury, pain, resentment... The list was endless. She methodically showered and brushed her teeth in the lovely bathroom a few minutes later, narrowing her eyes at her reflection in the mirror over the sink. He was angry with her, that much was obvious, and why? Because she hadn't slept with him. It was as simple as that. And why hadn't she slept with him? She rinsed the toothpaste away and then sipped at a glass of water as she looked into the large violet-blue eyes in the mirror. Because he had stopped making love to her.

She shut her eyes, but when she opened them again the reproachful look was still there. After all she had said, all her high intentions, that was what it boiled down to. He could have had her back there at his house and she wouldn't have stopped him, and he had known that—he had. So, if that was the case, how dared he blame her for the ugly end to the evening?

She glared ferociously into the mirror, her brow wrinkling. *He* had stopped, *he* had started talking about substitutes and goodness knew what, and then he had blamed her for it all, acting as though she were a tease, as though she expected him to beg. She hadn't realised how much that word—'beg'—rankled until he had left. How dared he? How *dared* he act like that?

Then later, as she lay curled up in bed with Ann's steady, rhythmic breathing mocking her wakefulness, the tears came. Hot, scalding tears that burnt her face and stung her eyes. And much much later, as dawn began to make its way across the window in a pink-grey glow, she realised she had to leave this place, get as far away from Jacques Challier as possible. Immediately.

'How are you getting back?'

She came back to the present with a jolt and forced herself to smile at Ann as she replied as lightly as she could. 'By plane. It's quicker and less time-consuming. I've got a taxi coming at eleven to pick me up.'

'As organised as ever.' Ann glanced over the rolling lawns and tree-filled grounds as she spoke.

'I've always had to be, haven't I?' There was a slight

touch of bitterness in the words. Since their parents had died, and she had taken on the role of both mother and father to her younger sister, all the onus had been on her to guide and direct their lives. And although she hadn't minded that, recognising that Ann's placid, quiet nature wasn't able to cope with any big decisions, the responsibility had been enormous at times. And after Ian's death it had been worse, somehow—infinitely worse—because she had doubted her ability to make even the simplest decision for a time, her self-esteem and faith in herself at rock-bottom.

'Are you going straight back to the States?' Ann now asked as she turned to look at her again, her hands on the mound of her stomach and the expression on her face one of quiet repose. 'I thought if you went back to England first you could settle the matter of the flat and—'

'No, sorry; I'm going straight home.' Sandi straightened as she spoke. She needed to get as far away as she could, and England wasn't far enough. Not that she thought Jacques would come after her. Of course he wouldn't—he had made it perfectly clear last night exactly what he thought of her—but nevertheless...

She just wanted to get back to her small apartment, her little car and her job. Normality. Safety. Everything that she suddenly desperately needed. 'I brought everything with me to France so there's no reason to go to England—it would be a waste of money. You only need to settle the matter of the flat by phone, anyway—you always pay a month in advance so there'll be no problems, Ann.'

'No, I guess not.' Ann smiled at her suddenly. 'And it's about time I started doing a few things on my own initiative, isn't it? Especially with junior on the way. Emile always said I would be capable of far more than I realised if I just pushed myself a little.'

'He was right.' Sandi stood up and moved round the

small table to give her sister a hug. 'But don't push yourself too much in your condition,' she added wryly. 'Just take it nice and easy and everything will work out fine.' She suddenly felt as if one great weight had been lifted off her mind. If Ann could begin to think along those lines it boded nothing but good for the future and her child.

The other great weight, however, remained firmly in place, and she wrinkled her eyes against the image of Jacques Challier which confronted her the whole time she packed.

The taxi drew into the Challier estate on the dot of eleven, and Sandi left the château amid a host of hugs and kisses from Ann, Arianne and Odile, Claude and André having already left for the vineyards. Anna-Marie, Suzanne and Antoinette were particularly loath to let their new-found friend go, each little girl insisting on a long cuddle and kiss and making her promise that she would come back soon and see them.

'I shall come back and see all of you—and your new cousin when it's born,' Sandi assured them as she climbed into the taxi, her eyes bright with unshed tears as the three infants stood in a row by the door, their dark curls and huge brown eyes making them appear angelic. As their mother translated her words to them they all nodded with gusto, and then the taxi was drawing away. After waving through the back window until she could see them no more she leant back against the upholstered seat, swamped by a wave of misery.

She was confused, bewildered and unhappy, and somewhere in the back of her mind she felt that she had been dreadfully unfair to Jacques—although she wasn't sure how. He knew she wasn't game for a little light affair—she couldn't have made it more obvious from minute one—and she had been honest with him—almost. He had jumped to the conclusion that she was still in love with Ian, and although admittedly she had gone along with the supposition the end result would still have been the same even if she had told him the whole truth. Which she couldn't have done.

She twisted in the seat as she hugged her waist tight, the pain engendered by her thoughts almost physical. She just couldn't have done. The humiliation of that time, the terrible abasement and degradation she had felt—she couldn't expose them to the light of day for anyone, ever. She couldn't.

Once back in America, Sandi settled into the daily panic and drama of advertising life as though she had never been away, although even in the midst of the worst pandemonium and bedlam she was conscious of a deep, hard ache in her chest that just wouldn't go away. She worked late every night, only leaving the offices when she was ready to drop with exhaustion, knowing that that was the only way sleep could be guaranteed.

Even so, when she awoke each morning as soon as it grew light she was aware that she hadn't slept well.

But she was happy. She told herself so every morning without fail when she glared fiercely at her reflection in the mirror as she got ready for work. Happy, and contented with the way her life was going. *She was.* The blue-eyed reflection didn't argue but the violet gaze was always misted with tears when she eventually turned away.

She phoned Ann three or four times a week and was more reassured each time she spoke to her sister that she was going to be all right. So—everything in the garden was lovely. Of course it was.

She had been back in the States for four weeks when she opened an envelope one morning in order to process some shots from a top fashion show the day before and Monique's cool, unsmiling face stared back at her from the catwalk. She sat staring at the beautiful redhead for a full minute before she raised her head and buzzed the

main office for Andy, the young assistant she had sent
with the photographer for that particular shoot. 'Andy?
That fashion show yesterday...'

'Yes?' He was immediately by her desk. 'Is anything
wrong? They're doing something with those models
each day this week for the Zac promotion, so if you
don't like these shots—'

'No, no—the photographs are fine,' she answered absently. 'You say the girls are here for the week—all of
them?'

'That's right.' He stared at her, puzzled.

'OK, thanks, Andy.' She sat staring at the prints for
a full minute more before bundling them together and
sending them to one of her co-executives to process. She
didn't feel she could be unbiased. She was determined
that personal feelings wouldn't interfere with her professional judgement, but somehow she felt that the redhead had invaded her world deliberately.

She was still thinking about the photographs when she
arrived home that evening, parking her neat little car in
the underground car park before walking into the foyer
of her apartment block.

'Miss Gosdon?' The uniformed security man called
her as she prepared to enter the lift without looking to
left or right, her mind a million miles away. 'This gen-
tleman has been waiting to see you for the last three
hours.'

Whether it was the fact that Monique's appearance in
America was still firmly in the forefront of her mind or
that she had been thinking about Jacques Challier—con-
sciously and subconsciously—for every minute of the
day and night since she had left France she didn't know,
but as she turned and saw him standing to one side of a
large coffee-table littered with magazines and empty paper cups she found that she wasn't as surprised as she
should have been.

'*Bonjour*, Sandi.' The voice was deep and silky, with

that little edge she remembered. Oh, how she remembered it, she thought shakily as she looked into the hard, dark face with a feeling of impending doom.

He looked wonderful—but then of course he would, she thought bitterly. He was obviously accompanying Monique on her modelling assignment and enjoying every moment, if that cool, confident smile was anything to go by. His personality was powerful enough as it was, but the fact that his world was clearly right on course infuriated her still more because she felt that hers, for whatever reason, was most definitely not.

'Jacques? What a nice surprise.' She forced herself to walk forward with her hand outstretched and her voice polite, and she stitched a smile onto her face with tremendous effort. 'What brings you to this neck of the woods?'

'Business.' He looked down at her as she reached him and his eyes were warm. 'They say all good things come to those who wait, and have I been waiting!' He ignored her outstretched hand, gathering her into his arms and kissing her very thoroughly for one long, heart-stopping moment before letting her go. 'Where have you been? It's after nine.'

'Working.' She was hanging onto her composure by the skin of her teeth, but the interested face of the security man kept her voice bland and her face pleasant. 'You should have let me know you were coming. I'd have told you I was busy and bound to be delayed.'

'Perhaps that is why I didn't let you know,' he said drily.

And *perhaps* she was being fitted in between Monique's modelling assignments? she thought tightly. He was transparent; he really was. Didn't he think she could put two and two together and make four? She wouldn't have minded if he'd called round merely in the role of Ann's brother-in-law while he was in America, but that kiss had suggested that he wanted far more than a brotherly welcome.

'How long are you here for?' she asked carefully as she began to walk to the lift with him at her side.

'How long do you want me to stay?' he countered swiftly, with a nod and a smile at the security guard as the doors closed.

'Jacques—' She stopped abruptly and took a hold of her temper, which had risen to boiling point when really she had no right to be annoyed. He was a free agent— he had never pretended to be anything else—and she had nothing to blame him for. All she had to do was be pleasant for an hour or two until he left, no doubt to meet Monique, and treat him courteously while keeping him very firmly at arm's length. It was up to her to set the tone. It was simple, really. 'Just answer the question.' She softened the words with a cool but not unfriendly smile.

'I am here for five days, Sandi.' He looked down at her, his dark face unreadable. Just the amount of time the modelling assignment for Zac Fashions was going to last, she thought silently. She should have known.

He was standing leaning against the side of the lift now as he watched her through dark, narrowed eyes, his hands thrust in the pockets of his fashionable loose-cut trousers and his open-necked shirt displaying the tanned, hard line of his throat.

'And what exactly is the business that brings you all the way to New York?' she asked carefully as the lift doors glided open at her floor, displaying a quiet, wide corridor with ankle-deep carpeting and pale cream linen walls.

'"Exactly"?' His tone mocked her words and he didn't answer immediately, stepping out of the lift and glancing round as he nodded slowly. 'This is very chic. I like this.'

OK, so you like it, she thought snappily as she indicated a door halfway down the corridor with a wave of her hand, but just answer the question, will you? Smooth-talking Frenchman or no, he was going to have a job to explain this one.

'I am here to iron out the details on a new contract with one of our wine merchants that was recently taken over,' he said lazily as they walked side by side to her front door. 'I could have accomplished this by phone but it is always better to do business face to face in these circumstances, besides which…' he glanced down at her as she fitted her key into the lock, but she missed the look on his face as she opened the door '…I wanted a few days away from the vineyards and America seemed the perfect place.'

Well, he hadn't exactly lied—she had to give him that, she thought silently as she waved him into her apartment. She didn't doubt for a moment that the explanation of the contract with one of his merchants was true, but he hadn't explained why America was 'the perfect place'.

Monique's beautiful cat-like face rose up in front of her, and her smile was grim as she followed him into the large, comfortable sitting room. She had given him his chance to come clean and if he wanted to play it close to his chest then she was blowed if she was going to force the issue. But she was grateful to the powers that be that she had seen those photographs this afternoon, otherwise she might have thought— She gave a mental shake of her head at her own naïvety. She might have thought he had come all that way to see her.

The knowledge that she could still be such a fool, after all that had happened, made her mouth tight and her eyes strained as she watched him glance round her home. The apartment had already been furnished to a high standard when she had moved in, but although the decor was in neutral, pale shades of cream and beige she had added nothing of herself to make it more personal.

The home she had shared with Ian had been vivid and vibrant, her love of fabric and eye for colour creating a warm oasis that had been both pleasant to live in and beautiful to behold. But when her marriage had exploded in her face something within her had died. She wasn't aware that she had purposely stifled the desire to make any sort of nest, but Jacques, as he glanced around the immaculate, beautiful and sober surroundings, wondered at the puritanical austerity.

'The apartment was furnished when I came.' She was immediately annoyed with herself for feeling the need to explain anything to him, but as he had turned to stare at her she had sensed something in his attitude that she didn't like, almost a kind of pity. 'I find it restful.'

'Yes.' He nodded slowly. 'It is tranquil after all the hurly-burly outside, yes?'

'Exactly.' Her cheeks were burning now—she could feel it—and as she walked through to the small kitchen she found that her stomach was clenched in one giant knot. Why couldn't he leave her alone? She didn't want him here—she didn't. Poking about with those piercing, knowing eyes. Why had he come anyway? Surely Monique was enough for any man to cope with?

'Coffee?' She called the question over her shoulder through to the sitting room, but his voice sounded deep and lazy just behind her in the doorway.

'I have had enough coffee in the last three hours to last me for some time. But please, if you would like one...?'

'A glass of wine, then? Or maybe something stronger?' She nerved herself to turn and face him as she spoke, but was still shocked into immobility for a brief moment at the sight of him, big and dark and sardonic, in her small home. He had brought something with him, quite what she didn't know, but it was turning the air electric and creating a whole horde of tumultuous emotions inside her, not one of which she wanted to examine.

'Wine would be lovely.' He watched her as she turned to the fridge and extracted a bottle from the bottom shelf. 'Have you eaten?' he asked casually as she reached for two glasses from the small cupboard above the long, wide breakfast bar.

'Eaten?' She stared at him as though he had just spoken in a foreign language instead of very acceptable accented English.

'Eaten.' He repeated the word with a patience that bordered on the insulting. 'You know? With a knife and fork, a spoon, your fingers. Transferring food to your mouth—'

'I know what eating means, thank you.' She glared at him and was slightly taken aback when he returned the glare.

'Then could you just say yes or no?' he asked tightly. 'You're as jumpy as a kitten, for crying out loud. What do you think I am going to do? Leap on you and take you here and now on the kitchen floor?'

'Don't be—'

'No, don't you dare use that word again,' he interrupted angrily. '*Ridiculous.* I had never been called ridiculous in my life until I met you, but you know something? You make me feel ridiculous,' he said furiously. 'Ridiculous for bothering to come here, for caring about how you are getting on, for wanting to see you. I did not, for one moment, expect to be received with open arms, but I did expect a little courtesy—'

'I've been courteous!' She was stung into a denial that was more shrill than she would have liked. 'I've invited you in, haven't I?'

'Oh, thank you—thank you so much,' he drawled sarcastically, his voice icy. 'The fact that you are a walking block of stone on two legs is supposed to make me feel good, is that it?'

'I didn't know I was expected to make you feel good,' she said coldly as her heart pounded so hard that she was sure he must hear it. He had Monique for that, surely? she thought bitterly.

'No?' She was suddenly afraid of the coiled tension evident in every line of his big body as he glared at her, his eyes dark and glittering in his angry face. 'Well, perhaps it is up to me to make us both feel good, yes? A little therapeutic lovemaking, maybe?'

She opened her lips to fire back a reply but he moved in the same instant to take her mouth in a fierce, ruthless kiss that spoke of pure, undiluted rage and frustration. She struggled, using her hands and feet as she fought, but he didn't even notice as he moulded her soft shape into the hard lines of his and kept his mouth fixed on hers. And then, in spite of herself, it was happening again. That soft, irresistible melting of her will and her body to his.

One minute she was fighting him with every ounce of her strength, and then she was moving almost wantonly against him, her eyes closed, her face entranced and her body speaking eloquently of her need. His hands were moving all over her body and she wanted them to—wanted him to touch her intimately, fully, to explore every part of her.

'That is enough therapy for now.' She couldn't believe he was moving her from him again—*again*. As her eyes opened dazedly to fix on the hard, ruthless face in front of her she was quite unable to speak, and such was her humiliation and shame that it blinded her to the way his hands were shaking as he deftly adjusted her clothing. 'Now, we will drink a glass of wine and consider which restaurant I am taking you to tonight, yes?'

'No.' She stared at him in disbelief. He didn't really think she was going on a date with him, did he? After the way he'd just behaved, and with Monique lurking somewhere in the background like a tall and very elegant lady vampire? And after rejecting her for the second time? 'I wouldn't go out with you if you were the last man on earth,' she said hotly.

'A little extreme, but I do get the message.' He smiled, apparently not in the least put out. 'In that case we will eat here. I will arrange to have food brought in.'

'I am not spending the evening with you—'

'Oh, but you are, my sweet little English icicle,' he said silkily, his mouth hardening. 'And there is no need to be so incensed because you respond so beautifully to me. It is not a crime to enjoy the pleasures of love, I do assure you. And one day, when I know it is *my* body you are seeing and enjoying and *my* voice you are hearing, I shall not stop. You understand?'

No—no, she didn't understand, she thought helplessly as she glared back at him, but it was clear that he had no intention of leaving, and, short of calling Arthur, the security man, and having him evicted from her apartment, she really didn't know how she could make him leave. And even that wouldn't work, she acknowledged weakly. She doubted if anyone had ever made Jacques Challier do something he didn't want to do in the whole of his life, and poor old Arthur, with his rotund stomach and bad back, would be no match for the younger man.

'You're a pig and a bully,' she said a little desperately.

'And you are being very childish.' He glanced over her with soft mockery, his temper and aplomb remarkably restored after his lovemaking. 'I really don't know whether to smack you or soothe you.'

'You'd better not try either,' she said hastily.

'Don't tempt me, Sandi, and never throw a challenge like that to a man who has just behaved in a chivalrous fashion quite new to him and at great personal cost,' he said with sardonic coolness. 'Now, where is your telephone directory? I will arrange for a quantity of dishes to be brought here. Would you prefer Chinese, Italian, Indian—?'

'No.' As he opened his mouth to speak again she went on hastily, 'And I'm not being awkward, really. I'll cook us something if you insist on staying; your family *are* looking after Ann, after all.'

'Not the most gracious invitation I've ever received,' he said drily, 'but it's a deal. And while you're organising the food I will go and get some decent wine.' He had picked up the bottle of cheap plonk she'd had in the fridge and eyed it with something akin to horror as he had spoken. 'Red or white?'

'White…or red. Either. I don't mind.' She was flustered and stammering, and she could have kicked herself for letting him affect her the way he did. She didn't like the way he made her feel, but she couldn't do anything about it either. Every nerve in her body was sensitised to the point where it was raw and painful, and the flutters of excitement in her stomach and the thudding of her heart were further evidence of her body's betrayal.

Amazingly, in view of the state of her nerves, the soufflé was cooked to perfection, as were the accompanying vegetables. The wine that Jacques had chosen was mellow and fruity and potent, and although the dessert was nothing more exciting than fruit crumble it was, nevertheless, delicious.

She was overwhelmingly thankful that she had gone shopping the night before. Living on his own as he did, Jacques would surely appreciate that her rustling up such a meal at short notice meant that she was both organised and capable as well as independent, she thought hopefully. All reinforcing her image as successful businesswoman? The fact that the night before the fridge had harboured nothing more exciting than two tomatoes and a lump of stale cheese was incidental.

'How did I know you'd cook like an angel?' he asked softly as she prepared to serve him the last portion of the fruit crumble at his request—his third serving.

'You didn't,' she said flatly, placing the bowl in front of him along with the jug of fresh cream.

'Oh, but I did.' He eyed her consideringly. 'I really did. Perhaps it's something to do with that old adage about the way to man's heart being through his stomach?'

'I think they got the part of the anatomy wrong,' she said drily. 'Most of the men I know have their sights set a little lower.'

'I'm shocked.' He laughed at her, his eyes mocking and soft as they wandered over her flushed face.

'Now, that I do doubt,' she said with cryptic wryness. 'I don't think there is much that would shock you, Jacques Challier.' It must have been the wine that had loosened her tongue, she thought a second later as she wrenched her eyes from his bright gaze and drank the last of the richly rounded liquid from her glass.

'In this you are right.' She glanced up to see a strange expression darken the handsome face. 'Not now, at least. But I think it is not good to be…what is the word? Unshockable? Can you say that in English?'

'You just did.' She smiled at him but he didn't return the smile. Instead he leant forward, taking her hands in his as he stared into her face.

'I want to tell you something, Sandi,' he said flatly. 'It may help you to understand the sort of man I am, perhaps to comprehend what you cannot condone.'

'I don't think—'

He stopped her, one hand lifting to her mouth as he placed a quiet finger on her lips. 'Please. You are Ann's sister and a member of my family now whether you like it or not, and I do not think this antagonism between us will be good for the niece or nephew we share.'

Antagonism? she asked herself wryly. Was it antagonism that caused her to melt at his touch? She wished it were—oh, she did. Antagonism she could have coped with, but this sexual attraction that seemed to spring to life every time she saw him—that was something alto-gether more dangerous.

'When I was younger—much, much younger,' he added with a wry smile, 'I was engaged to be married for a time.' She felt the shock of his words register right down to her toes, but forced herself to remain absolutely still. 'The lady in question was my age—I had met her in my first year at university and we were together every moment from that time.'

'Every moment?' she asked carefully, and he let go of her hands and moved to stand with his back to her as he gazed out of the window at the New York skyline.

'Figuratively speaking,' he said flatly. 'Jacqueline was a free spirit, but by unspoken mutual consent neither of us took other partners.'

'Oh.' It didn't matter—of course it didn't matter, she told herself frantically. He was nothing to her, was he? She didn't even understand why he was telling her this.

'We graduated on the same day, found a flat in Paris, and with money both my parents and hers had loaned us started our own business—a little bistro that did ex-tremely well. After a couple of months we set the wed-ding date for the beginning of November, when business would be slacker, and on the thirteenth of October she was found dead in the street in an area well-known for its drug addicts and pushers.'

'Drugs?' Sandi stared at his broad back in horror.

'Apparently she had started on the mild sort when she was at university,' he said flatly, his voice expression-less. 'The police discovered she had moved to heroin only a few weeks before her death. The fact that the business was doing so well had enabled her to try some-thing more expensive.

'Her parents were devastated. She was an only child, and, perhaps naturally in the circumstances, they blamed me. They could not believe I hadn't known what she was doing. My own parents were more understanding, but then I was alive—they had not lost their child.'

'But—' She stopped abruptly. 'There weren't any signs?' she asked helplessly, wishing he would turn round so that she could see his face.

'None that I noticed. The final irony was that it was our best friend—a man I had gone through university with and regarded as a brother—who had been the pusher from the start. His guilt at her death led him to make a full confession to the police after they picked him up for another offence. He had, it seems, unknowingly sold Jacqueline a bad fix. His supplier had mixed the heroin with other substances. I understand more than five people died from that one batch.

'But the thing is...' he turned to face her now, and his face was strange in its lack of expression '...I didn't know. I had no idea—about her, about him, about any of it. I had known them both for three years, lived with Jacqueline for five months, and yet I didn't know the first thing about them. You have no idea how that felt.'

Oh, yes, I have, she thought painfully. I have.

'So—I did my penance for a time. The remorse, the guilt, the bitterness—all of it.' Just for a second the mask slipped and she saw a wealth of pain in his eyes. 'And then I decided to get on with life, but under my terms. No more involvement, no more commitment, no more trust. I had tried all that and it hadn't worked, so from then on I decided I would expect nothing and give nothing, and that way, if I made it perfectly clear from the onset, no one would get hurt.'

'Has it worked?' she asked softly.

'Yes.' He looked straight at her. 'Until recently.'

He meant Monique. The shock of what he had told her, the bitterness of betrayal she had glimpsed briefly in his eyes had had her wanting to go to him, to comfort him in some way, to tell him that she *did* understand, but now the thought of the other woman froze her tongue and her heart.

He had made it clear that he had revealed what was obviously a painful and difficult confidence to her because he was worried about the effect their stormy relationship was having on Ann and ultimately her child. That was all. *That was all.* This fiery sexual attraction that flared up between them he could and did control, and to a man like him it meant nothing beyond brief fleshly satisfaction. He had just been most explicit about the way he conducted his life.

She had to accept the fact that he trusted her enough to disclose his past and leave it at that, and as her heart thudded like a sledgehammer and her mind cried out against the unfairness of it all she raised her chin proudly. She loved him. The knowledge was there inside her and she felt no surprise. She had loved him from that moment when he had stood naked before her at his home, after comforting her in her agony of weeping, and had smiled at the joke against himself. She had known then but her mind had fought against the knowledge every step of the way.

'Thank you for telling me all this, Jacques—' Her voice broke but her dignity held intact as she smiled shakily and rose from the table. 'I'm sure it will help us get on better in the future and make things easier for Ann.'

'Ann…' He stared at her, his voice flat.

She turned her head away as though she couldn't look at him, and it was true—she couldn't. The sight of him standing there, the knowledge that she loved him, that she had committed the equivalent of emotional suicide, and the burning jealousy that was filling her whole being at the thought of him with Monique, were too much. 'I'm just going to the bathroom. I won't be a moment.'

He called her name as she left the room but she didn't stop. If she had he would have seen the tears streaming down her face, and that would have been the final humiliation. She had brought this on herself, she had no one else to blame, and now all she could do was get through the rest of the evening with a modicum of self-respect and poise. It would be hard, but then she had faced and overcome so much in the last three years that this one final hurdle would not be beyond her. She couldn't let it be.

CHAPTER EIGHT

'SANDI?' Andy's voice was right in her ear before her brain acknowledged the sound, bringing her back from her miserable reflection on the night before.

She had been a full ten minutes in the bathroom before she'd been sure that all trace of her tears had vanished, and when she had re-entered the sitting room Jacques had been sitting in an easy chair close to the window, contemplating a night sky that was alive with high-rise blocks in which small squares of lights had glowed brilliantly against the dusky blackness.

He hadn't smiled as she had joined him—in fact he hadn't smiled for the rest of the fifteen minutes or so that he had stayed—and had left almost immediately after a polite, cool speech of appreciation for the meal that had been stilted and formal. She had sat for hours after he had gone, the littered table and half-drunk wine remaining exactly as they were, before eventually stumbling to bed after she had cried herself dry, there to lie awake with wide, burning eyes until it had been time to get up.

'I'm sorry, Andy.' She forced herself to concentrate as her junior's concerned young face peered down at her. 'I was miles away.'

'Are you all right?' He had never seen his boss anything but one hundred per cent efficient, and this wan, lethargic woman who had been on a different planet all morning was worrying.

'I'm fine, thank you. Now, what's the problem?' Sandi answered briskly, appreciating the concern but knowing that the slightest show of sympathy this morning would have her howling like a baby.

'It's these photos for *Rage* magazine. I don't think they'll do…'

By the end of the long day her head was thudding, she felt hot and unbearably sticky, in spite of the excellent air-conditioning, and more exhausted than she could ever remember having felt. The final straw was Reception calling through just as everyone was leaving and telling her she had a visitor, which caused her to snap down the phone, her voice terse, 'There is no way I can see anyone this evening, Belinda. Tell whoever it is to make an appointment for tomorrow.'

'I don't think I can.' Belinda, that model of ice-cool efficiency and chilling sternness, who fended off unwanted visitors every day of her life, sounded ruffled. 'He's most persistent.'

'I don't care.' Sandi closed her eyes suddenly and took a hold of herself. Poor Belinda—she must sound like a real shrew. 'Look, I'm sorry. If he's being difficult I'll send Andy down with my appointment diary and fix something up for tomorrow, OK? Don't worry.'

'Right, thanks.' Belinda sounded most relieved, and Sandi shook her head and leant back in her chair for a moment, shutting her eyes against the pain in her skull. It was unusual for anyone to throw their wonder of a receptionist; he really must be determined. Damn—she hadn't even asked his name, she thought suddenly. Now, why on earth hadn't Belinda told her?

She ground her teeth with an irritation which heightened as she caught sight of Andy through the glass partition which separated her office from the main one. He was just walking out of the door, deep in conversation with several colleagues, the door closing behind them in the next instant.

Oh, wonderful—the perfect end to a perfect day, she

thought tightly. Now she would have to go down to Reception herself, and she still had at least another two hours of work to get through before she could go home. Her brain just hadn't seemed able to retain any information today, and everything had taken her twice as long.

Should she ring down and ask Belinda to send this person up? she wondered. She might as well, otherwise she was going to have to go down to Reception to see him. She sucked in air between her teeth in an irritable sigh. Well, she'd give him ten minutes and that was all. She was going to be here till way past seven as it was.

She was immersed in a long transcript of a dissertation from an important Japanese link that tentatively promised an enormous potential contract when the sharp knock at her open door snapped her head upright.

'The formidable Belinda said I was admitted to the holy of holies,' Jacques drawled laconically, and watched her mouth and eyes open wide.

'You?' She gaped at him before realising she must look like a surprised goldfish, whereupon she shut her mouth quickly.

'Me.' He entered the office with lazy assurance and seated himself in the chair opposite her desk.

'But—' She stared at him for a second more. 'She didn't say—you didn't say—'

'If you are trying to ask if I gave my name, the answer is no,' he said without a shred of embarrassment. 'I told her I was your boyfriend, who'd arrived in the States for a couple of days and wanted to surprise you.'

'And she believed that?' Sandi asked in amazement.

'Of course.' He smiled mockingly. 'I can lie very convincingly when I want to, and the knowledge that you would send me away with—what is that revolting English expression?—a flea in the ear if I told her who I was made me most persuasive.'

'How do you know what I would have done?' she

asked tightly as the blood pounded in her ears and her heart thudded against her ribcage like an imprisoned bird. Be calm, be cool, she told herself silently. Don't give yourself away. But it was hard to return to their old pattern of verbal sparring when all she wanted to do was fling herself into his arms.

'*Touché*, Miss Gosdon.' He bowed his head slightly and his black eyes continued to watch her. 'Would you have?' he suddenly enquired. 'Sent me away?'

'No.' It was out before she could stop it, and she followed on hastily, 'Of course I wouldn't. You are Ann's brother-in-law, for goodness' sake.'

'Damn Ann's brother-in-law!' The words were in the form of a mini explosion and she winced at the force of them. 'I asked you if you would see *me*, Jacques Challier,' he said with icy control after taking a long, deep breath. 'That is quite different and you know it.'

'Jacques—'

'Do not bother to reply.' The smile was as cold as his face, which held no amusement in its arctic depths. 'Your face adequately speaks for you.'

She hoped not—oh, she did hope not, she thought painfully as he shifted in the chair and glanced round the outer office, his profile hard and unyielding. If her face was portraying even a glimmer of what she was really feeling at this moment in time he would be horrified, she thought bleakly. Horrified and embarrassed to think he was being burdened by anything more than mutual sexual attraction.

'So this is where you work.' He turned his gaze back to her, but she could read nothing, good or bad, in the black eyes. 'I am impressed.'

She shrugged and smiled, not knowing how to reply even if she could have forced words past the constriction in her throat. She hadn't expected to see him again until Ann's baby was born, if then, and now here he was not a foot away from her. She wanted to drink in the sight of him—the black curly hair, hard square jaw and big, masculine shoulders—but she forced her eyes to drop to the papers on her desk before she gave herself away.

'When will you be finished?' He waved his hand at her desk as she glanced up at him. 'I would like to take you out to dinner—just dinner,' he added sarcastically as she flushed hotly. 'I will pick you up about eight at your apartment, so be ready.'

'How do you know I haven't got something planned already?' she asked shortly as the cool male arrogance, the imperious assumption that she was free, made her suddenly mad.

'Have you?'

'No.'

'Eight, then.' He rose as he spoke and reached the open door before turning round to survey her through glittering eyes. 'And it would make for a good evening if you could at least pretend to enjoy my company for once.'

'If you feel like that, why ask me out to dinner in the first place?' she asked, with more than a touch of acerbity in her voice. And to think she had spent a sleepless night and a miserable day over this monster. She was crazy, stupid—

'I would dearly love to know the answer to that question myself.' He eyed her sardonically. 'Put it down to the fact that I can't bear the thought that there is a woman who is oblivious to my accomplished charms. Will that do?' He raised his dark eyebrows as he watched her struggle to form a reply, and left while she was still spluttering.

That evening set the pace for the next three, until he left for France. He would arrive at her apartment block just before eight and whisk her away to a different venue each night.

That first evening they dined at a quiet little restaurant

tucked away in a back street, where the food was out of this world and the proprietor was fat and jovial, coming to sit at their table when they had reached the coffee stage and regaling them with quite horrifying stories of his youth in Sicily when, it appeared, most of his contemporaries had been recruited or murdered by the Mafia. It was blatant fantasy but fascinating none the less, and they left the restaurant to collapse with laughter in the dark street outside, feeling that the evening had been better than a trip to the theatre.

The second evening was spent at an exclusive, top-class nightclub, where the floor show was riveting and the food less so. They finished up at a hot-dog stand just after midnight, eating greasy junk food and sipping hot tea in elegant evening clothes, much to the amusement of several down-and-outs who emerged from cardboard boxes and under newspapers in an alley leading from the thoroughfare. Jacques treated them all to food and drink before their taxi driver persuaded them to leave, clearly feeling he was in danger of being murdered any moment, and they drove away with the smell of hot-dogs and wildly expensive perfume mingling in the back of the cab.

Sandi had spent a full week's salary on the fragrant scent that day in her lunch-hour, but Jacques hadn't even seemed to notice.

And it was the same story on the third and fourth night. He entertained her, wined and dined her, laughed with her and proved himself a captivating and charming companion, and all the time kept her very firmly at arm's length. No overtures, no approaches, sexual or otherwise. Just a friendly kiss goodnight outside her door when he escorted her back to her apartment and a cheerful smile of farewell.

And it got to her. It really, really got to her. It was useless telling herself, night after night in her chaste little bed, that she wouldn't have it any other way—although logically it was the truth. The fact that he suddenly seemed to view her as something in the region of a cross between a maiden aunt and a sister was aggravating, irksome, hurtful and most of all insulting.

And where was Monique in all this? she asked herself a hundred times a day. Even if he spent some hours in the day with the tall redhead, every minute of his evenings were spent with her, Sandi, and from what she'd seen of Monique it was not the sort of situation the beautiful model would accept without a fight.

What sort of relationship did they have anyway? She didn't understand it. She didn't understand any of it. And the more she tried, the more confused she became. And overall, second by second, minute by minute, hour by hour, her love for him was growing and it terrified her.

She didn't want to love any man, let alone Jacques Challier—a self-confessed cynic of the first order, who regarded women as necessary but expendable pleasure-givers, nice to have around, but for a short time only. Monique was the only one who had lasted the course, and even that was the strangest liaison in history—free love or no free love, she thought miserably.

Every morning she determined in her heart that she would tell him she knew he was here with Monique and ask him exactly how things stood between him and the lovely French girl. And every evening she spoke about a hundred and one topics except the one closest to her heart.

And now it was ten past two on a hot New York afternoon and she was sitting in the airport terminal close to where he would check in, waiting... Waiting for what? she asked herself weakly. To catch him out arriving with Monique? To prove that she wasn't quite the blind, gullible fool he thought she was? To show him she didn't care? He had no idea she would be here—she had led him to believe she was tied up with an emergency rush job at work all day—but she had had to come, to see for herself.

She saw him long before he saw her, his big, broad body and dark head standing out from the crowd even in the melting-pot of the air terminal.

'Hello, Jacques.' She had moved swiftly and quietly to his side and now he swung round to look at her, his handsome face breaking into one of his rare smiles as he beamed down at her.

'Sandi?' When, in the next moment, she felt herself being lifted into the air in a massive bear hug and swung round before being drawn close to his face as he took her lips in a scorching kiss, she almost decided to say nothing. But almost didn't count...

'It's good of you to come and see me off. I didn't expect you to do that.' He lowered her to her feet as he spoke, his face warm as his eyes held hers. 'Did you get finished earlier than you had expected?' he asked tenderly.

'Finished?' His transparent delight at seeing her there, the hug, the kiss—this wasn't what she had thought it would be like, she told herself frantically. And where was Monique?

'Monique?' She must have spoken the words out loud, although she hadn't realised she was doing so. 'How on earth would I know where Monique is?' He looked down at her in blank surprise.

'But she's here...' She stared up at him, her eyes cloudy with confusion.

'Is she?' He glanced round the massive terminal filled with scurrying bodies. 'Where?'

'In New York. Monique is here—but you know that.' And then, as she saw the black eyes harden and freeze and a dark mask come down over the autocratic features, she knew. She knew she had just made a terrible mistake.

'I know that Monique is in New York?' he asked expressionlessly as he bent to pick up the suitcase he had dropped when he had first seen her with one hand, his other holding her arm in a tight grip. 'I think we need to talk, Sandi.'

He led her over to a quiet corner and placed the massive suitcase on the floor before straightening to face her. 'Well, let's have it,' he said tightly. 'Why are you here? And why were you expecting Monique to be around? And, more especially—' and now his eyes chilled into black stone '—why did you come at all if you *did* expect her to be here? I had thought you two hadn't exactly hit it off.'

'I—' She stared up at him as her mind went blank. What could she say? What could she possibly say that wouldn't make it look as though she had been spying on him? Because... And here her face flushed scarlet and her heart began to beat like a tom-tom. Because that was precisely what she had been doing. But she hadn't meant it like that—she hadn't... Had she? She felt the heat rise up into her hair, and still her eyes were glued to his.

'Well?' The word was razor-sharp.

He clearly wasn't going to give any quarter, and she forced herself to answer with all she had...the truth. 'I thought you were here in New York with Monique,' she said flatly, her heart racing. 'On the day you arrived I saw she was working here for a few days and I thought you had come over with her.'

'But I told you I was here on business,' he said grimly.

'I thought you'd combined business with pleasure.'

'Pleasure?' This was getting worse, she thought frantically as his face turned an ugly shade of puce. 'Just a minute; let me get this straight. You thought I had brought Monique over to New York, that I was *with* her in the fullest sense of the word? Is that it?' She nodded miserably. 'And the evenings? When I was with you? How was this possible?' he asked, his French accent very pronounced as he ground the words out through gritted teeth.

'I thought—' She stopped helplessly. She hadn't thought at all, and the realisation was blinding. She had just allowed all the bitterness from the past to corrode the present. 'I thought you were with her in the day and me in the evenings,' she finished weakly.

'*Zut!*' After the one violent oath he was quiet for a full thirty seconds as he struggled for a self-control that was all but gone.

'Jacques—Jacques, I'm sorry—'

He cut off her apology with a sharp, vicious movement of his hand and she fell silent, looking up at him with huge, luminous eyes.

'So this is the sort of man you think I am?' he asked with a terrible lack of expression in his voice. 'You think I would bring one woman to New York for the week, sleep with her, make sport with her, and then entertain another in the evenings?' It sounded impossible now, when he put it like that, but that was exactly what she had been thinking, and she had no defence against the scathingly fierce anger in his face. 'Answer me, Sandi. Is this what you thought?'

'I suppose so.' She shook her head faintly. 'But—but I wasn't sure—not really—that's why—'

'That is why you came here today,' he finished, his eyes blazing with fury. 'And to think I was pleased to see you, that I thought—' He stopped abruptly. 'What a fool. What a fool I've been.'

'I didn't mean—'

'Do not say another word.' She was frightened now, desperately frightened. She had insulted him, accused him of all manner of crimes and she had been completely wrong.

'Jacques—'

'I mean it, Sandi—not another word or I will not be responsible for my actions.'

'Please listen to me,' she begged brokenly, but his face was as hard as granite, his big body held rigid and taut.

'Like you listened to me?' he asked with a bitter cynicism that smote her heart. 'When I told you about Jacqueline, shared my innermost feelings with you, bared my heart only to have you walk away as though I had just said something obscene? And even then I blamed myself, told myself that I was going too fast for you, that you were not ready to handle anyone else's emotions with your own so raw after your husband's death.

'But it is more than that, isn't it, Sandi? More than your longing for a man who has been dead for three years, more than your unwillingness to step back into the living world again. You do not like me. No—more than that. I do believe you actually hate me.'

'*I don't.*' The words were wrung out of her in a quiet plea but his face didn't change; in fact he took a step back from her, his eyes icy now and full of a pain that she could hardly bear.

'Well, you have come and you have seen,' he said with a dreadful finality. 'You were wrong. But do not let this worry you. There are all manner of diverse crimes of which I have been guilty in the past, and I am sure you can dig those up if you really try. No doubt there will be more in the future too. As I have said before, I am not a saint. I never have been and I am not sure I ever could be. There, you have it. I confess.'

He was furiously, viciously, blazingly mad, and she knew her legs wouldn't hold her much longer against the force of his rage. 'But this need not concern you, need it?' he went on. 'As you have said, I am merely Ann's brother-in-law—a relation to her only through marriage and nothing to you. We need not even meet again. I will make sure that when you visit France to see your sister I am not present. Does this suit you?'

'No—' She wanted to reach out to him but she really wasn't sure that he wouldn't knock her hands away, so great was his rage. 'I don't want that, believe me, Jacques. Let me explain—'

'But I—I want that,' he said proudly, his face closed against her. 'Goodbye, Sandi.'

She wanted to scream and shout and cry, to run after him, throw herself in front of him, grovel at his feet— anything to make him understand.

But she did none of those things as he walked away. She had thought she had been through the worst that could happen to her when she had found out about Ian, but that was nothing, nothing to this pain that was tearing her apart now.

If she had loved Ian, or the man she had thought he was, it had been but a pale reflection of the emotion she felt for Jacques Challier. He was her heart, her blood, her life, and she felt that he was taking all those things as she watched him disappear into the crowd without a backward turn of his proud head. And she had been responsible for this. It was all her fault, all of it. She wouldn't be able to bear it...

She gave a convulsive groan, careless of the glances around her, and stumbled to the ladies' cloakroom where she locked herself in the loo for a long time—how long she never did remember. She sat in a frozen state of stunned misery, hearing the excited laughter of children, the grumblings of over-stressed mothers, the wails of babies being changed, the giggling of animated teenagers—all the things that made up the flow of humanity—as she went over and over their conversation in her mind. On and on, relentlessly torturing herself, until she felt as if her heart had been ripped out at the roots.

And no matter how she thought of it, how she tried to justify herself, to bring some excuses to bear, there simply were no excuses. He would never forgive her. That knowledge was seared into the whole of her body. Never.

Eventually she left the tiny, safe little box, walking like an old woman to the car park and finding her car among the myriad of others, and it wasn't until she was in the driving seat, travelling far too fast along the freeway, that she asked herself how she was going to get through the rest of her life.

CHAPTER NINE

'SANDI?' Arianne's voice was anxious but excited. 'Thank goodness I have reached you. I tried to contact you at your office, but they told me you had left for home.'

'Ann?' Sandi's stomach had just turned over.

'The baby is on the way. Claude and I have just brought her into the hospital—'

'But it's early,' Sandi protested weakly. 'A month early. Is anything wrong?'

'No, no; please do not distress yourself. Everything is fine.' But the other woman's voice, in spite of its attempt at cheerfulness, was not totally reassuring.

'Has she definitely started?' Sandi asked quickly. 'I mean—'

'The waters have broken.' Arianne's voice was quiet now. 'There is no doubt that the baby will be born some time soon. Once the waters have broken the risk of infection is too high for her to be left.'

'Is she having any pains?' Sandi asked numbly.

'A little, just a little. Would you like me to ring you in an hour or so, when I know a little more? The doctors are with her now—'

'No. I'm coming over.' Sandi sat down with a little plop on the chair near the phone as her legs gave way. 'I'll be there as soon as I can—I'll ring the airport now. If I'm delayed in any way I'll phone you at the hospital. You will stay with her?' she asked anxiously.

'Of course, Sandi. Do not worry,' Arianne said swiftly. 'She is our daughter now, and this is Emile's

157

child. We will look after her as you would until you get here. She is perfectly safe.'

'Thank you, Arianne. I'll be there as soon as I can. Give my love to Ann.'

She put down the phone and stared at it in stunned shock for a moment before grabbing it again and dialling the number of the airport with shaking fingers. Incredibly, miraculously, they had a cancellation on a flight leaving for France that night, although she would be hard-pressed to make the airport in time. She rang for a taxi-cab before throwing some things into a case and phoning Andy with a list of hasty instructions, and then left the house within ten minutes of receiving Arianne's call.

Through the mad dash to the airport and the race to get on the plane she had no time to think, but once settled in the massive aircraft with all the panic behind her her thoughts were all of Ann—Ann and a certain tall, dark Frenchman who had vowed never to set eyes on her again.

The weeks since Jacques had left had been horrendous. For the first few days she had moved from one day to the next in a state of suspended animation, her mind stunned and frozen by the enormity of their confrontation. And then the wound had begun to bleed, slowly at first, before opening up into a gushing flood that had had her walking the flat at night until the early hours, quite literally holding her head in her hands as she had moaned her anguish out loud.

The knowledge that she had destroyed anything they might have had, completely and irrevocably, was unbearable. The fact that he hadn't been in America with Monique must have meant that he had come to see *her*. That was the thought that was driving her mad. And now she had lost the chance to be even on the perimeter of his life through fear—fear and cowardice. Fear that history would repeat itself and he would leave her, like Ian, and cowardice in that she hadn't opened her eyes to see him, the real Jacques Challier, without the spectre of Ian sitting on his shoulder. In that, she hadn't given them a chance.

But she had to concentrate on Ann now. As the plane rose majestically into the air with a slow whoosh she willed her sister to feel her love over the thousands of miles separating them.

This baby meant more than it would ever know. It had pulled its mother from the brink of the abyss Ann had glimpsed when Emile had been killed, had forged a link of steel wrapped in a silken thread with its father's estranged family and provided Ann with loving, doting in-laws and other relations, including Odile and her children, whom Ann spoke of often in her telephone calls and letters. Nothing must happen to this baby; it was too precious, too cherished, too loved.

For the whole of the seven-hour journey Sandi sent her prayers heavenward, unable to sleep or even doze in spite of the endless nights of cat-naps she had endured for the last few weeks.

When she arrived in France she felt like a wet rag, and a great sense of despondency and foreboding kept her silent and tense on the long drive from the airport to the hospital, which was situated several miles from the Challier château.

The July morning was already wide awake and one of glorious sunshine, although it was still only seven o'clock, but as the taxi ate up the miles Sandi didn't notice the scenery outside the windows. Her whole self, her very being was homed in on Ann and the tiny infant who was being born a month too soon. She told herself over and over again that that was nothing these days. They were saving babies at twenty-six weeks now—twenty-four even—modern technology was wonderful… But it didn't help. Nothing helped. She just wanted to get to her sister's side.

As the taxi drew up outside the hospital her stomach muscles clenched in a giant knot. Jacques had told her that the small private hospital was second to none, beautifully and expertly equipped, with the added advantage of boasting the finest obstetrician in all of France on its board. She hoped that consultant had been with her sister during the night—oh, she did.

As the taxi driver hauled her suitcase out of the boot she opened her bag to sort out the fare, whereupon a large male hand was placed on top of hers. 'Do not worry, Sandi; I will see to this.' She smiled up at Claude Challier, touched that he must have been looking out for her. 'Go now—go and see Ann.'

'Is she—?' Her voice faltered; his face was giving nothing away. 'She's all right?'

'I'm under orders to say nothing, but I can tell you she is well—very well.' He beamed at her, and for a moment he looked so like Jacques when he had first seen her that fateful day at the airport that she felt her face freeze. 'Go on. It is straight through the front doors, down the hall, first left and the room number is four.'

He gave her a little push as she stood transfixed, and then she was hurrying into the plush interior of the building where the perfume of flowers and thick, soft carpets competed with the faint but unmistakable smell of antiseptic and things medical.

'Ann?' She had entered the room on a little rush of excitement and anticipation before realising that her sister might be asleep, but Ann wasn't asleep. She was sitting bolt upright in bed, her eyes on the door and her arms cradling a very small bundle swathed in a lacy blanket.

'Sandi—oh, Sandi. I've been dying for you to get here...' As her sister's eyes filled with tears so did Sandi's, and the two smiled shakily as Sandi sat carefully on the bed before giving Ann a fierce hug. 'Here, say hello to your niece.'

'A little girl?' Sandi gazed wonderingly at the minute crumpled face topped with a smudge of wispy black hair, at the tiny eyelids closed tight and the diminutive little hand resting against one cheek. 'Oh, Ann, she's so small.'

'She isn't that small!' There was a wealth of feeling in Ann's voice. 'She weighed in at a full eight pounds, and that was more than enough, I can tell you! If she'd waited another month she'd have been stuck in there for ever.'

'Was it awful?'

'Bad enough.' Ann grimaced feelingly. 'But Arianne was wonderful. She was born at five this morning and Arianne stayed with me the whole time. She's just gone to organise some breakfast for you, but I think it was really to let us have a few minutes alone.'

'What are you going to call her?' Sandi asked as Ann placed the tiny infant carefully in her arms. The baby felt warm and smelt wonderful—a mixture of baby powder and something indefinable that brought a choking feeling to Sandi's throat. She was so beautiful and so tiny and— And she would never have one. She pushed the thought back into the recesses of her mind and concentrated on Ann fiercely.

'Emily.' Ann's mouth quivered, and Sandi reached out one arm to hug her close again. 'It's as near to Emile as I can get.'

By the time Arianne and Claude arrived ten minutes later, bearing a large tray for Sandi, both sisters' emotions were under control, although their eyes were pink-rimmed. The four of them were sitting chatting, Emily still fast asleep but now cocooned in a neat little glass crib at the side of the bed, when a knock at the door caused Ann to call out an immediate 'come in'. And Jacques came in.

Sandi's heart stopped for a moment, and then ran on at a speed the rest of her body couldn't keep up with.

She felt faint, giddy, and for a second really felt as if she might pass out, but the fact that when she looked into his face the dark, glittering eyes stared straight through her put iron in her backbone and brought an upward tilt to her chin. She took a long sip of the hot coffee she was finishing, stitched a polite smile on her face and said nothing.

'Where is this new arrival?' Jacques's eyes were soft as he glanced at Ann, who was trying not to look overly proud. 'May I see her?'

'Of course.' Ann gestured to the crib and right on cue, as Jacques bent over her, Emily opened her eyes and yawned. 'Pick her up,' Ann encouraged. 'It's all right.'

The sight of him cradling the small infant was almost too much for Sandi, and the lump in her throat threatened to explode in an avalanche of tears, but she excused herself quickly, after they had exchanged a brief nod and polite greeting for the sake of the others, on the pretext that she needed the bathroom. And when she returned ten minutes later, the armour of self-control firmly in place, he had gone.

All that day and the next, when Ann returned home to the château with Emily, she expected him to call—if only to exercise his right to ignore her as he had done to such good effect at the hospital. But by the end of the second day she realised he wasn't going to come. She didn't exist for him any more. And with that knowledge a rage came, and with that rage pride, and a painful dignity that she hugged to her like an all-enveloping cloak.

He was just like Ian. He hadn't really cared. He had wanted her for a brief sexual fling, nothing more, otherwise he wouldn't have been able to dismiss her with such coldness, without letting her explain. And she hated him. Loathed, detested and hated him. Ian had wanted only her money; Jacques had wanted only her body. And of the two she felt that Ian had served her least harshly.

The next morning she booked her return flight to New York, happy in the knowledge that she was leaving Ann and the baby in good hands. The Challiers, all of them, were clearly over the moon with their new family member, and the fact that she wasn't a boy was clearly as unimportant to them as to the proud mother. They loved Emily because she was part of Ann and part of Emile, and Ann was blooming under their devotion.

'You're leaving us tomorrow, Sandi?' They had all just finished dinner and had retired to the magnificent drawing room for coffee as the dusky evening sent the scents of summer through the open windows, the last of the dying sunlight falling in stark beams across the room. 'You are welcome to stay longer.'

'I know that.' She smiled at Claude. 'But I've had quite a lot of time off recently, and my company has been very good about it. I don't feel—'

When, in the next instant, the door to the drawing room was flung aside rather than opened, Arianne actually gave a little squeal of alarm before she saw her son framed in the doorway. *'Oh, mon Dieu!* Jacques, what on earth do you think you are doing, frightening us all like that? What is wrong?'

And for the first time in his life Jacques Challier neglected the lessons of his privileged childhood, the conventions, the polite propriety, the decorous good manners that were as much a part of him as breathing, and walked over to stand in front of Sandi without looking to left or right, his eyes blazing. 'You were going to leave? Tomorrow? Early in the morning? Without telling me?'

'I—' Her hand was at her throat as she struggled to make sense of what he was saying. 'I—'

'How dare you? How *dare* you think you could do this?'

'Jacques—?' As Claude rose to his feet, his eyes flying between Sandi's shocked white face and Jacques's countenance, which was as dark as midnight, he put out a hand to his son, only to remove it a second later as Jacques turned to look at him, his eyes blazing.

'Do not interfere, Papa. This is between Sandi and me.' He swung back to face her, his eyes narrowed. 'Well? You are going to leave tomorrow?'

'Yes.' She stood up now, her face pale, but her own fury at his arrogance burned in two bright spots on her cheeks. 'And why shouldn't I? You haven't called round or phoned—'

'How could I, when I was in Paris?' he snarled ferociously. 'You could have phoned me—I gave you the number.'

'The number?' She stared at him blankly, and at the look on her face he swung round to Arianne, who had just uttered a soft cry of dismay.

'You gave Sandi the letter?' he asked swiftly.

'Oh, Jacques, I am so sorry, but with the baby... I forgot. I still have it in my handbag.' Arianne was clearly horrified.

'*C'est impossible!*' He turned back to Sandi, his voice just a tone or so quieter. 'I gave my mother a letter to give you that day at the hospital. I had to go to Paris; there was no way I could get out of it. The letter explained it all.'

'I am so sorry.' Arianne's voice was tragic, but Jacques ignored them all now, reaching out and taking Sandi's arm then practically frogmarching her across the room.

'You are coming with me. I will have no more of this—this *ridiculous* situation,' he snarled softly. 'You did not receive the letter but you clearly made no enquiries about me, asked nothing about where I was, what was happening. You were just going to disappear again, weren't you? *Weren't you?*'

'*Again?*' Her voice was so shrill that Emily, asleep in her frothy pink crib in the corner of the room, wailed with shock. 'It was you who left me, remember? You wouldn't let me explain, tell you—'

'Sandi?' Ann's voice was utterly bewildered, and as they turned to face the rest of the room from the doorway, Jacques's hand still tight on her arm, Sandi saw the look of almost comical amazement that was on her sister's face mirrored in the expressions of the others. 'You've been seeing Jacques?' It said a lot for Ann's state of concern that she hadn't sprung to her newborn offspring at the first cry. 'Without telling me?'

'I haven't been seeing him,' Sandi said quickly. 'It isn't like that—'

'The hell it isn't!' Jacques glared at the rest of the room as he pushed Sandi through the doorway. 'Sandi is staying with me tonight. That is all any of you need to know. And whether she will be returning to America tomorrow is doubtful, so I would suggest one of you rings the airline and tells them—'

'You'd better not! I'm going back...' As Ann and Arianne and Claude heard the sound of Sandi's voice fade away and the front door bang shut Odile and André rushed into the room, their faces full of alarm.

'What on earth is happening?' André glanced over to where Ann had lifted Emily from the crib and was rocking her in her arms soothingly, murmuring a host of nothings as she did so. 'I thought something was wrong with the child.'

'Emily's fine.' They all turned to look at Ann, and as Arianne absorbed the look in her daughter-in-law's eyes she smiled slowly. 'And I think perhaps now Sandi is going to be fine,' Ann went on. 'I should have guessed, noticed...'

'Well, I didn't and I am his mother,' Arianne said quietly.

'Would someone please tell me what is going on?' Claude stared from one to the other and shook his head slowly. 'I am fast losing my grasp of what is real and what is not. And please, I do not wish anyone to say anyone else is fine, all right?'

But Sandi felt far from fine as she sat beside Jacques in the silver beast of a car. That he was blazingly, furiously angry was obvious, but what was really terrifying was the emotion that was running through her veins now. Because the temptation to say, to do anything she could to make everything all right was painfully strong, but even stronger was the knowledge that it scared her half to death that he had come for her like this.

It spoke of something more than mere bodily desire, and in spite of all her ragings, all her accusations, spoken and unspoken, the thought that she might be able to trust him, be able to reach out to him, the thought that there might be something between them, was too frightening to contemplate. She loved him, there was no doubt about that, she thought silently, but she didn't trust him. She doubted if she could ever trust any man again.

When he had, as she had mistakenly thought, flaunted Monique in front of her eyes, a tiny part of her, unacknowledged until this precise moment of time, had been relieved. It had been an escape route, an excuse to keep that secret place at the very depth of her hidden, and, yes, she had been relieved. She couldn't face the thought of opening up, of committing herself again, only to be ripped apart. She really couldn't.

'Where are we going?' she asked in a very small voice when the electric atmosphere in the car became unbearable.

'You know exactly where we are going,' Jacques said tightly without glancing at her. 'To my home.'

'You can't do this—'

'I just have.' Now he did spare her a swift glance, and she shivered at the burning intensity in the dark eyes. 'I have made myself the fool for you. Now are you satisfied?'

'Please don't say that.' She had made up her mind three years ago as to the route her life would take, and it didn't include a tall, dark, handsome Frenchman who would always have women flocking round him like flies. She couldn't, she just couldn't handle this, whether he wanted her for one night, one month, one year...

'Why not? I have never been afraid of the truth. You know I care for you, and you are attracted to me in spite of this obsession you have with your late husband.'

'I do *not* have an obsession with Ian.' Well, perhaps she did, she thought miserably. But certainly not in the way Jacques meant. 'You don't understand.'

'Because you will not let me understand.' It was so near the truth that she couldn't answer him. 'I was mad at you in America; I will not deny it. When you told me what you had suspected all that time you had been with me—' He stopped abruptly and drew a harsh, ragged breath through his teeth. 'I could have throttled you there and then, especially as I had told you things I had never told a living soul—about Jacqueline, about the way I felt.

'I had been miserable since you had left France, had engineered a visit to America purely to spend some time with you, and I felt you had betrayed me in some way. That may not be so, but that is the way I felt. But once I was home I began to see that I had tried to rush you again, to force the issue, and we had been doing so well. You enjoyed our evenings in New York?' he asked softly.

'You know I did.' And she had, so much.

'And I was most restrained, was I not? The polite goodnight kisses, the no touching? I could not believe that this was the Jacques Challier that had been in my skin for thirty-six years!' The self-mockery was soft but with a cutting edge that told her he had found the going really tough. 'So I decided that what had been accomplished once could be accomplished again, in time. I could be patient—hell, I had no choice. I would wait until you came over to see Ann and then I would continue the softly-softly approach until I had won. It was simple.'

'Jacques—'

'But you, you are not simple.' He glared at her now. 'What is it about me that you hate so much?'

'I don't hate you,' she said flatly, her heart thudding.

'You treat the people you *like* this way?'

She was saved the necessity of a reply to the sarcastic taunt as the beautiful car nosed carefully into Jacques's courtyard. As before the geese put up a show of cackling displeasure at having their quiet serenity interrupted, before retiring, feathers ruffled, to a far corner, from where they glanced balefully over their shoulders as Jacques led the way into the house.

'I want to go back, Jacques.'

'No way.' He turned in the middle of the sitting room and shook his head slowly as he let his eyes run over her slender shape. 'And you've lost weight.' He moved swiftly to her side and looked down at her intently. 'Why have you lost weight? You were too thin to start with.'

'Thank you *very* much.' The criticism took care of the weak tears that had been in danger of falling as she had glanced round the lovely farmhouse she had never expected to see again. 'And you—you're perfect, I suppose?'

'As near as damn it.' He smiled, but she just couldn't smile back.

'You were horrible at the hospital the morning Emily was born,' she said flatly. 'Absolutely horrible.'

'I was petrified,' he said soberly, shaking his head slowly as her eyes flew to his. 'You find this hard to accept? You think I am a man of stone, is that it? Well, I can assure you I was scared to death when I walked in that room, Sandi. Part of me wanted to ignore everyone else and take you in my arms and force you—*force* you to care for me. Another part, the sensible part, was telling me I had to follow the route I had planned and play it cool and slow. Another—'

He raked back his hair abruptly. 'Oh, hell, I could go on all night but that will not help us now. For once in my life I was out of my depth and unsure how to handle things—you... I was supposed to be in Paris mid-morning and it was an appointment I could not miss, one of vital importance. I put the number of my hotel in the letter and asked you to ring me.'

'I didn't know.'

'Would you have rung if you had?' he asked quietly as he looked her square in the eye. 'Would you, Sandi?'

'I don't know...' She broke the contact and sank down onto one of the big easy chairs, shaking her head helplessly. 'I thought—'

'I know what you thought,' he said tightly as he continued looking down at her bent head, her hair shining like liquid gold in the dim light of the wall lamps dotted about the large room. 'You made it absolutely clear on the morning I left New York what sort of man you thought I was, but I hoped that the realisation that you were wrong about Monique would perhaps allow you to consider that you might be wrong about everything else as well.

'Monique is a beautiful, sensual woman—' her eyes shot to his face as he spoke the redhead's name '—and utterly spoilt, vain, irritating, egotistical, shallow... Need I go on?' he asked sardonically.

'But you were so friendly with her,' she protested faintly.

'Sandi, she is the daughter of my parents' best friends,' he answered patiently. 'What did you expect me to do? Spit in her eye? Her mother has been trying to engineer some sort of match between Monique and me for years, but Monique knows full well how I view

that. I frequently put her in her place—she needs someone to keep her in order—but that is as far as it goes.'

And that would make him even more of a challenge
to Monique, Sandi thought with sudden intuition. The
beautiful model was used to having men fall at her feet;
the fact that this one was immune to her charms would
drive her crazy.

'Have you ever—ever taken her out?' she asked tentatively, not really wishing to know the answer but having to ask anyway.

'A few times, when she was younger and a slightly
more mellow character,' he answered, with an offhand-
edness that told her there was no involvement on his
side at least. 'Parties of joint friends, that sort of thing,
but only on a friendship basis. I have never enjoyed her
company.'

He looked her straight in the eye now as he dropped
on his heels to crouch in front of her. 'That is the truth,
Sandi. There has never ever been any sort of relationship
between us beyond one of platonic friendship. I know
Monique's type. The world is full of beautiful, spoilt
women who think the sun and moon revolve around
them alone. I have not been an angel, but you know this
already; I have not tried to pretend otherwise. But
Monique? No. Nothing like that was ever on the cards
and she knows it.'

'I see.' She stared at his dark face so close to hers
and her heart went haywire. She believed him, and she
knew now that Jacques was not the sort of man to be
involved with more than one woman at a time, but...
There was no way she could be that woman. She
couldn't handle being just one in a long stream of affairs.
Eventually he would tire of her—his sort of man always
did—and then—

'"I see"? Is that it?' She was unaware that the play
of emotions over her face had caught at him with knife-
like pain. 'This does not affect you in any way?'

'Jacques—'

'No—no more "Jacques, this", "Jacques, that",' he said abruptly as he rose again to stare down at her with flashing black eyes. 'You always speak my name like that when you are withdrawing a little, doing this thing you do so well of shutting me out. I expected too much when I told you of Jacqueline, I know that. I felt I was giving you privileged information, which was unquestionably a great presumption on my part.

'You did not ask to be told, I decided to tell you—and the fact that it did not make any difference to the way you looked at me was not your fault. I should not have expected this. I acted like a spoilt child and was so concerned with *my* feelings, the way I felt you had rejected me when I had honoured you so mightily—' his voice was dripping with self-contempt and self-mockery '—that I did not consider you at all. In this I was wrong, I admit it, but I will not let you shut me out any longer, Sandi, whether you like it or not. You are attracted to me, I know this, and that is a start.'

'I can't let myself be attracted to you. I'm sorry,' she said miserably.

'You can.' He eyed her hotly. 'However much you loved your husband, however much you miss him, he is not here and I am.'

His words were meant to be brutal, to shock her out of the brokenness he felt she was feeling, but they got no reaction and it puzzled him.

'I love you, Sandi.' The words were torn out of him and brought her eyes to his. 'I've fought against it, railed against it, told myself I was foolish to ever get emotionally involved with another woman after Jacqueline. But this is not a mind thing, it is a thing of the heart, and I have no defence against it. I did not intend to tell you, but I must. And I will not let you bury yourself, spirit, mind and body, in the way you have done for three years. You might never feel the same about me as I feel for you, but at least I can make you start living again.'

This was killing her. He didn't know it, but he was killing her, she thought blindly. The final nail in the coffin. He had just destroyed the last defence she'd had with three simple little words. 'I love you'. 'Don't say these things, Jacques—'

'Why? Because you do not feel they are the truth?' he asked softly. 'Is that it? But I do love you, Sandi. I am helpless before this feeling I have for you. It makes me vulnerable, exposed, wide open, and I do not like this but I can do nothing about it. I did not love Jacqueline like this and I shall not love again like it. You are the love of my life—'

'No!' Her voice was an agonised cry against herself. She was being offered heaven and she didn't have the courage to take it. She couldn't—she *couldn't* do what he had done and open herself so completely to another human being again.

'I want to marry you, Sandi, to commit myself to you,' he went on relentlessly, sensing that some sort of breakthrough was near. 'I want to share my days and my nights with you, to have children that are a part of me and a part of you—'

'I will never marry again.' She shrank inwardly, her stomach shrivelling into a tiny, tight ball. 'Never.'

'You loved him that much?' And it was the pain in his voice that broke the dam.

'Loved him? I hated him, loathed him,' she said as she closed her eyes against his face, her voice quivering with anguish. 'He was a monster from hell.' And she began to talk, to tell him all of it, with her eyes tightly shut and her voice so full of pain and agony and humiliation that Jacques's face was wet when he suddenly took her in his arms, pulling her against him with a fierceness that stopped her words and her breath.

'No.' She freed herself with a quiet firmness that

stopped him more effectively than any demented struggling would have done. 'You must hear it all.' And he did, every last word, until all she had said was branded on his mind and he would have given the world, all he possessed, for one minute with the man who had caused her such pain.

'And I love you, Jacques. I want you to know that now.' It was said with such flatness, such a strange lack of emotion that it stopped him from the reaction the words would have caused minutes ago. 'I never really loved Ian—I didn't even know the real man at all—but I do love you. And because I love you—' she raised her eyes to his now '—I want you to forget me, to find someone else who can be what you want her to be.'

Jacques had thought that he had been through every emotion known to man in the last ten minutes, but now he felt a new one, compounded of fury and resentment and sheer anger that she could speak in such a way after what they had just shared. He didn't move, and her words hung like something unclean in the stark silence that followed, filled with their own vibrating energy which pounded against his eardrums with a force that was unbearable.

And as she looked into his face she saw a stranger metamorphose in front of her—a dangerously angry, blazingly mad stranger, with eyes that were fire and a mouth that was a straight line in the hardness of his face.

'How dare you? How dare you say I should find someone else?' he ground out slowly through clenched teeth, and she backed away from him until she was standing against the wall. 'What do you think this emotion is that I feel for you? Something that can be turned off and on like a tap? I love you, dammit. I want to marry you; I want to have children; I want you to be their mother.

'I cannot change what Ian has done, heal the scars you bear in your head from his treatment of you; all I can promise you is that I will not be the same. That I will love you, cherish you, protect you all the days of my life. Do you believe this, Sandi? Do you?'

She felt paralysed by the raw emotion in his face and voice, unable to move, to make any response.

'Do you, Sandi?' His voice was softer now, calmer, but with a terrible determination to wring an answer out of her. 'Do you believe in my love, believe you can trust me?'

'No…' Her reply was a long scream of anguish and pain and loss. 'I can't. I can't—don't you see? I can't say that when it isn't true. I don't know if I'll ever be able to say it! *I don't! I don't!* I can't be what you want me to be; it's too late for that. I want to trust you, to believe we'd always be together, but I can't—I can't feel it in here.' She pounded her chest with her fists until he caught her hands in his, drawing her against him as he slowly stroked her hair with cool, firm fingers, his voice soothing and calm.

'Enough, little one, enough. You are making yourself ill and I do not wish this. You are too tired to talk any more—enough, now. No more crying.' She hadn't realised she was weeping until he had spoken, but now she became aware of the tears flooding down her face, and when he gathered her in his arms and began to walk up the winding staircase she was too tired to resist, her head falling against the hard wall of his chest as she relaxed against the male warmth of him.

She didn't want to lose him. The thought was all around her as he walked with her into a pretty bedroom and laid her gently on the big four-poster, his eyes soft. She didn't want to lose him but she would. She had to. But they could have one night together—surely one night wasn't too much to ask to last her a lifetime? When he went to turn and leave she caught at his hand, her voice still trembling from the force of her weeping.

'Don't go, Jacques. Please don't go.'

'It is all right. Everything will be all right.' He was quick to reassure her as he sat on the side of the bed, stroking her hair back from her damp face, but she didn't want this fatherly care; she wanted—she wanted him. She needed him. Just once, that was all she would ask.

'Make love to me.'

'What?' His hand stilled on her forehead, his eyes wide with surprise.

'I want you, Jacques.' She reached up to him, drawing his head down to hers before he could reply and pressing her mouth against his as she quivered against him. 'I love you. I do...'

For a moment she thought he was going to resist her, and then he responded with a fierce, desperate urgency that had her moaning against his lips as his hands explored her body. Their kissing, their touching was frantic and fierce, and she was lost in the mounting whirlpool that was carrying her to its core, hardly aware that he had removed her blouse until she felt his lips burning on her bare skin, creating fire wherever they lingered.

He was lying next to her now, as he kissed and stroked her, the little words of endearment and love that he whispered against her skin adding to the entrancing magic of his intoxicating lovemaking. She felt a tenderness that she'd never known before blossom into being as she saw his dark head against the pale skin of her breasts, and then a languorous, burning warmth began to seep into every part of her and she began to tremble helplessly, her body shaking against his. As his mouth found hers again she kissed him back wildly, wantonly, until they were both trembling, his body rock-hard and fierce against hers and his eyes narrowed slits of black light.

'You're wonderful, incredible... You see how it will be for us...?' He was on the edge of losing control, she knew it, and she wanted him to take her—wanted to be as one with him for one glorious night.

'I love you...' She murmured his name as he kissed

her bare flesh hungrily. 'I want to be able to remember this all my life…' And the moment she had spoken, the second the words had left her lips, she felt him freeze against her, his mouth still on the warm swell of her breasts for a timeless second before he raised his head slowly, his eyes seeking her face.

'All your life?' He raised himself on one elbow, his body still shaking from the force of his desire but his control rigid. 'Why all your life, Sandi? There will be many more nights, days, shared between us, because I intend to live a long, long time.'

And then she realised he had misunderstood when she had reached for him, asked for his love. He had thought…

What he had thought was blazing in his eyes now, his mouth hard as he rose from the bed to look down at her from his great height. 'You thought I would be content with one taste of you? That I would give you a parting gift—something like that?' His voice was very tight now, very controlled.

'Oh, no, Sandi; get that out of your head. I am going to have you, all of you—heart, soul and body; you can get used to that idea right now. I don't care how long I have to wait but you will be mine, and with a gold band on the third finger of your left hand too. You are not some cheap affair, some liaison that I can walk away from with nothing more than a warm memory, and I will not be that for you. I will not allow it. You will not reduce us to that. Now, go to sleep.'

He wasn't going to leave her? To calmly walk out and leave her? 'Jacques—'

'I said go to sleep, Sandi.'

'I shall be leaving in the morning.' The words were both a plea and a warning, and his face closed still more as he looked at her from the open doorway. 'I mean it, Jacques. I'm going back to New York, to the life I have chosen. It's the only thing I can do—you must see that.

I wouldn't be any good for you—I would destroy anything we might have—'

'Have you finished?' His voice was cold now, cold and remote, and she sat up jerkily on the bed and pulled her clothing around her, her face flushed and embarrassed at the state of her undress.

'Yes, I've finished,' she said dully, and she had. She could never be the kind of wife he wanted, the kind of wife she would have given the world to be. How could she be when the very basis of her love for him had the element of trust missing? It would be like a canker, eating into both of them until it ended in heartbreak and confusion and pain.

And she wouldn't pretend—couldn't. He deserved the best and she wasn't the best; it was as simple as that. Something had been torn out of her when Ian had betrayed her, something soft and vital and warm and magical. It had gone, and although she had searched for it—more and more over the last few weeks—it still eluded her. She couldn't trust him.

'Goodnight, Sandi.'

The door closed behind him and she sank back against the pillows of the big bed, aware that she was shivering uncontrollably. It was the end. Tomorrow she would walk out of his life for ever. *It had to be this way.*

CHAPTER TEN

'I UNDERSTAND your flight is at midday?'

She had heard the telephone ring last night, just after Jacques had left her room, but had been unable to determine who was calling even though she had crept to the door of her room and listened to his voice filtering up from the hall.

'Yes.' She glanced at him now as they sat on the patio, which had already been warmed by the early morning sun, having a breakfast of fruit and toast. At first she had felt she couldn't eat a thing, but then, at the sight of him digging in with gusto, pride had come to her rescue, and she had managed an adequate, if small, breakfast. 'But I need to get back to the château in time to pack and say goodbye to everyone.'

'This is understood.'

She didn't understand him this morning—she really didn't, she thought wearily as she lay back against her chair and pretended to enjoy the remainder of her coffee.

'There are a couple of calls I have to make and then we can leave,' he said coolly, rising to his feet. 'You will wait here?'

'Yes.' Her voice was lethargic, dull, but that was how she felt inside. She hadn't slept for more than half an hour during the night, and that had only been as dawn was breaking. She felt tired, crumpled and a mess without her make-up or even her lipstick.

The bathroom *en suite* had provided shampoo, soap and the basic necessities, including a small comb that had proved painful when she'd tried to untangle her thick curls, but she knew her eyes were swollen and pink-rimmed and her face was pale and washed out. Still, perhaps it was for the best that she would walk out of his life looking like something the cat had dragged in, she thought painfully. No false illusions about looking radiant in the morning, anyway!

Jacques, on the other hand, had looked the picture of health as he sat at the table when she had tentatively made an appearance downstairs. Freshly shaved, black curls slicked back but already beginning to flop across his forehead, eyes bright and hard mouth smiling. She could have hit him. And kissed him. And—

Stop it, stop it, she told herself firmly as her heart began to thud and pound at the thought that she would never see him again. She mustn't think, mustn't feel. She just had to get through this day the best she could and then take stock. Of what, she didn't know. The rest of her life stretched out in front of her like an endless nightmare. If only he hadn't told her he loved her, that he wanted to marry her, she could have tried to pretend it was just a thing of the flesh and maybe got by. But now—

'Oh, God, help me.' She actually said the prayer out loud, her eyes desperate. She had to be strong for a few more hours at least. She couldn't ruin his life as well as her own.

'OK.' He appeared in the doorway, smiling again, as though he hadn't a care in the world. 'We are ready to leave, yes?'

'Yes.' She stood up abruptly, her dignity gathered round her like a cloak, and marched past him with her head held high. His eyes were soft on the back of her head as she walked out to the car, but once he had opened the door and settled her inside the same remote, cool mask he had worn all morning was firmly in place.

She sat in numb misery for the first half an hour, utterly lost in her own pain. He had given up. Well, she was glad, *glad*. Of course she was. She just wished he hadn't done it so quickly and apparently with such ease, that was all. She shut her eyes at the unfairness of her thoughts. What was the matter with her? The man had offered to marry her and she had refused—several times. What had she expected anyway? He had said once before that he wasn't the type of man to bang his head against a brick wall, and she couldn't blame him.

'Jacques?' Another half an hour had gone by and, as once before, when he had taken her to his home instead of the château, she felt that something was wrong. 'Where are we?'

'Where are we?' He gave her one lightning glance and she knew immediately that she was right: they weren't going to the château. She glanced anxiously out of the window now, before swinging her head back to his dark profile.

'Yes, where are we?' she asked shrilly. 'This isn't the way back.'

'It is the way back to where I want to go,' he said smoothly, his voice silky and soft. 'We are heading for Soane et Loire; does that help?'

'Of course it doesn't help,' she said tightly. 'Because you know full well I haven't the faintest idea where that is.'

'It is in Burgundy.' His tone was helpful. 'OK?'

'No, it is not OK.' She couldn't believe it; she just couldn't believe it—it was in quite the wrong direction. 'What about my plane?'

'What plane?' he asked innocently.

'The one I am supposed to catch today.' Driver or no driver, she was going to hit him in a minute, she thought hotly.

'I told Ann to cancel that when she rang last night,' he said coolly, his voice bland. 'At the same time I arranged for your suitcase to be delivered to my home just after breakfast. I thought it would spoil our time together if you weren't able to feel comfortable in your own things—'

'*Our time together?*' She had given up trying not to shriek, and he closed his eyes for the briefest moment as the sound reverberated round the car.

'That is most unattractive, you know that, don't you?'

She answered him with a most unladylike oath that caused him to tut-tut deep in his throat. 'You can't—' She stopped abruptly. 'This is crazy, Jacques. What are you going to do? Keep me prisoner somewhere until you get your own way?'

'Exactly.' And now there was no amusement or mockery in the swift glance that burnt across her stunned face. 'For as long as it takes, my love.'

'I don't believe this.' She shut her own eyes now, leaning back against the seat helplessly. 'I just don't believe this is happening to me.' He said nothing, concentrating on the road with just a narrowing of his eyes against the brilliant sunlight outside the powerful car. 'What's at Soane et Loire anyway?' she asked after a few electric moments had ticked away.

'Lunch.' The deep voice was unforgivably unconcerned.

'Lunch?' She sat bolt upright again. 'Then where is it we're going? What's our final destination?'

'My family's little log cabin in the mountains,' he said calmly. 'That's where we were when Emile—' He stopped abruptly. 'That is our hideaway, our retreat,' he continued smoothly after a few seconds had passed. 'No telephone, no TV—heaven…'

'And where, exactly, is heaven situated?' she asked with enormous self-control as she forced her voice a few tones lower than it wanted to be.

'Savoie, in the French Alps.'

She shut her eyes and said nothing. There was nothing to say, after all.

* * *

They lunched at a charming hotel built next to a Romanesque church with a wonderful backdrop of mountains and forest behind, and an enchanting vista of deep valleys with colourful meadows from the dining room. The steak *au poivre* melted in the mouth, and the *ananas au kirsch*—fresh pineapple chunks soaked in kirsch liqueur—was out of this world.

By now the tension of the last few weeks, the trauma of her dash to France, her lack of sleep the night before and the presence of Jacques still so firmly in her life had reduced Sandi to a mindless robot that walked and talked and obeyed almost without question. She was utterly exhausted, mentally and physically and emotionally, and Jacques knew it, glancing at her anxiously once or twice when they were back in the car after their meal.

'Here.' He drew into a small lay-by on a winding road that overlooked a massive monastery, which was sleeping in the blazing hot sun and surrounded by orchards and sweet-smelling meadows. He adjusted her seat into a reclining position. 'Go to sleep. It will take us some time to get to Savoie—we have to go through Burgundy first, and then Rhône—and you look awful.'

'Huh…' It was all she could manage, and within seconds of lying back and shutting her eyes she was sound asleep, her hair falling in riotous abandon about her face and throat and deep mauve shadows staining the honey-coloured skin under her eyes.

When she next opened her eyes, dazed and light-headed from the hours of much needed sleep, it was evening and they were approaching the region of Savoie. The evening was mellow with dusky golden sunshine, fresh pure air streaming into the car through the open windows and the banks at the side of the road and the meadows beyond alive with brilliant wild flowers. 'I—I must have fallen asleep,' she murmured as she struggled to come fully awake.

'Like the proverbial log—except logs don't snore.'

Jacques glanced at her with a wry smile and his words brought her jolting upright.

'I do not *snore*,' she stated emphatically, hearing his dry chuckle with a feeling of helpless panic. This was too cosy, too…nice… The word Jacques objected to so much mocked her, but it was true, she thought painfully. It was all too, too nice and he mustn't think— 'You can't keep me in this log cabin for ever, Jacques, and you must know there is no chance of anything permanent between us,' she said quickly.

'Must I?' He didn't seem in the least perturbed as he glanced at her briefly through narrowed black eyes.

'I mean it,' she stated flatly. 'This is all—all—'

'Ridiculous?' he put in helpfully. 'That is the word you would normally choose, is it not?'

'It *is* ridiculous,' she said tightly. 'All this is ridiculous. We are ridiculous—'

'No.' Now the car swerved off the road and came to a halt overlooking a picture-postcard village behind which snow-capped mountains rose majestically into the vivid blue sky. 'Not us. The situation may be—but that is your fault, not mine.'

His voice was angry and throbbing with something she didn't dare question, and for the first time that day she realised that the control she had thought so steel-like was only skin-deep.

'You are going to stay at the cabin with me, Sandi, and you are going to talk to me, dammit. I am not going to make love to you. Pleasurable though that would be for both of us, it would confuse the issue right now— and we have the rest of our lives to enjoy each other's bodies.'

'Jacques—'

'And so we are going to talk—really talk. You are going to open up that little Pandora's box and tell me all about your fears, your anguish, your feelings of humiliation and pain, the grief…I want all of it—all of it right out in the open where I can see it and deal with it, and you will be healed. I am not Ian, Sandi—I think you could probably travel the whole of the world before you found a skunk like that again—but I am not a mind-reader either, and I can't help you until you communicate with me.'

'I don't want help.' Her eyes were blinded by tears.

'Well, I do.' His voice was gruff and husky. 'Because I can't face the thought of letting you go now I've found you. It might be hell with you, if we don't get this thing sorted, but it would be utter torment without you. I love you, Sandi; I need you. The least you can do for me, if you love me as you say you do, is talk to me.'

'And if that doesn't change anything?' she asked brokenly. 'If I still don't feel I can trust you, marry you? What then?'

'You will.' He looked at her with a wealth of love in his eyes, his dark, handsome face serious and intent. 'I can't believe we have found each other against all the odds only to have it fall apart before it's even begun. I won't believe that.'

'Jacques—'

'No more words, not for now. We will find the cabin, we will have supper and we will sleep. Tomorrow is a new day.'

And the next day, when she awoke in the beautiful red-roofed *gîte* and walked out onto the wooden balcony that overlooked the crystal-clear waters of the shimmering lake just yards away, with nothing but distant cowbells to disturb the peace of the timeless Alpine valley, she remembered his words. Tomorrow was here—now. The thing was, was she brave enough for the soul-searching Jacques had spoken of?

And so a bitter-sweet, disturbing, painful and magical time began. A time of long walks hand in hand through Alpine meadows covered with carpet upon carpet of wild flowers, of swimming in their own secluded lake through long, hot summer days, of horse-riding along narrow mountain paths on mounts borrowed from the small riding school-cum-farm on the outskirts of the tiny village from where they fetched their food, and of evenings spent on the veranda of the cabin with the air gradually cooling as dusk filtered into the scorching blue sky.

And through it all Jacques was true to his word. Beyond holding her hand and brief, controlled kisses there was no lovemaking, although Sandi invited it time and time again as her love for this proud, strong man who had turned her world upside down grew deeper and deeper. And slowly, very slowly, she found herself beginning to talk of everything that held her bound.

It was traumatic, frequently harrowing for both of them, and there were times when Sandi raged and shouted at him for putting her through it, but...it was helping. More than she would ever have dreamt possible.

And still Jacques kept his distance. She had long ago ceased to worry about her work—what Ann had told them she had no idea, but that all seemed in another world, another universe. But still, *still* she couldn't say the words Jacques wanted to hear from her heart. Something was holding her back, keeping her from taking that last step of faith, and as they neared the end of the first week she felt she never would.

'Enjoying it?' Jacques's voice was lazy as he glanced at her through narrowed black eyes.

'Uh-huh.' She smiled back as her hair blew in a golden cloud about her tanned face. They had decided to try and find a particularly enchanting valley that Jacques remembered, accessible only on horseback, and now, as the horses picked their way carefully along the wide mountain path with steep gullys on both sides, she wondered how long this could go on. Because she couldn't change; she knew that now. She could never marry again; it was too big a step of trust—even with Jacques.

And then it happened. One moment they were drinking in the pure, clean air laden with a thousand summer scents, the sky a vivid deep blue above them and the horses lazy and contented, and the next a small, twisting snake slithered across the path in front of them, sending both horses demented. Sandi felt herself begin to slip as her horse reared up with a frantic neigh, made one desperate clutch at its mane, and then she had gone, falling onto the path for one brief second before the force of her fall took her over the edge of the gully towards the ravine a hundred feet below.

Somehow her hands clutched at a small prickly bush a few feet down from the edge of the path as she fell, and although she felt the sharp thorns tear into her flesh she hung on with all her might as she screamed Jacques's name.

'Sandi?' He was peering over the edge in the next moment, and she saw him shut his eyes for an infinitesimal second at the sight of her clinging to the bush which was the only vegetation for miles on the hard granite rock where nothing survived the heat of the day. 'Thank God. Keep still. I'm coming.'

'You can't come down here—you'll fall; you'll be killed,' she sobbed in terror.

'I'm coming down. Just wait a moment.' His head disappeared, and within seconds loose pebbles and dust were falling in her face as he began to descend towards her inch by precarious inch, using the few small footholds and slight indentations in the rock-face as he came.

'Go back, Jacques; please go back. We'll both be killed. You can go and get help—'

'You won't hold on much longer.' She knew that, but the thought of him dying too was unbearable. 'Now, keep calm and do exactly as I say,' he said, with a control that was formidable.

'Jacques, the bush is beginning to loosen.' She screamed in terror as it gave a little, but in the next moment he had grabbed her wrist, his flesh hard and firm on hers.

'Let go. Let go of the bush now, Sandi, and I will get you up.'

'I can't.' She was crying, almost hysterical with fear, and the pain in her lacerated hands and the thought of trying to climb up the sheer rock-face with only a few niches in which to put her feet and bleeding hands were too much for her.

'Give me your other hand,' he said calmly, his voice strong and cool. 'Reach out to me, Sandi.'

'I can't—I can't let go…' The bush shuddered and moved again as she clung on, Jacques's hand holding her other wrist in a grip of iron.

'If you don't let go it will take you with it. Let go, Sandi.'

'I can't—I can't!' She had never known that fear such as she was feeling now could exist. It was numbing her mind, her body, sending her mindless.

'Then we'll both go together.' The shock of his words brought her out of the hysteria, and as she raised her head to look up at him she saw that he meant it.

'Let go of me. Save yourself,' she said faintly. 'It's pointless us both dying.'

'I can't live without you, Sandi.' He spoke without any emotion, in contrast to her breathless sobbing. 'I love you and you love me. In life, in death, I want to be with you. I can get us both out of this if you trust me, Sandi. Do you? Do you trust me?'

His face was blurred through the tears streaming down her face from a combination of pain, panic and shock, but as she felt him gripping her wrist with steel fingers she knew this was real. This was the end, the ultimate, the final challenge, and now it was here she wondered how she could have hesitated for so long.

'Yes…' Her voice was a soft whisper through her tears, and then she drew in a deep breath as she reached out with her other hand, knowing they were both dependent now on the kindness of God and the mountain. 'Yes, I do trust you, Jacques. I trust you absolutely.'

By the time they had inched their way to the path, slowly and painfully, they were both drenched with their own sweat and smeared with grey dust and blood from her bleeding hands. They lay for long minutes in each other's arms without moving or speaking, their hearts pounding like sledgehammers and their limbs like lead. And then a bronzed, dirty hand turned her face towards his and she saw that he was smiling, his eyes warm as they devoured her tear-stained face.

'I told Ann I was going to make you trust me whatever it took,' he murmured softly. 'Can you remind me to watch what I say in the future?'

'Oh, Jacques, I love you. I love you so much,' she said shakily.

'And trust me?' he asked softly.

'And trust you,' she promised huskily.

'Then you may kiss me.' He pulled her on top of him, holding her very tightly, and as her mouth sought his the kiss deepened and held. 'And you will marry me?' he asked against her lips. 'Straight away?'

'Tomorrow, if you want,' she agreed breathlessly.

'I don't know if I can wait that long,' he said gruffly, his voice filled with a fierce exultation that stirred her heart. 'Oh, my love, my love. I'm going to make it all up to you. You're going to be loved like no woman has ever been loved before, do you know that?'

'Yes…' She was laughing now, her heart and mind free at last from the shackles of bitterness and pain. And then, as he groaned his need of her against her lips, his mouth taking hers with a fierce passion, there was only the blue sky above and the soaring mountains beyond, and two hearts entwined and ready to continue down the road of life, together at last for eternity.

Modern Romance™
...seduction and
passion guaranteed

Tender Romance™
...love affairs that
last a lifetime

Sensual Romance™
...sassy, sexy and
seductive

Blaze.
...sultry days and
steamy nights

Medical Romance™
...medical drama on
the pulse

Historical Romance™
...rich, vivid and
passionate

29 new titles every month.

*With all kinds of Romance for
every kind of mood...*

MILLS & BOON®

Makes any time special™

MAT4

MILLS & BOON®

Christmas
with a Latin Lover

Three brand-new stories

Lynne Graham

Penny Jordan

Lucy Gordon

Published 19th October